SCAVENGER

The Place

Dana Stewart Quinney

ISBN: 1546496912
ISBN 13: 9781546496915
Library of Congress Control Number: 2017907706
CreateSpace Independent Publishing Platform
North Charleston, South Carolina

For my mother, Bernice Stewart. *Everything.*

BOOK 1

The Place

CHAPTER 1
LAST DAYS

B en Elliott tried to keep his eyes on the cream-colored tile floor as he pulled packages of old-fashioned cloth diapers off the shelves in the supermarket. "Please, don't let anyone from school see me," he asked desperately of any and all powers. "Gramps has lost it this time, for sure," he told himself. "Why are we going to need all these diapers? Couldn't we just get little towels instead? Or washcloths? And couldn't we get them in Twin Falls?"

So quickly that they fell into his cart with a series of soft thuds, he added several big shakers of baby powder and half a dozen packages of large safety pins. Pushing one cart and dragging the other behind, he reached the checkout stands. The self-scan lanes both had long lines, so he willed himself to be patient while the checker scanned the baby things and stuffed them back into his carts.

As soon as she handed him the receipt, Ben maneuvered the two carts through the automatic doors at the best speed he could manage, out to Gramps' gray Ford pickup in the parking lot. He began to breathe a little easier as he tossed the packages of diapers into the bed. "Made it," he thought, turning to get into the cab. "Nobody saw me."

"Hey."

Ben's heart sank. Flat-footed on the asphalt stood Turk Thomas, Mason Patelski, Andy Johnson, Mose Twohorses, Tom Cress, and Carlos Aguirre. Football practice must have let out early today.

Turk reached around Ben and hefted a package of diapers. "Well, if it isn't the Scavenger, scavenging! Have a secret mistress, Scavenger? Gonna be a baby daddy and nobody gave you any diapers? No, that's not it. You are probably too small to wear Attends and these are for you. Incontinence incorporated. Shit city. Wee wee wee." His white smile was blinding. Turk winked one very blue eye and tossed the package to Tom, who tossed it to Mason and then to Mose. All of them were taller than Ben, and kept the package away from him with ease. He felt ridiculous, powerless. They laughed, not kindly.

Big Mose jumped up and fired the diaper package back into the bed of the pickup, a set shot. "Two points," he said coolly, as if bored. "Come on, guys, let's get out of here." They turned away.

Though he didn't watch them moving on, Ben could hear the joking remarks, the cutting laughter. This would be all over the high school by morning. And it was only Wednesday. *God.* But what else was new? At least he'd paid for the diapers. He hadn't scavenged. Not *this* time.

He got into the pickup, slammed the door, and shoved the key into its slot. The truck was warm from the late afternoon sun; he sent the window down.

"Hey, Ben." Ben's breath caught. He couldn't take another one of the jocks right now. But no, it was Gary. His best friend, Gary Scott. His almost still-friends friend. His departing friend. What was that word that Mrs. Phillips had used? Erstwhile. His erstwhile friend, Gary.

"Hey, Gary," Ben said. "What's up?"

4

"Have to get a couple of things from the store for Mom before dinner," Gary said, sauntering over to the pickup, leaning with his spine against the hood and his elbows braced at what looked to Ben like an impossible angle. "I saw those guys, the jocks." Gary took a couple of steps and peered into the pickup bed before returning to lean on the hood. "Holy crap, you *do* have a truck full of diapers. Has your Gramps gone even more fringe than usual? Or is it just you this time? Diapers, I ask you."

Ben sighed. "Gramps says that the end is coming fast now," Ben said, though he knew Gary didn't want to hear it. Nobody wanted to hear it, not ever, so Ben had learned to keep his mouth shut. "He thought we might need these. They are cloth diapers, so we can use them for lots of different things." Ben could feel his lips thinning to a tight line. He sounded stupid, even to himself.

"Sure," Gary said, barking a short laugh. "Sure, you can use diapers." Gary shook his head, making his stiff red curls bob just a little. "The end is nigh, huh?"

"Very close," Ben replied. "I know you don't think that anything's going to happen, but . . ." The thinly veiled disgust on Gary's face was obvious. Gramps kept saying that everyone would disbelieve, and that they both should smile and nod and go about their business. But Gary—Gary was, had been, Ben's friend, and didn't he have to try to make Gary understand? He had to try, because the alternative could be very dark. Very dark, indeed.

"Sure," said Gary again, as if he couldn't think of anything else to say. "Survivalist stuff. I get it: same old. Look, I wanted to tell you that I'm going out Friday night. Ha. Survive *that*."

"Yeah? Who with?" Ben asked. Gary, out on a date. Yes, Gary was moving on, leaving his nerd-class, *outcast*-class friend behind.

"Cindy Green," Gary said somewhat smugly, attempting to smooth his carroty hair. "Dinner and a movie. *Werewolf's Blood*, so with any luck she will clutch me."

"That's OK," said Ben. "Fairly shiny, actually." He took in his friend with a sidelong glance: long legs and slim hips in worn jeans, a gray t-shirt with wiry arms emerging, all topped by a narrow face with a prominent nose and high cheekbones. Blue eyes studied Ben from under dark red brows. And then above a high forehead, the wavy cliff of untamable red hair stood like a strangely curled wire brush. "If I can't get Gary to come with us, I'll want to remember him this way," Ben thought, didn't want to think.

"Well, envious one, got to get moving," Gary said. He shoved himself off the pickup hood into an upright stance, seeming to readjust a number of loose bones.

Ben acted upon a decision he had thought about for weeks, months—a decision he hoped he wouldn't regret, hoped Gramps wouldn't regret giving him permission. He had actually made this decision two weeks ago, when he had printed out copies of the maps.

"Wait, Gary." Ben fumbled in the glove compartment and came up with several sheets of folded paper. Through the window, he handed one to Gary without unfolding it. "Take this. Don't show it to anybody. But when things go bad, well—this is a map. A map to me and Gramps' Place." Ben could hear his own voice; the words seemed to bounce back at him from the roof of the pickup. He sounded flat, emotionless, unpersuasive. Unconvincing, because he was trying to be casual. But this was *Gary*. Ben had to do better than this at convincing him. Casual might be cool, but casual didn't carry any weight.

Ben went on, trying for some urgency, some sense of validity. "It's a few miles, but you could walk there in a couple of days. Or I could come get you. Just call me, Gary. I'll have my cell, and Gramps says cells should be good for a little while even when things start to go wonky. Pack up what you want to take and have it ready for bugging out. You know—a bug-out bag. Might be best to memorize and then destroy the map. I don't want it getting around."

Gary raised a reddish-brown eyebrow. "Paranoia, brother, you are there," he said, shrugging uncomfortably, a shrug that involved his entire upper body. "Bondian, James, note: the sky hasn't fallen and there's no Spectre. Walker, note: Zombies not crawling up, out, or away, even." He folded the map into a tighter rectangle and shoved it deep into a front pocket of his jeans without bothering to look at it.

"I know you think Gramps is senile and that I'm a few bricks short of a load," Ben said as Gary took a step away from the pickup. He reached for Gary's arm, saw the look in his friend's eyes, and let his hand drop. "But you and I have been friends for so long. I just want you to make it. Don't take this wrong. Just say you will keep the map and not toss it."

Ben knew he sounded desperate now, truly paranoid. He took a breath, tried to be matter-of fact. "I have some stuff to do for Gramps in Twin Falls the next couple of days, so you aren't going to see me at school. Gramps is going to call me in sick." Gary was silent, fidgeting from foot to foot; Ben could tell Gary wanted to get away; it was time to shut up before things between them went even worse. "Have fun at the movies," Ben said. "Don't get any popcorn. You need to keep your hands free for other things. Gary--" The word hung in the air, heavy enough to fall.

Gary took two steps toward the store, three. "Roger," he said.

Ben said nothing. He had tried, but it was too late now to do things differently, and he knew it wouldn't do any good to beg.

But Gary stopped in his tracks, then turned to look closely at Ben, his forehead wrinkled, his blue eyes troubled. "OK. OK, Ben," he said slowly. "I will keep your precious map. For old time's sake. And when things *don't* blow up, you might consider getting back to normal again. Normality is nice. My old friend Ben was normal." Gary trotted toward the glass doors of the supermarket, passed through the shadow there, and the gaping doors swallowed him whole.

Ben squinted into the sun just as it began to slide behind Carbonate Mountain on the far side of the store's parking lot. Gary had been fading from their friendship for some time, and it seemed that the only way to get him back would be to ignore Gramps, to defy Gramps even, and to forget about the coming crash.

Defying Gramps wouldn't be that difficult these days, Ben thought with a small coldness congealing in his stomach. Gramps wasn't as strong as he used to be. Just lately Ben had noticed Gramps getting tired way too fast, and that was more than a little scary. But still, Gramps was *right*. Wasn't he? "How many times have I had this debate?" Ben asked himself.

Gary thought Ben should try being normal, did he? Fat chance of that. Here it was early October. October was a time of year when normal guys were into football, girls, hiking even, going hunting maybe, hitting the drive-in for a burger and fries after school, doing the social network thing, gaming, or just having some friends over for pizza and watching football or a movie, or doing some games. And instead, here he was, almost sixteen, driving a pickup load of diapers home. Holy crap, indeed.

Shaking his head, Ben started the engine and got going.

Along Wood River, the cottonwoods were turning to gold, and shadows moved on the road as their long leaves fluttered in a light breeze. Up ahead, Ben saw Lainey Adams and Turk Thomas walking together, very close, with Kaylee Field and Shandy Johnson trailing a few steps behind. Ben had History with Turk, and History and English with Lainey and Kaylee, but they weren't his friends. To them, he was just the idiot who scavenged for throwaways and bought twelve packages of diapers after school. When Ben passed them, they didn't wave. "I printed out four copies of the map," he thought grimly, "and I have only one friend. Sort of. Pretty stupid."

⊨⇥ ⇤⊨

Artemisia Ames pedaled her bike home slowly, the heavy books in her daypack slapping against her spine every time she hit a bump. In her view were the narrow streets, the leaves on the trees turning to yellow, orange, brown, and amber, the neat and not-so-neat houses set well back from the street, the asphalt of the road, the occasional car, and behind everything, the huge gray shoulder of what she called Thing Hill, a large presence nearly treeless and patched with the sagebrush that was her namesake, *Artemisia.* "That's what I get for having a Forest Service botanist for a mother," Artie thought for the ten thousandth time.

The air was warm with a hint of crispness as she rode through shadows of houses and trees that stretched long and blue across the road at day's end, the way they always did late on sunny afternoons. The sun slid toward the blade-sharp, shadowy ridge to the west, Carbonate Mountain. She turned left onto the street where she lived.

Artie's street looked the way it always did toward the end of the day. On her right, she could see Carlos Aguirre's little brother Manny running across their lawn chasing a soccer ball. Mrs. Williams drove by in her new blue Jeep Wrangler, probably on her way downtown to the Starbucks in the Albertson's for her daily late-afternoon mocha. The Drews' brown tabby cat, Mabel, sat on their porch soaking up the last rays of the sun, licking her paws. Everything looked all right.

But there was something wrong here, something Artie felt high in her throat, making her feel slightly choked, making her want to breathe too fast and to swallow over and over.

Artie was an observer. She had always been the curious one in her family, wanting to know why and how everything worked and the names of all the plants and animals, rocks, mountains, rivers, birds, flowers, dogs, cats, horses, and people. She wanted to know how and why the world operated, and what was in it. She also wanted to know what bloomed when and what the seeds were like, what animals did and why they did it, what made up the rocks and soil and how the landscape got that way, what people thought and felt and why they did the things they did.

Artie had learned some years ago that her never-ending stream of questions made people uncomfortable, so she had stepped back a little from the front of life and began to watch.

She knew the town of Hailey fairly well now, she thought, and many of the people in it—plus the surrounding hills, gulches, canyons, and mountains. Artie knew which creeks had which kinds of trout, where the coyote dens were, where the pine grosbeaks nested, what tiger swallowtail caterpillars looked like, on which hillsides she could find agates, and what gulches had wild bluebells and lupine in May and June. In addition, for several neighborhoods Artie knew who worked where, what they did, what cars or trucks they drove, how late they stayed up at night, what movies they went to see, how often they drove to Twin Falls or Boise or Stanley, what dogs and cats and horses and canoes and snowmobiles and children they had, and who was—or at least seemed–happy, and who was obviously not content. And although this fall things looked almost—almost--the same as always, something was wrong.

Ever since she could remember, Artie had always had a sense of when something was going to go bad, an edgy feeling when something ill was in the wind, on its way, just about to arrive. She remembered the time when she'd felt strange when she was ten and her mom was planning to drive to Salt Lake City for a conference. Artie had begged her mother not to go. And two hours after her mother had set out, a range fire, whipped by the wind, had engulfed the highway. Her mom had been fine, but she had been stopped on the highway for four hours.

One afternoon last spring Artie had refused to ride Gram's horse across a little bridge over an irrigation canal. That day she had been riding with Shannon Peterson, and Shannon had been very irritated when Artie had turned Merry back and cut short their ride. But later that afternoon the bridge had collapsed, the bank undermined by the current in a place hidden from view. So Artie knew, just *knew* something was wrong now, and that the something was something big, and that it was something gathering force, something dark that was out there but coming closer. *Or did she? Or was it?*

She had tried all summer to put her finger on what seemed wrong, to give it a name. The economy was a mess, of course. Some people her parents knew had lost their jobs. Many others were afraid of losing their jobs. Her dad was one of those. Was that the wrongness? Maybe. But what was it about the town that had made her feel the wrongness in the first place? Whatever it was eluded her, kept dancing just out of reach.

Over everything, she felt a shadow, a shade that took the warmth from the sun, a difference that prickled a chill up her spine now and then, that made her shiver for no reason. Artie had told her mother, finally, when the feeling began invading her sleep with nightmares. Her mother thought those feelings were what she called "teen drama." Or "adolescent runaway emotions, caused by hormones." Or even, as her mom had said just last week, "You are becoming an adult, Artie, and you are realizing that the world is full of problems not easily solved."

Even Artie's best friend Rosa Mendez didn't think anything had changed. Was Artie the only one to feel it? Was she just putting a dramatic twist on things to make her life a good story to tell? Nevertheless, Artie felt that it would be idiotic to ignore what she called her "bad-thing radar."

Several things seemed different about Hailey, changes so tiny that perhaps they weren't changes at all. To Artie, people seemed to be walking a little faster, and their fuses seemed to be shorter.

But the things that made the goosebumps rise on Artie's arms were stupid things, things that she hadn't noticed at first, things that had come to her attention gradually over the past summer. People hadn't gone on picnics much this year. They didn't go fishing or camping very often. There had been fewer flowers in front yards than she had seen in past summers, and more weeds. Their neighbor Mrs. Grant didn't take her book and her iced tea out onto the patio on the warm July and August evenings. The Tanners didn't give their big summer barbeques. Mr. and Mrs. Wizner had let their apricots and apples go unpicked, and the fruit had fallen into the lawn, rotting and attracting wasps. Mr. Feldson hardly ever walked his beagle any more, just left Boppy in the back yard. And his son Billy, a high school senior, had started the summer washing his car every Saturday night, but somehow he had stopped doing that well before the 4th of July. Hardly anyone whistled or sang. Even Artie's mother had stopped singing in the shower. So many little things, little tiny things . . . Shadow things.

Today, this afternoon, the shadow things seemed crushing, almost overwhelming. "I wonder if I'm sliding into mental illness," Artie thought suddenly, as she reached her own driveway and the fluttering shade of the aspens there. "I feel so odd right now, like there's a heavy weight over my head that's about to fall any minute. I wonder if this is how people who have clinical depression feel. Is this what paranoia is like?"

Artie pulled up to her own open garage and snorted as she wheeled her bike inside and hit the plastic pad to shut the door behind her. "I must be crazy. There's nothing wrong," she told herself, also for the ten thousandth time, as she swung herself and her daypack around the doorjamb and into the bright kitchen. "But, today it's different," her mind whispered. "But . . ."

⊷⊷ ⊶⊶

Gramps was sitting in his big leather chair with the flat wooden arms, as he often was these days, when Ben came in. Fending off the three Shelties jumping on and around him, Ben toed off his shoes and collapsed onto the couch.

"Did you get them?" Gramps asked. "The diapers?"

"Sure, Gramps. And the baby powder and the big safety pins. They are still out in the pickup," said Ben, taking Molly, the tricolor, into his lap. He noticed an empty bowl and spoon on the arm of Gramps' chair. "Is there anything to eat?"

"Beef stew in the crockpot," Gramps said. "Sorry I didn't wait for you. I forgot about lunch and got hungry."

Ben nodded. Gramps was doing a lot of crock-pot cooking these days, but that was all right. Gramps was good at it. Ben took Gramps' empty bowl back to the kitchen, set it in the sink, ran it full of water, and brought out a clean bowl of steaming stew for himself. "Smells good. How are you feeling tonight, Gramps?"

Outside, twilight had come. Twilight fell rapidly in October, and the living room was on the west side of the house, long fallen into the shadow of Carbonate Mountain as the sun moved on its sure path to the west.

Ben switched on a couple of lamps and looked carefully at his Grandfather while he ate his own stew: narrow shoulders, thin arms emerging from rolled-up plaid flannel sleeves, the long hands with long fingers a little swollen at the joints. They were veterinarian's hands—Ben knew well the raised white scar on the left index finger that Gramps had said came from a mean mare with sharp teeth. The little finger on that same hand was permanently bent from an encounter with barbed wire, rope, and a tangled cow. Gramps had a straight nose and generous lips in a square, lean face, white hair a little sparse on top, and heavy white eyebrows over clear blue eyes. He had never been a big man, but just lately he seemed stooped and shrunken. Tonight Gramps looked more tired than usual, Ben thought.

"I'm OK," Gramps told him with a flash of blue eyes, as if reading Ben's mind. "Not to worry."

Ben spooned stew. "Some of the jocks saw me loading the diapers into the truck," he said without meeting Gramps' eyes. "Not much fun."

Gramps gave him a look through the white eyebrows. "I know it's not fun, boy. I wouldn't put you through all this if it weren't necessary. I'd have picked up those last diapers myself, but I just get worn out so fast these days. Trying to save my strength for the move."

Gramps tapped the shirt pocket where his cell phone lived. "I've been talking to Cuda and Beezer today. Couldn't reach Simon and Phil--or Lucy--and that scares me a bit. Well, not so much Simon and Phil. They quit their jobs in July, retired at last--about time—and they sold their Frisco house in August and have been hauling things to their cabin in northern Cal every weekend since. Their cabin doesn't have phone service, landline or cell, and Simon did tell me they were going to leave San Francisco for good sometime this month. So those two are probably just fine and settling in for the winter. I just wish they had called me first, though. But I am quite concerned that I haven't been able to raise Lucy. She's supposed to be all packed into her new 22-foot travel trailer and closing up her house this week. Ready to roll, you know? I should be able to get her on the cell, but she hasn't been answering. She hasn't answered texts or email, either. She's supposed to get to the Place on Saturday.

Lucy has driven to the Place before, so it isn't like she lost the map or anything. Huh," Gramps sneezed into his hand.

"Don't like it," Gramps continued. "Cuda's been in D.C. watching, but he's going now. He has got his family loaded and he's heading out tonight for his place in West Virginia. Cuda was worried, Ben. He thinks we might have left it too late. Told me he was going to go black after today and for me not to try calling him, not for six months, anyway." Gramps took a deep breath. "Not until spring. Beezer left Houston yesterday. He called me from Las Cruces this morning. He's going to ground, too, and is no doubt out of cell range by now. His cabin is in a side branch of one of those deep canyons."

Gramps touched Ben on the arm and held his eyes. "I wish I knew exactly what is going to go on so I could tell you," he said. "But I trusted these guys in 'Nam and I trust them now, so I hope you will, too, as time goes by. And Lucy. Though Rob has been gone for a while, as soon as I saw her for the first time all those years ago, I knew that we could trust his Lucy. I stood up at their wedding and knew she was as brave and true and smart as my Benerita, and I was right; that's all. The only thing I know with any certainty is that the major geology thing that's coming is almost here, as Lucy has been predicting all this time, and that will cause a crisis of resources and a crisis in government--and people that don't raise crops or meat, who don't work in the factories, who live in the smaller towns, are going to become dispensable. 'Excess,' as Cuda puts it. 'Expendable. Too scattered and too hard to govern; taking up resources without producing any; too hard to keep in line.' We're mostly a resort area, so that means us."

"Excess," Ben repeated softly. He'd heard most of this many times before, but the dire combination of events coming had seemed a freight train hundreds of miles away, unseen and unheard, a train that was out there somewhere but would never quite arrive at their own station. Was it really, actually about to happen? He put his bowl on the floor, where Molly and blue Moonie immediately began licking up the remains of his stew, until Bear shouldered them away and took the last lump of potato for himself.

"So," Gramps went on, with the hard-edged cheerfulness of someone less confident than he hoped to appear, "it is nearly time for us to scoot. I'm going to stay here for the next couple of days and rest up for the last trip. I see that you have a duffel and your daypack filled already. That's good; one less task to do here. I'll finish packing my suitcases while you are in Twin Falls buying things. I wish Hailey were large enough so we could shop together for the last push—but no, that would raise too many eyebrows. And to shop here in town would be too expensive as well. 'Under the radar' is our motto, don't forget. It should be easy enough for me to get my stuff here in order while you do the final buying. There's not much left here, anyhow. The suitcases and a cardboard box or two ought to do for the remaining things I'm going to take. And the shotgun, of course. So, you will go buying tomorrow."

Gramps passed a hand over his wispy hair, smoothing it. "I called a few stores in Twin Falls a couple of weeks ago and ordered in some of the items on our lists, and I've done some online ordering, too—things to be picked up at the stores in Twin. I think almost all of the things I've ordered are in now. If the rest of those things don't come in by Friday morning, well—we just won't have them, period. I imagine somebody will be glad enough to get them, eventually."

Gramps stroked the white stubble on one side of his jaw with slender fingers. "I gave them all a story that I was stocking up for a new youth camp. That ought to be a good line for you to use if you get any questions on the quantities. But maybe the stores are getting used to preppers by now. And, Ben--dress older than you are, when you go down to do the buying, so nobody wonders why you aren't in school. Button-down shirt, long sleeves, not a tee. Your good shoes. Khakis, not jeans, OK?" Ben nodded. He'd heard this before, too. Gramps continued, "I figure we should be out of Hailey for good before Friday sundown." Gramps' eyes crinkled with his smile. "Friday night at the Place, that's the plan. I'll bake us a pie."

From the flat arm of his chair, Gramps lifted a little green notebook, much worn and dog-eared. "I called the bank today. Looks like there's a bit over $49,000 in there, Ben. I cashed out my Idaho Power shares last week. I had the bank move what was left in savings, into checking. All of it. Good thing I know Alf Rangel down at the bank so well; used to take care of his horses and those two white nanny goats of Eve's, remember? Saanens, they were. Nice to work with, Saanens. So Alf didn't give me too much fuss about moving all the money. I've been busy today. I revised the lists of things for you to get in Twin Falls."

Gramps tore half a dozen pages from the notebook and handed them to Ben. "Here they are, the last lists. Take 'em. I made copies here in the notebook."

Ben smiled. Gramps lived by lists, had done so ever since Ben could remember. It seemed that most of his own life had been spent getting things or doing things written on one or another of Gramps' lists. He didn't believe for one moment that these lists would be the last.

Gramps said, "I'm sorry you'll have to do this last shopping for us alone. But time is running out, has just about run *all* the way out, and that $49,000 isn't going to do us any good after things hit the fan, so we might as well get some use out of it. Life savings, they call it–ha!" Gramps pretended to be laughing, but his eyes said something else.

"Your Uncle George is going to come over in about an hour to help you put the shell back on the pickup," Gramps went on.

"I told him we were going hunting this weekend and wanted to sleep in the truck. Duck hunting down by Carey, I said, so you'll know what to say if he asks. But with the shell on, the truck can carry a lot more stuff, and you can go from store to store without tempting someone to steal anything from the bed."

Gramps sighed and said, "First thing in the morning, you can take off for Twin Falls, and be careful. Under the radar, remember? When you've got a full load, go to the Place and unload. Fill 'er up again until the money is gone, however many trips it takes. And after you've got everything bought, you can finish stocking the caches, too, on Friday. But--first things first. Go at first light. Be back here before dark tomorrow night, by 1600 sharp. I don't want anyone seeing our lights on the road to our Place. Don't want anybody remembering that. I figure you can do two trips from Twin Falls to the Place in a day, if you need to. It's less than 250 miles for a round trip. Two, maybe three trips should do the whole thing." Gramps let his head fall back against the chair cushion as if this long speech had exhausted him.

Ben nodded again. Gramps often reverted to military time. Sixteen hundred translated to four o'clock in the afternoon. That was good; it would still be light at four.

"Don't spend so much that you don't have enough for gas on the last afternoon. I want the pickup's gas tank pretty much full when we get to the Place on Friday night," Gramps said. He added, "Before you leave Twin on Friday, after you've got everything on these lists, if there's any money left and any time left, get yourself some things for fun, something for those long winter nights, so be thinking of what you might want. I hope there will be some money left for you to splurge a little. There should be a bit of extra, at least a thousand—maybe more. If there's a lot left, get more books. Got my calculator?"

"Yes, I have it. Everything will be fine," was all Ben said. It was no use telling Gramps that he didn't need to take that little calculator; he could use the calculator in his phone. Ben didn't say much these days. He thought, "If I didn't believe Gramps, this would be utterly, totally insane. But I do believe him. Unfortunately." He added suddenly, "I ran into Gary after school, at the store. I wish it was going to be more than just us, Gramps."

Frank Elliott smiled in a way that lit his face and made him seem, for the moment, much younger. "I wish your mom and dad were still alive. And your grandmother, of course. And both you and I tried to convince some others a while ago, didn't we? Doc Funk, for one. He and I have been friends for 40 years, but he still doesn't listen to me. And the few hard-core survivalists here seem to be all about blowing people away after the apocalypse and sitting on their piles of goods watching other people get desperate. The preppers I've talked with absolutely don't understand that they won't make it if their 'safehouses' are their homes in town. So I've never felt like getting in with them. There were a few others I tried to tell a couple of years back, good people, too. With the possible exception of Eleanor Phillips, they think I've lost my mind, even your uncle George. Glad I haven't told any of them the location of the Place. With any luck, they won't remember I was serious. If they do remember, they'll probably come here looking for our stuff, and won't find it, or us. 'Crazy old Frank Elliott,' they say now. 'He's a hoarder. He's obsessed.' So it's just us, kid. And Lucy, when she gets to the Place this weekend."

"And the dogs," Ben added, ruffling Moonie's gray fur. "Dogs are better company than most people."

"Yes. And I figure we'll have more people, eventually," Gramps said, the light still in his eyes. "People who are a little less gullible than the average, a few who are a little smarter and more observant. Or luckier. A few more will come after a while--or else after the first winter, if we feel that it might be safe by then, we can go out looking. So!" he said, pushing the plaid flannel sleeve farther up his left arm.

Ben knew what was expected, and lifted his right arm next to Gramps' left. "Stand fast," they said together. "Stand Fast," read the simple, small tattoo on each of their arms. Gramps and Ben then lifted their opposite arms, each of which bore the same single word. "Hope."

CHAPTER 2
SPENDING IT ALL

B en was up before the sun and out the door, dressed in a blue long-sleeved cotton shirt and crisp khaki slacks. He felt a little weird, but that was all right. The pickup started easily, and, armed with his debit card for the joint checking account that was really Gramps' account, Ben turned south onto Main Street and headed toward Twin Falls.

At dawn the town of Hailey was awake and moving--people on the sidewalks, cars and trucks on the streets, a school bus skirting a stalled truck, the ever-present SUVs. Hailey and its air-field fell behind as Ben drove south. He drove slowly through the smaller, sleepier town of Bellevue, a known speed trap, and then he was out in the farmland, with little traffic so early. Finally he crested Timmerman Hill and entered the soft gray and tan expanse of the sagebrush desert, where he could really make some time.

Ben was glad enough to avoid school this morning, after that disaster with the diapers yesterday. "Scavenger," nearly everyone at school called him. He could just hear Turk and Carlos, Tom and Mason, Andy and Mose sniggering over the story of the Scavenger's diapers, and he could just see how the girls they told would smirk. Still, it was beyond strange to think that he might not be going back to school, that there might not *be* a high school to go back to. Because on the surface, life was still shiny. This morning, things were running along the way they always did. Normal. Boring.

There was a football game Friday night, an away game, in Filer. And Gary was taking Cindy Green to the movies that night instead of going to the game. A history test loomed next Wednesday, and a report for English was due at the end of that week, on the following Friday. Mrs. Phillips had been much dissed for assigning that paper's due date at the start of this year's Homecoming festivities, but she hadn't budged. He smiled; Ben liked Mrs. Phillips. Weird old bat that she was at times, she knew her stuff, and if you took her class, you had better know it, too. Besides English, she taught art, and that's where Ben kept his heart.

Ben wondered if Gary would have a good time Friday night and would ask Cindy to the Homecoming dance the following weekend, and if Cindy would go with him. If so, that would be still more distancing between Gary and himself. But—Gary had looked so happy this afternoon.

That whole girl thing was simply outside Ben's range, though not exactly by choice. Gramps had kept him so busy for so long that going to a dance, or even just going for a coffee, feeling close enough to a girl to *ask* her even, was just a fuzzed-out dream, beyond him somewhere. Way out there. It was pointless to care, anyway. For one, he couldn't dance. For two, the whole dance thing sounded boring, "Boring as all hell," Gramps would say. For three, he had no idea what he could talk about to a girl. And for four, what self-respecting girl would go anywhere with *Scavenger*—or would even let herself be seen talking to him?

Gramps had started what Gary called "this survivalist stuff" for reasons that he hadn't tried to explain then, about eight or nine years ago. People had found Gramps a convenient alternative to the landfill. "Hey, Joe," Gramps would say as he pulled up to a house where a neighbor was carrying an old screen door to the curb on garbage day, "Want me to take that off your hands?" Gramps had sharp eyes, sharp ears, and was always on the lookout for throwaways and giveaways.

And Gramps would tell him, "Benny, why don't you run down to Mrs. Grover's and pick up a box of empty coffee cans she has saved for me. And don't forget the lids." Or, "On your way home from school, swing by the back of Mr. Danner's store. He's going to give us an enamel camp dishpan that he can't sell because it has a dent in the rim." Or, "Come on—we're going to take the truck down Broadford Road to the Youngs' place. They've got a dozen gallon jugs for us, glass jugs. They had a big Halloween party and drank a lot of cider. Those jugs will be just the thing for storing wheat and rice."

When he was a little kid, Ben thought these gathering activities were ordinary things that some people just *did*, something like a hobby. Some guys collected coins or knives, some guys had a couple of old cars they thought they were restoring, some guys had signed baseballs from the big leagues that they kept in glass cases, some guys built a lot of birdhouses. Gramps was just a guy who collected things, Ben had thought when he was just a kid. But Ben knew better now. Now he knew that Gramps was known as the town nutcase. Gramps was Crazy Frank Elliott, Fruit Loop Frank, Idiot Elliott. He was the old geezer who used to be a great veterinarian, but who started going gaga just before he retired. Such a shame.

Ben was about eleven when the other kids started calling him "Scavenger." He had told Gramps how they laughed and pointed and whispered, and Gramps had sat him down with half a gallon of huckleberry ice cream and told him about the coming changes and how they had to work hard to gather and prepare everything they would need to make it through the first years after the end, when other people would be dangerous to them and everything would be scarce. "Your parents left you to me, Benny," Gramps had said then, "and we owe it to them to be smart, survive, and be around to rebuild."

The gray sage blurred past, and Ben slowed for the strange little town of Shoshone, whose wide-open heart was barred with a dozen railroad tracks. He saw a school bus on the road ahead as it began turning off the highway, and thought again of Mrs. Phillips. The last art piece he'd done in her class had been a pencil sketch of some aspen leaves on the ground, curling slightly as they dried. He'd tried to make wind go through the sketch, just the tiniest breath of wind, a stirring. She'd seen that. He'd been astonished that she had seen it.

A sudden thought struck him, and he knew it was right. Gramps might have a fit later, but that would be later. And after all, she wouldn't come--and so Gramps would never know.

The Shoshone Post Office was only a little out of his way, a one-story box of a building made of tan brick. The low building looked temporary next to one of Shoshone's original black lava stone storefronts.

Before he could change his mind, Ben pulled up to the Post Office. He took one of the folded maps and a pen from the glove compartment and wrote a note in the top right corner: *Everything ends on Friday, but you can come here. Just you. Don't tell.* He signed with his initials, BE. She'd know. In art class, he always signed his sketches that way. On the back of the middle fold he wrote: *Mrs. Eleanor Phillips, Wood River High School, Hailey, Idaho 83333.* "That ought to do it," Ben thought. He didn't know the address of that big old house where she lived by herself, but it wasn't as if Hailey had another high school, or even another zip code, after all.

As Ben slid from the pickup with the map in his hand, he remembered Mrs. Phillips bending over his last drawing, her gray brows drawn together and her small hand splayed flat on the plastic-woodgrain surface of one of the long tables, where he sat in art class with twelve other students. "Those leaves are moving, aren't they?" she had asked, but it really wasn't a question. She knew. "The wind is pushing them just a little," Mrs. Phillips had told him then. "It's not enough of a breeze to lift them into the air, is it? But they are vibrating, getting ready for the wind to move them along the ground." She had turned her face to his, very close. He had seen in great detail the soft, slack skin beneath her jaw and the precisely cut wrinkles that fanned from her eyes. In that moment, she wasn't "Mrs. Phillips" to him but *Eleanor*. The intelligence in her gray-blue gaze had transfixed him.

"Yes," he had whispered, a breath, so that no one else would hear, "the wind is touching them." Mrs. Phillips had nodded. That had been enough for Ben. A rare wave of pure happiness had flooded him and he'd sat motionless in the classroom, feeling for the rest of art class as if he were floating in a pool of sunshine.

Yes, he'd send Mrs. Phillips this map, all right. Gramps said she was a widow; if she'd had any children, they were somewhere else now, because Ben had never seen her around town with any family.

He pushed the bar on the heavy glass door and entered the cool stillness of the Post Office. A smiling clerk, looking pleased at some traffic so early in the morning, sold him a single stamp and used a bit of tape to close the folded paper. The map went into the "out" slot and the deed was done. Ben jumped back into the pickup. "You never know," he told himself, slamming the door. "You really never know."

He drove south out of Shoshone; Twin Falls was close now. Ben set his face in a grim smile. "Four maps and two friends," he thought, and couldn't help adding, "sort of."

A few miles later, the pickup reached the Perrine Memorial Bridge. Ben put his foot down on the accelerator; the bridge had always scared him a little, the long man-made span seeming so fragile between the sheer black cliffs of the Snake River Canyon-- and the river, gray-green and sluggish below, seeming so very far down. Five hundred feet down. He always sped across the bridge. When he was small, the bridge had been frightening; now it just made him uncomfortable.

Five hundred feet was so far to fall that you would splat on the water like it was a table of solid metal before you broke through the surface and sank, already smashed and dead. At least that was what Gary always said. *Gary.* It would be so much better if Gary were going to the Place with them on Friday. Fat chance. He knew that Gary's parents were among those who called Gramps "Crazy Frank."

"I won't think about that. At least I've given Gary the map," Ben told himself as the dark south rim of the canyon fell behind and the pickup gained the stretch of highway beyond the bridge. "Sometimes strange things happen. Maybe Gary will come after all—not right away, but eventually. As soon as bad things start to happen. When things start to change."

And then Ben slowed. He was rolling into Twin Falls.

Last night Ben had studied Gramps' lists and had rewritten them into individual lists for each store as he figured out where to go for what, to save time. Seeing how many things Gramps still wanted to get, Ben was heartily glad for everything that he and Gramps already had stashed at the Place during the last few years. For so long, renovating and stocking the Place had eaten most of Gramps' military pension and Social Security checks and whatever Ben had earned in odd jobs here and there, not to mention their time and energy.

After a long phone conversation with Dr. Lucy three years ago, Gramps had sold out his half interest in the veterinary clinic (which he had kept after he had retired), and he had also sold four empty lots in town that he had owned since forever, to give them some serious money to pour into the Place. That's when the Place's buildings had acquired their gray metal roofs, and that's when Gramps had bought the new pickup, among other things.

But it wasn't until last spring, when Gramps had sold their own house--the house Gramps had had built for Grandma so many years before, the house where Ben's dad and Uncle George had been born and where Ben himself had grown up—that Ben had realized just how very serious Gramps was about "that survivalist stuff." Besides the cash, the sales contract specified that Gramps and Ben could occupy the house for up to three years after the sale if they wished, rent-free. Then Sky and Mountain Development, L.L.C., would take over. Ben had hated the thought of some impersonal company owning *their* house. The sale of the house had precipitated Ben's first serious fight with Gramps, but Gramps had gone ahead and signed the sales contract. Ben still hated it. He knew that Sky and Mountain would probably move the little white house to a small lot in the flat country somewhere north of Shoshone and build some multimillion-dollar home on top of Gramps' vegetable garden--or even put up an apartment building there. He'd seen that kind of thing happen several times. He hoped they wouldn't cut down all the trees. He loved those trees.

This infusion of cash allowed Gramps to pick up the pace of preparation during the summer just past, and almost every day saw bags, boxes, cans, stacks, piles, cases, rolls, bottles, barrels, and bundles of things bought and ferried to the Place: stacks of metal fenceposts, bottle after bottle of antibiotics that Gramps could order because of his veterinarian's license, heavy bags of wheat and rice, cases of canned food, plus bandanas, canvas, paint, rope, spools of barbed wire, tools, and countless heavy plastic barrels, most of them blue, fifty-gallon barrels that still smelled faintly of the cider they once had held.

The past summer's warm and comfortable days had not been spent fishing or hiking, but had seen Ben and Gramps driving these things to the Place and stowing them safely there.

The list of things already at the Place seemed almost endless, everything from butternut squash to shingle nails—and yet, Ben thought with a wry grin, here he was in Twin Falls with still more lists, really long lists. "The *last* lists," he said aloud, "whatever that is going to mean."

The Co-Op Bulk Buy store was his first stop. Gramps had listed a goodly amount of heavy stuff for Ben to buy at the Co-op, mostly canned foods; Ben decided that those should go on the bottom layer in the pickup, so Ben had come to the Co-Op first. And because the pickup's shell was attached now, he thought he could probably fit in all the lighter items needed from Fred Meyer on top of the Co-Op stuff, and maybe everything from Home Depot as well. He figured that the Co-Op, Fred's, and Home Depot things were probably all he'd be able to take today–but maybe he would hit the garden store as well. Seeds were light and didn't take up much room.

Ben found a parking space close to the doors of the Co-Op. He was early. The doors wouldn't open for another fifteen minutes, so he unfolded his lists and read through them again.

Co-Op Bulk Buy
200 packets of bread yeast
30 pounds of baking powder (called ahead)
5 cases of canned salmon
10 cases of canned pumpkin
3 cases each of canned apple, blueberry, peach, and cherry
pie filling plus cans of whatever looks good that is on sale

Ben grinned. Gramps loved pie, and had taught himself
to make good pies after Grandma had died.

Home Depot
20 hammers
20 saws
35 assorted screwdrivers
12 chisels
25 metal files, various, both round and flat, coarse and
fine assorted paintbrushes, at least 20
25 metal buckets

Fred Meyer
25 winter parkas
50 each, winter hats and neck scarves
50 pairs of winter gloves
4 or 5 dozen t-shirts, whatever is fairly cheap but looks well
made; can get more at ShopKo if they don't have enough
at Fred's
50 sweatshirts
50 pairs of jeans
30 pairs of flannel lounge pants
35 polarfleece jackets
Get various sizes of all the clothes, but most in our sizes.
6 large stainless steel bowls
12 can openers
15 big stainless steel spoons
25 big daypacks
300 skeins of yarn
four dozen knitting needles
25 sharp kitchen knives
25 blankets

25 pillowcases, colors (not white)
25 twin size flat sheets, no fitted, colors (not white), 12 flannel, 12 cotton

Cowboy and Ranch Outfitters
4 Dutch ovens, small ones
12 pairs tall rubber boots
5 boxed sets of enamelware, 4 each: plates, cups, bowls
5 enamel coffeepots
50 pocketknives (ordered ahead)
25 compasses
2 cases of Sterno canned fuel
Note: most of the things on order have come in: the hand water pumps, the crosscut saws, the pulleys, the two wire stretchers, the game cart, the wire snares, the scythes, and the two hand meat grinders.

Sportsmen's Warehouse
35 sleeping bags (order came in)
12 pairs of Carhartt overalls
6 Carhartt jumpsuits
50 flannel shirts
25 ceramic water filters (order came in)
Note: the six crossbows and all the bolts have come in

Harper's School Supply
Chalkboard to hang on wall
Check out what else they might have that we would like

Shopko
100 bottles of dish soap
100 large cans of Crisco shortening (called ahead), 8 small cans

100 cans of peanuts
25 big containers each of cinnamon, ginger, black pepper, chili spice, sage, basil, and cloves
a dozen salt shakers
35 pairs of sneakers
35 pairs of cheap knitted gloves
200 pairs of socks, heavy and light
50 plastic raincoats (called ahead)
100 bars of Ivory soap
50 packages of needles, called ahead
3 dozen packs of permanent markers
200 notebooks and packages of pencils
100 big bottles of aspirin (called ahead)
100 big bottles of vitamin C (called ahead)
20 hot water bottles (called ahead)
Bunch of hard candy
Some chocolate

Mohler's Corner Garden Supply
Vegetable seed packets, 12 or so of each: every variety of peas, beans, carrots, parsnips, squash, corn, pumpkins, tomatoes, gourds, cabbage, turnips, lettuce, kale, chard, spinach, green onions, radishes, zucchini, peppers hot and sweet, sunflowers, and whatever else looks all right.
Herb seeds, several packets of each: comfrey, basil, cilantro, chives, chamomile, sage, rosemary, thyme, dill, arnica, echinacea, mint, fennel, marjoram, tarragon, sorrel, summer savory, chives, and whatever else they have
4 bags each of potato and onion sets (order came in)
Flower seeds: 25 packets of blue flax (called ahead)

Rocket Man Used Books
Some westerns--early Louis Lamour and Tony Hillerman for sure
Bunch of cheap books, use up whatever money is left; get two copies of things that strike your fancy, for trade, if the money is holding up. Here's a list of classics we don't have, or we don't have two of, so try for some of these if there is time:
The Hunger Games trilogy
Wuthering Heights
Jane Eyre
David Copperfield
Bleak House
Pride and Prejudice
Emma
Moby-Dick
Treasure Island
Robinson Crusoe
Last of the Mohicans
The Pathfinder
Tales of Edgar Allan Poe
Book of old English and Scottish poems and ballads
Book of poems by the Romantic poets: Byron, Keats, Shelley
Books of later English and American poems, including Matthew Arnold, Emily Dickinson, Walt Whitman, Siegfried Sassoon, Rupert Brooke, Wilfred Owen, Alfred Noyes
Some art books with photos of famous paintings
Anything by Zane Grey, but especially:
Riders of the Purple Sage
Betty Zane
The Last Trail

The Spirit of the Border
Nevada
Forlorn River
Wildfire
My Friend Flicka, Thunderhead, Green Grass of Wyoming
Anne of Green Gables books
Tales and Rhymes of Mother Goose
Aesop's Fables
Smoky the Cowhorse
She
King Solomon's Mines
The King Must Die
The Bull from the Sea
Bulfinch's Mythology
The Call of the Wild
White Fang
King of the Wind
Ring of Bright Water
Lad: A Dog
Game of Thrones books
The Iliad
The Odyssey
Plays by Aeschylus, Aristophanes, Sophocles, Euripides
The Harvester
Girl of the Limberlost
The Black Stallion
Dune
Ender's Game
Alas, Babylon
A Canticle for Leibowitz
anything we don't already have by C.J. Cherryh, Harlan
Coben, Louise Penny, Lisa Unger, Lisa Gardner, Linwood
Barclay, Greg Iles, William Kent Krueger, Laurie R.

King, Ray Bradbury, Robert Heinlein, Andre Norton, Cordwainer Smith, Fritz Lieber, Josephine Tey, Helen McInnes, Gerald Durrell, Konrad Lorenz, Fritz Lieber, Zenna Henderson, Niko Tinbergen, Steven Jay Gould, Roger Zelazny, Farley Mowat, Dana Stabenow
Book on how to raise rabbits
Book on how to raise chickens
Book on goats and sheep
Book on cows
Book on training horses
Book on spinning and weaving
Book on tanning and curing leather
Book on how to knit, and book of knitting patterns that has sweaters, socks, mittens, scarves and hats
Books on geology of the West
Genetics textbooks
Books on history of USA and history of Idaho
The Mistress of Mellyn (This was Benerita's favorite romance, and I can't find her copy.)
Some of the Nero Wolfe mysteries by Rex Stout
Conan the Barbarian stories by Richard Howard
To Kill a Mockingbird
Brave New World
1984
Tom Sawyer
Huckleberry Finn
some books of crossword puzzles
some books on vehicle engine repair
book on cheesemaking

Some of the quantities had seemed odd to Ben at first. He had asked Gramps why they would need so many things like hammers, files, pocket knives, saucepans, chisels, compasses, sleeping bags, coats, daypacks, water filters, meat grinders, and metal buckets. Gramps had replied, "For barter, Benny. Some of these things will be for trade." That made sense.

After studying the lists for several minutes and playing with Gramps' old-fashioned pocket calculator, Ben was reasonably sure that there would be enough money for everything on the lists, so he decided that instead of waiting until Friday afternoon, as he went to each store, he would get a few things just for fun (as Gramps had suggested), as well as a few things to surprise Gramps later on. It would be faster to get the fun things as he went along, Ben thought, instead of having to backtrack on Friday. He would just have to monitor the money very closely.

Ben looked at his phone: 9:00. He saw someone on the inside unlocking the Co-Op's door. Again Ben thought of Gary, but Gary would be in school now, in Mrs. Phillips' English class, probably with his elbows on the table, his head propped between his hands, sitting there behind Kaylee Field and Carlos Aguirre, trying to stay awake. Gary was a midnight gamer. Hello, Halo; goodnight, English class.

Gritting his teeth, Ben pocketed Gramps' calculator and headed into the Co-Op. "First things first," he told himself. He sighed and stiffened his back when he reached the sidewalk. But when he his hand closed around the door handle, Ben smiled. He'd bet that no one he knew had ever got to spend almost $50,000 in two days. It could be a kick.

At the Co-Op, for his fun things Ben scored ten turkey breasts in enormous flat cans. "Thanksgivings," he had thought. "And Christmases." The other things were easily found and loaded into the pickup. At Fred Meyer, for his extras Ben went a little wild. He opted for a dozen plastic bottles of bacon bits, 25 bottles of ketchup, 20 jars of mayonnaise, 12 squirt bottles of mustard, 25 bags of caramel squares, a dozen little boxes of birthday candles, 12 big cans of cranberry sauce, and 15 huge bags of dog treats. And at Home Depot, though he came up short on the metal buckets, he picked up eight strings of small LED lights, four white and four multicolored, expensive because they were solar powered.

On his way to Lowe's for more metal buckets, Ben found himself passing Mohler's Corner Garden Center, so he stopped there first. Fall was evidently a good time to buy seeds: they were all on sale. He was pleased to find many packets of seed that were half-price, or BOGO--buy one, get one free. "That should save some money for buying the fun things," he thought. And evidently Gramps had called Mohler's about the blue flax seed because there wasn't any in the racks, but as he worked his way around the store picking up vegetable seed of every kind, Ben saw a stack of flax-seed packets rubber-banded and waiting on the counter, as well as bags of potato and onion sets, which he knew weren't usually offered in the fall.

Acting upon some impulse he couldn't name, Ben grabbed a random handful of flower seed packets and a large net bag of daffodil bulbs, tossing them in with the many packs of vegetable and herb seeds already in his cart. As he was checking out, a display of bulbs on a revolving rack caught his eye, and when a woman turned the rack, a small bag fell to the floor. He offered it to her: "Is this yours, ma'am?"

"Not mine," she said kindly, with a smile that included her eyes. "You can have it, young man."

So into his cart went the paper bag, another impulse. When he was stuffing the Mohler's things into the back seat of the pickup's extended cab, he noticed the bright label glued to the little brown bag of his impulse purchase, and saw pictured there a cluster of lavender starlike flowers with petals slightly curled and faintly striped with dark purple. "24 Ixiolirion Bulbs" was printed on the photo label. Ben had never heard of ixiolirion. "Ixiolirion," he said aloud, hearing the word for the first time. The word sounded like poetry, sounded like something Elvish from *The Lord of the Rings*. "Ixiolirion," he repeated. "You are going to bloom at the Place next spring."

The metal buckets had been a problem, and Ben was running late as he drove north across the sagebrush desert toward Hailey. Home Depot had had only eight of them, and it had taken him more than an hour to track down four more buckets at Lowe's and two at Ace Hardware. Ace was going to get him some more buckets from their store in Burley; the store manager told Ben he could pick them up in Twin Falls tomorrow before noon.

But he had bought everything else on Gramps' lists from Home Depot, as well as everything from the Co-Op, Mohler's Garden Center, and Fred Meyer. The pickup was crammed to the top of the shell and the extended cab stuffed until he'd had to muscle the back doors shut. Even the passenger-side front seat and floor areas were filled, packed with stacked sweatshirts on the seat and a tumble of boots in the footwell.

Now as Ben drove the long, slight incline leading to the Wood River Valley, the truck felt sluggish with the added weight. He decided not to pass anyone if he could help it.

Ben had already downed the burger he had picked up on his way north out of Twin Falls, and he was just polishing off the last of the large order of fries. He looked at the clock on the dash for the twentieth time. No, if he went first to the Place and offloaded, he would not finish until after dark, and Gramps had told him specifically not to be on the road in the dark. Something had to give. Up ahead on the right, a dirt road branched off, and Ben slowed and turned in there. He stopped after thirty yards and pulled out his cell. Gramps had trained him not to talk on the phone while driving. Sometimes the Gramps rules were irritating, but today this rule was all right, *especially* today. "Under the radar, under the radar," he thought.

"Hey, Gramps?" he said when Gramps picked up. "Hey, I am only making one trip today. Had a bunch of trouble getting enough buckets. Took too much time and put me behind. But I figured out how to get them."

"Yes?" Gramps said. "I really want those buckets."

"Yeah, it's good," Ben went on. "I got 14 today, and Ace Hardware is going to have nine more waiting for me tomorrow. Even though it's one trip, I got more than half the stuff today. And that story you thought up about me helping you buy things for a new youth camp? I didn't even need it. Nobody even asked why I wasn't in school, can you believe? Must have been my clothes. But I'm not even to Timmerman Hill yet and it's going to get dark about the time I would get to the Place. What do you want me to do, come on home with this load?"

There was a long silence that made Ben uncomfortable. "Nooo," Gramps said at last, drawing out the word as though he were still thinking. "No," he repeated more briskly. "Just go to the Place now and unload what you've got. Spend the night there. The keys to the Place are in the glove compartment. The woodbox by the stove is full. You can cook yourself some dinner."

"I got myself some fast food on the way out of Twin," Ben said. "So I'm OK. You OK?"

"Yep," Gramps said at once. He added, "You can take off from the Place first thing in the morning for Twin, and I will see you tomorrow afternoon. I'll be ready to go when you get here. Leave a little room for my suitcases, your two bags, and the dogs. Remember, get here well before dark, 1600 sharp."

"OK, Gramps, will do. That will be fine and I will see you tomorrow. Night."

"Night."

Ben ended the call and pulled back onto the highway. 1600 sharp, tomorrow. He hoped he could buy the remaining things tomorrow, get all four of the caches stocked, and be home by four o' clock. He shook his head and smiled: Gramps and his military time.

There ahead he could see the little bump of Timmerman Hill, the gentle rise marking the northern limit of the desert. As he drove down the north side of Timmerman, he saw below him, fading toward dusk, the patchwork that was the Wood River Valley, with its five-to-ten-mile-wide band of farmland, cottonwood-bordered river, and mountains on all sides except the south, where the landscape gentled into mild sage hills like Timmerman—almost home, but not quite.

At the northern base of Timmerman Hill, Ben passed the rest stop and turned west onto the state highway. The sun was very low now, low and sinking, but that was all right. He turned down the visor flap to shade his eyes. He would be at the Place before dark. *Under the radar.*

CHAPTER 3
THE PLACE

Just as twilight at last became darkness, Ben arrived at the Place. As he drove the pickup into the barn, the soft black silhouette of a Great Horned Owl swooped low overhead, and he felt a little spooked, wishing that the dogs were with him tonight--not to mention Gramps himself. A small shiver tingled down his spine. He shook himself. "Fool," he said aloud. "This is the Place. Nowhere is safer than the Place."

He swung the big wooden doors shut behind the pickup. Groping in the darkness of the barn, he found his LED head-lamp hanging from its nail and strapped it on. Though he was very tired, he wanted to unload tonight. He wouldn't put every-thing in its final place, not yet. Later, Gramps could help him figure out where to store what. He just wanted to get everything out of the pickup and the vulnerable things stashed safely away from the eager teeth of deer mice and woodrats, inside the hard plastic barrels, for temporary safekeeping. If he did that tonight, he wouldn't have to start out tomorrow being tired or late, and an earlier start would mean he would be sure to get everything done so he could easily pick up Gramps and the dogs in Hailey by four.

Ben worked swiftly, the beam of his headlamp turning the blue plastic barrels already stored in the barn into a wall of turquoise and indigo as he stowed the day's haul. It took him almost an hour to get everything somewhat sorted and moved out of the pickup so he would have room for tomorrow's big buy.

Most things went into empty barrels. The tools, cans, and bottles he simply stacked on the barn floor. He would have to re-sort and move most of the things soon, but for now the items that needed to be, were safe from the woodrats and deer mice.

As he worked, he could hear the owls hooting to each other from the cottonwood tree near the west side of the barn. They had nested in the trees there for years.

Ramona and Patrick, Gramps called the pair, after two lovers he had known whose car slid off an icy road one winter night and drowned them in the Salmon River before they could escape. "Patrick was dark and very tall," Gramps had told him more than once, "but Ramona was pale and fair like frost, almost an albino, with long platinum hair." Patrick and Ramona were hooting tonight. Great Horned Owls hooted until almost Halloween, and Ben knew from experience that after the end of October, throughout the winter, Great Horned Owls didn't usually hoot, they screamed. "Thank God for small favors," Ben thought as he made his way to the ranch house and unlocked the back door. He didn't feel like hearing any screaming tonight.

Once inside the house, Ben locked the door behind him and left his headlamp on. He and Gramps never locked the door unless they were leaving, but tonight it felt right.

The Place didn't have electricity. Gramps wanted it kept off the grid entirely. And though there were some new solar panels in storage in the new bunker, Gramps didn't want solar arrays winking glassily to any plane flying over Spear Creek Gulch. Not for a while, at least.

Ben didn't bother to open the shutters, light one of the oil lamps, or put wood from the kitchen woodbox into the stove and start a fire. He was too tired. His headlamp would be enough to see him to bed, and it wasn't cold.

Still feeling slightly spooked, Ben headed for one of the two bedrooms and, using the combination he had memorized long ago, opened the gun safe that took up most of the closet. From a shelf inside, he took a .357 Smith and Wesson revolver, loaded it, and locked the safe, twirling the dial away just as Gramps always did. Tonight was weird, and he didn't have a dog to alert him if something happened.

This bedroom held a bookcase and two single beds with a night stand between them. Rolled up on each bed sat a fat sleeping bag. Ben untied one of them, shook it out, and crawled in, slipping the gun between the sleeping bag and the mattress, at the head of the bed. "This is really stupid," he thought. "I have slept here hundreds of times, maybe thousands. Nothing weird or frightening has ever happened. This is your Place, idiot brain, safer than town, safer than anywhere," he said to himself. He turned off his headlamp. *But you have never stayed here alone,* a tight little voice in his head told him. *Never without Gramps, and never without dogs.*

"Shut up," Ben said to the voice. Switching on his headlight again, he scanned the nearby bookcase and pulled out one of Gramps' old paperback Andre Nortons that he had read before and liked: *Star Man's Son.*

The voice whispered along in the back of his mind for a while, scrabbling at him like a woodrat in the wall, whispering things that had been floating around in Ben's brain, like, "*What if someone knows you know about the coming meltdown and has followed you here? What if this whole thing is a stupid joke and you have just spent the last of Gramps' money for a bad reason? What if nothing happens and you have to put your tail between your legs and go back to school, and everyone thinks you are a hilarious, pitiable freak and you flunk out? What if, what if . . .*

But after a few pages, Ben walked with *Star Man's Son,* and half an hour after the scrabbling voice grew silent, Ben turned off his headlamp and slept.

⊨⊨ ⊨⊨

"It's not going to freeze tonight," Artie thought, shoving her sleeping bag out through her bedroom window and onto the small second-story balcony, where she often slept during the summer and early fall, hidden from below by dense and leafy aspen branches. She went back for her book, pillows, and flashlight, and pulled on a pair of purple and orange fuzzy socks to round out her outfit of bright orange flannel pajamas and fuzzy orange knit hat. She liked to wear things that matched.

She pulled her curtains and her window shut and stepped outside.

Artie smoothed out the sleeping bag and wormed inside stomach-down, zipping it all the way. Hunching her shoulders, she packed a pillow on each side of the sleeping-bag opening to keep out cool night air, flipped on her light, and began to read.

Tonight the air held only the faintest chill, and the sky she could see through the aspen branches was clear and starry. "I know Dad won't let me sleep outside when it starts to get really cold," she thought. "I had better do this while I can." She propped her chin on her hands and opened the book she had chosen. It was time to read *The Lord of the Rings* again. She reread it every autumn, because that was when *The Fellowship of the Ring* really began.

A slight breeze rubbed the a branch of one of the aspens against the railing of the balcony, making a familiar creaking sound, and Artie smiled. She imagined the hobbits in the gentle woodlands of their home, starting out on familiar paths with bulging packs, little knowing what awaited them even in the supposed safety of the Shire. She shook her head with a delicious shiver.

A soft thud brought Artie's head up, but it was only her cat, Sally, jumping out of one of the aspens to join her on the balcony. She felt Sally turn around and lie down somewhere near her feet. After a minute, Sally's rich, comfortable purr filled the air. Artie smiled in the darkness; she knew Sally liked these open-air nights, and would leave the balcony several times before dawn to shinny down one of the aspens for small cat-expeditions in the neighborhood. Sally had a good cat-life.

"My person-life could be worse," Artie thought. Artie was tired, more tired than usual, and she had eaten more than her share of ice cream after dinner. She felt a shadow between herself and the stars, though they were shining as brightly as ever. The shadow felt like something impossibly dark about to creep over the world. "I'm just full and sleepy. That's all it is. But I'm not going to fall asleep for a good while," she told herself. "I finally made it to Friday night and I'm going to read my way into Saturday morning."

She looked up at the stars, clean and bright, for a long moment, feeling again as if something ominous were hovering over her head. She blinked, hard. "Probably one of the Nazgul, you geek," she told herself, and then she plunged into the Shire.

The morning light found its way through a crack in a shutter and pricked Ben's eyes like the smallest blade of a pocketknife: sunup. He woke suddenly, lifting his head from the book and swiping his hand at a drool stain on the open pages.

He went to the outhouse and then to the barn, where he sorted through the blue storage barrels and the stacks of canned food, putting a few carefully chosen things back into the truck.

Then he dressed again in the blue shirt and khakis. He left at once, wanting to get moving, wanting the day to be over. Leaving this early, he'd be in Twin Falls before most of the stores opened, but that was all right.

The truck left a plume of dust behind him on the narrow road. Ben hoped he was the only one to see it.

CHAPTER 4

CASH OUT, CACHE IN

Once in Twin Falls, Ben drove to the first Starbucks he saw and plumped for a venti caramel latte with whipped cream, plus three sausage biscuits and a blueberry muffin. He smiled as he gathered up his order. "I'm filthy rich for one more day," he thought. He sat inside at a little table as the cool early sunshine spilled through the window, and ate his breakfast while he took out a stack of receipt slips and Gramps' calculator. While he ate, he totaled the receipts from yesterday's buy. He was good. The total was considerably less than he had feared, so today wouldn't be as anxious.

Friday's big buy went much faster.

ShopKo was the first destination, and he easily found everything on that list. He got more candy than he thought Gramps might have bought, though candy was on the list--two dozen big bags of full-sized chocolate bars, twenty bags of bite-sized bars, and also a variety of cheap hard candies--bags of everything from gummy worms and peppermints to lemon drops and Jolly Ranchers. Ben had been a big fan of grape Jolly Ranchers since the third grade. Gary had always nabbed the watermelon-flavored

Ranchers in the multi-flavor bags, and that was fine; even back in the third grade, Ben had thought them disgusting.

A baseball-sized conglomeration of colorful rubber bands appealed to him as he went past an end-aisle, and he took that, too, as well as a large clear-glass vase (what if he wanted to paint some leaves or flowers sometime?), a heavy glass goldfish bowl (or if he wanted to paint some fish or diving beetles?), some bags of marbles and jacks, and several bags of little plastic horses with cowboys and Indians. He had loved those when he was small, and he just *wanted* some. Who would see him with little plastic horses and cowboys at the Place? And who was to say there wouldn't be a child or two at the Place someday?

With that thought, Ben bought a stack of coloring books for adults and for children, grabbing them willy-nilly from the rack. He loved crayons and took ten big boxes of them, as well as a stack of jigsaw-puzzle boxes and some very small toy boats. He could picture the boats bobbing down Spear Creek, going faster than he could run alongside.

Near the checkout stand, he saw a bin filled with on-sale boxed cake mixes. Gramps had said many times that flour and sugar would stay fresh longer than the mixes, but Ben thought, "So I'll eat a lot of cake for the first month or two, and then it won't matter." He piled two dozen boxes of cake mix into one of his overloaded carts.

ShopKo was nearly empty of people so early in the morning on a weekday, and checkout was fast. Ben came out of ShopKo far ahead of the schedule he had set for himself while he was driving from the Place to Twin Falls.

Cowboy Outfitters went fast, too. After he found everything on that list, he bought himself and Gramps each two beautiful, soft shirts of microfleece with quilted linings of thick brushed flannel, both of his in a mossy green, and the two for Gramps a deep, rich blue. Ben also bought a dozen heavy-duty hunting slingshots with extra bands. Gramps had once told him that you could bring down a lot of small game if you were good with a slingshot, because a slingshot made almost no noise. Ben wondered why slingshots hadn't been on Gramps' lists, but they were inexpensive—and, he thought, a good thing for barter. And the Place had an unlimited supply of creek pebbles for ammunition.

Sportsmen's Warehouse had the sleeping bags Gramps had ordered, but each bag wore a plastic-bag overcoat and paper liner and had been packed flat in order to hang up, so Ben spent nearly an hour in a back room with one of the clerks, removing the papers, rolling the bags tightly, and stuffing them into their drawstring carry sacks.

As his extras there, Ben grabbed spools of fishing monofilament and flyfishing line in several different weights, plus fifty each of his two favorite patterns of fishing flies, Adams and mosquito, two fly reels, and six boxes of plain hooks, sized 6, 8, 12, and 14. He knew already that his and Gramps' fly rods, two more that had belonged to Ben's father and his grandmother, and some other fishing supplies were already stored at the Place, but he couldn't remember where at the Place Gramps had stored some of them. "Better safe than sorry," he told himself.

At Harper's School Supply, he found a sturdy, wood-framed chalkboard all ready to hang on a wall, and bought two boxes of white chalk as well, although he knew he could pick up some yellow chalk-rocks along the creekbed at the Place when he had time. Ben also discovered and bought two big wall maps of Idaho— one showing the standard towns and roads, and the other one a colorful geology map, labeled with all the rock formations.

At Ace Hardware, sure enough, the manager had the buckets ready for him, an easy stop. Ben also grabbed two pairs of sturdy barbeque tongs from a display as he came up to the checkout stand, grilling tools being closed out after summer's end. The tongs had a useful look he couldn't resist.

Ben's last shopping stop for Gramps' lists was the used bookstore, Rocket Man's, where he loaded up on both hardbound and paperback books. "No more ebooks for a while," Ben thought with a sigh.

For years, Ben and Gramps had stopped at Rocket Man's to buy books nearly every time they had gone to Twin Falls. With the help of the owner, Mr. Bee, Ben eventually found every book on Gramps' list, and more. Some of Gramps' book selections seemed rather odd, but they were cheap, and Gramps wanted them. Maybe these would be good for barter, too. With Mr. Bee's help, finding things on the shelves was fast, and Ben thought Gramps would be pleased that he had managed to get everything on the list, plus a stack of westerns and some additional science fiction. Almost accidentally, Ben lucked into a box of new paperback crossword puzzle books that Mr. Bee said he had bought as surplus from another store. He had been ready to take them to recycling because they hadn't sold, and was glad to find a buyer: the extra-low price was a bonus.

Dr. Lucy had been predicting a large, bad geology thing that was coming very soon, and Ben knew it had to do with volcanoes, so Ben sought out and bought several geology texts on volcanoes, plus a thick paperback titled *Roadside Geology of Idaho*. He also got several coffee-table books on dinosaurs, complete with paintings of the reconstructed animals. Another illustrated book that appealed to him was *Fish Families of the World*. *Horse Breeds and Horse Colors* looked equally desirable, as did *Mammals of the Great Ice Age*, *Birds of Paradise*, and several art books. "For those long winter days and nights," he told himself.

And just like that, he was done. And it was still early.

Relaxing in the warm autumn sunlight, Ben sat for some time in the truck with the calculator and the long curls of store receipts. He had picked up all the orders, found everything on the lists, and had added a few things as well. And as he had hoped and as Gramps had predicted, even though he had already bought a number of fun things not on the lists, there was still some money left over.

Ben filled the truck with gas. And then smiling, he stopped at Blue Lakes Mall and ran in for eight hundred dollars' worth of art supplies from the Blue Art shop: sketch pads, pressed-paper tablets, pencils, brushes, charcoals, oil pastel sticks, fixative, tubes of paint, palettes, a tackle box, an easel, several frames, and two large portfolios to contain finished work. This stuff would *really* help those long winter days and nights go faster.

After buying the art supplies, Ben figured that a little more than $300 remained in Gramps' account, but that was all right. It was close, pretty darned close. "I'll make it closer," he told himself, and he pulled into the parking lot of the nearest store, a Target, and picked up nearly a hundred and fifty dollars' worth of little things that took his fancy--boxed board games, notebooks, packages of needles, some Hot Wheels cars, and two dozen candles— six each of orange, black, red and green—for the holidays.

On his way to check out, he passed displays of Halloween decorations and suddenly wondered how, or *if*, he would be celebrating his October 31ˢᵗ birthday this year. He thought, "Well, Gramps would be OK with my getting some of this stuff. And so would Gary, seriously, if he's at the Place by then. Why not? There's still some money left. And it's going to be just us." A foot-tall tabletop witch sporting a pointed hat and a raven on her shoulder went into his cart. He saw a stack of plastic tablecloths, and thought of the round oak table at the Place and its ever-present red-and-white-checked oilcloth. He chose an orange tablecloth printed with black spiderwebs and spiders. Ben smiled—he could just see Gramps and Gary—and Dr. Lucy, too--sitting around the Place's kitchen table at midnight on Halloween, drinking cocoa and eating candy by candlelight and telling ghost stories, with the Shelties right close, asleep on the floor. Maybe Mrs. Phillips would be there as well. Outside in the dark, the wind would be howling, but there would be a fire in the fireplace and a fire in the stove, and the Place would be toasty warm. "This year I can tell the one about the wolf skeleton that comes alive," Ben thought. "Bet Gary hasn't heard that one."

A plastic candelabrum with a skull base would do nicely for some of the candles he had just found, so that went into the cart along with a bag of small black plastic spiders and a package of spiderweb material. He could put the spiders here and there— on a pillow, on a windowsill, in the sink. A spider in the sink might get a little jump and a scream even from Gary.

A store clerk was filling a bin with black plastic bats, and Ben took two dozen bats as well as some bags of Halloween candy and two strings of solar-powered LED lights—one orange and one purple. Ben surveyed his cart and added in his head. Yes, he was finished.

Ben sat in the truck in the Target parking lot for a few minutes, punching numbers on the calculator. After running the numbers twice, he figured that only $23.96 remained of Gramps' $49,000. He blew out a long breath. "Wow," he said aloud. "I did it. All gone."

Suddenly he smiled. It hadn't occurred to him—or probably Gramps, either--that if the end was coming soon, he could have bought anything and everything he wanted, because the credit card bill would never come. "Why am I still thinking that I shouldn't overdraw the account?" Ben asked himself, "if everything is going to slide to hell by this weekend?"

Gary was right. Ben and Gramps were not normal at all. And old habits died hard, Gramps always said. Ben tightened his fingers on the steering wheel. A frightening number of their habits might suddenly become old habits, useless habits, obsolete.

"Will that really happen?" he thought. And he found that at least at this moment, he thought that it would. And he didn't regret the spiders and bats one bit. Without realizing it at the time, he had even bought enough fishing line to hang them from the ceiling. Gary would like the bats.

Gary would be on his lunch break now, probably sitting in a booth at the drive-in on Main Street, maybe even with Cindy Green, chewing his way through an order of chicken strips and onion rings, being normal as normal except for the amount of ketchup he used. "At the same time, the Scavenger leaves Twin Falls with a truck full of sleeping bags, slingshots, dish soap, plastic hanging bats, and hundreds of crayons," Ben told himself. If only Gary would eventually think about what Ben had said, and would just *come.*

Thinking about Gary and lunch made Ben hungry, and on the way out of Twin Falls, he stopped for some fast food. $23.96 would buy a satisfying lot of fast food. Pleased with himself, Ben went through a drive-in and got himself a Coke and two cheeseburgers with double large fries, and the same for Gramps, too.

It was noon when Ben drove north over the Perrine Bridge and left Twin Falls. The pickup was stuffed full, but because of all the sleeping bags, was not nearly as heavily loaded as it had been yesterday. He could finish stocking the caches and would still be home well before four. Then he and Gramps could load up the last few things from the Hailey house, pile in the dogs, and they would all be at the Place long before dark.

A few miles after he passed through Shoshone, Ben began looking for a little-used dirt road leading east into the sagebrush. The road had faded in recent years; weeds were taking over.

Ben remembered that when Gramps had first taken him to the lava tube cave several years before, the road had been wider, clearer, more sharply defined—but the last time they had come, last spring, the road had looked disused and narrower, overgrown with tumbleweeds, cheatgrass eating at its sides and fuzzing the midline. Ben gave his rear-view mirror a hard glance and slowed the truck; no one was behind him.

"There it is," Ben said aloud in relief when he saw it, one of the few dirt roads in the area that didn't lead to a ranch and didn't have a gate. He pulled off the highway and bumped very slowly over lumpy basalt for half a mile until he saw a two-foot-high cairn of piled black rocks twenty yards off the north side of the road, drove to it through the cheatgrass, and rolled to a stop.

Ben spotted the next cairn fifty yards away in a jumble of black lava, and jumped from the truck. Then he opened the back of the shell and lifted out a bucketful of things he had taken from the Place this morning, plus several items from the day's shopping, and his headlamp. He walked toward the first cairn. The weeds had had a good summer, and now he couldn't see even a vestige of the path he remembered from last spring.

Ben was heartily glad Gramps had insisted on building the cairns. This place was lumpily flat, with miniature hills and valleys created by an old lava flow. The miniature "hills" were about the size of trucks, and the valleys shallow and small, like dry-rock swimming pools. He could walk here, but it was too rocky to drive.

He reached the visible cairn and scanned the horizon. He saw another, taller cairn ahead to the east and headed for it, stepping with care. The jagged lava made for treacherous walking. The last thing Ben wanted to do was to put his weight on a thin plate of the stuff and fall through into a cave. But the cairns showed him the way. He knew he would be fine if he walked straight from cairn to cairn.

He could hear Gramps' voice in his head as his feet took him from cairn to cairn, lava hump to lava ridge, around fernbushes and sage, through little runners of dry cheatgrass, over odd folded boulders, up and down and northeast.

"Your grandmother found this lava tube cave when she was a girl," he seemed to hear Gramps telling him from years ago. "She was about your age, Benny, about ten years old. Her dad, that would be your great-grandfather Felix Balboa--had his truck break down on the highway that day. He had to flag somebody down and get to a place where he could call for help, so he told your grandma to go out in the sage and play. No cell phones then, my boy. He told Benerita to stay close enough to his truck that she could hear him call when he got back, but far enough away so she wouldn't noticed from the highway. It was spring and she was picking flowers. She got a bit farther away than she realized, but she wasn't one to worry about getting lost.

"Your grandmother had a built-in compass, Benny. She always knew exactly where she was. I could take her deer hunting in a place she had never been before, walk all day in the hills, up and down, in and out of half a dozen drainages. We would turn around and walk back when it was time—and she always came out within twenty yards of where I'd parked the truck. Always. It was uncanny. And so she remembered finding this cave as a young girl. When she mentioned it one time, I thought it might be a good place for a hidey-hole. And she found it again, perfectly, took me here with no false steps at all, though it had been well over forty years since she had seen it."

Ben smiled at the story, wishing his grandmother hadn't died, wishing she would be going to the Place with them. But at least she had given them this cave and its name.

Finally Ben saw the dark cave in a rocky hollow ahead, the opening arched with a shallow curve like a strung bow. He bent low to enter. "Gramps and Ben Cache 1, Benerita's Ice Cave, final stocking," he said aloud. He was glad that it was too late in the year for rattlesnakes. Gramps had told him that unless it was in spring and summer, there were always a few rattlers around the cave entrance and to watch out and carry a poking stick so you could make them rattle and find out where they were.

Just inside the entrance, Ben looked for the little flat place on the cave wall, in a thin layer of volcanic clay next to the lava, a few feet to the north side of the entrance. His headlamp found the two-inch-high words that had been scraped into the dry clay with a sharp rock: Benerita's Cave. Gramps had done that years ago.

Eighty feet back, well past the cave's cold twilight zone, Ben saw the gleam of two aluminum garbage cans, and smiled. One can was already stocked with two tightly rolled sleeping bags, two changes of clothes and shoes plus a daypack and hat each for him and Gramps, a waterproof tarp and two-man tent, two old-fashioned metal canteens with long shoulder straps, a ceramic water filter, several boxes of matches in two glass jars, a pair of inexpensive binoculars, two pocketknives, a first-aid kit, a set of wire snares, several maps sealed in large plastic bags–and on the very bottom, a big jar of sugar, a sealed tin of powdered milk, and a two-pound can of good coffee. On the cave floor against one side wall and beneath a layer of piled rocks lay a Ruger .22 pistol and two boxes of ammunition in a sealed plastic box, but Ben had no need to check the gun in its dark resting place now; the cave floor looked undisturbed, and he knew he should keep it that way.

The back wall of the cave was oddly pale; it almost seemed to glow. Ben stepped toward the wall. He reached out with the flat of his hand and met a surface both slick and cold. Yes, the ancient ice, remnant of another age, was still here, the source of water for this cache, hidden and permanent, priceless in the wide desert, pure and chill and strange.

He wondered if there had been long-haired scurrying ground squirrels or heavily furred badgers and weasels living here in the time of the mammoths and mastodons. Or—this was better by far—a sabertooth cat and his mate lived here in the cave and terrorized the surrounding countryside. He could just picture the cat crouched at the entrance in full snarl, his body half in shadow, guarding the cave against--what? Giant cave bears maybe—with a stormy sky overhead, maybe even a blizzard, the air full of snow. No, not snowing, Ben decided. That would be too hard to paint.

Quickly Ben opened the other garbage can, which was empty, and unloaded the contents of the bucket he carried–a saucepan and coffee pot, two fork-spoon sets, two enamelware plates, cups, and bowls, a can opener, a bottle each of aspirin and vitamin C, a bottle of antibiotic capsules, a couple of notebooks and a package of pencils, one of the slingshots, a towel, a bar of soap, two pairs of gloves, and four pairs of socks. He went back to the truck for paperback books, two LED headlamps with extra batteries, a small shovel, and a number of food cans and jars of nuts. In one more trip--carrying a ten-pound bag of dog kibble, four cans of Sterno, a small can of Crisco, a dozen candles, two plastic raincoats, two polarfleece jackets, two bags of candy, and a compass--he had filled the garbage can.

Ben jammed the lid of the can down tightly and dusted his hands together. "Benerita's Ice Cave, Cache 1, fully stocked," he said aloud to make it seem official. "Now for Number 2."

As he left the cave, Ben had a sudden vision of himself and Gramps lying on rolled-out sleeping bags, eating savory beanie weenies from the cans and drinking hot coffee, reading by headlamp or candlelight, with the Shelties sprawled around them in the semidarkness. Maybe this whole deal wouldn't be so bad after all.

Back on the highway, Ben crested Timmerman Hill, rolled down into the Wood River Valley, turned west onto the state highway, and drove until he came to a small dirt road, barely visible in tall sagebrush. Opening a rickety gate in a barbed-wire fence and closing it behind him, he drove up a dry gulch. He checked the truck's clock; he was still making good time.

After a mile, the road became a two-track trail, nearly overgrown with bunchgrasses and sage. Another mile found the truck on a steep sidehill, the track now very sandy, requiring extreme care as well as four-wheel drive. Soon he could see a wet stain in the dirt alongside the track, and a few yards later, he parked the pickup at the only place on the hillside where it was remotely possible to turn around.

The mouth of a hundred-and-fifty-year-old mine tunnel, shored up with axe-hewn timbers, gaped black in the hillside, and from it issued a tiny trickle of water that oozed over rocks and disappeared into a short tongue of darkened sand beside the road. "Gramps and Ben Cache 2, Lovely Luna Mine," he said. "Final stocking."

The mine was not much more than a serious test tunnel, Gramps had told him. Two brothers had last worked it for several years in the early 20th Century, during the Great Depression: using only pickaxes, they had mined some galena ore—a combination of lead, zinc, and silver that Dr. Lucy had taught Ben to recognize during one of her rare visits a few years ago. Ben knew that the Lovely Luna had been abandoned since before Gramps himself was a kid. Ben set the emergency brake, jumped out onto the dusty ground, and filled his bucket from the truck.

It was cool in the mine; even at the entrance, the breath of the mine was chill and dead. The dusty floor showed no new footprints, not even coyote or woodrat tracks, and that was good. It had been several months since Ben and Gramps had visited Lovely Luna.

Sixty feet back the tunnel began to bend gently toward the south. Twenty steps farther and the entrance was obscured. Against one rocky wall Ben found the two garbage cans in the dim coolness, and in two more trips had filled the empty can.

This cache's handgun box was buried in the rock spoil against one wall near a supporting timber, and its resting place looked just as undisturbed as had its counterpart in Cache 1.

"Just like Benerita's Ice Cave, Lovely Luna is another one you'd have to wait until dark to get into if you wanted to be secret," Gramps had told him the first time they had come here. "There's not much cover on this hillside, and after the world falls apart you sure wouldn't want someone with field glasses three miles away seeing you go into this tunnel, because there's only one way in and out." Ben thought he must have been about twelve then, and remembered that he'd thought about outlaws and posses and lawmen coming after, about ridden-down horses and stolen gold--instead of a meltdown of civilization, of starving people, of neighbor against neighbor and a government turned sour and useless. He shook his head. It had been nice to be twelve, but that time was past.

Ben replaced the can lid and pushed it down firmly. "Lovely Luna Mine, Cache 2, fully stocked," he said. "Now for Number 3."

With great care and some anxiety, Ben turned the truck around on the narrow track and drove down the hillside. Once back on the state highway, he continued west for several miles and then turned south, bumping slowly down a slight incline on a well-traveled, rocky dirt road heading toward Magic Reservoir.

He emerged from a shallow gulch to park on a dusty flat where fishermen came to unload their small boats and put in for an afternoon of fishing the narrow reservoir. To Ben's relief, the flat was empty of cars and trucks. On the northeast, the reservoir was bounded by a low lava rimrock about twenty yards above the high-water mark. Ben filled the bucket and walked along the water's edge toward the dark, low cliffs until he was out of sight of the parking flat.

Above him at the base of the rimrock grew a chest-high knot of currant bushes. He headed for it.

Ben climbed a tumbled slope of lava boulders, then pushed currant branches aside and entered a low cave in the rimrock, its entrance a black slit just wide enough for a 32-gallon garbage can to be pushed inside. He entered and saw them at once, for the accessible part of this cave was only 25 feet long: two aluminum garbage cans. This cache had roof, floor, and walls of black lava. The dark stone soaked up the light from his headlamp until it seemed weaker than a penlight.

At the back of the small chamber, a wide crack led further into the darkness. Ben had tried exploring the crack once, but after a few feet, had come to a squeeze that he couldn't force his body through. At that farthest point were buried this cache's pistol and ammunition. His light had once told him that the crack widened again beyond the narrows, so maybe he could bring a hammer and chisel sometime and widen the crack. There was one flange of lava he just might be able to break into pieces.

Again, Ben unloaded the contents of his bucket into one of the garbage cans, and after making two more trips, replaced the lid with care. "Magic Reservoir Rim, Ben and Gramps' Cache 3, fully stocked," he said. "One more to go."

This time, the turn from the state highway led north up a narrow gulch along a small stream bordered by squat bush willows, on the way to the Place. The stream was too small and shallow to have fish; the stream went dry by autumn in some years. The streambed and banks had been heavily trampled by cattle, and though the cows had recently been gathered out of the hills for the winter, their stench still hung about the damp soil and yellowing autumn grasses.

At a place in the small meadow where the stream took a sharp bend, an old metal livestock watering tank lay dusty and empty in the dry grass, bent and riddled with holes where someone with a rifle had shot it up for amusement. Long ago, some cattleman had cut the steel tank in half lengthwise, laid it on its side, and had brought stream water to it with a pipe, since in the late summer and fall, Gray Creek was only an inch or two deep. The tank had been there for years, as long as Ben could remember.

Ben stopped the pickup and ferried several buckets of material across the narrow meadow to the streambank next to the old tank, lifting aside a mat of fine willow roots. He got down on hands and knees to enter a shallow dirt chamber where the stream, during some long-ago high-water flood, had hollowed out a little cove.

The ceiling of this hidden cubby was not quite high enough to allow Ben to stand, but the space was fairly large, a dozen feet long and half as wide. The stream had since eaten its way down through the soil as overgrazing had increased erosion in the streambed, and the small room was now high and dry above the level that the stream might flood, walled with dirt on three sides, roofed with dirt densely laced through by heavy roots, and floored with rounded stream gravel and a drift of narrow, pale brown willow leaves. Ben inhaled the scent of water, willows, and cow as he got down on his knees to enter the fourth cache.

This one had always been his favorite, because he had found it himself when he was in the seventh grade, dinking around one morning while Gramps changed a flat tire during one of their trips to the Place. How cool would it be to disappear from the middle of a meadow? One moment you are there, standing in the grazed-to-nothing grasses. Blink--and you are gone like a twist of smoke in the wind.

At the far end of the scoured-out space, two garbage cans appeared. Behind them, dug into the dirt wall behind a gnarled willow root, he knew that the plastic box with the pistol rested unseen. Ben lowered his supplies into the empty can and left the bucket in a little niche behind the cans.

"Gray Creek Meadow, Fourth and Final Gramps and Ben Cache, fully stocked. All done," Ben said with some satisfaction.

But in reality, he felt rather strange. Had he truly thought that this day would come, ever? And did he truly think they might someday need the caches if something happened to push them out of the Place? Today he didn't have time to speculate. Ben scuttled backwards out of the cache pocket, lowered the curtain of tangled roots over the opening once more, and trotted back to the truck.

The afternoon was growing old. Low sagebrush branches vibrated stiffly in a brisk wind, and their shadows spiked long across the close-cropped grass. Ben started the pickup.

Now for home, home to Hailey for the last time. Would it really be the last? In a flourish of dust, he left Gray Creek meadow and headed home to Gramps and the dogs.

CHAPTER 5

GRAMPS

It was exactly four o' clock in the afternoon when Ben pushed through the front door. He felt the oddness at once, even as he sang out, "Gramps, I'm home! I brought you a hamburger!"

The dogs weren't jumping and barking; the three of them were huddled together in the middle of the living room looking at him. Their ears were flat back, their heads lowered as if they had just been scolded.

Then Ben saw Gramps. He heard his own voice saying, "Gramps, Gramps, *Gramps!*" as he ran across the hardwood floor to where Gramps sat slumped in his big chair. Ben shook Gramps' shoulder and felt his hand. The familiar hand was not cold exactly, but too cool and too white. The skin of Gramps' hands where they lay on the arms of the chair was wrong, the wrong color. His fingernails showed yellow against the pale gray of his skin.

Time stopped for a moment.

Ben became aware that he was still shouting, "Gramps! Gramps!" and made himself stop. The three dogs pressed close to Ben's sides. He could hear them breathing. He patted at Gramps' cheeks—wasn't that what you did to wake someone up?

Then Ben lifted Gramps' head and looked at the face he had known so well for so long. Gramps looked younger somehow, his face smoother. His cheeks felt wrong where they touched Ben's hands. And he looked–*gone*. Far gone. Gramps wasn't breathing. He wasn't anything. No, he was cooling; that was it. Gramps hadn't been Gramps for some time.

Ben let Gramps' head fall gently and said, "Gramps is dead." Ben felt heavy, almost paralyzed, and slid to his knees. Bear pushed his black muzzle against Ben's face and licked him on the chin. Ben wanted to scream and run, call 911, call Uncle George, do *something*. "Not *now*, Gramps," he thought. "Oh my God, don't die *now*." But that is exactly what Gramps had done.

Then Ben heard a slight crackle and noticed a sheet of notebook paper on the floor at Gramps' feet. Molly had stepped on it with a front paw. A pen lay there, too. Ben took the paper, saw Gramps' familiar writing. The page was crumpled as though it had been crushed in a fist with some force. Ben smoothed the paper across his knee and read.

"Benny. Something is bad wrong with me all of a sudden," the notebook page read. "I think I'm going out like a candle. Today. I will try to wait for you, but don't know if I can. If I'm gone when you get here, don't call anyone. Don't tell your Uncle George. Don't stay here. Don't stay here. Take the dogs and get out. Leave at once, at once." That sentence had been underlined so forcefully that the point of the pen had ripped through the paper. "Be at the Place by dark and stay there. DO NOT LEAVE THE PLACE. I have always loved you more than anything." Instead of signing "Gramps" as he had done on so many notes to Ben over the years, Gramps had signed the paper with a shaky flourish: "Franklin R. Elliott."

Ben folded the paper and shoved it into a back pocket of his jeans. The repeated words "Don't stay here. Don't stay here," seemed to hang in the air. For a fleeting moment he thought again of calling his father's brother, his Uncle George. But it wouldn't be right to ignore Gramps' last wishes. And he was certain that Uncle George would not let him go to the Place.

If only--but things were what they were. At least Dr. Lucy would come in a couple of days. She could even come tomorrow. She could help sort things out. And maybe this whole danger thing would come and go in a week or two or a month or two and then he could come home. But Ben had been trained so well that his body was already moving. It would be dark soon. He had to be at the Place by dark. His mind closed on that thought and held it tight. *Don't stay here. Be at the Place by dark.*

Ben noticed then that Gramps, with typical Gramps' efficiency, had placed three packed suitcases on the floor near the front door, along with two small cardboard boxes. Ben checked the boxes and found books, shoes, a package of sponges, a pair of scissors, Gramps' binoculars–he stopped looking and closed the leaves of the boxes.

Six feet away from Gramps' chair, he found the cell phone. Had Gramps tried to call and dropped it? Or had it fallen from his hand or pocket? Wasn't he able to get out of the chair so he could pick up the phone and call for help? *God. He couldn't think about that now.* Ben dropped the phone into his shirt pocket.

Gramps had been all ready to go to the Place. The pain of it, the irony hit Ben somewhere in his gut and doubled him over for a moment. Had Gramps given himself a heart attack lugging these suitcases into the living room?

Ben couldn't have the pain right now. He sucked it down and tried to plan his next move. His own duffel was already packed, too, leaning with his daypack against the wall in the hallway. He had packed both of them days ago.

In several trips, Ben ferried the suitcases, duffel, pack, and boxes to the pickup and shoved them inside the shell on top of the load of things from Twin Falls.

Trailed closely by the three anxious dogs, Ben dived into his bedroom and stripped two pillowcases from the pillows on his bed. Into the pillowcases went several pairs of his shoes and jeans, a dozen of his books, his winter parka, his laptop and its charger, his e-reader, and two framed photos from the walls. He also pulled the blanket from his bed. Moving to Gramps' room, he took a thick cream-colored photo album and looked for the older album with the brown cover, but it wasn't there, nor was the little box where Gramps had always kept the few good pieces of Grandmother's jewelry. He realized that Gramps must have packed them in the suitcases. But the two boxes of shotgun shells that he knew were under the bed, were still there, along with the shotgun itself, and he took them to the pickup, too.

From the kitchen, Ben tumbled into the pillowcases whatever odd things, cans, and packages of food he could grab quickly from the pantry and refrigerator, two boxes of dog treats, the leashes hanging just inside the pantry door, the dog dishes on the floor, and Gramps' address book from the counter. The pillowcases were heavy now. He grabbed the shotgun and called the dogs.

The four of them spilled into the front yard, and Ben was shocked to see that outside everything looked fine, bright, and normal. Even while putting the suitcases into the pickup Ben had felt as if darkness were closing in, but now he could see that in the front yard it was still sunny and warm. Lazily, a handful of golden aspen leaves drifted to the lawn from one of the trees Gramps and Ben had planted when Ben was six. The world outside looked as if nothing had happened.

Ben slung the filled pillowcases inside the pickup shell. He took a minute to wrap the shotgun in his blanket, and laid it gently beside the suitcases there.

The three dogs hopped into the back of the extended cab, where they were used to riding. Ben shut the dogs inside the truck and stood irresolute for a moment beside the pickup, and then ran back into the house, where he stood for a moment near Gramps' body. "I love you more than anything, too," he said, and with shaking fingers, pulled the big ring with the square-cut garnet from Gramps' right hand and transferred it to his own. It fit exactly on the third finger of his right hand. He knew Gramps would have wanted him to have this ring. The thin gold wedding band on the other hand he didn't touch. He took the green notebook from the arm of the chair and left the house.

Ben turned back once in the yard trying to memorize everything, desperately hoping that this wouldn't be the last time he ever saw the only home he could remember: narrow white siding, deep front porch, door with its graceful oval of beveled glass, the tall windows, the steep roof, the big spruce tree on the west side, the walkway though the grass made from flat lava rocks picked up in the desert by Gramps and Ben's father long ago. *Home.* Damn Sky and Mountain Development. But the Place was home, too. Now, it had to be.

Ben threw himself into the driver's seat and started the engine. Bear's intelligent black face, ears lifted in inquiry, appeared over the seat back and Ben said automatically, "No, Bear. Stay there."

Ben pulled out his phone and called Gary; Gary wasn't picking up. Ben sent a text message. "Going the Place now. It gets bad use yr map or call n I'll come." He took several deep breaths and began repeating softly, "Under the radar, under the radar." It wouldn't do to drive stupidly now. He had to be calm. Ben backed the pickup out of the driveway.

It was almost five o' clock. School was out for the weekend, today was a beautiful autumn day, and the sidewalks were full of people. Artie Ames waved to him as he passed her on her bike. They had English, Math, and History together; she seemed a halfway decent girl; at least she would speak to him in school.

She didn't call him *Scavenger.* That wasn't much, but it was something, *had been* something. He lifted a hand to Artie and drove on. He hoped she wouldn't remember seeing him in the truck. But, then, few ever noticed Scavenger.

Ben looked for Gary as he drove out to Main Street and stopped at the stop sign to wait for an opening in traffic so he could turn south, with the vague idea that if he saw Gary, maybe he could persuade him to come along. But Gary wasn't on the street. "Cindy Green tonight," Ben thought. "Gary is probably taking a shower and seeing if there is anything he can do to his hair." Gary's red hair was so wiry and springy that it seemed to have a life of its own. Over the years, Ben had watched Gary try every hair-taming remedy in existence on his forest of red frizz. Ben shook his head. Maybe Gary would come, maybe tomorrow, after his date was over. When things got bad. *If.*

A big yellow school bus passed by, filled with high-school football players and cheerleaders, heading south as well, to the away football game in Filer.

"Normal," Ben thought. "Normal Friday-night things." He laughed, but it became a cough and then a sob. "Under the radar," he muttered and kept muttering. "Driving, going under the radar, leaving, going, driving under the radar." The mantra kept him from thinking. He saw an opening in the traffic on Main and took it, heading south. Ahead, the school bus accelerated as it left town and disappeared from view.

⊷⊹ ⊹⊶

The sun was setting behind the western hills when Ben reached the Place and opened its gate. He drove through and locked the chain behind him. The Place was situated oddly, a long, narrow 160-acre homestead parcel that hugged a small creek and its meadows.

During past millennia, Spear Creek had carved a shallow gulch for itself less than two hundred yards wide. From the dirt road, even from a hundred feet away, it was impossible to see the house and outbuildings of the Place, crouched as they were under the rather steep shoulder of the east side of the gulch, the barn nestled against a tumble of rounded granite outcrops there.

The road went serenely on past the Place, heading up into the mountains to an old mine. Spear Creek Road was not used much any more, Ben knew. A wildflower-lover or three might meander through these hills in the spring. A few cattlemen used the road during the summer; the whole area, outside of the few homesteaded ranches, was part of a huge Bureau of Land Management grazing allotment. None of the ranches for many miles around, with the exception of Horner Ranch three canyons west, had had a resident family for decades. And hunters occasionally drove the road in the fall. In the winter and in spring snowmelt time, Spear Creek Road was unplowed, unmaintained, and undriveable.

The Place had been a 1920s homestead like many in southern Idaho, anchored by a thread of permanent water in dry sage hills where there was much sagebrush and few trees, and water was scarce. From the dirt road that ran past it, the Place looked like many abandoned homesteads from that era: an ancient gate in a tumbledown fence, several tall cottonwood trees, a gnarled old apple tree bent almost to the ground, a few ragged Douglas fir planted decades back, some aged lilacs, a tangle of yellow pioneer roses, a line of mature cottonwoods, and up the gulch a little way, a grove of aspen, as well as a string of short and bristly native willows near the creek bank, straggling down the center of the thin meadow--and no visible buildings. So many of these homesteads had no buildings at all now, leaving only traces of roads, fence remnants, and long-ago-planted trees to tell the tale that people had once lived there. The weathered wood of such cabins and barns was sought after as "barnwood." Many old buildings that weren't pressed to the ground by many years' weight of heavy winter snow, had been disassembled and the wood taken by contractors catering to the rich who built luxury homes near Sun Valley Resort, and wanted their new houses to "blend in with the landscape" and "look western."

But, of course, the Place was more than it appeared from the road. Because of the steep drop-off of its eastern hillside, the house and other buildings of the Place were invisible from the road, not to be seen until a person was well inside the gate, one of the reasons Gramps had bought the Place thirty years before. Someone had to be very determined and very close to see the buildings.

In all the weekends and summer days and nights they had spent at the Place, Gramps would never let Ben start a fire until it was dark. Gramps had never let Ben bring a friend here, either, though many times Ben had begged him to let Gary come. Even when Ben was small, before the scavenging began, Gramps had told Ben that isolated cabins were sometimes burglarized or vandalized and that was the reason they had to keep it a secret that the Place was habitable.

Ben had never come to the Place in the winter. The snows-- and in earliest spring, the mud--made the Place inaccessible except by means of skis and snowshoes, and a weekend wasn't long enough to ski or snowshoe in from the state highway and get back to Hailey in time to go to school on a Monday morning, though Gramps had been planning to buy a snowmobile.

The buildings all had new metal roofs pitched to slide off the snow, so they would not collapse in the winter from the weight of snow and ice, and the windows were new triple-glazing, all with heavy wooden shutters that were fastened securely in the fall so that the weight of snow pressing in toward the walls would not burst the glass.

A long time ago, Ben had gone on a picnic with Uncle George, Aunt Cora, their son (and Ben's cousin) Neil, and another family. When the marshmallows came out to be toasted around the fire, the adults began talking about what they would do in the face of nuclear fallout, war, plague, or some other major emergency.

"Well, it's obvious," Uncle George had said, pausing in the act of lifting a bottle of beer to his lips. "Go up into the mountains, into the forest, and find some cabin no one is using, and wait it out. Plenty of trees for fuel and you could hunt deer." The other couple had agreed. Ten-year-old Ben had listened, astonished, very tempted to quote Gramps at them, finding it difficult to believe how dumb they were. It was just as Gramps had told him many times, "Everyone will scramble to go up into the mountains during a disaster, Ben," he had said. "They all think it would be fine to live in a forest cabin, melt snow for water in the winter, and live on venison. That is so crazy. What do you think it would be like to hunt deer in five feet of snow on a steep slope when it is below zero? A good percentage of the deer and elk would be long gone to the lower country by winter, unless it happened to be an open winter. Would there be enough deer and elk to feed all those people if they could manage to get close enough for a shot? Do those people have experience with guns? How much wood would it take to keep warm during all those 20- and 30-below nights in an uninsulated summer cabin? And are they going to try to burn green wood when all the fallen wood is covered by five feet of snow? No, thank you. What you want is a little place on the edge of the desert in some forgotten gulch hidden in the middle foothills, a place that's high enough that it's almost impossible to get to in the winter and too unscenic to be a destination in the summer, a place where there is a small source of permanent water and a cabin that can't be seen unless you are almost on top of it. You can eat rabbits and voles in the winter, dig camas or have a garden in the summer, and burn sage if you have to, to keep warm. Why kill yourself trying to keep warm at 7,000 feet when you can have life much easier at 3 or 4,000 feet? The mountains are beautiful, but they are hostile. Even so, people will flock there like idiots." Ben had bitten his tongue at that picnic and kept silent. He had become very good at keeping silent.

The sun seemed to go down hastily, with only a flash of gold quickly swallowed by indigo clouds. Ben drove to the barn, stopped the truck inside, and let out the dogs. It was a good thing that Shelties were a little too large to be prey for great horned owls. He could hear the owls hooting already.

The dogs made a beeline for the lilac bushes near the barn to do their business. They had been to the Place many times, had been coming here since they were small puppies, and they loved the Place. Seeing their eager rush from the barn, tails wagging, Ben let go the tight band around his heart that he had put in place while driving, and opened his heart to the Place, swiping the side of one hand at a few hot tears.

Ben shouldered the shotgun and dragged out the two heavy pillowcases to carry inside. Standing in the barn's doorway, he took a moment to look at the fading sky. There wouldn't be a moon tonight. Patrick, or maybe it was Ramona, skimmed silently over his head in the deepening twilight and vanished behind the barn.

When he got to the house, the dogs came running as soon as he reached the back door, trotted inside with him, and stood expectantly in the kitchen while Ben found the matches in their tin holder on the wall and lit the oil lamp that always sat in the center of the round oak table. Since the shutters were still fastened, the house was almost pitch dark inside, but the golden, finger-sized flame from the lamp chased the shadows to the corners of the kitchen.

He turned down the wick the way Gramps had taught him. The yellow light made him feel warm, and it felt good that everything around him was familiar. He took in and let out a long breath. This was better.

Ben fished the dog dishes from a pillowcase and turned to the pantry to fill them with kibble from a five-gallon can there. "Good thing Gramps and I bought tons of dog food last spring," he said to them. "You guys are set." He remembered that most of the dog food was safe in several dozen industrial-grade plastic barrels, sealed with silicone, in the old henhouse. At the sink, he filled the water dish that was always there on the floor behind the door. At least they would have cold running water in the kitchen for a couple of weeks, maybe a month, until Spear Creek froze.

Bear, Molly, and Moonie crunched happily at their food while Ben made three more trips to the barn and brought in his duffel, his pack, the cardboard boxes, and the suitcases.

Then Ben took his time unloading the pillowcases and finding places for the last-minute things he had grabbed from the house in Hailey—two loaves of bread, two sticks of butter, some packages of cereal and granola bars, dog treats, leashes, books, the blanket from his bed, his laptop and pad, the two framed photographs from his bedroom wall, and a number of other small things, some of which he had no memory of taking.

In one pillowcase he found a white paper bag with the cold hamburgers and fries, the food he had brought from the drive-in for Gramps, somewhat squashed but still clean. He shook his head; he didn't remember putting the fast food bag into the pillowcase, but, of course, he must have done it. "Gonna eat them," he said to himself. Bear looked up at him for a moment as if he knew that things were strange. "It's OK, Bear," Ben said. Bear held Ben's eyes a little longer and then returned to his own food.

Ben retrieved *Star Man's Son* from the bed where he had left it that morning, propped it open on the table with a saltshaker, and read while he ate. "Tonight we are not going to think at all," he said to the dogs. "We got here before dark. We are safe. Nobody saw us or followed us after we left the highway. We did what Gramps wanted us to do. We aren't going to think about anything until the sun comes up in the morning."

Thoughts pushed free of his self-imposed barrier and he found himself wondering, "How long should I stay here? What if Gramps was wrong and everything in the outside world goes along just fine? Will I flunk out if I stay here over the winter?" And an icy shiver rolled down his back. "Gramps is gone, and our house isn't even our house any more. Will I have to live with Uncle George and Aunt Cora—and Neil? God, living with Neil, that sneaking little weasel. That would be beyond horrible."

He could just see Neil now, pale and thin, whining and whining. "Hey, Mom. You said Ben could have a couple of cookies, and he ate four." "Hey, Gramps, it's not fair for you to take us fishing on Saturday. I don't like fishing. It's super boring. You should take us to Blue Lakes Mall." "Hey, Ben, I didn't really steal that ten-dollar bill. I found it in your room." "Hey, Ben, I'll pay you fifteen dollars a month if you'll feed mom's horse every night. It's such a boring—" Ben cut off his own stream of thought. Tonight was awful enough without thinking about Neil. "I'd rather stay at the Place forever than live with Neil," he decided. "It would be so good if I never saw him again."

Ben ate slowly, making the cold food last. As he downed the remaining fries, suddenly he felt tired, exhausted, as if he had been shoveling gravel or digging post holes for hours. He took out his phone, then put it back into his pocket, wondering how long the battery would last. Gary hadn't called. But it was only seven-thirty, much too early to go to bed--at least it would be too early on an ordinary night. Gary would still be on his date; he'd never forgive Ben for interrupting. If things were still ordinary.

Ben carried the lamp into the living room and found the old wind-up clock on top of the bookcase. He wound it tight, setting the time the way Gramps had showed him. He wasn't sure why, but he knew his phone—and Gramps' phone—could die in a few days, and it seemed important that he should know what time it was. He told himself that he'd have to look for the portable solar charger right away. Gramps had bought the thing a year ago, and what had come out of the shipping box was a smooth lime green-and-gray plastic unit looking much like a miniature vacuum cleaner, attached to a flat solar panel that came with several stakes. Gramps had stored it somewhere here at the Place. But where? Ben shrugged his shoulders. That was a question for daylight.

Even though it was so early, Ben could hardly keep his eyes open. He checked the front and back doors to make sure they were locked and took the lamp into the bedroom he had used the night before.

It felt odd, staying here with locked doors. Except for last night, during all the times Ben had stayed at the Place, he and Gramps had never locked the doors of the house or clicked the lock shut on the chain for the barn doors, not until they were leaving. This was their Place, and it had always felt safe. Ben shook his head. Things felt different now. He squeezed his eyes shut against the pain of loss. *Would* things be different outside the Place after today? Oh, god, *would* they?

Was he a fool? Had Gramps been a fool all along? And what about those friends of Gramps', the people who had fed Gramps' obsession all these years: Beezer, Cuda, Simon, and Phil? Rob, who was gone now, like Gramps. Not to mention Lucy. Ben had met the other veterans a few times: gray-haired men, competent and confident, but without any time to share with a boy. He had seen a very old photo of them in one of Gramps' albums, all of them young, all of them sort of half in uniform, some kind of bright green field behind them with rows of plants in water, and then a wall of dark, unfamiliar trees beyond that. Rob had been in that photo—tall, stoop-shouldered, long-legged Rob who had married Dr. Lucy and had died three years ago.

Dr. Lucy was the only one of the group Ben had actually talked to very much, and she hadn't had much time for a boy, either, but had made time for Ben. She'd had a little time for Ben, had showed him the difference between basalt and rhyolite and a few other things. Was Lucy on her way to the Place? She had better be.

Ben pushed his chair away from the kitchen table and took up his book and the oil lamp; he would go to bed now and read himself to sleep; he picked up his headlamp from the kitchen counter. The dogs followed him out of the kitchen.

Setting his book and the lamp on the bedside table, Ben stripped off his khakis and was sliding his feet into the sleeping bag, when his phone rang.

⊨⊧

CHAPTER 6
TIMOTHY

B en was so startled that he cried out, fumbling on the floor for his slacks and grabbing the phone from his pocket so awkwardly that he was afraid he had cut off the call.

He looked at the screen. He knew the caller, but it was a surprise. It wasn't Gary, or Dr. Lucy, or even Uncle George. The call was from Mothy, one of his classmates, one of Gary's geek gaming friends, Timothy Rich. Ben hadn't talked to Mothy for at least a week, maybe longer. He touched the phone to answer.

Ben took a breath before speaking, but before he could say a word, he heard Mothy's voice seeming to burst into the room from the glassy surface of the phone, a voice high and soft and breathy. "Ben! Ben, are you there?"

"I'm here," Ben said, suddenly wondering if he should have answered at all.

"Thank God, thank God," said Timothy. "Listen, everything is awful, it's terrible, there are shots, something is wrong with the water, people are dead--" Timothy was running his words together, gasping.

"What?" was all Ben could think of to say. "What? What do you mean? What is happening? Where are you?"

"There are guys in uniform and people are dying, and people are dead, my mom is dead, and," Tim stopped to take a breath. "I'm in the bushes on the west side of the high school," he said. "I'm under a bush, kind of inside a bush, on the ground. Gary-- Gary said this afternoon that you have a place to go to be safe. A safe place. So I went to your house, but your Gramps–"

"Yes, I know," Ben interrupted. It hurt to say it; his throat burned. "I know Gramps is dead."

"*Do* you have a place to go, Ben?" Mothy gabbled, relentless, terrified. "Can I come? Are you there now? Can I get there?"

Ben pulled the phone away from his face and looked at it as if it were something he had never seen before.

"*Holy crap, holy crap, holy crap.*" Ben felt his lips silently mouthing the words. "Unbelievable," he thought at the same time. "*It's real.* It's happened, what Gramps said. And Gramps said we'd have to be prepared to take in a few people. But of all people, why does it have to be *Mothy*?"

Timothy had been in Ben's school class since they were in the first grade. Mothy was and had always been a smart, small, spindly, poorly coordinated nerd, always more than a little weird, the butt of everyone's jokes. Hardly anyone ever talked to Mothy or hung out with him--except equally nerdy Carl Wilson, Gary, and Ben sometimes, Gary much more than Ben, because both Gary and Mothy were serious gamers: Halo, Endless River, WW, Orgaboo, Sackery. And maybe one or two of the geek girls might say something to Mothy now and then. Or one of the teachers. Sometimes. Ben and Mothy had never been at all close. Mothy was too needy, too irritating. And Ben hadn't had time for friends, other than Gary. *Gary. Where was Gary?*

But Ben and Mothy had been assigned a school science project last spring, as a team of two, and they had worked on it for two weekends and several school nights, so Mothy's cell number had found its way into Ben's phone—and, evidently, vice versa.

"Ben, Ben," Mothy was whispering from the phone. Bear wagged his tail uncertainly and the flame of the lamp wavered, moving the shadows on the wall. "Where are you, Ben? Do you have a place? Do you? I'm desperate. I don't know what to do. Can I come? Can I come? Please tell me that you have a place. Please."

Ben sat motionless on the bed, staring at the faces of the three dogs. Mothy looked like that sometimes. Ben thought of Gramps and took another breath. Really, there was only one answer. "OK, Mothy. Yes, I have a place and you can come here," he said at last. "Have you seen Gary tonight?"

"No, no," Mothy told him, and in his thin voice Ben heard the sharp edge of fear. "I've called Gary and texted, over and over, but he doesn't answer. Nobody answers."

"Find Gary if you can," Ben said. "I gave him a map. And I will give you directions now. But be careful and don't you guys be followed, and I mean it, *don't* be followed. Hear me? Don't be followed. I'll tell you the directions now. You have to memorize them. And promise you won't tell anyone else. You and Gary can come. That's all."

"I promise, I promise," came Mothy's voice. "Who would I tell, anyway, except Gary? And I'll be careful."

Ben told him the directions to the Place and made Timothy repeat them three times. "It's going to take you an hour in a car or maybe two or three days to get here on foot," he said. "After you get to the turnoff from the state highway at Horner Ranch Road, if you are driving, stop there for the night. Don't drive here until it gets light tomorrow morning." Ben didn't want a lost Timothy or a stuck Timothy anywhere near the Place. And like Gramps, he didn't want car lights on the dirt roads. *Under the radar.*

"No car. I don't have a car. Do you have GPS coordinates for where you are? I have my Garmin," Mothy asked unexpectedly.

"Once a techie, always a techie," Ben thought with a wry smile. That was Mothy. Trust Mothy, who rarely went anywhere outside the valley, to have his own GPS. He pictured Timothy's small, pinched face with its smooth cheeks and hazel eyes under a spill of mouse-brown hair. "Coordinates?" Mothy repeated. His voice broke.

"Yes, yes, I do have them," Ben said. "Wait a minute."

Ben vaulted from the bed and carried the lamp into the living room, holding it close to the 7.5-minute US Geological Survey map Gramps had stapled to the wall beside the front door. Gramps had put an X on the Place and had written its UTM coordinates at the top of the map. Ben read them to Timothy and made him repeat those, too.

"Cool. My pocket Garmin is even charged," Mothy said.

"If things are as scary as you say, don't call me back unless you get lost," Ben said. "You know cells can be traced."

"Yes," said Mothy. "Thanks."

"Good luck," Ben said, and ended the call. "Cell phones can be traced," he repeated to himself. He wished he had taken the trouble to learn exactly how those traces worked.

"Gary," he thought immediately. He had to try to reach his best friend again, now, no matter what the consequences. Quickly he brought up Gary's name and sent the call. It rang and rang, and then he heard Gary's voice in the recorded voicemail greeting: "Hey, lay it down gently."

"Gary, I'm at the Place," he said. "Get here! Mothy Rich is looking for you, so call him. He's close to the high school. Don't let anyone see you. Call me! Use your map! Use your map!"

Ben waited half an hour, but the phone remained silent, and the living room was growing chilly enough to bring up goosebumps on his arms, or maybe he had goosebumps for another reason. He didn't want to run the phone battery down right away if he could help it. If Gary called, he could leave a message.

Finally Ben turned off his phone, went to the pantry, and laid the phone inside the steel can on top of the dog kibble. He turned off Gramps' phone and put it into the can as well. Maybe the metal of the can would block a trace; he didn't know. He fitted the steel lid to the can and pushed it down.

Back in the bedroom, Ben sat half inside his sleeping bag for some minutes, his mind awash with questions. Though it wasn't going to freeze tonight, he felt more than chilled. Mothy on the run, hiding in the bushes at the high school? Shots fired? Soldiers? People dying, people dead? And what was it Mothy had said about the water? It was too much. "Tomorrow I'll get out the hand-crank radio and see what's on the news, or what the emergency network says, if anything," he thought. "I just can't face it tonight."

He stared at the small flame of the lamp and sat stiffly upright in the dim bedroom for some time, wondering, hardly daring to think what might be happening in Hailey, but unable to keep his thoughts from the possibilities. "Gramps kept telling me that things were going to go bad, fast," Ben thought. "I thought I knew what he was talking about. I had no idea, not really. None." He stared at the little flame, golden at the top, blue at the bottom, slightly trembling. "I hope Mothy can find Gary," he said aloud, as if that would make it a spell with power. "I hope Mothy finds Gary."

Half of him wanted to throw on his khakis and shoes, drive the pickup out of the barn, and go roaring back to Hailey to get Gary, Gary and Mothy. But, Ben realized, if Mothy, if *Tim* was on the high school grounds, he was little more than a block from Gary's house. If Gary was home, or when he got home after his date, Tim would get to him. And then they'd come, both of them. And Gary had a vehicle, a good one for dirt roads, a Jeep Rubicon.

If what Tim had just said was true, it would be very, very stupid for Ben to blunder around Hailey in the dark without even knowing what or where the threats were. Soldiers? Shots fired? Ben felt goosebumps prickle on his arms again. And, of course, what had he just told Tim about having lights on the dirt roads near the Place at night? Gramps had thought that very important *not* to do. *Gramps. Gramps' note had said DO NOT LEAVE THE PLACE.*

Eventually, Ben wormed all the way into the sleeping bag, patted the bag for the dogs to jump onto the bed and sleep with him, and blew out the lamp. "Now we know Gramps was right," he said to the dogs. "It has started." Ben shook his head and repeated the words, hardly believing them. "Gramps was right. It has started."

He pulled Bear up to his face and rested his own chin in the silky place between Bear's ears. It was good to hear Bear and the other two dogs breathing beside him in the darkness and feel the firm pressure of their bodies. He could still detect the smooth bump of the gun under his head between the sleeping bag and the mattress; he liked that, too. Molly and Moonie felt warm on his back and behind his knees. He was very comfortable, but sleep did not come for a long time.

CHAPTER 7
DEATH

At eight in the morning, Artie was ready to start her Saturday. Yesterday she had waved to Ben as he drove by in his pick-up, and she thought he had waved back. That was a good sign, a happy thing. Maybe he would nod to her or even smile in the hall Monday morning before English class.

After breakfast and chores, she planned to make herself a sandwich and take off on her bike up Quigley Gulch, where she hoped to find a good place to sing, practicing for the Fall Choir Concert coming up just before Halloween, and maybe she could collect some bright leaves of aspen, yarrow, and wild geranium to press for winter crafts. Also, she had an idea for a poem or some song lyrics chasing around in her brain, and she needed to be somewhere away from town to work that out.

"It's good being a plant nerd and a word nerd in the fall," she thought. As Artie sat up, her sleeping bag pooled around her waist and she took a deep breath of the crisp morning air. She liked spending the nights on her pocket balcony, but it was getting a little late in the year to be sleeping outside, and the forecast was for rain. "The forecast said no rain until this evening, though," she thought, rolling up the bag, pushing up the sash of her window, parting the curtains, and stuffing the bag into her bedroom. She climbed inside after it and pulled down the sash. Golden sunlight spilled in behind her; time for breakfast.

In the Ames household, night owl Artie was usually the last one up, and as she took the stairs two at a time down to the kitchen, Artie was surprised not to hear the usual Saturday bustle and chatter. There was no smell of coffee, either—not even the scent of toast.

Artie rounded the corner from the hall into the kitchen and stopped in her tracks. Flat on her back lay her mother, still in last night's blue shirt and jeans. Broken glass surrounded her head like a fragmented halo, glass in her auburn hair. Not two feet away in his striped pajamas lay her little brother Turner, face down. Artie let out a short scream and rushed to them, calling "Dad, Dad, come here!"

Her mother wasn't breathing. Her face and hands were cold, and her eyes were open but fixed in place. The surfaces of her mother's eyes looked dry and a little cloudy. Artie had never seen that before. There were no wounds, no blood visible. She tried to lift her mother's head, but it was stiff and her neck wouldn't bend. She moved to Turner, and found that he was not only dead, but even more wooden than her mother. "Stiff as a board," she thought. "Dad," she screamed. "Dad!"

She ran for her parents' bedroom, and coming around the bed, saw a large bare foot, bottom up, on the floor of the bathroom, just inside the open bathroom door. "Dad!" she screamed again.

Her father, wearing his brown and black plaid pajamas, was dead on the tile floor with a plastic glass in his right hand. He had a tube of toothpaste in his other hand, and a long, smooth rope of blue and white goo trailed from the tube onto his arm and from there onto the tan tiles of the floor. His hand was clenched, as if it were still squeezing. He, too, was cold and wooden.

Everything was wrong; she couldn't stay here.

Artie ran upstairs for her phone and called her grandmother. It rang and rang, and finally went to voicemail. She called her grandpa's cell—the same. She took a deep breath and left a message. "Gran, Grandpa, I'm coming over right now. I need help. Something really, really bad has happened." It would take only minutes to drive to Gran and Grandpa's place. She could call 911 from there, since it was far too late to help her family. When the police got here, she wanted Grandpa and Gran with her.

Artie stood in the middle of her room and made herself take more deep breaths. "This can't be happening. It can't, it can't!" she thought. She could feel her heart racing; it was difficult to breathe.

Maybe one of the neighbors could help, Mrs. Gregson or Mr. and Mrs. Wilder. She ran downstairs again and went to the front door. To her horror, the front door stood wide open. In a corner of the front porch, a white mound of fur crouched oddly over the water bowl that was kept there. "Sally," she whispered, looking around nervously before going to her cat.

Sally, too, was dead--but not yet stiff, limp and still warm, her head turned to the side and half submerged in the dish of water. Artie called her grandparents again and got no answer. She looked up and down the street. It was deserted, eerie. She backed slowly across the porch to the front door, closed it behind her, locked it, and leaned heavily against the polished oak. She should do something. *Something.* What was happening? Whatever it was, was no accident.

Artie went to the rack on the kitchen wall for car keys, but no keys hung there, not even the key to the shed. This was odd. Never mind. She would use her own car keys from her purse. She'd be at Gran and Grandpa's in fifteen minutes.

She stepped into the garage and found the doors gaping open and both cars gone.

She felt as if the world had slipped sideways into insanity. How could both cars be gone when both her parents were here? "Someone has done this," she said to herself. "I've got to get out of here." The feeling of wrongness that had been so irritating yesterday, now overwhelmed Artie like a cold and suffocating flood. She had to get out of this house.

Alert for any sound, Artie ran upstairs to her room and changed from pajamas into jeans, sneakers, a t-shirt, and a gray hoodie. She pulled her hair back into a ponytail, and stuffed it into a black watch cap.

She emptied her schoolbooks from her daypack but left in her purse, then packed in her journal, and, with some tugging, managed to get her scrapbook inside as well. She was damned if she was going to leave her parents and her little brother here, even for an hour, if murderers and maybe thieves were around, without having some photos of them.

She took her water bottle and the pack, and forced herself to go down to the kitchen. With her hand shielding her eyes from looking at her mother's body, Artie was about to fill her water bottle at the sink when her mind flashed images so rapidly that they fell through one another, superimposed: glass from a tumbler lying splintered on the kitchen floor near her mother's head. Dead Turner in his pajamas. Turner often came downstairs for a glass of water after he had been put to bed. Dad, sprawled in the bathroom, the plastic glass in his hand. Sally, dead in her water dish, her mouth still open. Sally's gray spiky tongue and neat white teeth seen clearly under the water in her dish outside.

"The water," Artie whispered in dawning horror. *"There's something in the water."* She thought of how very close she had come to brushing her teeth before coming downstairs, and her hands began to shake.

Dazed, Artie tried to jam her water bottle, still empty, into her daypack, then dropped it on the floor. She was drowning in the flood of *bad thing*. "Focus, you have to focus," she told herself. Her eyes found the knife block on the counter, and she nodded to herself. She selected a medium-sized, sharp knife. She wrapped the knife in the dishtowel hanging on the oven door-handle and shoved both into the top of her now-bulging pack.

For no reason that she could understand, Artie began to feel hurried, like she was running out of time. She stepped into the garage warily. Though the cars were gone, her bike was still where she had left it yesterday afternoon. She pulled her bike upright and stood motionless in the shadowy garage.

After looking up and down and across the street for a long moment, Artie climbed onto her bike and began pedaling, very fast, in the direction of her grandparents' house. "Gran and Grandpa have a well," she thought. "They have well water, not town water. They should be all right." Their house was just over three miles away, on a small acreage a short way south of town, not far from the river. "It won't take me any time at all to get there," she thought, "and *then* we'll see. Gramps can call the police."

Four blocks later, Artie was thoroughly frightened. She'd not seen a car on the street, not a person, not a cat, not a dog. She felt exposed. She had never felt like this on her own street. Was everyone dead, just like her family?

Jumping off her bike, Artie wheeled it into the narrow alley behind the houses on her street and continued moving in the same direction, but fairly well hidden from the street by the houses and sheds. At one house, Mrs. Worthing's, an upper window had been pushed open, and between the dark curtains she could see something white, something like a hand and a pale sleeve dangling over the sill. She got back on her bike and went for speed.

Artie had to cross Main Street to get to her grandparents' house. When she came to the intersection she thought she would use to cross, she felt an odd chill go down her spine, so she leaned her bike against the red brick wall of the Evans Bank and willed herself to be invisible in the deep shadow there, between two enormous and densely branched potted evergreens that some-one had placed near the wall, while she watched Main Street for some time to see if it was safe to cross. Nothing moved on the street. Nothing at all. But her mind began repeating, *bad thing, bad thing.*

"I can't stay here all day," Artie told herself finally. Just as she gathered herself to make her move, shots rang out.

Artie heard four shots, *crack, crack, crack, crack,* one after the other, not far away, and pushed her bike close to the wall behind one of the potted trees. She crouched, hugging the pot of the other tree, wedging herself into the narrow space between the pot and the brick wall. "Rifle," she thought. She had twice been deer hunting with her grandfather, and had gone with him, Gran, and her mother to the shooting range many times. "Firing awfully fast," she told herself. "Too fast, but not a full automatic. Must be more than one shooter."

Shots fired in downtown Hailey? She held her breath. A moment later a man came running toward her across the intersection from the opposite side. *Crack!* The man dropped like a stone and was still. Artie shoved her fist into her mouth and bit down on her knuckles so she wouldn't cry out. *What was happening?*

"Bad idea to cross Main Street," she thought, nearly choked by the feeling of wrongness. "Bad idea to be out in the open at all. I will wait here until dark, and then I'll go clear down south to where that big culvert goes under the highway near the south end of the airfield, and I'll cross in that. It's half a mile out of my way, but that's all right." With her back against the brick wall, she settled down to wait. She was very glad she had put on her gray hoodie and not the blaze orange one she had decided to wear on her planned hike up Quigley Gulch, when she was thinking about it last night. She felt in her pocket for her phone. Should she call 911 now? Something told her *no, bad thing*. Time to try Gran and Grandpa again, and she should call her friend Rosa as well. "Wait," Artie thought. "I'll text." No one could hear her if she texted. She'd tell them not to drink the water.

⊶⊷

Ben got up slowly and took the dogs outside. He had slept longer than he had intended, and the sun was high and bright in the east. Toward the west there was a hint of cloud on the horizon, and Ben remembered that rain had been forecast for tonight. He'd heard it on the radio coming home from Twin Falls only last night. Now he would be on his own with weather forecasting, but Gramps had taught him a few things. He would manage somehow.

Gramps. The pain of it was so harsh that he felt like screaming. Instead, he looked at the tattoo on his right arm and read it aloud: "Stand Fast."

He couldn't help Gramps or himself by standing here in the yard like an idiot, holding down two prints of flattened meadow grass with the soles of his shoes. "I want you to survive," Gramps had said countless times, so at least for now, that's what Ben would attempt to do.

Ben trudged to the barn. He swung both doors open to let in the light, and began sorting and re-sorting the goods he had brought from Twin Falls. The dogs followed. Bear was sticking especially close to his side, and that felt comforting; it was wonderful to have the dogs here. With Gramps gone, he felt that having the dogs was keeping him from going out of his mind.

The barn smelled sweetly of hay and dust. The walls of the barn were insulated with bales of hay, stacked four deep against the walls and higher than he could reach. Molly, Moonie, and Bear hopped onto the first tier of bales and found places to curl up and watch. Ben sighed and tackled the barrels into which he'd shoved his recent Twin Falls purchases, pulled everything out onto the old plank floor, and began to sort. Eventually, he began to unload yesterday's purchases from the pickup and added them to the sorting piles bit by bit.

After everything had been sorted into piles, Ben took several of the empty, heavy blue barrels and lined them up along the east wall of the barn. He pushed the chosen barrels against the wall of bales there and began to fill them with the things from Twin, making sets of similar things in a way that made sense to him. Out came Gramps' green notebook and a permanent marker.

Using the marker, Ben numbered the barrels, and after he had filled each, wrote on each lid what was inside, also copying that to a page in the notebook. One barrel he filled with sweatshirts and coats; one with flannel lounge pants, overalls, and jeans, one with shirts; one with socks, gloves, hats, and scarves; two with pillowcases, sheets and towels; another six with sleeping bags; two with packages of diapers; one with soap; one with yarn, knitting needles, and pattern books; four with books, toys, puzzles, and notebooks; four with kitchen things and small tools; and so on until most of the goods were stowed.

He found the garden cart behind the barn and piled it with canned food to take to the house; he knew better than to leave cans in the barn, where they would freeze when winter came. It took several trips to get all the cans into the house, and that was good; he had to concentrate and work hard. Ben didn't want to think.

He stacked the food cans in the back of the pantry, along the wall in the sleeping loft, under the beds in the two bedrooms, in the bottoms of the closets, and in the cool basement under the house, which already held thousands of cans of food from several years of stocking.

Once everything was stowed and recorded, he was tired and it was past time for lunch. Ravenous, Ben stood at the kitchen table and wolfed a cold can of Vienna sausage and another of pork and beans. He gulped some bitingly icy water straight from the kitchen tap.

He tried again to call Gary, but didn't reach him. Ben left another text message and put his phone back into the dog food bin.

"Well, I can't put it off any longer," he told himself, sighing. From the top of the bookcase in the living room, Ben took the hand-crank radio. He felt perfectly divided in his mind, almost frozen. He needed to know what was going on in the world outside the Place, but he didn't want to know. His hands felt clumsy, stiff, as if they had decided they weren't able to operate the radio.

Ben sank onto a chair at the kitchen table and began to turn the handle slowly—then whirled it faster and faster, until the tiny green LED came on. Gritting his teeth, Ben turned the black knob. Gramps had made certain he knew how to access the emergency channel.

He turned the dial until it rested on the right frequency, noticing that no other stations were operating. He held his breath, at first hearing only static. After so long that he had to crank the radio again, he heard a voice. "—not panic," the voice was saying. "Violent sunspot activity has knocked out most communications--" Static. He cranked until his arm cramped. The voice eventually came again, "—knocked out most communications and flight navigation systems. Stay home and remain calm." Static. "—over in a few days. Do not panic. Violent sunspot activity—" Ben let the voice cycle through its message twice more to make sure he had heard it all, and then stopped cranking. He turned the dial through the other channels, through its entire frequency: nothing but a few crackles. He turned off the radio.

Was sunspot activity truly what was happening? Then why had Mothy said, "People are dead?" And what had he meant by "guys in uniform," and "shots"? Ben didn't understand, but something frightening was definitely going on in Hailey, and probably everyplace else, judging from the radio. He was very glad to be at the Place and not in town.

Ben got up and went outside. It was time to do some checking and to remind himself of the other things that he and Gramps had brought to the Place together. Hopefully he could locate the solar charger. He took the dogs on a walking tour.

The outhouse looked all right, and the bucket of powdered lime that sat inside was clean and full, its lid on tight. The barrel that held new rolls of toilet paper and the empty plastic bucket beside it were still in place, their lids tight as well.

The long henhouse was packed to the rafters with more than two hundred and fifty of the heavy plastic barrels, stacked two deep. Many of these had been in place for several years and were marked in Gramps' bold printing: DOG FOOD, DOG FOOD, DOG FOOD, HEN SCRATCH, ROLLED OATS, WHEAT, RICE, POWDERED MILK, PASTA, LIME, SALT, and many more.

The huge loafing shed, half open on one side, held still more barrels, hundreds of barrels, these covered with brown plastic tarps held down by large rocks. Ben peeled back two of the tarps and saw that these barrels were in good order, too: ROPE, WIRE, HAND TOOLS, UNDERWEAR, MOTOR OIL, TOILET PAPER, and so on, read their labels.

He followed Spear Creek two hundred feet upstream to check the penstock, a long wooden open-topped box in which the water was collected from the stream and diverted into a PVC pipe that took it to the kitchen sink. Ben saw that the penstock was working well and was free of debris, although when the creek began to freeze, he knew he would have to take the box out and drain the pipe, leaving them high and dry in the meadow until spring, the way Gramps had done every fall.

Farther upstream, a tiny spring trickled into Spear Creek, its five-foot-long channel cushioned with emerald moss. The place where water bubbled up from the ground was a sand-floored pocket at the base of a willow, holding only a scant cupful of clear water. The sand grains at the bottom of this little spring were always dancing about, and the water was clear as rock crystal.

During the past summer, Gramps and Ben had dug a yard-wide and foot-deep square hole in the damp soil next to the spring, and had lined it with granite rocks from the hill behind the Place. A length of copper pipe lay in the sedge nearby. In the dense shade of the short willows, Gramps was planning to make a springhouse cooler here, a box made of screening where perishable foods could be kept in summer away from insects and small animals, a run of water from the spring to be trained through the copper pipe and made to run down one or two sides of the screened box, where both the cool water and evaporation would lower the temperature inside. To this end, Gramps had collected several discarded screen doors and window screens, still in their aluminum frames, now leaning against the west side of the barn. Ben and Gramps had planned to finish the springhouse next spring. "Right," Ben thought bitterly. Under the sleeve of his flannel shirt, Ben felt at itch, and he pushed up his sleeve to scratch at it. "Hope," the itchy patch of skin told him. He swiped at the tattoo with a fingernail and tried not to think about it.

The wind sliced past the stems of the meadow sedges near the creek with a harsh hissing sound. To the west, more clouds were slipping over the horizon. A storm was coming in. Yes, it would rain tonight.

Downstream and closer to the house was the waterwheel he and Gramps had built several years ago, when Ben was only a kid. The five-foot wooden wheel was running easily, slick and slimy with algae and dark-spotted with snails, turning and turning, lifting and spilling water back into Spear Creek. Gramps' original idea had been to use the waterwheel to generate electricity for the house, but they had never gotten around to making that happen. The waterwheel didn't turn in the winter, of course, when Spear Creek was silent and locked in ice. Somewhere at the Place, Ben remembered, Gramps had stashed a book on how to generate electricity using a waterwheel—something else to search for before winter. He imagined that he would have lots of time to discover where Gramps had put which books, and to read them—but he suddenly realized that he should figure out all the books he wanted and locate them before the snow fell.

The woodshed was full of split pine from up on Cat Mountain, and the two axes, the heavy wedges, the maul, and the hatchets were where they were always kept, heads sunk into a big bucket of oily sand just inside the shed door. Much more wood, wood that needed to be split, was stacked against three walls of the shed outside, and outside along one side of the barn. Split wood also lined the house's covered front and back porches, stacked against the walls of the house. With a pang, Ben remembered the long days of hot work splitting that wood, and the cold drinks he and Gramps had shared, sitting in the meadow grass in the shade of a willow tree.

Ben saw that the chain link dog run attached to the south wall of the woodshed was intact, its gate shut and the corrugated tin roof in good repair. One side of the run was a wall of the woodshed, and crosscut rounds of pine were stacked six feet high on two more sides of the dog run, outside the chain link, wood that Gramps had bought last spring from a firewood dealer. "You will have to keep Molly and Moonie somewhere safe when they come in season," he could hear Gramps saying.

"Gramps," Ben thought miserably. His stamp was everywhere at the Place. How could Gramps be gone forever? His death didn't make sense. This was Gramps' Place. He should be here.

Ben hadn't been to the old bunker yet, the first shelter Gramps had built, or rather improved, finished before Ben had even been born. The bunker, dug cavelike back into the hillside, concrete-lined, beam-supported, and linoleum-floored, was part of the original homestead and was where Gramps and Grandma had stayed when they first bought the Place, before they had fixed up the old ranch house itself. They had enlarged the bunker. It had once been an interesting den, cool in the summer, where Ben could play or read on hot days. But this year the old bunker had been stacked nearly to the low ceiling with food and other things. He had yet to find the solar charger, but Ben didn't think he could handle going into the old bunker today. Nor could he face going into the other dark place. He walked back to the house.

Before going inside, Ben stood on the back porch with an armload of split wood and took a critical look at the sky.

The western sky was now crowded with piled dark clouds, and they were moving eastward rapidly. The air smelled wet; Spear Creek sounded louder than usual. It would rain tonight, was supposed to rain all night and all day tomorrow, the truck's radio had told him yesterday. "Good," Ben thought. "Nobody likes moving around in a rainstorm." But then he thought of Timothy Rich and wondered if Mothy could possibly follow the directions or the coordinates, keep himself out of sight, and actually find the Place: Mothy, out in the rain. Mothy, who was usually glued to a monitor, mouse, keyboard, pad, pod, phone, or joystick. Mothy, who never went camping, or fishing, or hiking.

And Gary. Did he still have the map? Could he find the Place, too? Or by now had he connected with Mothy? On foot, it would be cold and unpleasant getting to the Place during a serious rainstorm. But Gary was far more at home in the outdoors than Mothy. And he had his old Jeep. Gary would be all right, if he would just *come.*

Then there was Dr. Lucy. Gramps had said she was driving down from Montana. Lucy was a no-nonsense, capable person; she would make it, rain or no rain. He had expected Lucy today, but surely she would get to the Place in the morning.

When it was almost dark, Ben called in the dogs, lit the oil lantern, and laid a fire in the big, black Majestic wood stove. The old house creaked and groaned as buffets of wind swept in; the storm had arrived.

It began to rain, softly tapping on the metal roof, and Ben remembered happy summer nights here, snug in his sleeping bag, listening to rain on the roof, while Gramps snored gently in the next bedroom. *God.*

"Well," he thought. "Rain is good. An hour of rain and most of lower Spear Creek Road will turn to soup. Any tracks the truck might have left on the road will be gone, and no one will want to drive up here. It's a safe night, and obviously Dr. Lucy won't be coming until it's light. She is no doubt holed up somewhere." The storm had brought with it early darkness and chill, and Ben lit the wood in the stove.

Ben held the oil lamp inside the pantry and found a can of pork and beans and a big can of coffee. He dumped the pork and beans into a saucepan, filled the familiar gray enamel coffee pot with water, scooped in some coffee, and slapped each onto a round stove lid.

A clap of thunder brought hammering rain and sent the dogs scurrying under the kitchen table. Ben laughed at the dogs and picked up *Star Man's Son* while he waited for the fire in the stove to heat his meal. "Poor Mothy," he thought, listening to the downpour. "But he's not stupid. He will find a place to hole up tonight, too, just like Dr. Lucy will. And Gary will call me and leave voicemail or a text," he told himself, not quite believing. *Hoping.* The woodstove was beginning to send out pleasant waves of heat. "Cozy," he told himself.

Ben fed the dogs, put his head down on the table, and sobbed.

It was dark and raining in Hailey. Every few minutes thunder boomed and lightning lit up the sky brightly enough that Artie could see the corridor of tall cottonwoods along Wood River to the west, and the outline of the tall hills beyond.

Artie had worked her way south of town, where she was stumbling along in the barrow pit on the east side of the highway, opposite the airfield. She was wheeling her bike, splashing in puddles, falling now and then. Her hoodie and jeans were soaked through, and water sloshed squishily in her shoes. The only vehicle she had seen today had been an unmarked white semi, driving north in the late afternoon. She had hidden behind a clump of wild roses while the truck went by.

Artie shivered and wished she had thought to bring a flashlight. Or not. It would be very tempting to keep it on, if she had one. But no, she didn't want to be seen.

Another flash of lightning showed a silver gleam ahead, close, and Artie gave a little start of relief. The culvert at last!

Lights. Artie whipped her head around. Twin headlamps.

A vehicle, still a mile away, coming her way from the south. Clutching the handlebars of her bike, she sprinted for the culvert, hoping it was as large as she remembered. Grabbing at the culvert rim with one hand, she swung in, slipping on mud underfoot and pulling her bike in as well. After seeing that man shot in the street, how was she supposed to know who was decent and who was dangerous? It could be that the vehicle coming from the south had in it the sheriff and some deputies that would make everything right. But all day Artie had felt that hollow feeling she always got when things were going to be bad, and she had learned never to ignore it.

A narrow stream of water was rushing through the bottom of the culvert. Artie found that if she laid her bike down crossways, she could sit on the frame and be out of the water, a foot planted on each side of the stream and taking part of her weight. Artie heard the vehicle pass overhead with a hissing rumble. She was wet and cold; her shivering turned to shaking.

She withdrew her arms from the hoodie's wet sleeves and hugged her own ribcage, cursing herself for not bringing a raincoat. Of course, when she had left home this morning, she had figured to be at her grandparents' house in less than half an hour.

Another flicker of yellow light from the far end of the culvert surprised her. Another vehicle? A minute later she felt it pass over. Another flicker, another rumble. And another. And another. She had reached the culvert just in time. A convoy of some kind was going north into Hailey. Vehicle after vehicle rolled overhead. "Holy crap," she thought. "Holy-oly crap. I had better stay here for the night."

⊷ ⊷

CHAPTER 8

FIRE AND RAIN

Sunday morning Ben was up well before daylight, stoking the dying fire in the kitchen stove, feeding it a little more wood so he could start the day with hot coffee and toast. He made the toast simply by laying slices of bread flat on the stove lids for a minute on each side, then forking the slices onto a plate and spreading them with a small amount of the now-precious butter, plus generous quantities of grape jelly from the pantry. The bread came from one of two loaves he had brought from Hailey, having scooped them into a pillowcase at the last minute, along with the butter.

"I had better enjoy this bread while it lasts," he thought. "Pretty soon I'm going to have to learn how to make bread. Arrrgh, me making bread." He shook his head. Gramps had always done most of their cooking, and had always told Ben that when they went to live at the Place, that would be time enough for Ben to learn. But Gramps had never made bread. And butter? What about butter, *here*? That was another thing entirely. Ben shook his head and took a bite of toast; he was really going to miss butter. And Gramps himself. *Gramps.*

Ben remembered Sunday mornings in Hailey, waking up to the fine smell of bacon and the sound of it crackling in the pan, the bacon-smell mingling with the rich aroma of strong coffee. Gramps always made a great Sunday breakfast—oatmeal with real cream, bacon and eggs, fruit, toast, orange juice, and really good coffee. And Gramps' idea of a good Saturday breakfast was equally fine, though not as big a spread: cold pie with whipped cream, and lots of coffee. Gramps *did* make pies, excellent pies, on a regular basis, often on a Friday night. *Gramps again.* Ben sighed, then gritted his teeth. He had to get real, to understand that Gramps was truly gone.

"Cookbooks," he forced himself to think. During the past few years, Gramps had bought several to stash at the Place. Along with other books, most of the cookbooks were stored in barrels somewhere in the old chicken house or the barn--but maybe one or two could be lurking close by, in the bookcase around the corner in the living room. Ben sighed again. There were countless things he'd have to locate before the snow came.

The hard rain had gentled sometime during the night. It was still sprinkling softly outside and the sky was roofed with black, not a star to be seen.

Over the snapping of the fire in the stove, Ben could hear coyotes yipping somewhere to the east of the cabin. He wouldn't let the dogs out until it was fully light. The three Shelties sat on the kitchen floor near the door to the back porch and stared, waiting: black and white Bear and the two females, blue Moonie and tricolor Molly. They were ready for the day to begin, but they knew how it was at the Place. They waited, staring at the back door.

"Looks like it's going to rain all day," Ben said to them. He still had Hailey things from Gramps' suitcases and his own duffel bag and daypack to stow somewhere, so he could work on that for a while inside the house. He might be able to handle dealing with Gramps' things today.

He would have to unpack and stow them sometime, and it would be best to get the things put away before Mothy and Gary got here, and Dr. Lucy. "Never let anyone see you cry," Gramps had said many times. "I know it's not the current thinking, but I'm old-school, and the world is going to be old-school again within your lifetime, Benny. Don't show weakness; that makes you safer." Ben wanted any of that possible weakness to be well over before Mothy and Gary showed up. *If Mothy and Gary showed up.*

When his coffee was poured and the full light of the cloudy day filtered through the kitchen windows, Ben let out the three dogs and took his last cup of coffee into the living room, where he began emptying the suitcases. He opened Gramps' suitcases on the long leather couch and began to unpack them.

Gramps' clothing and shoes went into the closet and dresser of the bedroom that had been Gramps' when they had stayed at the Place together. "They'd be a tight fit for me, anyway," Ben thought. Gramps was, *had been* a little shorter than Ben, with smaller feet and narrower shoulders. "Maybe Mothy can wear some of these," he thought. Not Gary. Gary was considerably taller than either Gramps or Ben.

Gramps' prescription heart pills went into the kitchen pantry, all ten vials and twelve bottles of them. Ben looked at the labels; yes, Gramps had double-dipped and had gotten his prescriptions filled at several different pharmacies at about the same time, only last week.

At the bottom of the smaller suitcase, Ben found two things he had hoped to find, a photo album with a brown cover and a polished box about eight inches by four inches by six inches, made from some reddish wood inlaid with copper and mother of pearl in an exquisite leaf and vine pattern. He slid the little copper hook from the loop and lifted the lid with care. This was an artifact of his family, his family that was.

Ever since Ben could remember, this box had occupied center stage on the dresser in Gramps' bedroom at home, the bedroom Gramps and Grandma had shared before she died. The box was lined with pale blue satin gathered, fanned, and folded richly in the lid, sides, and bottom of the box. The box was old, perhaps older even than Grandma; the satin showed a darker blue inside the folds and gathers. Gems winked at him, and a brass key poked up through Grandma's necklaces, bracelets, rings, and earrings. He fitted the key into its slot, wound it, and let it go. Delicately *The Blue Danube* waltz tinkled through the air and caught him in the throat with memories.

He remembered each piece of the jewelry: the bracelet of round, faceted garnets set in gold. The square-cut amethyst ring. The opal pendant mounted in silver with a tiny diamond above it, the brass-wire combs jeweled along the tops with marcasite and peridot, the white-gold pin in the shape of a bow sparkling with diamonds, the aquamarine earrings transparent as drops of water, dangling from silver filigree. All of these had fascinated him as a child. And, since five years ago last September, Grandma's engagement ring had lived in the box, a fiery, brilliant-cut orange sapphire set in rose gold, flanked by two radiant yellow diamonds.

Every year on Grandma's birthday, September twenty-first, Gramps would take out all the jewelry, spread the pieces on a towel on the kitchen table, and clean everything gently, a ritual of remembrance.

Gramps liked to talk while he did the cleaning. He'd told Ben many times which pieces had come down to Grandma in her family, some all the way from Spain; which ones he had given her for Christmas, for an anniversary, for her birthday, when Ben's dad was born; which pieces she had worn when they'd gone to the opera in San Francisco, or when they'd had dinner at the governor's mansion so long ago. "Your grandmother was one of a kind," Gramps would say.

Ben could almost see Gramps holding the engagement ring, his eyes too bright. "No colorless diamond solitaire for my best girl," Gramps would tell Ben every year. "She loved the fall and wanted her ring to remind her of autumn leaves, the aspens and cottonwoods—so I had this ring made for her in Twin Falls, at Levinson's Jewelry, that little corner store with the jade elephants in the window. Levinson's is gone now. That corner is a McDonald's these days. But Hale Levinson knew what he was doing—bought in and set the stones himself. And just look at it!" Gramps would hold the clear and sparkling orange sapphire and yellow diamonds up to catch the light before stowing the ring away in the wooden box for another year. Ben twisted Gramps' garnet and gold ring on his own finger. It still felt odd there, not right. He pulled off Gramps' ring and nestled it in the box next to Grandma's diamond-and-sapphire ring. That felt better.

Ben could remember Grandma well; her image was clear, only slightly faded: iron-gray hair pulled away from her face and coiled low on her neck, tumbling to her waist on the rare occasions when she let it fall. Narrow, aristocratic nose and thin lips, high cheekbones, her whole face long and narrow. Fine-textured skin and large, deep-set brown eyes beneath arching brows that stayed as black as her hair had once been. Long neck, slender body, long, tapering fingers with a gentle touch. Benerita, her name was, a Basque name. Gramps said she had been Benerita Balboa. Ben had been named for Benerita and for her most-loved place, Bennett Mountain.

Ben's fingers found his favorite in the box, a pin in the form of a spray of small flowers on delicately curving gold stems. The leaves were of gold, and the petals were light blue sapphires.

"Forget-me-nots," Gramps had told him. "Those were her favorite flower, too. Your grandmother loved this brooch. She had it down from her own grandmother. You will have to find a good woman to wear this someday. This and the ring." *The Blue Danube* stopped, slowly plinking itself into silence in the middle of a phrase.

"Yeah, right," Ben thought. "Find a good woman, when I've been Scavenger all these years? Sure. And what are my prospects from now on?" But Ben knew it wasn't fair to blame Gramps for that. Without Gramps' foresight, Ben would be back in town hiding and terrified with Mothy, or out in the cold rain with nothing to eat and no place to go--or crouching in some basement hoping no one would discover him, or perhaps simply dead, simply *gone.*

And to be honest with himself, Ben thought sternly, he didn't know—somehow had never learned--how to talk to girls, so he avoided them, which, for the Scavenger, hadn't been at all difficult. The girls he knew from school seemed for the most part to be ruthless, status-focused creatures, unkind and untouchable, silly, with a great deal of surface shine and little depth, their sweet bodies and lovely faces desirable, but their minds and hearts closed to the things he loved: art, birds, the sky, trees, dogs, wildlife, rocks, flyfishing, open country, books . . . To girls at school he was just *Scavenger*; almost mute, not athletic, shabby, weird. He wondered: could that be over now? Could he be just *Ben* from now on? Or were any of those girls still *there? Was* there a there, even?

No, he'd had more important things to do than get involved with other people his age. He had found out last night from Mothy how important those important things were.

Timothy had said people in Hailey were dead now. Ben felt his fingers grip the jewelry box, hard. But what did that mean? He should have asked Mothy. It was stupid that he had been too shocked last night, too surprised to think straight. Were *some* people dead? Or was *everyone* dead, everyone but Mothy? And maybe, *maybe* Gary? Ben wiped a hand down one side of his face.

"Never mind," he thought stubbornly. "My job for now is simple: make it through the winter, and that's what I am going to do." He locked the jewelry box and photo album inside the gun safe, where they fitted nicely on a top shelf next to boxes of bullets.

At a brisk pace, Ben sorted the things from the suitcases, boxes, pack, and duffel, his own things as well as Gramps'. By midday he had everything put away, had refilled the suitcases with food cans, and had stashed them in the attic sleeping loft overhead.

The rain got serious. It fell relentlessly, now unremarkable, now smacking hard onto the metal roof in huge drops. The dogs scratched to be let in, shaking water all over the kitchen.

Ben built up the fire in the stove and for lunch, heated a can of chili. He put on more coffee and he tossed the dogs each a treat. Lighting the stove's firebox gave him serious pause, but he went ahead. This was the first time he'd ever had, had ever even *seen*, a fire in the stove when it wasn't dark outside, but he figured that the rain made it safe. No one would see smoke coming from the stovepipe in this hard rain. And the dirt roads to the Place would be quite muddy by now—Horner Ranch, Gray Creek, lower Spear Creek; no one but Mothy, Gary, or Dr. Lucy would be close, anyway.

Ben stared at the two cell phones lying lifeless atop the kibble in the steel can like dead child's toys. After a long moment's hesitation, Ben punched his on and checked: no missed calls, no texts, no new voicemail; the same was true of Gramps' phone. Ben's battery was holding well; it might be good for three or even four more days—more, with the emergency reserve they all held. Gramps had bought a small gas generator two years ago; and along with several five-gallon cans of gasoline, it was hidden in the new bunker. "I have my cell charger and some extension cords," Ben thought. "If I can't find the solar charger, maybe I can figure out how to charge a phone using a gas generator. But– would that be wise, now?" The question was unanswerable, and without thinking about it any more, Ben called Gary's number yet again. When after many rings it went to voicemail, he turned off the phone and replaced it inside the kibble can.

Outside, the gray clouds lowered and the rain fell in sheets. Yes, he was certain that the rain would disguise any smoke from the stovepipe. Ben was more tired than he should be and despite the warmth radiating from the big stove, he felt cold. "I feel weird," he thought. "It might be shock," he told himself. "Shock, weirdness, and two nights of bad sleep."

He brought in more wood from the front porch and stoked the firebox again. Then he took the red plaid throw that lay folded over the back of the couch, wrapped the thick wool around his body, and sat at the kitchen table near the stove, with fresh coffee at his elbow, his book on the table, and the damp and gently steaming dogs lying at his feet. It wasn't long before Ben's head lay down on *Star Man's Son,* and he fell asleep.

"Artie? Artie, you get out of bed this instant!" her mother called up the stairs as she often did on school mornings. Everyone in her family, except Artie, was a morning person. Artie floated down the stairs already dressed in a navy blue sweater and fairly new jeans.

Before she knew it, she was in school, at her locker in the east hallway, ferreting among the books and other odds and ends for her lunch bag. The next locker to the left belonged to Lainey Adams, and before lunch Artie always tried to get to her own locker right away, diving in and out before Lainey and her friends got there. But today she was running a little late and here they came, almost too lovely to be real.

Lainey had braided her long, strawberry-blonde hair into a fat twist down her back with some sort of glittering purple necklace woven in. She wore a long-sleeved blouse of black lace with a gauzy lavender scarf around her neck, and painted-on black jeans. Under the lace blouse, Artie could see that Lainey was wearing a purple bra: this ensemble passed for high style among the elite at Wood River High.

Lainey turned her back to Artie while she tossed books into her locker. Lenore Holman and Kaylee Field stood patiently behind Lainey, waiting for her, chattering away. Artie was invisible to them. She had always been invisible to them. They stood inside her personal space as if Artie weren't a person at all.

"—her to the Homecoming Dance," Lenore said. Lainey, Kaylee, and the other popular people called Lenore "Lenny." Lenny always seemed to speak in sentence fragments. "Going?" One slender hand smoothed her tailored black skirt.

Kaylee was in black as well; she had on a black turtleneck over a short purple skirt and black tights, and wore a number of jangling silver bracelets. Together they were Lainey, Lenny, and Kaylee, the Three Musketeers of the in-group, the Triumvirate of Taste, the Princesses of Popularity: Lainey, the blue-eyed strawberry blonde; brown-eyed Lenny, her hair dark auburn with red highlights; and Kaylee, the hazel-eyed golden blonde, three colors that knew they were worth it. "It must be Goth Day in Popularity-Land," Artie thought, waiting silently, as usual, for them to be gone.

"Of *course* I'm going--with Turk," Lainey answered, shoving something into her black crocodile shoulder bag. "What did you expect?" Lainey slammed her locker door almost in Artie's face (Oh, does the nonperson have a face?), and the three of them drifted away, laughing.

They were always laughing, and Artie was always invisible to them. That's the way it was and had been for years. Lainey,

Lenny, and Kaylee were no doubt on their way downtown for lunch, most likely to meet up with the two other cheerleaders, Shandy Johnson and Paige Wills. Only the lame, the dumb, and the ones nobody would ask out brought their lunches.

It was cold in the hall today, really cold; that was odd. Artie grabbed the jacket she had hung inside her locker door. The locker yielded up her lunch bag, finally; she shut the metal door with a tinny clang, and set off down the hall to find Rosa and . . .

Artie fell forward off her bike and nearly planted her face in the muddy stream in the center of the culvert, before she caught herself. She had tried to stay awake, but at the fag end of this evil night, she had fallen asleep at last.

It had been the most miserable night of her life. For hours, images of her dead family had darted around in her brain like sharp arrows, not to be shut out no matter how she tried to distract herself. She was still shivering; no wonder she had felt the cold in her dream.

However, perhaps things were looking up for her exit from the culvert. Her clothes were drier, though not yet dry. No vehicles had driven over her for a long time. At least, Artie felt that the loud rumbling overhead would have jolted her awake, if there had been any more vehicles.

Both ends of the culvert showed deepest indigo now. Dawn was not far off. It was time to move, before it was fully light.

She righted her bike, shouldered her pack, and crept to the western mouth of the culvert. Outside, rain was still falling. "Great," she said to herself. Then she smiled a little; maybe the rain would help her get to her destination unseen.

She looked both ways, listened, and then left her shelter, wheeling the bike as rapidly as she dared, crossing the open, closely grazed area beyond the southern boundary of the airfield, and then, as the sky began to grow gray in the east, sliding the bike and herself under a barbed-wire fence and into a rough pasture, where she kept to a straggling line of cottonwood trees along an irrigation ditch.

After twenty minutes of walking through slippery, saturated grass, Artie could make out the dark, vague shapes of a house and outbuildings ahead. All the windows were dark. She leaned against a tree and watched for a minute or two: she heard no sound but the rain, saw no movement.

Cautiously walking a little closer, she came to a shed painted white with dark trim, and things fell into place. This was her grandparents' neighbors' place. The Petersons. Mrs. Peterson worked at the Post Office and Mr. Peterson drove a UPS truck. They had a daughter in grade school, Shannon. The Petersons also had two sorrel mares, Latte and Jinx. Artie had gone riding with Shannon a number of times.

"I should wake them up and tell them what happened," Artie thought, but already she knew that she didn't want to be seen by anyone; she just wanted to get inside her grandparents' house. *And what if the Petersons were already--what if they were all*—she couldn't think it.

Artie was close to the river now; she could hear its dull wash of sound below the pattering rain, just barely. The day was graying into dawn and a low mist breathed into the air, rising from the pastures.

Artie, thoroughly soaked again, crouched to hide herself in the curling mist and moved as quietly as she could past the Petersons' outbuildings, across their corral, and into her grandparents' back pasture. Their two horses, Merry and Slim, a bay and a palomino, had taken refuge in the loafing shed to get out of the rain. They lifted their heads toward Artie and nickered. The horses weren't nervous. They didn't seem upset. That was excellent. She let out a sigh of almost-relief and wheeled her bike into the shed, leaning it against a wall behind a lawnmower. This would be a good place to leave it for now.

She approached the house from the rear. It, too, had dark windows, but that was nothing unusual. Her grandparents were retired and liked to sleep late sometimes. They were night owls, too. "You get that from us, Artie," Gran had said so many times.

After a long stop near the back fence to look and listen, Artie opened the familiar gate and let herself into the back yard. The rain had slackened, but the mist continued to curl and thicken. The garage loomed, a dark and blocky shape. She knew their garage door didn't lock.

Holding her breath, Artie shoved the garage door up. Empty. The garage was empty. Gran's sedan was gone and Grandpa's pickup was gone. Artie's heart sank. She pulled the garage door down behind her and thought, "This is like it was at home." She felt the boiling fear, simmering for several hours, rising again in the back of her throat.

Artie came to the door into the house and held the tarnished brass doorknob in her hand. Should she knock? Should she just go in? Well, she was here. What else was there to do?

Artie turned the knob and the door opened. The house was dim inside, but she knew it so well that she left the lights off, calling softly, "Grandpa? Gran?"

Five minutes later Artie sat herself on the bottom stair with her head in her hands and let a few tears come. The house was empty. The rooms were neat and clean, the beds were made, the fridge was full of food, and the television was on but muted and turned to The Weather Channel. Grandpa loved The Weather Channel. Everything was as it should be, except that she had found her grandmother's everyday handbag on the floor in the upstairs hall, and inside were Gran's wallet with her driver's license, debit card, and credit cards. *And her asthma inhaler.* That was not right—Gran not here, her car not here, but her wallet and inhaler left lying in the hall.

Movement near the far wall startled Artie into crying out, but it was just Callie, their calico cat, pushing inside through the cat door. Callie wouldn't come to Artie. Instead, she paused a moment to shake drops of water from her fur and headed for her food bowl in the kitchen. Artie could hear the crunching. At least Callie didn't seem to be worried. That had to be a sign that whatever might have happened here was at least a few hours in the past.

But what now? What should she do? Resolutely, Artie pulled out her cell and called first her grandmother and then her grandfather. Both their phones went immediately to voicemail. That was terrible, frightening. She didn't leave a message.

She took a deep breath and after a long moment poised between fear and desire, finally called 911. After a moment she heard a man's voice, a recording: "All circuits are busy. Please leave your name and number and we will get back to you as soon as possible. We urge you to stay calm, stay indoors, and wait for further information. Tomorrow morning, turn to the emergency information channel on your television or radio. All circuits are busy . . ."

Artie ended the call and turned her phone off. She hefted it in her hand, seeing nothing but moving reflections in its blank surface, and then shoved it into the pocket of her jeans. That took her two attempts; her hand was shaking. *Wrong.* Yes, something was as wrong as it could be.

Outside, it was as light as it was going to get until the rain stopped. White mist hid everything except the vague shapes of nearby trees and fences. Artie thought, "Should I stay here? I have no idea what to do." But there *was* something she could do. She was cold, wet, and very hungry. She could fix that, certainly.

For the times when she stayed over, Artie kept a few of her things in the downstairs bedroom: a few clothes, an extra pair of sneakers, underthings, some books, a brush, and some lotion. She could change clothes.

Artie dumped the entire contents of her damp daypack onto the couch and spread the things to dry. She felt, she *knew*, that she shouldn't advertise her presence, so she decided not to run the washer or drier or turn on any lights.

In the guest bedroom, she peeled off her wet clothing and put on dry clothes and shoes from her stash there. Crumpled on the floor, her clothes looked like the molted skins of some strange alien—and most definitely showed that someone had been in the house very recently. She kicked them under the bed.

Then she returned to the kitchen, opened the fridge, and standing up, wolfed three pieces of leftover chicken and half a bowl of her grandmother's excellent potato salad, finishing up with a Snickers bar and a Coke. That helped. She hadn't had anything yesterday but a couple of granola bars that had happened to be in her daypack, and, after dark, some water from a rain puddle.

In the downstairs bathroom, Artie toweled her hair and brushed it, and put in a new ponytail. She still felt too wary of tap water to brush her teeth or wash her face.

Then she ran up the stairs to her grandparents' bedroom and opened their closet. The small gun safe there was open, emptied; Gramps and Gran's target pistols, her mother's target pistol, the two shotguns, the Remington .22 rifle that Artie herself liked to shoot, and the deer rifle, all were gone. The ammunition was gone, too. Artie had to bite her lip to keep herself on track; she felt like running out into the rain, felt like screaming.

Two deep breaths and she was thinking again. "I'm almost the same size as Gran," she thought. "I need a raincoat." In the closet she found Gran's heavy, hooded raincoat, the one with the quilted flannel lining, and tossed it onto the bed. She also found a pair of black pull-on rubber boots, a lightweight parka, and a good-sized dark-gray daypack. Feeling like a thief, Artie rummaged in their dresser drawers and added to her loot a long gray polarfleece neck scarf with its matching hat and gloves, and two pairs of thick socks. The king-sized bed with its tumble of decorative pillows was so inviting that it made her feel sick, wishing she could dive into it, heap pillows onto her head, and go to sleep. But she didn't feel safe here. At all.

Outside, one of the horses whinnied, and Artie jumped, ran to the south window, and stared blindly out into the white mist. What would be a safe place now? Was any place safe?

Artie put on the light parka and tugged the raincoat on over it. After finding the guns missing, she felt the same way she had felt at her own house yesterday morning, like a clock was ticking, like she had to get out. Artie was listening to herself very carefully today; when that ticking clock told her *time to go*, she would go.

She decided to repack, provision herself, and find a good place to hide where she wasn't likely to be discovered, so she could get some sleep. The previous night of cold, stress, grief, and broken sleep had left her very tired.

Quickly she took her plunder downstairs, along with a fleece blanket pulled hastily from the linen closet at the top of the stairs. She pushed the small blanket to the bottom of Gran's gray daypack and packed the socks, scarf, gloves, and her remaining few clothes from the downstairs bedroom on top of the blanket: a t-shirt, a sweatshirt, a pair of jeans, and a set of undies. She pulled the rubber boots on over her own shoes and wore Gran's hat.

In the kitchen, Artie gave herself the remaining chicken and potato salad, half a dozen Snickers bars from Grandpa's stash in a drawer, a dozen granola bars, a four-pack of little grape juice bottles, a handful of tea bags, two cans of concentrated soup, a spoon, two bottles of water with the seals intact, and several boxes of matches. She put the matches into one resealable plastic bag, the tea into another, and took a fistful of the bags as well. With sudden desire, her eyes lit upon a chubby box of black plastic garbage bags. She stripped away the box and stuffed the roll of bags into one of the oversized front pockets of the raincoat, taking a few minutes to run to the living room and wrap her precious scrapbook inside one of the bags.

She knew the drawer where Grandpa kept his flashlight and a few extra batteries, so those went into Gran's pack as well. Last night she'd thought about having a flashlight; it would be good to have one. Then she revisited her own clammy daypack and repacked it.

Finally, Artie took a large bag of cat kibble from its place in the pantry. She poured kibble into several of Gran's mixing bowls, which she placed on the kitchen floor beside the two cat dishes. This would help Callie for a while. Callie would be able to find water outside in irrigation ditches, at least for the next few days, and then there would be snow. Besides, it was only a hundred yards further west to the river. Eventually, Callie might have to learn to be a better hunter. "Or," Artie thought, though she couldn't quite bring herself to believe it, "or Gran and Grandpa could come back."

After the frantic activity, Artie felt wrung out. She would like nothing better than to fall across the guest bed and sleep for hours. Would it be safe to sleep *under* one of the beds? Or in a closet? She couldn't go home now—could she *ever*?

Artie did not want to leave the house, this familiar house she had loved all her life, where she and Gran had cried over sad movies and laughed over popcorn, where they had teased Callie by dragging lengths of bright yarn across the floors, where Grandpa had kept glancing at The Weather Channel on winter evenings while trying to tie fishing flies under the gooseneck lamp at his desk, where she had spent many an afternoon reading in front of the fireplace, or helping Gran bake chocolate-chip cookies, or cutting out paper bats to hang for Halloween, or spooning soil into little pots to start tomato plants on the windowsill.

Someone had come here and had driven Gran's cream-colored Toyota sedan away, and Grandpa's red Ford pickup, taking the guns and ammunition. Or had frightened Grandpa and Gran so much that they had left at once, instantly. But would they leave separately, in two vehicles? Would Grandpa and Gran take the household guns and the few bullets and shotgun shells they kept in the gun safe, but leave Callie?

And what about Gran's wallet and inhaler in her bag on the floor in the upstairs hall? And why hadn't Grandpa and Gran called Artie back? Something very much not good had happened here. Artie found herself hoping that her grandparents were still alive. If they had been here, dead on the floor . . . The thought was too horrible.

The house was warm, dry, and comfortable, but it was not a safe place to stay; she could feel it. A sudden rattle of harder rain beat upon the west windows. "Raining through fog," she thought. "Weird." Outside, where could she go in this rain? It seemed an effort just to think.

Artie looked into the front yard through the window in the door. The mist was still thick, cottony. That was good.

What about hiding in the basement? No, she could be cornered there; there was only one way in or out. The little playhouse Grandpa had built her years ago, now filled with garden tools and flowerpots? No. The roof leaked. Its floor would be mud by now. The garage? No, another dead end. And someone had been in there, had taken the cars.

Then she thought again of the horses. In one corner of the long loafing shed and under its roof, Grandpa had built a little tack room for the saddles, bridles, blankets, and grooming supplies. The tack room had solid walls, and was, as Grandpa often said, "mouse tight." And best of all, the tack room had two doors, one on the pasture side of the loafing shed, and one through the back of the loafing shed, opening into the small corral. The tack room would be chilly, but it would be dry, and she was getting desperate for sleep. The horses would be likely to warn her if anyone came close. And if she were going to move again, moving in the dark sounded like her best option, so she should sleep now and rest until dark.

It would do, and she was beyond anxious now; she felt that the invisible clock had ticked down and the alarm would go off any second—but she was so tired that she almost didn't care. That was dangerous, stupid. Artie zipped Gran's heavy raincoat to her chin. The coat was olive green, a good color for blending with grass and trees.

Artie stood irresolute in the middle of the living room floor. On the silent TV The Weather Channel presented its usual regional information. Green and yellow radar-generated blobs of rain covered most of Oregon, northern Nevada, and Idaho; as if she didn't know it was raining. Odd; the regional radar imager was playing over and over, but no weather reporters were to be seen. Artie took up the remote and flipped through the channels; maybe she could find some news. She saw channel logos only, one after the other. Some channels were blank, gone. "This is crazy," Artie heard herself whispering. This was something big.

"All right," she said aloud. "What is left that I might need—that I can carry?" She knew--her wet clothes. "When will I be able to get at my clothes at home? I'd better take what I've got now." She pulled another black plastic bag from the roll and retrieved her sodden jeans, hoodie, watch cap, underthings, shoes, and t-shirt from beneath the guest bed, squashing them into the bag and then stuffing it into the top of her own daypack. "I'll dry them out later," she told herself. Somehow, she had the feeling that she wouldn't be coming back—at least not for quite some time.

Shrugging a daypack onto each shoulder, Artie left the house.

Quickly she retraced her steps to the loafing shed. Merry and Slim were half-asleep, nodding over the manger; they barely noticed Artie as she opened the door into the tack room. She shot the bolts home.

The tack room was almost dark, with only a little light coming in through tiny cracks around the door. The air smelled of hay and horse.

The bulging packs would be good as pillows. Artie took the two saddle blankets from their hooks on the wall and covered herself as she curled up on the rough wooden floor. She squeezed Gran's daypack into a more comfortable shape and settled her head on it, inhaling the indescribably familiar and comforting scent of Gran's closet along with the clean, dry smell of horse. This was good, or as good as it could be under the circumstances. It felt good to her in the tack room, far from bad things. She was ready to shut down.

After a few minutes, Artie breathed more easily. Her legs began to warm under the horse blankets. Her tight muscles began to relax; her bad-thing radar was silent for now. Artie wondered if her radar was simply overwhelmed, pinged out of register by everything that had happened, but she could feel herself shutting down, regardless.

Artie decided she would watch and listen awhile, and then if it still felt safe, she would sleep. She knew from experience that she didn't think straight when she was too tired. Artie knew that if ever she needed a clear head, it was today. She would sleep and then think about what to do, where to go, after it got dark.

⊨⊰ ⊱⊨

The dogs woke him, scratching at the kitchen door to go outside. Groggy from an afternoon of unaccustomed sleep, Ben staggered to the back door and let them out.

It was still raining, cold needles coming down hard, and it was fully dark. Ben grabbed a raincoat from the bedroom closet, put on his LED headlamp, and went out with the dogs. Bear, Moonie, and Molly weren't large enough to fight off coyotes. He had to keep an eye on them while they did their business, and he could visit the outhouse as well. Gramps' words came to him from the old list tacked to the kitchen wall between the windows, "Never let the dogs out in the dark unless you stand right with them."

Ben paused for a minute to scan the sky. He knew that the eastern horizon was close here, a steep but small granite hill covered with sagebrush. To the north loomed Cat Mountain, the source of Spear Creek. The western horizon, he knew, was a longer vista, two miles or so, bounded by tall gray hills, the first blunt granite teeth of the Castle country. To the south, lower sage hills folded around Spear Creek, Gray Creek, and Horner Creek.

He knew the surrounding countryside so very well; he had walked it many times growing up. Ben knew where to find wild iris along Spear Creek in May, where granite hoodoos held up the messy stick nest of a pair of ferruginous hawks every summer, where flakes of obsidian had been left by the Shoshoni long ago, where an old mine bored into Cat Mountain as a typical, horizontal tunnel that was level for fifty yards--and then ended suddenly in a gaping shaft, at least 80 feet straight down, frightening as the open mouth of Hell. He knew this place.

But tonight, everything was black. There were no horizons, no vistas. Not a single star broke from the cloud cover. Tonight was a deep, anonymous, nobody-finds-anybody night.

The rain beat a sharp tattoo on Ben's raincoat, and after his visit to the outhouse, he called the dogs, who followed him into the kitchen wet and shaking their coats like little dervishes.

Ben locked the door, draped the dripping raincoat over a kitchen chair, lit the oil lamp, and built up the fire in the stove. He stared at the door for a long moment, still feeling odd about locking that door, but blackness looked in through the kitchen windows, and he let it stay.

"Dinty Moore canned stew tonight," he said to the dogs. "For you, it's going to be kibble again." As his hand reached the top shelf in the pantry and closed upon a squat can of stew, Ben wondered where Mothy was tonight in this rain, if his Garmin GPS unit was still working—and most importantly—he wondered if such a geeky and feeble kid, a kid who pretty much lived online and spent as little time outdoors as possible–if a kid like Mothy could possibly negotiate 45-plus miles of unfamiliar roads alone, in the dark, in the rain. But Mothy wasn't stupid, not at all; Ben had to give him that. Timothy had always been smart. Surely he could find the Place. After all, there were only four turns once he was on the highway going south. Surely Mothy would manage to get here.

Ben opened the can of stew, dumped it into a saucepan, and put it on the stove. He filled the coffee pot at the sink, added a scoop of ground coffee, and put that on as well. Tonight he would have cream; the pantry yielded a small can of evaporated milk. There were more cans of milk in the cellar and in the old bunker, and quite a lot of powdered milk in barrels in the ancient chicken house. He'd have to search out more milk sometime soon, and bring some in to the kitchen. He put the empty stew can on the floor and heard it rattle around as the dogs licked it clean.

Ben fed the dogs their kibble and found himself holding his cell phone. It still had a little more than half battery power. He checked both Gramps' phone and his own; there were no messages, no missed calls. Without hesitating, he called Mothy; it rang and rang. He left a text message: "U coming?" He tried again to call Gary; it rang only once and gave him voicemail. That was a change. A spike of anxiety tightened his neck muscles. Ben said, "Gary, come to the Place. Where are you? I will come get you." He shut off both phones immediately.

He decided not to call Dr. Lucy. She would come tomorrow, anyway. She *would*.

He wondered if Mrs. Phillips had received the map he had mailed on Wednesday from Shoshone before things fell apart, and if so, what she had thought of it, of him. Had she left Hailey? Could she be on her way to the Place? He had seen her old SUV in the parking lot at school; in that Explorer she could get here, even with the muddy roads. He remembered her penetrating blue eyes, the silver hair done up with pins on top of her head, and her soft, sagging cheeks. She must be very close to retirement, if not past the age at which she could retire if she chose. Mrs. Phillips was about the same age as Gramps; Ben knew that they had been in high school together. Mrs. Phillips was one of the few who had taken Gramps seriously, or at least had done him the courtesy of listening. Ben wished he had told Mrs. Phillips that she was his all-time favorite teacher. He shook his head. He wondered if he would ever see her again.

The kitchen windows were still black. All Ben could see by the light of the oil lamp were drops of rain rolling down the outside of the glass, streaming together like tiny rivers. Without a raincoat, without shelter, without a fire, it would be very cold out there tonight. Unpleasant. Ben could tell it wasn't going to be cold enough to freeze, but rain at night in early October, at over 4,000 feet? Cold.

"OK," he said to Bear, who had finished his food and was staring up at him. "OK, Bear, it is about 45 miles from Hailey to the Place." Bear cocked his head to the side and wagged; he liked being included in a conversation. "So, it was nighttime, Friday night, when Mothy called. Now it's Sunday night at about the same time: 48 hours. To get here, he'd have to walk about a mile an hour, if he started right away. Most people walk at about 4 miles an hour. Four miles an hour average walking speed was in a problem Mr. Reynolds gave us to solve last spring. Timothy is a pretty small guy." Bear licked his lips. "Let's say Tim didn't want to walk in the dark, so he didn't get started until maybe 7 o'clock Saturday morning. So that's about 40 hours. And let's say he walked only about two miles an hour because he's Mothy, after all. Two into 40 is 20; that would get him here in 28 hours. Let's say that every three hours he rests an hour. Three into 28 is almost 10. So that would get him here in 38 hours. That's almost now."

Ben found that he was pacing back and forth in front of the stove. He stopped occasionally to check the stew. Bear lay on the floor and watched him, head moving back and forth, back and forth.

Ben went on: "Let's give him 8 hours to sleep Saturday night. That would get him here in 46 hours." Ben stirred the stew. It had begun to bubble around the edges of the pan, and the hearty aroma rose into the kitchen with trails of steam. "So, throw in a little time for miscellaneous stuff, give him not 8, but 12 or fifteen, or even eighteen hours to be holed up today and tonight from the rain, maybe some more time for hiding or something like that, maybe for missing a turnoff and having to double back, and he should absolutely get here tomorrow, before dark. If he doesn't get here by dark tomorrow, then by the first thing in the morning on the day after tomorrow, I will have to . . ." He would have to think about some way to find Mothy. If Mothy didn't get here, he would do *some*thing. Why wasn't Mothy answering his stupid phone?

Ben had been trying all this time not to think about Gary. Gary was in much better physical shape than Mothy, and was much more an outdoor person. Gary had had his map more than two days longer than Mothy had had the directions from Ben. And unlike Mothy, Gary had a vehicle, a Jeep, even. If everything in Hailey were as bad as Mothy had said, where *was* Gary, then? Why didn't he call? Even with the mud, he could at least have driven to where Horner Ranch Road took off from the state highway, right away. So why wasn't Gary here now?

Ben had a sudden vision of Gary messing around in his, Gary's, bedroom on a rainy night last spring, trying out some kind of smelly green gel that made the wiry red hair stand up in spikes, sticking out his tongue for the mirror and laughing at himself before collapsing backward onto his bed.

Ben jerked the stew pot off the stove almost fiercely and placed it on the thin piece of wood Gramps kept on the table as a trivet. Ben fished a spoon from the utensil drawer. He would eat straight from the pot.

The coffee was done, too. Ben poured himself a mug and added evaporated milk generously. "Well, crap," he said sharply. "If Mothy and Gary don't get here by the day after tomorrow, I will call them first thing. And if I don't connect, I will have to go looking for them." Typical Mothy. He would slow Gary down. "Yes, that's it," Ben thought. "That must be it. They got together and Mothy is slowing Gary down. Or they ran out of gas. And I have got to find that solar charger for the phones before they go dead." Ben attacked the stew.

⟨+ +⟩

Full darkness had crept into the tack room. Artie sat up abruptly, suddenly awake. Something was wrong. She lurched to her feet on cramped legs. Pounding, that was it, a dull thundering. But it wasn't thunder.

It took her a moment to realize that the thudding was hoof-beats, horses running in the dark. But she could still hear rain beating on the roof of the loafing shed. What was happening? Artie pulled back a bolt and cautiously opened the nearest door.

Yes, something was wrong now, close. She could feel it in the back of her throat. Night had fallen, but toward the house she could see a strange, inconstant light spilling from the windows onto the lawn, and she smelled smoke. She put on her own pack and grabbed Gran's pack by the straps, sliding out of the tack room into the dark pasture. She left her bike. It was too much to handle with both packs and in the dark.

Outside, she could hear crackling and saw bright flames shooting from one of the living-room windows. *Grandpa and Gran's house was on fire.* Stunned, she stumbled to a tree and held onto the trunk. "But it's raining," she thought. "How can the house be on fire when it has been raining all day?" She knew she hadn't turned on the stove.

The horses kept running and running in the dark pasture. She could hear the splashes and dull thumps of their hoofbeats. Slim flashed by, pale in the early darkness. Merry was a black blur behind him. Of course; horses were terrified of fire. But they should be safe; the pasture would be pooled and puddled with rainwater by now.

She heard—and felt—a *whoomp!* not far away—the Peterson's house was burning. Shocked, she realized that someone was here *now* and was setting houses on fire *now*. "I have to get out of here," she told herself, moving before she had finished the thought.

Artie had grown up visiting this place often and playing along the river nearby. She knew the area, in light or darkness. She needed a refuge where she could hide away from roads and buildings, and immediately thought of an old logjam left near the river by some long-ago flood but now high and dry, a place where she had played many times when she was small. Caught and held by still-living trees, the old logs formed an irregular wall nearly four feet high and twenty feet long. The logjam was about six feet thick, with an odd little space inside near one end that was almost as tight as a beaver lodge, an old hiding place of hers. The hidden space would probably be fairly dry. Even if the place weren't dry, it would be a place to hide. And Artie had a raincoat now. She wondered why she hadn't thought of the log-jam before. "That's what being too tired does to my brain," she thought.

The light from the two burning houses was growing; another small explosion told her that one of the Petersons' outbuildings had caught fire. Fire meant light; light meant exposure. She had to get away at once.

Artie stumbled through the trees along the pasture fence and came out on the familiar road to Gran and Grandpa's, Broadford Road. The orange light showed her the narrow barrow pit, now filled with rainwater, and she jumped it. After looking both ways and seeing nothing moving, she ran across the north-south road. This is the way she would have come on her bike yesterday if she hadn't seen that man shot on Main Street. Broadford led south from Main, away from town and into small-acreage suburbia, then farmland and pastureland.

Once on the other side, she half-slid, half-fell down the grassy slope of a neighboring pasture and went to her knees briefly as she stepped into slick, wet cottonwood leaves that had drifted several inches thick on the ground beneath the river-corridor trees. She slipped through an old barbed-wire fence and went on, west.

She could hear the river's noise strongly now, the water rushing a little madly after all the rain. As she moved closer, the sound of the river drowned out all other sounds except the intimate pattering of the rain on her raincoat and on the leaves near her feet. She groped her way ahead, sliding her feet through the leaves and pasture grass, arms in front of her face.

Once Artie was well inside the river's cottonwood corridor and away from the light of the fires, she retrieved the flashlight from Gran's pack and flicked it on for a moment to orient herself. Yes, there was the familiar half-fallen tree supported at an angle by two others. Beyond it squatted another landmark, the fat and flat gray boulder banded with white quartz, the one that looked like a designer ottoman with a slightly tilted top. That rock had served as table for many of her childhood tea parties. Artie had always loved the rock because it was a good-luck rock, since the white band went all the way around it without a break, keeping the luck inside.

"Maybe it is good luck after all," she thought, slogging ahead. Her feet sunk into the ground an inch or two with each step-- there was now coarse river gravel under the leaves.

She hadn't far to go now. Gran's pack was too heavy to carry by the straps for very long. Artie put her arms through the straps and put Gran's pack on her front; if nothing else, it was warmer that way, and she now had both hands free to keep her balance.

Swishing and sliding through the wet leaves, Artie came to the irregular wall of horizontal dead tree trunks, the trees caught there large and small, much of the bark weathered away and trunks smooth after so many years, white as bone, shining wetly in the brief gleam from the flashlight. The logjam.

She looked back toward Gran and Grandpa's, back toward Hailey. The whole sky to the north and east was aglow now, cottonwood trees looming black against an orange sky. "It's the end of the world," she thought. The feeling of wrongness choked her. "I don't understand." But she did know now that she had to stay away from buildings. That had just become obvious.

With wet hands, Artie felt along the ragged wall of tree trunks until she found a certain jutting branch, and pushed in. That tree trunk was hollow. Its shell had been battered and frayed until it was weak and flexible. She shoved again, hard, and part of the log yielded and opened a crevice in the wall of logs just large enough for her to slip inside. She dropped the daypacks through the rift and climbed in herself, fitting the odd, almost-broken piece of tree trunk back into the wall behind her. The sound of the river diminished to a steady, humming whisper as she shut herself into the darkness. She had discovered this secret place when she was five years old.

Artie found herself in a small, black space she hadn't been inside since she was much smaller herself. Once, she had been able to stand inside the logjam and lie down full-length. Now she could sit upright with her legs stretched out straight in front; that was all. But it was enough. The logs beneath her were damp, and though the odd roof of logs, gravel, bark, branches, leaves, and roots was fairly tight, she felt a steady drip, drip, drip onto one of her knees. This would be uncomfortable.

Then she remembered the roll of black plastic bags from Gran's kitchen, yanked it out of the raincoat pocket, and tore a bag off the roll, spreading it over her legs. She heard the drip tapping on the plastic, felt a trickle running off to the side. That was better.

Artie was fairly confident that she hadn't been seen, and thought that in the loose carpet of leaves, those disarranged by her passage would soon meld together again; it was good that here on the ground there was a thick layer of newly fallen leaves, with river gravel underneath instead of mud, in which she would have left tracks to this hiding place. She knew no one could see her inside this little pocket, even in daylight; hadn't she fooled Grandpa and Gran many times when she was a little girl? They had walked right past the logjam, calling for her, and had never known how close she had been. She hadn't even told Rosa about this hiding place.

Sudden heat flooded her face and she brought her cold hands to her cheeks. "Oh my God," she thought. "I wonder what is happening to Rosa." Rosa Mendez had been Artie's best friend for years, and Artie hadn't thought of Rosa since yesterday when she was hiding near the bank building, waiting for dark. Yesterday she had tried to call Rosa several times without success. She'd sent Rosa three text messages; there had been no answer. But today, after she had made it to Grandpa and Gran's, Rosa had fallen from her mind. What kind of friend was Artie, then, to forget Rosa for so many hours?

Rosa lived on the west side of Hailey near the river, with her mother, grandmother, and little sister. Artie lived—had lived?—on the northeast side of town. She hadn't been anywhere closer to Rosa's than Main Street since she had started running.

Rosa was bright and lively—and since an accident five years earlier, wheelchair-bound. With these strange things happening, Rosa would be especially vulnerable. Or had she poured herself a glass of water last night and died in her chair? "What shall I do about Rosa?" Artie thought desperately. Should she risk going back, going to Rosa's house? Or was the long white house with the green shutters already burned, Rosa and her family dead or gone, the place torched by whatever people were responsible for all this evil?

Fumbling with her phone, Artie called Rosa. There was no ringing; it went immediately to voicemail. Artie said, "Call me; I will help you," and ended the call. Artie saw with a sinking heart that her phone was almost out of battery. She should have charged it at Gran's when she had the chance; a charger lived in her daypack. Artie shook her head and replaced the phone in her pocket; she hoped she was thinking more clearly now that she'd had some sleep.

Narrow spaces between the logs of her chamber showed Artie the fiery sky to the north and she thought, "At least I am safe for tonight. But what about tomorrow?" The world had gone crazy, irrationally mad and frightening. Why was the water poisoned? Where were Gran and Grandpa? Who was setting Hailey on fire?

Sitting snug in the logjam listening to the rain, Artie hugged herself tightly as the feeling of wrongness, already strong, began to build again. She felt almost sick with feelings of evil to come. Her mother and father had always called Artie a pessimist, but what she felt sometimes was more than simply the attitude that all outcomes were bound to be the worst possible outcomes. And tonight she was absolutely convinced that she must hide and stay hidden--that if she went back into Hailey, it would be disastrous.

Back in her mind a little-girl voice was wailing, "What next? What should I do next, and why?"—asking a question she could not answer. But there had to be *some* answer. She must figure out something to do, somewhere to go, but there was no information, nothing solid that would anchor plans, to make things make sense. And there was no one to ask. She bit her lower lip, hard. No one.

It was October, and winter was coming. *Winter.* That was one certain thing in all this mess, and Artie focused on that. Winter would be here in a month or even sooner, and winters here were long and cruel. "Poor Callie," she thought, hoping that Callie had gone out through the cat door before the fire had started, and that somehow Gran's kitchen and the bowls of cat kibble would survive the fire.

Artie felt the ground-conducted vibration of the rushing river through the logs and branches on which she sat and thought about the winter to come, the river partly or wholly frozen over, the deep snow, the very long nights.

If Hailey was indeed being deliberately burned, Hailey would be no place to stay when winter came. In most years, the snow cover began in November and lasted into April. In other years, the snow came earlier and lasted longer. Nights of thirty below zero or even colder weren't uncommon in January and February. She thought about freezing and starving and darkness. Part of the answer to the unanswerable question was getting herself to a lower elevation before winter. "I will watch very carefully in the morning, and if it seems safe, I'll go on south," Artie decided eventually.

"Even if she's still all right and still at home, I can't just go get Rosa and wheel her to nowhere," Artie thought suddenly, a plan forming in her mind. "I will go south, out of Wood River Valley, and down toward Shoshone or Gooding. I'll keep going until I find some farmhouse with food and water, where we can stay. It's about 70 miles to the Snake River. Surely I can find a place for us to stay in the farmland between here and the Snake, where the winter won't be nearly as bad as it will in Hailey. I'll find a farm where some family will take us in—I can work--or if the farmhouses have been burned, maybe I can find a potato cellar where a family has stored some food. And—there are empty farmhouses, too, farms for sale. I could find one of those."

She brightened as a thought struck her. "Quite a few people are Mormon, and Mormons are supposed to keep a year's stored food and other supplies for emergencies. Maybe I could find a Mormon's place, one that has food plus a wood stove, or at least a fireplace, and its winter fireplace wood all stacked up. Then I will sneak back and get Rosa, and maybe Merry and Slim, too. Rosa could ride Slim. He's gentle. I could lead him, and I could get her to the farmhouse that way. With the horses, I could take her on dirt roads across the desert so we wouldn't be seen on the main roads. Or, if nobody else is in Hailey and Bellevue any more, I could steal us a pickup or an SUV when I come back for her. That way I could bring her chair. Together we could go to Gooding, or Shoshone, or Jerome, or even Hagerman, somewhere around there." It wasn't much of a plan, but it was a plan. And Rosa wasn't the only reason she planned to come back to Hailey.

"Us" sounded good. "Together" sounded even better. If she could find an abandoned farm with a well or a spring or one next to a stream or even near the Snake, with a stash of food, where she could bring Rosa and keep her safe . . . "Pie in the sky," she told herself. "But a pie-in-the-sky plan is all I have, for now."

CHAPTER 9
GARY

B en felt restless. "Cabin fever, already," he said to himself when he awoke to another morning of rain. "That's idiotic, the loner feeling lonely in just a weekend. It's barely October. But I had better get used to it." The Place wasn't, would never be the same without Gramps.

This morning the rain was fitful and diminishing. Today there was steady wind with the rain, and Ben could see, far to the west above the Castle Hills, that the cloud cover had begun to break up.

He tried Gary's phone once more, got voicemail, and shut it off. He debated calling Mothy, then decided that Mothy himself could make a call and leave a message if he found it necessary. Ben figured that he had perhaps three days left before the phones ran out of battery, if he used them as little as possible. He would keep the phones accessible until the batteries failed and then figure out somewhere to store them more securely. In the meantime, he would step up his efforts to find the solar charger.

Gramps' phone had no calls or messages, either, and after some thought, Ben decided not to call Dr. Lucy just yet. "Our cells can be used to track us, Ben," he could hear Gramps saying as they had driven a pickup-load of rice and oats to the Place two months back. The August sun had been hot, the sky cloudless. The pickup had bounced merrily over the washboard grooves on Horner Ranch Road, kicking up a billowy plume of dust behind them. Ben, as he often had, let Gramps talk on and on, thinking mostly about the meat loaf sandwiches and Cokes in the cooler behind the seats and about taking his lunch up to the granite rocks in the shady grove along Spear Creek once they got to the Place.

Gramps was on a roll. "You can't just leave your cell sitting out, Ben. Not after things start going wonky. Even if you think you have turned it off—well, if you were building little spy devices, wouldn't you include an app that made the phone turn off, look off, act off, even if it was still on? Nope, you have to think of things. You have to think of everything."

Paranoia. That's what Gary had called it. "Well, call me Mr. Paranoia," Ben thought, replacing his phone in the kibble can next to Gramps' phone and pushing the lid down tightly. "Bennett Paranoia Elliott, grandson of the one, the only, the famous Crazy Frank."

Then he tried the crank radio yet again and got static and fragments of the same message he'd heard Friday night: "Sunspots. Communications affected. Stay home. All well."

He tidied his bed and wiped the kitchen table and the stove, then rinsed the kitchen rag under the tap until his hands stung with cold. He hung it on the faucet to dry. Dr. Lucy had probably been held up by the rain and mud, but she should arrive later today, and he was looking forward to that. He'd seen Lucy on several visits, the last one more than a year ago. Dr. Lucy was much younger than both Gramps and her deceased husband, Rob, one of Gramps' Viet Nam veteran buddies along with Beezer and Cuda, and Simon. Ben thought that put Lucy in her early fifties.

Lucy was small, but looked stringy and tough, with a square face, iron-gray hair cut short, fresh-apple cheeks, green eyes with flecks of hazel, and a way of looking at you that was so direct that she made you squirm. She had a very paintable face, Ben had thought. He pictured her standing next to a rhyolite outcrop, rock hammer in hand, gazing into the far distance.

"Lucy is no-nonsense," Gramps had often said. "She's one of a kind, shoots from the hip, no head games, no games at all. And she's sharp." Ben had been surprised the first time he saw her. Dr. Lucy hadn't been even close to Ben's idea of a university professor. On each of her rare visits, she had showed up in old jeans and a t shirt, wearing battered but good-quality boots. Lucy never stayed longer than two days with them in Hailey or at the Place, and most of that time she would spend talking to Gramps, talking far into the night, so Ben didn't know her very well--but she seemed kind and intelligent. Gramps thought, *had thought* much of Dr. Lucy. The very fact that he had invited her to ride out the disaster here with them proved that.

Ben realized that he knew very little about Dr. Lucy other than that she was Rob's widow and for years had been a geology professor at Montana School of Mines. Dr. Lucy was one of a research group predicting the geologic event that was supposed to send the country into chaos. "Big, long-term government grant," Gramps had said. "Lucy's volcano research has been going on for over twenty years."

Ben wondered if she would bring a dog or maybe even a cat, or a bunch of geology books, more food, or a gun. She would be driving a big pickup and pulling a 22-foot trailer. He did know that much, so she would be bringing *something* to the Place.

Gramps and Ben had spent considerable time during the past three summers digging a second bunker into the side of the west hill and fitting it with heavy doors.

Hanging in front of the wooden doors were several layers of old and faded Army-surplus camouflage netting, which by semifortunate coincidence, from a little distance looked almost exactly like a scattering of mixed sagebrush and rabbitbrush.

In addition to providing a hiding place for Gramps' pickup, the new bunker was intended to swallow up Lucy's larger truck and her trailer. Dr. Lucy had sent Gramps the dimensions of both, including lengths for the tongue of the trailer, the hitch on the pickup, and their heights. The new bunker was finished now, and almost empty except for a few things stacked against the back wall in the earthy dimness—three 750-gallon plastic tanks of emergency water, cans of gasoline and motor oil, several solar panels, a small generator, and some tools. Three years ago Gramps had rented a skid-steer for two weeks to do the heavy earth-moving. Then Ben and Gramps had made four trips up on Cat Mountain with the chain saw to bring back lodgepole pine timbers for creating and holding up the walls and earth-covered roof. They had floored the bunker with mismatched, overlapping bargain-remnant pieces of kitchen vinyl.

After they had finished the new bunker, Gramps had parked the Place's ancient 1940s John Deere tractor, the old harrow, and the front half of a junked 1960s pickup right on top of the bunker's dirt roof, using their own pickup to drag the things onto that section of smoothed-off hill. The timbers had had to be strong to hold that extra weight as well as three feet of soil.

"Ground-imaging radar, Ben," Gramps had told him. "If they are searching for people, for holdouts like us, that's what they will have in their planes, ground-imaging radar. They'll get a blip of metal from the cookstove in the house right below where the stovepipe sticks out of the roof; that's why the gun safe is next to the stove, just on the other side of the closet wall. And they will get another blip from our pickup, if it's still parked in the barn-- but people expect barns to have old combines, trucks, plows, and such things rusting and forgotten inside. They don't expect to get a big metal reading where there's nothing but hillside, so that's why we're putting all this iron and steel on top here. When they fly over the Place, they'll see this metal, and their GI radar will blip. They'll understand that blip because they can see the old tractor and things. We don't want them to read more blips than they'd read in any abandoned farm, or blips they can't easily understand." Ben had asked who "they" were going to be. Gramps said he didn't know for sure, but that the government was getting weird and so were a few other groups, so it was best to be very careful and secretive. Ben had hoped he would never have to find out about *them* on a first-hand basis. He was still hoping.

At this point, Ben was glad that the new bunker's dirt roof had had a summer and a half to grow a crop of fluffy weeds and a few small rabbitbrush. The bunker's roof wasn't barren soil any more; if you didn't know how to read the landscape very well, Ben thought, it would look normal there, just part of a hill on an old ranch, a small hillside that looked like it had burned several years in the past, with tumbleweeds and tumblemustard blown under and around the old tractor, thistles grown up through the rusting harrow, a scattering of fire-blackened sagebrush skeletons Ben had gathered from an old fire scar a couple of miles south of the Place and had carefully planted in random groups last summer, and a ratty tangle of weathered orange baling twine placed by Gramps just behind one of the flat tires on the 60s pickup as an extra authentic touch.

But today Ben wanted to move the onion and potato sets to the old bunker, and also search there for the cell phone charger. The old bunker was the root cellar of the original ranch here, and Gramps had thought it had probably been dug in the1910s or 20s. Gramps and Dad and Grandma had enlarged it years ago, putting in better supports, heavy, lockable wooden doors, better shelves, and ventilation screened to keep the mice out. The old bunker was almost invisible, built into the eastern hillside. Over it, the sagebrush of many decades had grown tall, and the back half of the 1960s pickup provided a metal signature on the roof. The double doors were recessed, hiding in the shadow of a cut bank; a straggling vine of old man's beard hung over them like a tattered curtain.

Ben took the dogs and went to the barn for the onion and potato sets he had bought in Twin Falls. It was time to finish sorting the new stuff properly and to stash the remaining things in storage for the winter. This had been an unusually warm autumn, with only two light freezes so far--in Hailey, at least--and he knew he should take advantage of the decent weather to do some of the chores that had to be done before Indian summer was over.

A fresh wind swept up Spear Creek gulch, and overhead, narrow fissures of blue opened in the roof of cloud; the rain was almost done. "I hope the wind dries out the road for Dr. Lucy," Ben thought. He wouldn't think of Gary and Timothy for a while, he told himself, not until today's chores were finished.

"Gramps said to check the sawdust barrels in the old bunker every two weeks if we had to live here at the Place this winter," Ben said to the dogs. "And maybe the solar charger is in there." He was getting used to speaking to them out loud with non-doggy concerns; it made him feel much older somehow, and less alone.

Last fall had been the first time Gramps had stocked some of the sawdust barrels, just about this time of year, before the snow came. Gramps had said it was an experiment. He'd wanted to see how effective the sawdust barrels were at storing food over the winter. By the time the roads were clear enough that Gramps and Ben were able to drive back to the Place in mid-April, more than two thirds of the vegetables and fruits in the barrels were still sound and edible. Some of the apples had been quite wrinkled, but even most of those were still sweet. Gramps had called the experiment a success, and had admonished Ben to check the barrels, because when one vegetable or piece of fruit went bad, the slime of its rot contaminated everything close by. He had told Ben that it would be best to check the barrels often, smell them carefully, and remove anything that had begun to spoil. Ben and Gramps had finished re-stocking the barrels only the weekend before. It seemed a lifetime ago.

Ben lugged open one of the thick wooden doors of the old bunker; the damp smell of earth met him with a hollow chill and dead air. The bunker, also floored with old, overlapping remnants of kitchen vinyl, had once been a little home all on its own; Gramps and Grandma had lived there for several summers while they were refurbishing the ranch house.

Wooden shelves packed with jars and cans of food lined the walls. Some of the jars had been there so long that Ben thought some of the contents probably weren't safe to eat; years ago Grandma had put up peas and beans, tomatoes and salsa, plums and pears, sliced peaches and chokecherry syrup, apple jelly, raspberry and currant jam, salmon and steelhead. "Never mind," Ben thought. He liked seeing Grandma's jars there beside the canned food that he and Gramps had brought. And the fruit should be all right; he and Gramps had been eating Grandma's jelly, jam, and sliced fruit ever since Ben could remember.

Two old wood-framed cots had been stacked one on top of the other to save space, and the smaller of the Place's two generators, with its funnels and filters, had been shoved under one set of shelves to make room for the ever-useful industrial plastic barrels that now nearly filled the floor space. Four plastic-wrapped bales of clean sawdust slept on the cots, ready to hand.

Under the cots and under the shelves were packed hundreds of pumpkins and winter squash—acorn, butternut, hubbard, jarrahdale, turban, and others whose names Ben didn't know. For some time he searched the bunker for the solar charger, and finally concluded that it was stashed elsewhere. But where?

Ben turned to the plastic barrels. He pried up each lid and sniffed, checking for rottenness and smells of mold. Every barrel smelled fresh and fine; that was good, but these were very early days yet. He wouldn't expect rot after only a handful of days.

It had taken Ben and Gramps most of the two previous weekends to buy the fruit and vegetables in Twin Falls, transport them to the Place, and bed them into the blue barrels. Even then, Gramps must have known that they were going to spend this winter here for certain, Ben found himself thinking, though at the time Gramps had told him that the food was "just in case," and "they could always eat it in the spring."

Last year they had done up only three of these barrels as Gramps' first fresh-food-storage experiment, but this year they had filled eighteen. In each one, vegetables or fruits were laid down like spokes in a wheel, with care taken that no two items were touching: layer of vegetables, layer of sawdust, layer of vegetables, layer of sawdust. Two barrels were apples; one was small cabbages, the little heads tight as bowling balls; another was packed with oranges, lemons, and tangerines, with a few limes for good measure; two barrels held onions; three were filled with carrots and parsnips; one was half full of turnips and wax-coated whole cheeses; one held sweet potatoes and more cheeses, and the remaining barrels were filled with potatoes. Gramps had told Ben that his own grandparents had stored food like this, packed in sawdust in a root cellar just like the old bunker, and things never froze, but stayed cool and fine and wholesome all winter.

"Turnips," Ben said to himself as he shook more sawdust into the turnip barrel from one of the bales. "I have no idea how to cook turnips. I've never even *eaten* turnips. But Gramps said they were good food and one of the things that would keep, so I guess I will have to learn." He dropped the onion sets one by one onto the waiting bed of sawdust, added another layer of sawdust, and did the same with the potato sets, laying their empty net bags on top. "Next summer I will have to put in a garden." He groaned. "Oh, my God, that should be epic."

Ben had never done much gardening. He'd watered and weeded the little garden Gramps planted on the east side of the house in Hailey each year: green onions, peas, beans, lettuce, and a few tomato plants; that was all. He needed Gramps, *needed* him. But there was no remedy for death, no cookbook with recipes for whipping up a new family member, no survivalist directions for crafting another Gramps. He added a final layer of sawdust and replaced the lid on the barrel, then shooed out the dogs, closed up the old bunker, and took the dogs on a short walk upstream.

The waterwheel Gramps and Ben had built was lifting and spilling and turning slowly in Spear Creek as it had for five years. How long would Spear Creek stay unfrozen this fall? The latest Ben and Gramps had ever been to the Place was late November, two years ago, and the surface of Spear Creek had been frozen over. Ben smiled at the memory. That winter the snow had come late, but the cold had come early. They had spent Ben's four-day Thanksgiving vacation at the Place, with Bear, then a five-month puppy, and Molly. Moonie hadn't yet been born.

That had been a wonderful small vacation—only the two of them and the two dogs, the weather clear and bright and very cold--but just perfect. Gramps had made them Thanksgiving dinner in and on the old wood stove—a roast turkey with mushroom cornbread stuffing, mashed potatoes and turkey gravy, Brussels sprouts, canned cranberry sauce, and pumpkin pies with whipped cream. Gramps had made two pumpkin pies, two blueberry pies, and two apple pies. They had lived the next three days on reheated leftovers, reading books by the fire, talking far into the night, playing Scrabble, sleeping late in the mornings, and in the afternoons taking long walks up the gulch with the dogs. Somewhere stuck in a book was a small watercolor Ben had done of Gramps that weekend, Gramps in the leather arm-chair near the fire, sound asleep, a Louis Lamour western slipping from his fingers. "I'll have to look for that watercolor," Ben thought, remembering the frames he had bought in Twin.

A compact blur of black, Bear ran ahead along the stream, now splashing into the shallow water for a few steps, now stopping to shake his thick fur. The two girls followed more sedately. Moonie could tolerate water, but had no love for getting wet, not like Bear. And Molly would get her feet wet only under protest.

The wind was stronger now, sending the clouds to the east, breaking them apart. The iron-gray sky was shredding into a patchwork of less gray and more blue. "That means it will be colder tonight," Ben thought; he had better get moving. They had almost reached the aspen grove. "Come on, dogs," he called. "Let's go back." He had one more task for this afternoon. He hurried back to the house, racing the dogs down the meadow.

On each side of the house's front walk, placed where the morning sun would warm them every day, stood a wooden half-barrel, old and weathered, filled with soil. Dried weed stalks bristled from both of them now; they had been a project of Grandmother's a long time ago. Neither Ben nor Gramps had had any time or inclination when at the Place to deal with flowers.

Grandma's crocus and daffodils, grape hyacinths and violets, columbine and Indian blanket, still bloomed every spring in the flower beds in Hailey, and Ben and Gramps had watered and weeded them faithfully for years. Grandma's flowers would be on their own in Hailey from now on. Ben tried not to think of their leaves curling and drying in the hot July wind next year, the plants, without water, dying in their beds next to the house.

But the Place was home now, and the Place had nothing of tame flowers but a clump of Oriental poppies Grandma had planted, the even older line of lilac bushes along one side of the barn, and the tangle of yellow pioneer roses near the lilacs that Gramps said had been here long before he and Grandma had bought the Place.

Ben took the net bag of daffodil bulbs and the little brown paper package of ixioliron bulblets from the pantry shelf where he had put them when he'd carried the seed packages in from the barn. He squatted beside the wooden half-barrels each in turn, pulling out the weeds and tossing their dry stalks and shallow roots to the wind. The three dogs snapped at the weed stems as the wind tumbled them off the porch, making a game of it.

With the aid of a big spoon from the kitchen, Ben jabbed holes in the mud and planted the daffodils in the center of each half-barrel, and the ixiolirion, which were labeled as growing only six inches tall, around the edges. The mud in the barrels was cold and slimy from the rain, but Ben knew that in the bottom of each barrel was a layer of coarse creek gravel plus several drainage holes, so the bulbs wouldn't rot.

"I am going to live through the winter," he said, willing himself to believe, "and I will see these bloom in the spring." He felt good about getting the bulbs planted and the vegetable sets stored before the hard freezes came. In October, you never knew; the weather could turn cold at any time.

He remembered that he had once read, "Who plants a garden, plants hope." The two half-barrels weren't exactly a garden, but he imagined the daffodil petals, tissue-thin and bright, lit by a springtime sun, and the small ixiolirion flowers, a surprise in lavender. After the snow came, it would be good to think of the bulbs sleeping here, waiting. Next spring they would be a nice surprise for Dr. Lucy, too. Ben stood up and called the dogs. Today's chores had been only a small day's work, but at least they were done.

Before Ben went inside to see about dinner, he walked warily out to Spear Creek Road and had a long look as far down the road as he could see. No Mothy. No Gary. No Dr. Lucy. Nobody. But the wind was still strong and the pale, sandy mud of the road had already begun to dry.

This part of the road was mostly granite sand, and it drained fast; the lower portion would still be mud-glop city, he realized. Dr. Lucy would have that figured out, he decided; she had been here at least twice and was a geologist, after all. Maybe she was downcanyon sitting in her truck eight or ten miles away, or maybe even as close as Gray Creek Road, waiting for the mud to dry before trying to pull her trailer uphill to the Place. But if that were true, why didn't she call? No one had called Gramps' phone since Ben had taken it.

"Well, if I don't see any of them by tomorrow night, first thing the next morning I will climb the east shoulder of Spear Creek Gulch, up to the Hand, and look down on the southeastern part of the road," he thought. "And if nobody is there, I will go after them, at least as far as Timmerman Hill. I, *we* could even sleep in one of the caches on the way back, if it comes to that."

⟞⊹ ⊹⟝

Artie jerked her head back and blinked. So she had managed to fall asleep in her tiny cavity in the logjam. What had awakened her? Through the cracks in the logs, she saw orange light, faint orange, flickering and wavery like sunset reflected in a stream. Fire, still. But it must not be too close, because she couldn't smell smoke, just wet leaves, wet wood, and her own wet pantlegs.

Cautiously, she turned her head and shoulders so she would face north, and found a wider crack in the logjam. Yes, the whole northern sky was aflame in the direction of Hailey. She moved a little to ease her back. *Pat, pat, pat,* tapped the rain drip on her leg where the black plastic bag covered her jeans. Outside it was still raining. Her hands were shaking, and she didn't know why.

"Bad things are still coming," Artie thought. "There is more evil to come. I can feel it."

Suddenly a scream, a high, long, knife-edged scream, split the air. And then another. "God," she thought. "What is happening?" Her first impulse was to run, to break from her hideout and run away from town, to put as much distance as possible between herself and those screams. But running blindly in the dark, in the rain--that would be incredibly stupid. She felt rested now, and her mind was working better.

Artie held her place, listening so hard she had to remind herself to breathe. The screams had been horrible—but they had been distant, barely on the edge of hearing. Perhaps that's why she had awakened, the sound of a distant scream. The only sounds she heard now were the wind in the cottonwoods, the deep thrum of the river, and the patter of the rain on the logjam and on the black plastic bag.

"I do need to get out of here before it gets light," she decided. "I'm still too close to town." She had no idea how long she had been asleep, and so tugged her phone from her pocket, looked, then replaced it. She'd had the phone on vibrate-only since yesterday, desperately hoping Gran or Grandpa would call.

Ten after ten o'clock. Hours yet until dawn. No calls from Rosa, or from her grandparents—or from anyone else, for that matter. "OK," Artie told herself. "I'll wait until it has been about an hour since I've heard anything scary, and then I will move south. I'll stay inside the cottonwoods along the river. I'll be slow and quiet so I won't fall in the dark, won't be heard or seen. When I can tell that it's starting to get light, I'll look for another hiding place. And eventually, I'm going to find a good farm." Silently she blessed Gran's warm parka, rubber boots, and padded raincoat with its deep hood.

At eleven, Artie pushed her way out of the logjam, and with care repositioned the odd section of log that served as the entry to the small chamber. She stood for long moments listening and hearing nothing but the river and the rain, and then began walking slowly south, downstream, gliding from tree trunk to tree trunk, using brief flashes of Grandpa's light and the flickering orange of the sky to check her footing. Relentless, the rain continued to fall.

Artie stayed quite close to the river as she passed the town of Bellevue, not much more than a quarter of a mile away on a high bench above and to the east of the cottonwood corridor. Strangely, the whole town was dark, as far as she could tell from some distance away and through the trees.

When she left Bellevue behind, Artie knew she had walked almost three miles from Gran and Grandpa's place. "Tonight I'll try to get as far south as the state highway that goes to Fairfield," she told herself. "That can't be more than 20 more miles. And I can go west for a while and then turn south and go up over the City of Rocks hills and down to the farmland around Gooding." Artie couldn't remember when, or if, she had ever walked 20 miles in one stretch. Surely she had, going up Quigley Gulch and back to town, or in the Sawtooth Mountains on one of the family overnight fishing trips. Or had she? "I can," she told herself. "I'm going to. And then I will find a good place." She passed into the farmland unseen.

As she made her way among the cottonwoods and drifts of slippery leaves, Artie found herself thinking again of *The Lord of the Rings*, of *The Fellowship of the Ring*, and how the hobbits had hiked boldly away from Bilbo's house, feeling the warm, pleasant autumn sunshine on their shoulders and walking heedless in the security of familiar paths and trails. But that feeling had lasted little more than a day, and very soon they had found themselves pursued by nameless things in the shadows, things that soon proved to be fearsome and formidable indeed. Artie remembered that the hobbits had started out singing, but had soon become silent, feeling vulnerable and hunted. She found herself making up a tune and verses to a dark song, a song of hunted things, of mist and nightmares, of horses running in black rain, of skies on fire, of rough-barked trees, secret places, drifts of leaves, and the sound of a river. It was a good song, better than most she had created. She would write it down as soon as she got—got *somewhere*. She would call it "Running in the Rain."

Several times Artie bypassed houses and barns, sheds and corrals, feeling very glad that she had chosen to stay near Wood River, and that no one had built within 50 yards of the stream so that she could drift through silently in the night. It helped that it was still raining. Who would be out and about in the middle of an October night in the rain? Especially in a pasture or an alfalfa field?

Twice she passed farmsteads with security lights blazing from tall poles; she avoided those and kept very close to the river until their circles of light fell behind. Once a barking Labrador came out to challenge her, but thirty feet away, inexplicably the dog seemed to change its mind and turned to run toward a barn. She saw no one, no moving vehicles, no lights on the distant highway. Besides that dog, a few horses and cows, and in one small pasture, two llamas, she encountered no living things but trees, grasses, and shrubs. Artie was tiring, and her thoughts turned away from her new song and fell into a verse that kept time with her steps.

"Keep going 'til the sky turns gray. Then find a hiding place to stay," Artie kept telling herself, to keep other thoughts from her mind as her boots came down in the saturated leaves. The rain pattered on and on; her jeans were soaked to the knees, as her intermittent flashing of Grandpa's light and the clammy feeling of wet fabric on her legs told her. If she let herself think about her family, if she allowed herself to feel, she wouldn't be able to go on.

She found herself thinking her new rhyming words to music, to one of the two songs she was to sing solo at the high's school's fall concert this year. "Keep going 'til the sky turns gray. Then find a hiding place to stay," Artie sang under her breath over and over and in time to her steps, trying not to think, "What solo? What concert? What *high school?*" She had cherished her hard-won position in the front row of the concert choir, between the other two soloists, Melanie Carr and Rick Camarillo. The three of them were to sing Debussy's *Vocalaise* as a series of solos and as a trio, their portions arranged and divided into parts by the choirmaster, Mr. Dean. The remainder of the concert was to be a mixture of selections from pop, folk, rock, jazz, rap, and poetry readings, but the Debussy was to be the centerpiece. *Then. Yesterday.*

It seemed unbelievable that she had planned to spend yesterday afternoon up Quigley Gulch practicing for the concert and looking for bright leaves and late wildflowers to press for crafts. "I wanted yarrow leaves," she thought, keeping her feet moving, talking to herself to blank out the worst thoughts, "because they turn beautiful colors and look like little ferns. I wanted to find some wild geranium leaves, too, and fall asters, and some aspen leaves, to make cards and to use in my scrapbook. I wanted to work on an idea for a new poem."

She couldn't bear to think of what she wanted now. Yesterday seemed a lifetime ago, washed away by darkness and rain and death.

The fiery sky was far behind now, a slight glow to the north nearly obscured by the trees. Artie stayed inside the river corridor of cottonwoods and walked by and through pasture after pasture, passing along the edges of field after field, always with the rush of the river to her right. She was very tired, but felt that she was making good time even though the darkness made her progress slower than it would have been in the light.

From time to time, Artie would stop to listen with her light off just to make certain she didn't come upon anyone unaware. Once she heard cattle lowing and another time the sharp cries of a family of coyotes, far distant to the west, but that was all except for the flutter of cottonwood leaves, the sound of the rain, and under it all the broad thrumming of the river. "Keep to the plan," she thought, putting down one foot after another in the slick, wet leaves. "Walk until the sky turns gray, then find a hiding place to stay." She added a verse: "Walk until the sky's dark blue, then find a hiding place for you."

She kept on walking among the cottonwoods, now leaving Grandpa's flashlight on, since she had passed no buildings or driveways for some time. Eventually the rain pattered itself to a stop, and above, a few stars broke through the cloud cover.

Artie remembered that once, when they were walking home last winter after a study session at the library, Rosa had asked, "Artie, you act like you're not afraid of the dark. At all." They had stopped on the sidewalk in front of Rosa's house before parting ways for the night.

"Afraid of the dark?" Artie remembered answering. "No. I'm not afraid." And she wasn't. She had spent so very many happy hours roaming the hills above town in the dark.

"I am," Rosa had remarked then, looking around nervously and hugging herself. "You're lucky, Artie. The night scares me." Continuing home alone, Artie had wondered if being wheelchair-bound might make a difference in Rosa's feelings for the night, and had concluded that it might indeed, because the wheelchair limited Rosa to roads and sidewalks.

Artie had discovered something about darkness during her midnight rambles: in the dark, the hills were her own. People who went out in the night haunted the towns, not the gulches and ridges. Night prowlers had no interest in sagebrush slopes, or clumps of willows, or rock outcrops ideal for sitting while waiting for moonrise. Danger in the dark was near houses, in yards and parking lots, in the streets.

Artie had always felt a little odd about her parents. Other girls in her class had always said they felt closer to their fathers than to their mothers—that was something the psych-heads put forth, the mom-girl, dad-boy rivalry *vs* attraction thing. And you were supposed to have conflict with the parent that you were most like. But although she loved her father, Artie had always, always felt closer to her mother. The two of them were very much alike. They loved plants. They loved discovering things. They loved the mountains and trees and flyfishing. They loved singing and writing and reading, and they loved being alone in the night.

The first time her parents had awakened in the small hours to find their daughter gone, Artie had been seven or eight years old. Artie had slipped out of bed, dressed herself, and in the bright moonlight, had taken off up the nearest hillside, not for the first time, just the first time she was found out. She had been leaving a note on her pillow each time, in case someone came in to check on her while she was out in the night, but until that occasion, no one had come, so she would wad up the notes and toss them into her wastebasket when she would return toward morning, creeping silently through the house and up the stairs to her bedroom. But this time, one of her parents had come in to check on her and had found the note in the empty bed.

When Artie came home two hours later, her dad was shouting about calling the police, and her mom was sipping coffee in the kitchen and reading a novel. Dad was livid; Mom was calm. "I did that when I was her age, and now Artie is doing the same thing. She left a note, Mike. She's all right." Artie's mother had waited for her father to run out of energy, volume, and expletives, and continued, "I will teach our daughter how to keep herself safe in the dark." And she had done just that. Artie felt very comfortable in the dark, usually. Tonight was different. But she was very glad she wasn't like Rosa, afraid of the dark simply because of the darkness.

After a long interval, she noticed that the faint glow to the north was no longer visible. Artie realized that her progress was now somewhat robotic; she felt detached from her feet and seemed to be far above them, watching them step out, slide through the wet leaves, push down, and push off. Watching them.

"It's getting light," Artie thought, suddenly aware, realizing the meaning of her mantra. "I can see my feet now." Sure enough, though she could still see stars through the broken canopy of cottonwood leaves, the sky was now deepest indigo rather than black, and a grayness in the east began to grow and spread. She felt that clock ticking again, and scanned her widening field of view for possible hiding places. She switched off the flashlight and shoved it into one of the deep pockets of the raincoat; it would be good to save the battery.

She figured that at the rate dawn was coming, she had perhaps half an hour before it would be fully light. Her feet were heavy with fatigue now. She needed to rest. She continued south more rapidly in the deep dawn twilight, looking for another safe place.

A sharp little wind sprang up from the west, stirring the wet leaves. Artie stopped for a minute to look into a small hollow, filled with leaves and spanned by a recently fallen tree, a large tree. This might be a hiding place of sorts. She bent and scrambled into the hollow, then scrambled as quickly back out; the low spot under the leaves was full of rainwater. But that was all right. She still had some time before dawn.

A slight noise whispered up ahead. Artie took a step and then clutched the nearest tree, listening.

Ha-ha, ha-ha, ha-ha, ha-ha, came a shallow series of breaths, like a person—or an animal--breathing hard after running. *Ha-ha, ha-ha, ha-ha.* Only instead of the breaths becoming deeper and longer as the creature recovered from exertion, the interval stayed the same: *Ha-ha, ha-ha, ha-ha.* Artie felt her fingernails digging into the damp tree bark. What was this?

After some minutes, she could hear no change. Gray light was increasing rapidly now. Soon it would be sunup, by which time she wanted to be well hidden. Cautiously, Artie moved her head to one side so she could see around the tree. Nothing.

Wait. What was that large, dark blotch a few yards away in the fallen leaves? She risked another look, and another. Did it have legs? Weren't those legs and a head lying in the leaves? Dogs breathed faster than people. Perhaps it was a big dog that had been running and was exhausted. She slung off both packs and rummaged in the top of her own for the knife, unwrapped it from the kitchen towel, and held it fast. She left both packs at the base of the tree.

"Here, boy, here, girl," Artie called softly. "It's OK. I won't hurt you."

She heard a faint cough and then, unbelievably, a voice. "Artie? Artie, could that be you?"

She stepped away from the tree. That voice was familiar. "Gary?" she said, still not believing her ears. "Gary Scott?"

"Artie! It *is* you!" said the voice from the dark blotch on the ground. "Come here! Please come here."

Artie stabbed the knife into the tree and ran to him. Wild, spiky hair lay half-buried in the leaves. It was Gary, all right.

Gary lay on his stomach in the deep carpet of cottonwood leaves, his head turned to one side. He wasn't moving, and she could still hear his breathing, *ha-ha, ha-ha, ha-ha.* Something was very wrong.

Artie stood over him and in the blue-gray pre-dawn light; she could make out a hole in the back of his jacket, a hole surrounded by a hand-sized dark stain. "Can't you get up?" she asked stupidly, as if her tongue had separated from control by her brain. "What is that hole in your back?"

"Artie, I'm shot," he said.

She fell on her knees beside him in the thick carpet of leaves. "My god, Gary, what happened? The hole doesn't look very big. There isn't much blood. It's not bleeding now. I'll drag you somewhere safe and we will fix it. It will be all right. We have to move now. It's getting light fast." Artie realized that she was gabbling and shut herself up. She reached out to turn him over.

"No!" Gary almost screamed. "No," he continued. "Please, don't move me. The pain has kind of faded out and I don't want to move. That hole in my back is not the problem. I was shot in the back," he went on, "late last night. But it isn't that, it's where the bullet came out in front that's the problem. All the blood."

Bending close, she saw that Gary's face was ice-pale. But the eye she could see above the leaves was just as clear and alive as ever. One of his hands had been flung above his head and she saw now that the hand was dark with blood. "Who shot you? Why?" she had to ask.

"Friday night I saw the soldiers, and the white buses," Gary said with effort. "When I was going out to pick up Cindy for our date. So excited. What a laugh that is now. I hadn't driven two blocks when I saw them, the soldiers with their rifles, bringing people out of their houses, rounding them up. Shot a guy who ran. God, Artie, it was terrible. Just shot him." Gary coughed a little, still breathing rapid, shallow breaths.

He went on. "Turned around and drove home but my folks weren't there. Weird. I had left them not five minutes before, but--gone. Pot of potatoes on the stove, but the folks were gone. I turned it off, Artie. I turned off the stove. So our house wouldn't burn down."

Artie nodded silently, thinking of the fiery halo in the sky above Hailey hours earlier.

Gary continued, "I decided to get out of Hailey, but the highway was blocked by some white Hummers, so I ditched the Jeep and hid in a woodshed Friday night. I called my folks once but no answer. Phone wasn't charged, anyhow; it died almost right away. After a couple of hours, I got out of the shed and started to go south on foot, away from town. But too many soldiers and for a long time I hid. All night. All day. Couldn't move without being seen.

He paused for a few moments to breathe. "I was under some trees by a ditch near the airfield and stayed there until dark. All wet in the rain. Cold. Then I took off. OK for a while. Made it to Bellevue. No lights. But soldiers on the street. I got almost through Bellevue when one saw me and shot me. It knocked me right off my feet but I got up and kept going. It didn't hurt at first. Just felt like somebody socked me. Two of them came after me with lights, but I fell, I kind of fell down that hill. You know that bench that Bellevue sits on, where there's that steep slope to the west, almost up to the highway? I slid and rolled down that and lost them somehow in the dark in a bunch of bushes. Don't know how. I kept going for a long time and then fell by a log and went out. I woke up in the dark and kept going and falling and going. And now I can't get up. But I don't want to get up any more." After this long speech, he was gasping.

"I'll find some cover for us before the sun comes up," Artie said, "and I can work on you once we are hidden." She had so many questions.

"Soldiers?" she thought. "White buses?" But as wild as that sounded, Artie remembered her own family dead on the floor, the silent streets of Saturday morning, the man shot in the back trying to cross Main Street, Gran and Grandpa's empty house-- and she knew Gary was telling the truth. "Oh, no," she thought, remembering that she had crossed a pasture just south of the air-field in yesterday's early morning twilight. "If only I had known Gary was nearby, we could have, we could have . . ." She took in a sharp breath. "I was lucky," she thought. "Lucky that the soldiers were in Bellevue, not around the airfield, not down by the river." She reached for Gary again. Maybe she could drag him to cover.

His hand flopped in the leaves. "No, Artie, don't do that. I just want to stay here, not to move. Can't move, anyway. I have to tell you something." *Ha-ha ha-ha-ha-ha.* His breathing was very shallow now, very fast. Gary turned his head slightly so she could see all of his white face. "Look, you know Ben Elliott," Gary said. It wasn't a question. Of course she knew Ben.

"Yes," she reassured him. "I know Ben." How could she not? They had gone to school in the same class since kindergarten.

"Ben is my *best* friend," Gary said, with an odd emphasis. "He is my best friend, my best. I've been stupid. I haven't acted right, so I need you to make it. I need you to make it so you can tell Ben that he is my best friend, my best. That I'm sorry."

"Of course, Gary, I'll tell him," Artie said, puzzled and trying to soothe Gary. She had to get him fixed up; she *had* to.

"No, you don't understand," Gary said. "Ben has a safe place, and you can go find him and tell him that he is my best friend. You can get there. Find him." Gary's bloody hand flopped in the leaves, buried itself in them. "Artie. I have dogtags. I wear dogtags and I want you to wear them, to remember. And find Ben. To tell."

"All right, Gary. It's all right. I will find Ben," Artie said, trying to sound firm instead of scared out of her mind. She thought, "Gary is rambling. He has no idea what he is saying."

"No," Gary said, reading her tone of voice. "You still don't understand. *Listen,* Artie. Ben has a safe place and you need to go there and tell him I didn't make it but that he is my best. Was. Look," he said, gasping again. "I have a map. Ben gave me a map, and it's in the left front pocket of my jeans. Reach in there and get it. Map."

"A map," Artie said stupidly, her heart suddenly pounding like a triphammer in her chest. She was beginning to understand. "*Ben's* map."

"Ben's map. Map from Ben. Get it? Get it," Gary insisted, with a flash of his old wit. "Now. Reach in. I can't."

Artie felt under Gary and let her hand worm its way through the wet leaves beneath his body until she felt the waistband of his jeans. The pants were tight, but she managed to slip two fingers into the front pocket. Her fingertips felt an edge and she drew it out, a three-inch square of tightly folded white paper, stained with blood on one side. When Artie withdrew her hand and arm, she was shocked to find the sleeve of her raincoat covered with red, covered with bright ruby blood.

Dawn had caught them. The sun was coming up through the trees, bringing color back to the world, scarlet smears on the golden leaves and on her olive-green sleeve. *Red and gold, red and gold.* Artie could feel the burn of tears gathering behind her eyes; it was too much.

"Yes, yes," Gary was whispering. "That's the map, the map Ben gave me to his place. You have to go there and tell him. Go there!"

"I'll go, Gary," Artie said, leaning over to place her hand on his neck. His pulse there was slow, faint. She felt helpless. "I'll go to Ben's place, and I'll tell him, and we will come and get you." Artie had a thought, a thought that hurt. "Rosa," she said. "Do you know anything about Rosa?"

"Buses on Rosa's block," Gary said between shallow gulps of air. "People at gunpoint. Not many people. Not enough to be everybody. I drove back to my house before I hid in the Hultz's woodshed. Stove was on but Mom and Dad were gone. Potatoes."

Gary coughed and coughed, and Artie felt guilty for asking him her question. The coughing faded into his shallow breathing: *ha-ha, ha-ha, ha-ha.* "Don't go back to Hailey, Artie," he said between difficult breaths. "It's all bad there. Please. Don't go back. You have to go to Ben's place. To tell him. I was too dumb. He is my best. Has always been. Since we were little. Kids. Sorry. Promise."

"I promise," she said, whispered. Gary's face was changing, smoothing into blandness.

"Best," Gary said, a breath. His eyes closed slowly. There was no *ha-ha, ha-ha*. He wasn't breathing. "CPR," Artie thought frantically, and rolled Gary onto his back to begin. Did she remember how to do it?

Gary's jacket fell open and Artie saw the fist-sized wad of flesh pushing through his bloody shirt, the place where the bullet had punched out. She saw his whole front flooded and sticky and dark red with blood, fragments of a cell phone bursting from a torn shirt pocket. Artie knelt beside him, paralyzed. CPR wouldn't help. She couldn't imagine how Gary had gotten this far from the Hailey airfield with this terrible wound. "*Grievous*," she thought. She had read that somewhere. "*Grievous wound*." Sunlight streamed across Gary's body, the light striped with the thin shadows of branches.

Dawn, and she was alone and exposed.

"Dogtags," she remembered suddenly. "I'm supposed to take his dogtags. 'To remember,' he said." She reached inside his collar and found the silver ball chain that she had seen him wearing for years. The three attached dogtags dragged away from his chest and dripped bright blood on Gary's cheek as she pulled the chain over his head. Artie stuffed the dogtags into a back pocket of her jeans.

Artie bent to kiss Gary's forehead, then rolled him onto his stomach once more. She shoved the map deep inside a zippered pocket of her raincoat and then went through Gary's pockets, thinking, "He wants me to make it. He wouldn't care." She found two quarters, a black-handled pocketknife, his wallet, a set of keys, and a curious green-glass bead in the shape of a tiny frog. She took them all.

After a careful scan of the area, Artie scooped armloads of fallen leaves and heaped them over Gary before she left him. "I'll come back someday to bury you for real, Gary," she said. "I'll tell Ben what you said." She went back for the kitchen knife and her packs.

Suddenly she felt exhausted, and it was past time to find another place to hide. Artie wondered if life was going to be just that from now on: sneaking from hiding place to hiding place.

As she moved on through the trees, she felt cold tears running down her face and dripping off her chin onto the top of Gran's pack, tup, tup, tup. *God, god, god.* Gary dead, shot in the back. Gary, the class clown with the electric red hair.

She had known Gary since forever. Gary had been second base on their little-kid schoolyard softball team when they were eight, the year she had been shortstop. Artie had seen Gary fall down the icy front steps of the elementary school when they were nine, the time he had broken his big toe. He had won the class math prize in the fifth grade, a twenty-five-dollar check from the Hailey Chamber of Commerce. In the seventh grade, just before Halloween, he had dyed his stiff red hair purple for some reason known only to Gary. Unseen, he had put a moth in her jacket pocket last spring on the final day of school, and when she put a hand in that pocket, the thing had scared the absolute crap out of her. She could see that Gary now, doubled over laughing at how she had jumped, his dogtags dangling from the front of his shirt on their silver ball chain, his red hair wild and woolly. His chain was in her pocket now, stained with his blood; she could almost feel it burning there.

Now there was no Gary Scott. He was dead, just like her family. The world had changed overnight.

Artie wiped and wiped at her eyes as she trotted through the cottonwood gallery forest looking, looking. Before long, she was winded and stopped to breathe. She was desperate to examine the folded map but didn't dare to look until she had found another place to hide. Gary's bloody death had shaken her badly;

though she hadn't seen or heard anything threatening for hours, Artie went on with care, walking, looking. Looking, walking, listening.

After a mile or more, she came to yet another pasture fence, rusty and tangled barbed wire and blackened wooden fence posts that had seen a fire come through at some time in the past. Nearby was a very old gate of half-blackened silvery wood, partly off its pintels and leaning almost to the ground. All around it grew tall nettles and thistles. This would be a good place to rest (*Hide*, she thought, not rest, *hide.*) while she looked at the map.

Though the space under the gate was low, Artie could just manage to sit up under it, next to the gatepost. She pulled the back of her raincoat down so she wouldn't be sitting on cold mud.

With unsteady hands, she retrieved the map and unfolded it, smoothing the paper onto one knee. The map had been printed on ordinary white printer paper. Gary's blood had dried, dark and smeared, along the northern boundary. "That's where Hailey is," she thought with a grim smile. "Was?"

"MAP TO THE PLACE," she read in all capitals at the top of the page. Below, a strong line of red made an angular path across the paper and ended in a large X. Taking up most of the page was a map that looked like it had been lifted from Google Maps, probably re-sized in PhotoShop and printed out, with the red line and X added. Ben was good at PhotoShop; Artie knew that from school.

She traced the red line from Hailey's Main Street south on the highway past the airfield, through Bellevue, continuing south through the Wood River Valley's farmland, and to the bottom of Timmerman Hill and the intersection with the state highway, where the red line made an abrupt turn to the west.

The red path followed the state highway west for miles and then turned northwest onto a gravel road labeled Horner Ranch Road. A little less than five miles farther, Horner Ranch Road curved through a shallow valley and split, the Horner Ranch fork continuing almost straight west, and a smaller road, Gray Creek Road, heading northwest, climbing into foothills. Following Gray Creek for a mile or two, the red line then turned due north at the intersection of Gray Creek Road with a thin thread of road so faint that it was almost invisible beside the red line: Spear Creek Road.

Not far after that, the red line came to its end at the large X. It looked to Artie as if Spear Creek Road continued north past the X, where it ended high on Cat Mountain: a tiny crossed pick and shovel indicated an old mine there. She knew that there were thousands of mineral claims and diggings in the mountains of Idaho, most of them quite old. The map didn't give this mine a label, but the hand-drawn X in the Cat Mountain foothills did have a name: "The Place."

Artie stared at the map, transfixed. "I have been going the right way without even knowing it!" she said aloud. She peered out from under the gate, looking southeast. Wasn't that low ridge Timmerman Hill?

"I've come almost to the state highway!" she told herself. "And I am west of Timmerman already, so it's only twenty-five miles or so to Ben's Place!" The enormity of Gary's words and of the map she held in her hands came to her like a blast of pure oxygen. Before she found Gary, she had just been running south, running and hoping to find a place, any place before winter, any place away from the high country, a place where she could take Rosa, if she could find her later on. That was all. And now, this map. She hadn't fully realized until this moment what this map might mean.

She had a place to go.

Artie's eyes brimmed once more, and she wiped her cheeks with her fingers. A safe place, Gary had said. *Ben's place.* "Fate?" Artie thought. "This couldn't be fate." For Ben was the reason, the other reason besides Rosa, that she had planned to go back to Hailey after she had found a place where they could stay. She had been planning to go back for Ben, too, *somehow,* and bring him to someplace safe *somehow,* because although it had been from afar, she had loved Ben almost all her life.

Artie emerged from her shelter, stood, and took a long look, 360 degrees around.

Far to the north, a thin smear of smoke lay in the bottom of the valley: Hailey, or what was left of it. To the west, over a tumble of sagebrush hills, the sky was clear now. And to the southeast . . .

Yes, that low sagebrush-and-grass-covered ridge was actual-ly, truly, Timmerman Hill. The main highway continued south over the hill to Shoshone and Twin Falls. Artie had been over Timmerman countless times, usually with her mother at the wheel and Turner in the back seat playing games on his phone.

The state highway ran east-west at Timmerman's base, to Carey on the east and to Fairfield on the west. She was indeed, nearly a mile west of the state highway's intersection with the highway to Twin Falls; that was to the good. The state highway lay between her position and the Timmerman ridge. She would con-tinue south along the river and intersect with the state highway, then turn west and follow the highway to Horner Ranch Road.

Now oriented by the familiar ridge, Artie realized that the distance to the state highway from the old gate was little more than a mile of rough pasture dotted with small shrubs and shoulder-high willows, bordered on the west by the river and its corridor of cottonwoods. There were few buildings to be seen, only a tumbledown barn and two equally rickety sheds. "I'll wade Wood River instead of going across the state highway bridge," she told herself. "I'll be less likely to be seen if I'm not on the highway. But, first—"

Artie crawled under the leaning gate and rummaged in Gran's pack for the chicken and the potato salad. Time for breakfast, and then a nap. Artie had always had the ability to "set" herself to wake up after whatever sleep interval she chose. "I'll eat and then sleep two hours to rest my feet, and then I'll start walking," she told herself. "I have to be alert, and I'm too tired to be alert. When I get to the state highway, I'll walk a hundred yards or so north of the highway, parallel to it, and keep listening for cars. If I hear a vehicle coming, I can just lie down in the sagebrush and hide until it has gone past. That should work. And if I'm lucky, I can be at Ben and his grandfather's place before the sun comes up tomorrow!"

Artie laughed suddenly, for the first time since her world had fallen apart. She was about to trust her life to a crooked red line that had probably been drawn by Crazy Frank Elliott!

CHAPTER 10

MAP

After feeding the dogs, Ben heated a can of corned beef hash for himself for dinner. "Hmm," he told himself, savoring the aroma of the hash warming on the stove, "Gramps would make me eat some green vegetables, or something besides just meat and potatoes. Vegetables of some type."

He found a can of whole-kernel corn in the pantry and tapped its contents into the pot of hash. "Compromise," he told the dogs. "It may not be green, but at least corn is a vegetable that isn't a potato."

Gramps. His absence was still a searing pain; Ben wondered how long the pain would last, if it would be forever. Every once in a while, one of the dogs would trot into Gramps' bedroom looking hopeful, then pad back into the kitchen, crestfallen. Or all three would suddenly look at the door, and eventually sigh, and lower their heads once more to their paws. "I feel the same way," Ben told them. "Sometimes I feel like Gramps is going to walk right through that door and things will be normal again." Normal? He shook his head. Not likely.

Ben called Mothy; it rang and rang. Then, taking a deep breath, he called Gary again. This time, there was a click and a hum, no rings, no voicemail. Hurriedly he ended that call, took a deep breath, and called Dr. Lucy on Gramps' phone. Her phone rang twice and then went to voicemail. Flustered, Ben stammered, "This is Ben, it's Ben Elliott. Are you coming?" Ben switched off the phones and quickly replaced both in the kibble can. He wondered how Dr. Lucy would take it when she found out that Gramps was dead.

He poured coffee and held the cup in both hands, breathing the fragrant steam. Somehow, coffee made things seem less strange. He was glad that Gramps had loved coffee and had insisted on buying enormous amounts of coffee for the Place. "Coffee is a great barter commodity," Gramps had said many times. "It keeps well. And if there's no one else out there to trade something for it, Benny, you and I will swill coffee until we float away."

Far to the southeast, the coyotes began to sing. Bear lifted his ears and got up, staring at the door. Just outside, an owl screamed. Ben's scalp prickled, and he felt a faint chill down his spine. A screaming owl meant winter. Winter was coming.

Wishing for no one to find him and at the same time wishing for someone to find him—that was very odd, unsettling. "OK, Bear," Ben admitted, ruffling the Sheltie's thick black neck fur. "I'm a little creeped out tonight. What did Gramps always say? 'Like a goose walked over my grave.' I wonder why he always said it was a goose and not a wolf or a zombie." Ben retrieved the revolver from the bedroom and laid it on the table next to his coffee cup. You never knew.

In the end, Artie didn't wade Wood River at the state highway. The recent rain had turned the usually clear, thigh-deep stream into a muddy, brawling monster. She ran lightly across the bridge after long minutes of observation, and then hid herself in the willows on the far side for a while, just in case. But she neither saw nor heard any traffic, and soon was walking westward in the hard, bright sunshine, through the muddy sage hills, a hundred yards north of the state highway and parallel to it, headed for the Horner Ranch turnoff.

The mud from the rain made for rather heavy going. Artie was glad for Gran's rubber boots, though they were more awkward than sneakers alone. It would have been much easier to walk on the highway itself, but that idea made her very uneasy, so she kept to the sage, slogging and sliding up and down the little hills and through the yellowing meadows and small drainages between them.

The rain was long gone, swept eastward by the brisk wind. Artie stopped to put on Gran's soft, narrow scarf, winding it around her neck up to her ears. The raincoat blocked the cold wind nicely, though her nose and cheeks felt numb. Often, she would look down at the state highway a few dozen yards below her. The highway was empty and stayed empty.

Artie had driven this part of the state highway any number of times, usually when she and her mother were on their way to Boise for some special event or shopping trip. For the last year or two, Artie had been the one to drive this Timmerman-Fairfield part of the state highway on their trips because it was relatively flat and because it was the section with the least traffic, a good place to practice her driving skills. It was odd now, to be walking along this stretch and seeing no traffic at all, none.

Artie's mother had loved to visit the large Boise nurseries and garden stores in the spring and fall—in the spring to buy annual flowers for the flower beds and her oversized patio pots, and in the fall to buy chrysanthemums for the porch and for the sunroom, bulbs to plant for spring, and a house plant or two to brighten the long winter. The two of them would make an outing of it at least twice a year, staying Friday and Saturday nights in a Boise motel, shopping many of the plant places, and maybe taking in a new movie on Saturday night. They would have a pizza delivered to their motel room and watch late movies there afterward, or go out to dinner at some place with exotic food. On Sunday morning, they would visit the botanical gardens to see what was new and what was blooming and which birds were out. In the spring, they would stop to look at wildflowers along the way. They did their own kinds of girl things, plant-nerd things. Sometimes Gran would go with them, for a girl threesome. Turner and Dad, and Grandpa, would stay home in Hailey on those weekends with their own pizzas and movies or ball games to watch. None of the men in the family cared much about plants and flowers. Artie clenched her fists in Gran's gloves until she could feel her nails biting into her palms through the knitted yarn. Gone now, those times were all gone.

Fifty yards ahead, two ravens sat on a barbed wire fence facing the wind and letting the gusts rock them. The ravens, trim and shining, looked as if they hadn't a care; they looked as if the world was still functioning.

Artie stopped in her tracks. "Sometimes, things just move you along and you have to keep moving with them to save yourself," she thought. But under the open sky with the sage hills stretching in gray waves to the horizon, she found a centering stillness, and one piece of this strange puzzle fell into place. She took a deep breath and inhaled the familiar aromatic cleanness of the sagebrush. Somehow she felt like she belonged to these endless hills, the sage. "*Artemisia*," she said. "I am the sage. I have always been the sage. My god," she said to herself with sudden clarity. "I can be so dense; I can be such an idiot. *This* is what has been wrong all along, not just what is wrong *now*; *this* is what has been coming; *this* is why I have felt so strange all summer." She wondered if other people had known that the world as they knew it was closing, was pinching tight shut with poisoned water and burning houses, with soldiers and shots fired and white buses and deserted highways and death.

No, that couldn't be it; people couldn't have actually *known* this was coming. If they'd actually *known*, there would have been headlines, outrage, and people fleeing. They must have sensed a change without knowing. Artie nodded to herself. People must have sensed the coming change in the same way that animals feel an imminent earthquake or tsunami, or in the way that horses became uneasy when moved to smaller and smaller corrals. Everyone had felt that evil was coming without consciously realizing, had reacted to the faint tremors and threads of wrongness and had been fearful without giving those tremors or threads a name or a cause. That's why people weren't going on picnics, why Billy Feldson had stopped washing his car on Saturdays. And eventually that wrong thing had reared up like an enormous praying mantis and had caught them all.

Artie shook her head at the peaceful, empty hills. But Crazy Frank Elliott had known. Crazy Frank hadn't been so crazy after all.

Ben, she thought. *Ben.* Artie remembered the only time she had mentioned Ben to anyone in her family, mentioned him as being special to her. Last spring it had been, on a Friday evening. Her mother was making spaghetti, and Artie was putting together a big salad. Artie remembered trying to slice a cucumber while looking out the kitchen window at Sally the cat, grooming herself in a patch of thin April sunshine on the picnic table in the back yard. All along the fence, tulips lifted their heads in every color of the tulip rainbow. "Artie," her mother had said pointedly, "watch what you are doing. Do you want really short fingers?"

Artie had turned to look at her mother's face and warmed to the smile there. "Just thinking," she had said.

"Penny for your thoughts," her mother had commented.

"Well," Artie had hesitated, but Turner wasn't home from Little League practice. She had learned not to tell confidences when Turner was around; her little brother was a blabbermouth. "Well, today at school," she began slowly, and then the words tumbled out in a rush. "Today at lunch Rosa and I were at the west side of the front steps, and we were opening our stuff. Rosa had one of those little packages of potato chips, and the wind just lifted it out of her lap and rolled it about ten feet down the sidewalk. And here came Turk Thomas and Lainey Adams, and Carlos Aguirre, and some others, and Turk went to the bag and put his foot above it, ready to crush it flat. And then Ben was there, Ben Elliott, and he grabbed the bag right out from under Turk's shoe and gave it back to Rosa."

"That was kind," her mother said. "Good for him."

"Yes," Artie said. "Ben does things like that." She looked down at her hands and tore some lettuce into bite-sized pieces, dropping them into the salad bowl. "I like him," she added softly. She remembered the hard look Turk had given Ben that day, the sneer, the mocking comment. "Scavenging potato chips to-day, are we?" Turk had said. That must have hurt. But by the time Turk got the last word out, Ben was gone, vanished into the school building without a backward glance. Ben did things like that, had done things like that and then disappeared, since they were both very small.

Her mother was bright. It didn't take much to show up on her screen. "Sounds like a boy who would be easy to like," she said, stirring the spaghetti sauce.

"Yes," was all Artie said, dreaming a little over the salad greens. But then, as sometimes happened, her mother plunged ahead and went too far.

"Do you think he will ask you out?" Her wooden spoon made circular furrows in the thick red sauce.

"I—I don't think so," Artie had replied, feeling a sudden wave of heat in her cheeks. "His grandfather keeps him really busy. Ben doesn't ask anyone out."

"Well, never mind. There are plenty of guys, God knows," her mother continued, with a faraway look on her face. "Especially at your age, when school still has them all corralled. I remember that when I was a sophomore like you, I just died hoping Jim Gallagher would ask me to the Homecoming Dance." Her mother laughed a little. "He was tall, blonde, and cute, really cute—a starter on the football team, too, and a senior. I was in heaven when he actually asked me."

Her mother lifted the spoon and pointed it at Artie. A fat red drop splatted onto the stovetop and began to dry there in the heat. "When is your Homecoming this year, Artie?" Without waiting for an answer, she slipped back into her memory. "Homecoming itself was fun that year. I was envied, and that felt good. Jim was just gorgeous. The pictures from that night were perfect; I'll get them out sometime and show you. My dress was midnight blue with little silver stars." Her mother gazed out the window and her voice trailed off as she remembered. Then she came sharply to attention and stirred the sauce vigorously. "But, you know, Artie--the guy was boring. He was all hands and football talk—just bored me to tears after the second date, and his breath stank, too. I don't think Jim ever listened to a word I said. After another week, I'm afraid I dropped him like a hot potato."

Artie tried to laugh. High school must have been so different for her mother, with her willowy figure, enormous hazel eyes, cascading red hair, and natural beauty. Artie was—well, she was ordinary, and knew it. And she was a knowledge nerd, and that made people uncomfortable.

She remembered Turk's narrowed eyes when Ben had plucked the potato-chip bag away from Turk's descending foot at the last possible moment. Turk was blond and gorgeous, too, like her mom's Jim Gallagher, but there was something wrong with Turk. He had lived in Hailey little more than two years and had taken the popular crowd by storm. It didn't hurt that he lived in a huge home up its own gulch, and that his father, Zach Thomas, was not only a big-time Hollywood director, but one of the richest men in America. Turk's mother was famous, too: the stunning Talia Manners, star of several wildly successful romantic comedies, an A-List star at the top of the A-List--until she committed suicide by overdose--and Turk's father pulled him out of Talia's Beverly Hills mansion and brought him to the even larger house near Hailey, with a male nanny and a housekeeper to run the household when Zach Thomas was off on a film project.

Turk had been pretty much steady with Lainey Adams for most of those two years, but Artie wondered if he really cared for Lainey, or for anyone. There was something about his eyes that was off, as if Turk stood just outside the world and was looking at his friends, at everyone, through glass, and didn't care, didn't care about them a bit, as if they were toads in a terrarium. She shuddered; now was not a good time to think about Turk Thomas. Or Lainey Adams, for that matter.

Artie looked ahead, westward into the cold wind, and cast her thoughts farther afield. There had been a football game Friday night, or there was supposed to have been a football game. The bus with the players, coach, and cheerleaders aboard had probably left Hailey before all the bad things began. Where were they now? Did this evil extend 80 miles south to Filer? To the whole state? Or further? Goosebumps not entirely from the cold rose on her arms. It was more than just Hailey and Bellevue, for certain; she hadn't seen a car or a plane since Saturday night.

Artie kept moving.

Three hours later, her feet felt like blocks of wood. She began to look for a rock where she could sit out of the mud and have a granola bar and some water from one of Gran's bottles. One of the many small lava outcrops loomed on the edge of a small valley, and she made for it.

With the sound of a thunderclap, two sage grouse rose from under her feet and bulleted into the small golden meadow below. Artie screamed involuntarily and fell backward into the middle of a sagebrush, terrified until she realized what had just happened.

The big birds sailed down the hill on curved wings and disappeared into pale grass. A tiny creek trickled through the autumn grasses and dark sedge near where they had landed. Little round willows grew near the water, bristling with countless stems; points of light glinted from their yellowed leaves as the wind shook them. Along the far side of the meadow, flanking it, she noticed a dirt road. "A road!" she thought. "Could that be Horner Ranch Road?"

She sat on a black rock and took out the precious map. Artie looked from the map to the state highway, to the dirt road ahead. On the far side of the small valley, the dirt road wound northwest, leading deeper into the sagebrush foothills until it disappeared in a fold of gray sage. "That has to be Horner Ranch Road!" she whispered.

After chunking down a granola bar and gulping half a bottle of water, Artie refolded the map, stuffed it back into her pocket, and descended into the valley, sliding a little in the rain-saturated soil. Horner Ranch Road. Ben and his Gramps' Place was only a dozen miles away! She might even be there before midnight if she could keep going.

Artie slogged through the marshy little meadow, waded the tiny creek, and came to the cattle-track-pocked edge of the dirt road. The road was muddy from the rain; water pooled in the cow tracks. With regret, she decided to continue walking several dozen yards to one side of the road. She didn't want to leave tracks on the road, didn't want tracks on the road that could dry and preserve highly visible evidence of her journey to Ben and

Gramps's Place. She had no idea if Gary's soldiers in their white Humvees would search the dirt roads, but she thought it stupid not to play safe.

Artie's legs were weary. She stumbled through tall sage and bitterbrush, now and then stopping to rest, sometimes standing up, sometimes sitting on the edge of a small lava outcrop.

So far, the map had been easy to follow. She thought about Crazy Frank Elliott, Ben's grandfather. Frank Elliott was older than her own Grandpa Turner. She had seen Crazy Frank around town many times, and could even remember a couple of occasions, when she was still in grade school, when she and Mom had taken Sally to Dr. Elliott to have her shots and wormings. He hadn't seemed odd to Artie then, just kind, but she had been only a child. She knew—everyone in town knew--about Doc Elliott's obsession with survivalism, knew that her own parents (especially Dad) and most of her friends' parents, thought him crazy as a bedbug, as a coot, as a loon.

"That poor boy," Rosa's mother had said once last winter, meaning Ben. Artie and Rosa had been in Rosa's family kitchen baking cookies for a school choir benefit. They had seen him trudging by on the street, head down and chin hunched into his collar against the cold wind. "No mother, no father, and raised by that loco. Somebody should do something."

Artie remembered saying, "But Mrs. Mendez, Ben is OK. He doesn't seem starved or abused." Elvira Mendez had snorted. "Ha. Even so, the poor boy. Clothes from the Goodwill, I think. Needs a mother." Artie and Rosa had nodded. Yes. Who didn't need a mother?

Artie lurched over a rock and nearly fell. This was not a time to be thinking about mothers. Where was Mrs. Mendez now? And Rosa? And her own grandmother?

A fresh mound of dirt from a badger dig lay across her path, and she thought of her own mother lying on the kitchen floor in her long-sleeved cotton shirt, cloudy-eyed, stiff, and dead. "No," she told herself. "Not now. Not now. Think about it later." She couldn't think about Mom and Gran now, couldn't think about mothers, couldn't let herself think about her own mother. "If I fall and break an ankle, what good will I be to anybody, even my- self?" Artie told herself sternly. "Pay attention, or you are going to fall and get hurt."

The wind rose and hissed sharply through the sage. The after- noon was old now, and colder. There would be no clouds tonight to hold in warm air. Tonight would be colder than last night, though Artie didn't think it would get cold enough to freeze. She took a few swallows of water from one of Gran's bottles and picked up her pace; she could see the sun sinking toward a gray- velvet ridge. She intended to keep walking until she reached Ben and his Gramps' haven, but travel would be much slower after dark. "Make time now," she told herself. "Get moving."

Artie looked around for a way to focus on her surroundings. "I will say the names of the plants as I pass them," she thought. As a Forest Service botanist, Lisa Ames had known the plants very well, and from the time when they were small, had made it a game for Artie and Turner to identify them. After the first grade, Turner had grown very bored with their mother's "name that plant" game, but Artie had loved the game and still loved learning the names of plants on the family camping and fishing trips.

She had learned very early on that it was best to keep her knowledge to herself, however, though she couldn't always make herself do that. One of the very strangest things about school, she had discovered, was that although you were there to gain knowledge, if you ever showed your peers that you knew things that they didn't know, you were scorned.

Artie remembered the last time she had been stupid enough to identify a plant at school. Last spring Rosa had brought a wilted section of vine from home, and after lunch period, had retrieved the sprig from her locker so she could ask Artie what it was. Artie remembered the length of vine lying across Rosa's lap in her wheelchair, the black skirt draping over Rosa's knees, her soft cream-colored sweater with its long sleeves pushed up. They were early for history class after lunch and had stopped in the hall just outside the room. "Oh," Artie had said, taking it up for a critical look. "That's field bindweed, *Convolvulus arvensis.* It's in the morning-glory family."

Lainey Adams had been there, close, as if she had coalesced from the air at Artie's shoulder. "Well, la de da," Lainey had said. "Ms Einstein pronounces. Latin, yet. Toss that right into the need-to-know file for me, would you?" Her audience of Kaylee and Lenny was there, of course, along with Andy Johnson and Carlos Aguirre and Candi Strom. Lainey had twirled in place, sending her skirt belling out to show off her slender legs, already perfectly tanned to that peachy golden color that Artie's skin never achieved.

"Sorry, Artie," Rosa had said, after. "I should have waited until we were alone to ask you. I knew you would know what it was. I just wanted to show you and then throw it in the wastebasket on my way into class. My fault."

"No worries," Artie had said. But at that moment she had resolved—once more--that she wouldn't be tempted again to show her special knowledge. She always resolved the same thing. But when the next time came, she knew would find it impossible to resist coming up with the answer, if she knew it. Whenever something like this happened, Artie felt confounded. She supposed she would never understand why knowledge was supposed to be precious, but was actually despised, and why it was highly desirable to be better at sports than anyone or more beautiful than anyone, but undesirable to have more knowledge.

Artie looked down at her muddy feet. "Well, it's just me now," she thought. "I will name the plants close to my right foot every time I step." She took a step on the downhill slope. "Eriogonum," she said, one step. "Bitterbrush. Big sagebrush. Squirreltail. Phlox. Lupine. Wild rye. Bitterbrush." She kept walking. "Gray rabbitbrush. Cheatgrass. Bur-buttercup. Squirreltail. Sandberg bluegrass. Big sagebrush."

Ben came in from his last outhouse run of the evening and gave the Shelties each a big bone from his Twin Falls haul. After a few preliminary squabbles, the three settled on the kitchen floor for an interval of serious chewing. Ben took his headlamp and climbed the ladder into the sleeping loft.

Clambering over the two mattresses on the floor, he looked through the cans of food he'd stored there in Gramps' suitcases and in rows against the walls, located three cans of Spam, and brought them down. Then he checked on the remaining bread. He had enough to make several sandwiches. He had a plan.

First thing in the morning, while it was still dark, he would fry up the Spam and make some sandwiches. He'd put them in his pack along with some candy bars and dog biscuits, fill a couple of bottles with water, make coffee for Gramps' thermos, and climb the east ridge of Spear Creek Gulch, where he could sit on the granite rocks of the Hand and watch two miles back down Spear Creek Road. He'd have with him Gramps' binoculars and the .38 revolver. If he saw no one after the first hour or so, he and the dogs would take the pickup and head down toward the state highway and ultimately toward Timmerman Hill.

The pickup could reach Timmerman in half an hour. He'd take the phones and call Gary, Mothy, and Dr. Lucy from somewhere close to Timmerman. He'd call as soon as he was close to Timmerman.

During the day, while he was waiting for them to show up, he'd find a non-obvious place to park somewhere in the trees along the river, where he could monitor a good stretch of road. Ben didn't know where he would intersect with Gary and Mothy, but surely, surely he would encounter Dr. Lucy on the highway. Gray. Gramps had said that her pickup was gray, like their own. And surely Mothy and Gary would make it to the state highway before the afternoon was over. They'd probably be starving, so he'd have the sandwiches and candy bars ready. And they would all be back at the Place before dark.

It might not be smart to risk being seen on the road and to be using up gasoline from the Place's limited supply, but if he were going to do any searching at all, Ben thought, he would have to have some range—and a way to get people back to the Place quickly. Whatever he did, he'd have to do it before the snow came, and it would be best to do this exploratory trek now, while the cell phones still worked. "Damn," he thought. Where was that solar charger?

Outside, the wind was dying and he could hear Patrick and Ramona beginning to scream.

CHAPTER 11

DISCOVERY

The sun was setting.

Artie had pushed herself all afternoon, but she was going to lose the light soon; the sun was bleeding out on the next ridge to the west. She knew that twilight was brief in October.

Suddenly she caught a movement out of the corner of her eye and whirled to the south. On the hill she had just walked down, something was moving, and moving swiftly, through the sage. She froze until the thing emerged from behind a big rock. Coyote. As if on cue, a chorus of ice-pick howls stabbed down into the gulch, and Artie shivered. She had so very often walked the hills around Hailey alone in the dark, and had planned to walk far into the night tonight, but with coyotes about . . .

"Nonsense," she told herself. "Mom said many times that there have been very few attacks by healthy coyotes on adult humans. They won't come after me." Still, it was a little unnerving to be alone out in these endless, unknown hills in the twilight, with things moving, slipping half-seen through the sagebrush behind her back. Her own hills were familiar, comfortable, even in the dark, even with the occasional coyote. This place was a mystery. She wished she knew what was in the next gulch over, and the next. Now, *that* would make her feel comfortable.

Artie looked down at her feet. Mud covered her boots and her jeans to above the knee, was spattered on her raincoat. She had washed the bloody sleeve in a puddle, but traces of blood still showed at the seam and cuff. "I'm quite a sight, I'm sure," she sighed. "Mudgirl, bloodgirl. And I don't even want to think about my hair." Artie shook her head. "But what I should worry about is keeping Ben and his grandpa from shooting me on sight." She was only half-joking about that. Until now, she hadn't really considered her approach to the safe place in the dark, but indeed, it might not be a good idea to barge right up to whatever their place was. Survivalists, Idaho survivalists, would have guns, no doubt about that. Was their place a ranch? An earth-covered bunker? A mine? Artie shook her head once more.

The light was fading fast. Perhaps instead of pushing on in the dark, she should find a good place to spend the night.

Artie squinted as she peered into the sage ahead. A thin, uneven thread branched from Horner Ranch Road and she exclaimed, "Could that be Gray Creek Road?" She hurried forward, crossing yet another tiny meadow of pale grasses and dark sedge. A little creek, so narrow that she could almost jump over it, trickled through a culvert under Horner Ranch Road. Artie picked up her pace.

And a few dozen yards farther on, she came out on a smaller road, dirt rather than gravel. At the intersection leaned a low sign, almost lost in the grasses and sage. It was early twilight now, and Artie knew there would be no moon tonight. She flashed Grandpa's light. *Gray Creek* was incised into the weathered wooden Bureau of Land Management sign. Only three or four miles until the intersection with Spear Creek Road! She could make that before total darkness. She could. She climbed twenty yards up the hillside above Gray Creek Road and began walking, faster.

Behind her, the coyotes howled again.

Artie felt an infusion of new energy; she was close. The road below where she was walking was paler in places now, less muddy. Coarse sand was replacing the fine, dark mud of the road and of the hills, and here and there she could just make out outcrops of a different stone, stone not black and angular like the basaltic lava.

Huge rounded rocks, pale as sheep and smooth as the humped backs of whales, broke through the increasingly steep contours of the hills. The muddy granite sand, crumbly rather than sticky, made for easier walking.

Artie told her leaden legs to keep moving. Gray Creek Road was climbing.

Her mind returned to the former puzzle and she worried at it like a small dog with a big bone. How could she present herself to Ben and Frank Elliott in the darkness without getting herself shot? And would they let her in? Would they let her stay? Was there room enough, food enough at their place? Surely there was, since Gary had been invited *and won't be coming,* her mind added darkly. Surely. *Surely.*

Twilight deepened, and Artie could barely see her feet. She tried the flashlight; the beam was fading. She stumbled over a fallen sagebrush branch, caught herself, and went on. The next time she stumbled, she wasn't so lucky, and fell headlong into a sagebrush, branches scratching at her face. Her knees planted themselves with a thud into the stiff, sandy mud. "This is not a good idea," she admitted finally. "If Ben and his grandfather see me coming in the daylight tomorrow, that shouldn't be the problem it would be if I arrive in the dark. If I keep trying to walk through all this sage and these granite rocks in the dark, I will fall and hurt myself before I even get there. It's stupid."

Artie decided that it was time to find a place to spend the night. She would find a rock outcrop that would block some of the wind, and she'd build a little fire near it. She would find a place where she could lean back against bare rock, where the heat from a fire would reflect from the stone, making it easier to stay warm during the night. Since she hadn't seen or heard a vehicle for many hours, it was unlikely that anyone would find his way here tonight on this narrow and muddy road, unlikely that anyone would be close enough to see a small fire in these lonely hills.

Cautiously and slowly, Artie walked along the hillside, still paralleling Gray Creek Road, looking for more pale shapes of the granite outcrops that had become so common in the past mile.

An odd rock formation like two thick-necked heads thrust into the sky ahead, standing barely taller than her own head— just what she had been hoping to find. This outcrop would do very well. She could clear a little space on the uphill side for her fire, and near the rocks she'd be somewhat sheltered from the wind.

Artie dropped her packs at the foot of the outcrop and began to gather wood. Since she would be burning sagebrush, it would take a small mountain of fuel to last through the night; she knew that from many family camping trips.

Artie worked silently and as rapidly as she could for half an hour, using the dim flashlight to guide her, pulling dead sage from the ground and ranging farther and farther from the outcrop on her forays. Darkness had closed in with a vengeance, but at least the wind had slackened somewhat. The temperature was dropping, however. She told herself to move faster.

Eventually, she amassed a spidery, open pile of dead sagebrush, shoulder-high and perhaps eight feet in diameter. She found herself heartily glad she had stopped in a stand of sagebrush. If she had stopped in a stand of rabbitbrush or bitterbrush, she knew, she would have had to range far and wide for firewood. And neither burned well at all when damp, as sagebrush did. Stands of sagebrush almost always had a high proportion of dead plants, easily pulled from the ground, making it easy to find wood. "One more armload," she told herself, almost dead on her feet, "and then I will be sure to have enough for the night."

At the farthest point downhill from her woodpile, the flashlight beam seemed to pick out a gray line cutting through the sagebrush near Gray Creek Road. She blinked, hard. Was this real or an artifact of the deepening darkness? Could this be Spear Creek Road, its intersection? She had to find out before she settled for the night. She dropped her last load of sagebrush.

Using short flashes of her light to guide her steps, Artie made her way downhill. The pale line *was* a road! Was there a sign? So many of these old dirt roads had no signs.

Sliding in the muddy sand of the barrow pit and hauling herself up with handfuls of tough wild rye, she stood on the road in the dark and swept the flashlight around to get her bearings. Yes, there *was* an intersection. And yes, a faint road, small sagebrush and grasses growing in the center, branched off to the north here. Heedless for the moment, she ran down Gray Creek Road to the intersection.

Artie played her flashlight along the roadside. An old, rotting sign lay flat in the sage. She took off one glove with her teeth and pried the ragged slab of wood from the mud. "Spear Creek" was carved into the fissured slab of wood. *Spear Creek.* She had made it to Spear Creek Road! Carefully she replaced the sign in its sunken outline in the soil.

Artie had taken only one step back toward her discarded armload of wood when she heard the barking.

Suddenly, somewhere down Spear Creek Road in the dark, something was barking at her--yark, yark, yark—little barks. A fox? Coyote puppies? Surely the animal making the little barks was much smaller than a wolf. The barker sounded quite small. It couldn't be coyote puppies, she decided; coyote puppies were born in the very early spring and would be almost adult size by October. A fox, then. Or a *dog?*

"My god, I thought Gary was a dog," she thought. Artie turned on her heel and made her way back to her rock outcrop as fast as she could walk. The barking continued, seeming to follow her. She located the dropped wood, grabbed up most of it, and almost ran up the hill to her chosen outcrop.

When she reached her woodpile, Artie dropped the last load of wood and with scrabbling fingers pulled the kitchen knife from her pack. She lifted the flashlight and aimed its beam toward the barking. "Come on, now, I'm not afraid of you," she said, trying to make herself believe her own voice.

The barking increased in loudness and ferocity, and her flashlight showed two points of greenish-golden light, like little stars, downhill in the sagebrush, low to the ground. *Eyes.*

Artie moved toward the eyes slowly. She had to know what this creature was. Why didn't it slink away into the dark? She knew that it was long past the season for a fox or coyote den to have puppies that needed to be guarded. "Come here!" she called loudly, almost startling herself.

The golden stars blinked out, and Artie's flashlight beam caught a puff of gray moving away rapidly. Then the two stars showed again, smaller. And the barking started up again.

"Oh, my god!" Artie said aloud with a strangled laugh. "I have been scared nearly to death by a miniature poodle!"

"Come on," she said, coaxing, "come on, now." But the little dog retreated and retreated until Artie saw it fold up its toothpick legs and sit on a square sheet of brown plywood fifty yards past the intersection with Spear Creek Road.

Artie approached slowly. The small poodle lowered its head and lifted a paw as if to ward off some evil, but held its ground. Behind it something glittered in the sage.

Close now, Artie realized that the mound of brown "plywood" was not wood at all, but a flattened, very large cardboard box. And from under the box stuck out two shoes, sneakers with wavy, muddy bottoms, and two equally muddy jeans-clad legs. The poodle kept barking.

"I am not, NOT finding another dying person!" Artie whispered. "Wake up!" she called. "Sit up, wake up!" The legs didn't move, but the poodle jumped off the bowed cardboard and came to Artie, sitting just out of reach and shivering with nervous energy, the cold, or both. Ready to run at the first sign of a threat, Artie threw off the cardboard with one swift motion, tossing it into the sage.

A person, a rather small person in filthy t shirt and jeans, lay flat on the ground, face up. To her astonishment, the once-white t shirt read "Wood River High Chess Team" in bright green letters. A red baseball cap obscured the face and hair. Artie bent and lifted the cap.

"It's Mothy!" She exclaimed, hardly believing her eyes. "Mothy! Mothy!" She shook him by the shoulders. "Timothy Rich, don't you dare be dead!" Artie felt that she couldn't breathe. She felt herself climbing into hysteria. "I can't stand it if you are dead!"

She took a deep breath and put her hand on his neck, her ear to his chest. No, he wasn't dead, not yet. Timothy didn't move, but he was still breathing. He had a heartbeat. He had a regular pulse. His pale arms were chilled and clammy to the touch. The poodle hovered, shivering.

Artie knew what she had to do. She rolled Timothy over, searched for wounds, for blood. She saw none. "Fire," she thought. "He feels really cold. I hope to crap he hasn't had a heart attack or something." She took him by the wrists and pulled. Yes, she was strong enough to pull him to her woodpile; that was good. She dragged Tim through the sage. His head bobbed as if his neck were boneless. She imagined that his face and neck would later sport some scratches from the sage, not to mention smears of mud, but it was what she could do. The poodle followed.

Once at the rock outcrop, Artie tugged Gran's fleece blanket from the pack and spread it, folded, on the coarse sand. She rolled Timothy onto the blanket and pulled off his damp t-shirt, replacing it with her own sweatshirt that she had taken from Gran's guest bedroom. She was shocked by the sight of his narrow chest and sticklike white arms. His socks and shoes were mud-caked, so she removed them, pounded off the mud against a sagebrush butt, and gave him a pair of Gran's dry socks.

Artie retrieved the bag of matches. She pulled some shreds of bark from a piece of shaggy sage in her pile, made a tiny teepee on a space of smoothed sand, and lit a fire. As always, sage was easy to light, wet or dry. She fed the fire until larger pieces of sage began to flame and crackle, and then spread Timothy's shirt, socks, and shoes on the woodpile where they would catch the heat without being scorched.

Then she went back for the cardboard and for the metal thing she had seen glittering back in the sagebrush. The metal thing turned out to be a bicycle. "Aha," Artie thought as she righted it. "So that's how Mothy got so far so fast."

She smiled as she braced the cardboard on the bike and guided the wheels uphill through the sage. A bicycle would be good come morning. Artie propped the cardboard against the rock outcrop, on the far side of the sandy spot where she had laid Tim, a windbreak. She anchored it with two heavy rocks and the bicycle. That was good, too. Artie thought about rocks for a moment, and took time to gather a small pile of fist-sized rocks as ammunition just in case they were disturbed during the night. Then she settled to feed the fire.

After a few minutes, she pulled up one sleeve of the sweatshirt and felt Tim's arm, listened to his breathing. Wasn't his arm warmer now? Wasn't he breathing a little easier? But what could be wrong with him? Goosebumps roughened the skin on his arm; he had begun to shiver.

"Hypothermia?" she wondered. She had been so very cold that first night in just a t shirt and wet hoodie. But after that, she'd had Gran's parka and padded raincoat, not to mention waterproof boots, thick socks, a scarf, and gloves. And food. Why didn't Tim have a jacket? What if Tim hadn't had time to grab a coat before he left Hailey? Now, *that* was an unsettling thought. And how long had it been since he had anything to eat? She hadn't seen clothing, a bag, or anything else near the cardboard and bike. She thought of Gary and what he had said about the shots and the soldiers. Like Gary, Tim must have fled Hailey. He must have fled with only the bike, the clothes on his back, and his dog. Artie put more wood on the fire. "Warmth," she thought.

The poodle danced at the edge of the firelight, staring at Artie. What was Tim's dog's name? She tried to remember. She had seen Tim with the dog in town any number of times, walking it on lead. And calling it—what? The poodle was wearing a red leather collar, and a dangling tag caught the firelight. "Smoke," she remembered suddenly.

"Smoke," she said to the dog, extending her hand. "Here, Smoke. Come on, boy."

Smoke wagged his ridiculously tufted tail and picked his way through an edge of Artie's woodpile. He put a thin gray paw on her knee, and Artie scooped him into her lap. "Good boy," she said. "Wonder if you are hungry."

She fed Smoke one of the granola bars that didn't have chocolate or raisins, and gave him some water in her cupped hands. The poodle turned around twice and curled in her lap, tucking his head under the edge of her raincoat. She leaned down, tightened her arms around the gray fur. The warm contact felt so good.

"How the holy crap am I going to get Tim to the Elliotts' Place?" Artie asked herself as she stared into the fire. "Can I put him on the cardboard and drag him? Could I sling him in front of me on the bike? I can't carry him several miles, that's for sure." She looked over at Tim, flat on his back in the firelight. It was uncomfortable to see a person so vulnerable, but there he was, utterly defenseless, splayed like a starfish on Gran's soft beige blanket with gray stocking feet sticking out like two strange slugs beyond the muddy bottoms of his pant legs.

Artie studied him thoughtfully, considering. She lifted both his arms and placed them close to his sides to conserve warmth. "If Tim doesn't wake up by morning," she decided, "I'll hide him away from the road, behind this rock formation. I'll put the blanket and the cardboard over him, pile some sage on top, leave him some grape juice and candy bars and a note, and go to the Elliott place. Maybe they have a car or truck, a wheelbarrow, or even some horses. At the least, they will be able to help carry him." She felt better now that she had decided what to do.

Coyotes howled from the southwest ridge; Artie could barely hear them over the snapping of the fire. The wind had died away and the hillside felt calm and peaceful.

She felt secure enough to take off Gran's boots and her shoes. She set the shoes on the woodpile to toast near the fire and stretched out her legs to the warmth. She took off her raincoat and wore it as an open cloak to catch the heat. Then she ferreted out the precious map from the raincoat pocket and stowed it safely in a front pocket of her jeans. Artie fed the fire again. Now that the wind had died, she was feeling warmer.

Suddenly ravenous, she fossicked in Gran's pack and ate a Snickers bar. "Things are all right," she told herself. "We are going to be safe for the night." Artie placed the butcher knife on the ground near her pile of rocks.

Timothy turned to one side and groaned. Artie wasn't in any mood to be gentle. She took him by the shoulders. "Come on, Tim," she said urgently. "Come on, come on. Wake up!" He groaned again, and she smacked him on the shoulder with the flat of her hand. "Wake up, Tim! Mothy, wake up!"

Smoke pushed his muzzle forward and licked Tim on the mouth. "Aaaah!" Tim said, finally responding. "Off, Smoke; stop!"

Artie hadn't realized she was holding her breath; she let it out in a big sigh.

Tim pushed himself into a sitting position, his back supported by the rock. He swiveled his head on its slender neck, and Artie watched him taking in the scene: Smoke, Artie, the fire, the woodpile, the rocks. "What?" he demanded. "What is going on?" Timothy peered into Artie's face, squinting in the firelight. "Artie," he said. It wasn't a question.

"That's me." Artie had a sudden desire to laugh at the absurdity. She swallowed it down.

Timothy leaned against the rock and pushed his hair out of his eyes; Smoke folded himself into Tim's lap. "Artie, what on earth are you doing here?"

"I could ask the same," she returned, feeding the fire. "What are *you* doing here?" But, she thought for the first time since finding him--wasn't it obvious? Artie stared at Tim. She said, "Ben gave you a map."

"Yes, sort of," he said, wrapping his arms around his dog. "Artie, do you have any water? Anything to eat?"

"Sure," she said, reaching for one of the packs. "Here's a bottle of grape juice and a couple of Snickers bars. That OK?"

Tim grabbed for them eagerly, chugging the grape juice until the small bottle was empty. Then he attacked the candy bars. "I didn't get an actual map from Ben," he said between bites, "but I am headed to his place. I called him and he gave me directions."

"Can you call him now?" Artie asked eagerly. That would be the perfect way to tell Ben and his grandfather that they were coming.

"No." Tim shook his head ruefully. "I had my phone until sometime in the middle of Friday night. It fell out of my pocket in the dark somewhere between Bellevue and Timmerman Hill."

"Bugger." She shoved her hands into her pockets. "I have mine, but it's totally out of battery."

"Ben gave you a map, too, then," Tim said, finishing the candy bars and having the sense to toss the wrappers into the fire.

"Not exactly." Artie looked into the fire, watching the wrappers melt and curl. "I got my copy of the map from Gary."

"Gary!" Tim exclaimed. "Where *is* Gary? Ben wants me to find him. But I couldn't. It was too scary in Hailey to stick around, and it was dark, and Gary wouldn't answer his phone. When did you see him? Did he go on ahead?"

"I guess it's time for us to tell what happened in Hailey," Artie said. "Both of us. And how we got here. I'll go first and tell you about Gary, since you asked." She couldn't think of another way to say it. "Gary is dead." She drew up her knees and hugged them.

"Dead," Tim repeated. His eyes glinted in the firelight. "Gary is dead. You know this? You saw this?"

"I did," Artie said, and told him how she had found her family and her cat dead on Saturday morning, dead after drinking the water. How she had spent Saturday night in a culvert under Highway 75 and then had made it to Grandpa and Gran's house on Sunday morning and found them gone and their vehicles and guns gone. How the houses had begun to burn on Sunday night and how she had decided to run south in the dark, hoping to get to the lower country, to find a farm with food and water. And how she had found Gary at dawn and now had his map, the map that Ben had given him.

"God," was Tim's comment. He put a thumb in his mouth and Artie could see firelight gleaming on his teeth as he bit down on it. "Huh. Gary shot in the back, shot dead. And your family, dead. Unbefrigging. But I do believe you."

"Now you tell," Artie said impatiently. "Come on."

Tim took a breath. "OK. Well, my deal started Friday after school. We had Chess Club, and then I headed home on my bike. Funniest thing. I always go in through the garage and leave my bike there. But the headlamp was a little loose, and I wanted to fix it, put in a screw where one fell out, so I went around back instead and left the bike on the deck." Tim's hands tightened around Smoke's body.

"I went in the back door and there was Mom in the kitchen, sitting in a chair by the kitchen table. She almost always gets home before I do." He gulped and pinched the bridge of his nose for a moment before continuing. "Well, Mom, she had her head on the table, and a teacup with tea was broken and spilled all over the floor. I felt her hand, her—she was dead. Still warm, too, but dead sitting at the table, with her cheek down flat and one hand, one arm sticking out, just straight out on the table." Tim paused for a moment; Artie could hear him calming his breathing.

"And Smoke was in the back yard and he started barking," Tim went on. "And I looked out the kitchen windows and there were soldiers on the sidewalk out front, soldiers that looked different--and they pulled open the front door without knocking, and they hadn't seen me yet, so I ran out the back door. I grabbed Smoke in one arm and took the bike and wheeled it out to the alley and took off. I took off for Ben's. I didn't even stop to call him." Tim looked at Artie; she couldn't see past the miniature flames dancing in his eyes. "I got to Ben's house and pounded on the door. It wasn't locked. I went in and there was Crazy Frank sitting in a chair, deader than dead."

"What?" Artie couldn't believe it. "Frank Elliott is dead?" Tim nodded.

"Where was Ben? Is Ben all right?" Artie couldn't breathe. She felt like shaking Tim again.

"Ben wasn't there." Tim said. "Don't freak, Artie. Ben isn't dead. I talked to him on the phone after that."

Artie took a deep, shuddering breath. "Was Frank Elliott shot?" she asked.

"I don't think so," Tim replied soberly. "I couldn't see what killed him, but he was pretty freaking dead. He hadn't been dead all that long, either. I don't think so, anyway. I went through the house looking for Ben, but he wasn't there. Ben's room was kind of messed up. And their truck was gone and their dogs were gone, too."

Artie nodded, breathing more easily. "But why did you head to Ben's in the first place?"

"At Chess Club," Tim said, "Gary told me that Ben was leaving town, that he, Ben, had said that he was going to a safe place he and his gramps had been fixing up. That Ben had texted him that really weird stuff would be coming down, like immediately, and that Gary should drop everything and come with him. That it wouldn't be safe in town."

Tim looked up at Artie and she could see that he was blinking back tears. His wet eyes shone with trembling flames. "We thought that was *funny*, Artie. Gary and I. Funny, stupid survivalist stuff, we said. Dumb old Ben, brainwashed Ben, for falling for it. Crazy Frank Elliott. Hilarious." Tim swiped a hand across his face. "We laughed, even. Gary said he knew where their safe place was. Said Ben gave him a map a couple of days before. So that's why I went to Ben's. Ben's house is only a little ways from our house."

"I called Gary from under the big tree in Ben's front yard, but Gary didn't answer, so I took off for Gary's house. Smoke and I made it as far as the high school. You know that you can see Gary's house from the high school."

Artie nodded.

"About the time I got to the school," Tim continued, "I saw some white buses and some Humvees parked along Gary's street. The Humvees were white, too; I've never seen white Humvees all in a bunch like that before. There were soldiers with guns, and they were shoving people and making them get on those buses. I saw old man Larrabee and Mrs. Anshelm with the little twins get on. More soldiers showed up. That really scared me. You know that line of close-together lilac bushes down one side of the school lawn? Me and Smoke hid under the lilac bushes there. There was no writing on the buses or the Humvees, either, just huge numbers. One of the buses was 17, I remember. That's all. And the soldiers' uniforms. They looked funny."

"Funny, how?" Artie asked, fascinated in a horrified way. Gary had seen those Humvees and those white buses.

"Their uniforms weren't like the Army or the National Guard. They were whitish, like a camo pattern that was almost faded out. They almost looked like, like hazmat suits or something. Anyway, me and Smoke, we crawled under one of those lilac bushes and watched, and stayed for a long time. It got dark pretty fast. I heard a couple of shots, but by then it was so dark I couldn't see much. I called Gary a bunch of times but didn't get him. I called Jase, too, and Carl. I was scared shitless. I figured that it would be either useless or scary to call the police if soldiers were out there rounding people up. So I finally remembered that I had Ben's number in my phone from when we did that school project last spring, and called Ben and got him, and he told me the directions to his place. I don't have a map."

Tim held up something small, a blunt shape like an old cell phone. "But I always have my Garmin GPS in my pocket, and I got Ben to give me the coordinates!" he said in triumph. "Finally, the buses pulled out. They all went north. The soldiers got into the Humvees and went north, too. I took off on my bike then and knew I had to go south to get to Ben's safe place, so I just held onto Smoke and pedaled like a madman."

"Wait!" Artie couldn't believe it. "You went down the highway—you rode your bike right down the highway Friday night?"

"You got it," he said somewhat smugly. "Followed the dotted line in the dark. My bike lamp didn't even fall off."

"Unbelievable," she said.

Tim went on. "I only met a few cars, and I could see them coming a long way off, so I just slid into the barrow pit each time and waited in the weeds until they went by. Glad I did. Every one of them was a Humvee. Got to Timmerman before dawn and turned west on the state highway. After that I didn't see anybody at all."

"Me, either," Artie offered. "What about last night? Where did you spend last night? It rained all night."

"Sure did," he replied. "To go back to yesterday. By about an hour after dawn I was done in. I was on the state highway by the time it got light, and it started to pour. You know where that rock and gravel quarry place used to be just off the state highway after it leaves the river? In those little hills that are reddish? It's before the turnoff to Horner Ranch Road. They have kind of been filling it in lately."

Artie nodded. She had walked past the quarry only a few hours ago.

"OK," Tim went on. "By the time I got there, I had been soaked to the skin for a long time. The exercise kept me fairly warm for a while, but by then I was losing it. I saw a big piece of that corrugated tin roof stuff lying on the ground over where the quarry was, so we went over there and I lifted it up. It was dry underneath, just dry dirt. So Smoke and I crawled under it. There was room for the bike as well as us. I used the bike to lift the piece of tin off of us a few inches. We fell asleep and kind of slept the day away, and the night; no point in going out in the rain and freezing even more. And I didn't have a flashlight or anything, so I didn't want us to get lost in the dark and miss the turnoff road. We stayed put. We came out a few times and drank water from some puddles, but that was it. We were so cold." Tim rubbed his arms through the sweatshirt and glanced at Artie. "I see that you have a coat."

"Yes," she said. "It's Gran's. I took it from her house."

"Well, this morning when I woke up the rain had stopped, so we got back onto the state highway and started out for Ben's place again. And it was colder. The wind made it colder. And we were going to get there before too long anyway, so I thought I might take a nap and there was this old cardboard box thing in the brush by the road, and I just kind of pulled it over me for a nap." He stopped suddenly.

"Just a nap, huh?" Artie said. "It freaked me when you wouldn't wake up. I think what you had was hypothermia."

"Oh, come on," Tim scoffed. He stood up quickly, and just as quickly collapsed onto the blanket. Artie sighed and sorted out his arms and legs. After a minute or two, Tim's eyes opened. "Oh," he said.

"'Oh' is right," she repeated.

"Why is all this happening?" Tim asked, leaning back into the rock face. Orange firelight painted his face and hands. Of Smoke, Artie could see only a curly expanse of gray back. The poodle had jumped away when Tim got up, but now wasn't about to leave Tim's lap.

"I have no idea," Artie said slowly. She could feel heat from the fire on her face and knees, and the granite at her back was warming, too. "Why would anyone suddenly poison Hailey's water? Why would anyone burn perfectly good houses and take people away on buses? I don't get it. God, Mothy, if I had been sleeping in my bed Friday night instead of out on my balcony, they might have found me and killed me, too, when they came to steal the cars. They took our cars before I even woke up. And if I had stopped to brush my teeth before I came downstairs . . ."

"I know," he said, picking up a shaggy stick from the woodpile and poking at the fire. "If Smoke hadn't barked, and if I hadn't seen those soldiers out the kitchen window . . . I'm still not sure why I ran from them instead of asking them for help. And if I had put my bike in the garage the way I almost always do . . ."

"But I saw it coming," Artie said slowly. "Since last spring sometime."

Tim sat up straight, his eyes fixed on Artie's face. "What can you possibly mean, that you 'saw it coming'?"

"I didn't know what was coming, or why," she said. "But it seemed to me that people were wound tight, that they have been feeling worried and stressed, much more than usual."

"Hindsight is 20-20," Tim sighed, leaning back against the granite.

Artie didn't reply. It did sound stupid, that she had seen this coming. But nevertheless . . .

They sat silently for a time. Tim pulled a fold of Gran's blanket around his shoulders and leaned forward toward the heat. On the crest of the south hill, the coyotes shrieked and sang. Overhead, there was no moon, only the black sky dusted with stars. "It's beautiful here," Artie thought. "Beautiful and wild."

Tim broke into her reverie. "Do you have a weapon?" he asked. "Maybe a gun?"

"No gun," Artie said. "I looked at Grandpa and Gran's, but everything in their gun safe was gone. I thought you hated guns. I have a kitchen knife, though." She picked up the knife and showed it to him. The blade looked wicked in the firelight.

"A knife. Holy crap," Tim said. "I've been playing online with death rays and planet-killer disintegrators, and now--we have a kitchen knife."

"Well, it's a sharp one," Artie snapped, stung. "And I have a pile of rocks, too."

"Rocks?" Tim shook his head. "Welcome to the fourteenth century," he said gloomily.

"Rocks as weapons are way older than the fourteenth century," Artie retorted mildly. "By then, there was gunpowder." The coyotes screamed again, closer now.

Tim hunched his shoulders. "Will the fire keep the coyotes away from us?" he asked.

"It's all right," Artie said. "They won't come near us. I figure we are only a few miles from the Elliott place now. In the morning, we'll be there before you know it."

"Great," Tim said then. "And you do have matches. Matches and candy bars are way newer than the fourteenth century." He yawned. "Don't know why I feel so tired, but I can hardly keep my eyes open."

"It makes you tired to be cold," Artie said. "I think we're safe here tonight, but we should keep watch, and someone will have to feed the fire. You sleep and I'll watch. When I get too tired, I'll wake you up."

"OK." Tim said. He turned to one side, pulled the blanket over himself, and was out almost instantly. Smoke tucked himself into a fold of the blanket, a gray fur ball.

Artie looked up at the starry sky again. "Three people making their way to the Elliotts' place," she thought. "One down, two still going. And--" She still could hardly believe it "—Frank Elliott is already dead." She wondered who else would be at the end of this trek, if Ben had trusted anyone else with a map, who else might have been invited by Crazy Frank. "Not me," she thought ruefully, shaking her head. But then, how could Ben have known, have cared what she felt?

CHAPTER 12

FOUND

Ben was up long before the sun, frying Spam on the wood stove in a cast-iron skillet. He made coffee while he was slapping the sandwiches together. Coffee with evaporated milk went into Gramps' big Stanley thermos; then he got out some dog biscuits and a few candy bars. Ben stuffed his pack and locked the door of the ranch house.

By sunrise, Ben and the dogs were more than halfway up the east ridge of Spear Creek Gulch. The dogs forged ahead, excited by the prospect of activity after the days of rain. Ben struggled in the cold, sandy mud to keep up with the Shelties, but they nosed out a jackrabbit from under a sagebrush, chased it, and crested the ridge a hundred yards ahead of him.

Puffing and blowing, he made it to the granite formation atop the ridge that Gramps always called "the Hand," four round-topped fingers of gray granite standing upright next to two pillow-shaped boulders, one cracked and standing, one nearly as flat as a table, the Thumb and the Palm. Ben slung off his pack and sat on the Palm.

Catching his breath, he looked down on Spear Creek in its narrow valley, the stream curving away through the grassy meadow between small shaving-brush willows. From here he could see nearly all of the Place: roofs of the house and the chicken house, the woodshed, the loafing shed, and the water wheel. Only the outhouse and the barn were too close to the east hill to be seen from the Hand. Below, two ravens flew low and straight as they quartered the meadow, questing for prey. A hundred yards farther downstream, a kestrel hovered on the wind, doing the same.

Ben dug the binoculars from the pack and glassed the road, from the Place's driveway southeast to where Spear Creek Road disappeared behind the low shoulder of a sage hill. Nothing, no one. He felt his shoulders sag. But it was still early. Quite early.

He poured himself half a lid of coffee from the thermos, folded his fingers around the warmth, and settled to wait. The dogs abandoned their futile chase of the jackrabbit and flopped down on the Palm next to him, warm against his legs in the chill of early morning.

The two ravens spread the feathers at the tips of their wings and rose in the air until Ben could look straight into their clever black-bead eyes. Then they let the wind lift them over his head and flew north toward Cat Mountain.

After a long time, Bear turned his head and stood, facing downcanyon. He turned again to look at Ben, tail held out stiffly. Ben used the binoculars. "Yes, I see something, too," he told Bear. "Good boy." Maybe he wouldn't have to go looking for Gary and Mothy after all.

He could see movement on the road, but couldn't yet identify what was moving. A glint of metal flashed in the sun. He kept his binoculars trained on the road, excited, hoping. Gary and Mothy here! It had to be Gary and Mothy. Ben caught himself smiling. There would be good times now, or at least better times. *Much* better times.

Eventually, the movement on the road showed him one person moving slowly, and at his side, a child or small adult, with some sort of metal frame with them or around them both. A few minutes later, Ben could make out someone on a bicycle and another person holding the handlebars, walking alongside. "Gary and Mothy!" he thought in triumph. "It *is* them. Come on!" he shouted to the dogs. "Let's go down and meet them!"

Artie was tiring. She held tightly to the handlebars of Tim's bike and kept pushing. The road wasn't steep, but it was an uphill climb, and Tim and Smoke grew heavier with each mile. "We should be almost there," she told Tim, stopping for a moment to brush a strand of hair out of her eyes. She squinted, looking upcanyon: meadow, sagebrush flat, sage hills, a few trees. The Elliott place should be there somewhere. "I don't see any buildings," Artie said. "Check your Garmin again."

"Look!" Tim was pointing ahead down the road. "Isn't that someone standing on the road up there? And aren't those dogs?"

They hurried up the rise, as rapidly as Artie could manage. Before long she could see that the dark shape on the road was indeed a person, and, after another interval, that it was Ben standing there, Ben and three Shelties, two dark and one gray.

Artie's eyes stung. They had made it. Ben's place must be real—and in spite of all the death and fire and new strangeness of the world, there Ben stood, alone and unscathed, in a clean landscape of sage and sky and hills, and Cat Mountain, dark with pines, looming massive in the background. *Ben.*

When they were a hundred yards away, Ben's dogs ran to meet them, jumping and barking, spinning and whirling around them in a little storm of noisy muzzles and fur and wagging tails.

Ben walked toward them the last few yards as Artie and Tim closed the distance. "You made it, Mothy," he said. He looked at Artie, "You're not Gary," he said. "Come on." He turned and started away down the road.

Artie's eyes burned, and she blinked back tears. Well, what kind of welcome had she been expecting, after all? Her breath caught in her throat. Would Ben let her stay? Could she stay?

Ben turned back to them. "Here, Artie," he said. "Let me do this." She relinquished the handlebars to him, her heart pounding because he was so close. "Mothy, why aren't you walking or riding the bike on your own?" he asked, moving the bike along. "And that's your poodle, right?"

Mothy gulped. "Yes, I brought Smoke."

Ben asked again, "OK. But why aren't you walking? Are you hurt?"

"Tim's not hurt. He's just a little weak," Artie said. "He has hypothermia and hasn't had much to eat. He tried to walk for a while, but he was slow and pretty shaky, so the bike was a good solution." She was gabbling once more, and shut herself off.

"OK," Ben said again. They had reached a sagging ranch-panel gate, brown with rust, patched with pocket wire, and held shut by a heavy old chain and equally rusty padlock. Ben ignored the old gate. He lifted a loop of wire from a fencepost to the left of the gate and swung open a section of the barbed-wire fence. "Welcome to the Place," he said. He pulled the wire gate shut and refastened it after they had passed.

"But—but—there aren't any buildings here," Tim sputtered, his face falling. "It's just a flat place. Your safe house is a flat place?"

Ben smiled, continuing ahead down a steep little slope covered with tall sagebrush. "Wait for it," he said.

Suddenly the peak of a gray metal roof appeared over the sage, then another, then another. "Huh," Timothy said. "Stop." He disengaged himself from the bike. "I can walk now. There *are* buildings here. Thank God," he finished. Smoke jumped down from his arms to smell the Shelties. Stiff whiskers and upright tails ensued, but no growls.

"Yes," said Ben, pointing out each one. "The house. The barn. The outhouse. The chicken house. The loafing shed. And the woodshed."

Ben led them to the house and unlocked the back door. The kitchen was still deliciously warm from the early morning cooking.

"Well, I got inside," Artie thought to herself nervously. "Step one."

She looked around at the tidy kitchen, dominated by a huge, black cast-iron stove and a round oak table with six wooden chairs. Near the stove sat a wood box filled with split pine. On the adjoining wall were ordinary kitchen cabinets, plus a narrow wooden countertop and a large galvanized metal sink. Two small windows looked out onto Spear Creek's meadow to the west; another faced north, toward the barn and Cat Mountain. The kitchen still smelled faintly of coffee.

So this was the Place.

They sat at the table. Ben fished the Spam sandwiches and the thermos from his pack and set them out, then got three mugs from the pantry and filled them with hot coffee from the thermos.

Artie cradled her mug, inhaling the fragrant steam. "Better than Starbucks," she said. "Ahhhh." A sudden thought struck her. "You must have dog food here," she said. "Smoke is pretty hungry, too."

"We have tons of dog food," Ben said. "Probably literally, tons. Here." He got up. "I'll feed them all so they won't growl at Smoke and try to steal his food." Sounds of contented crunching soon rose from the floor.

"Now," Ben said, looking from Tim to Artie and back again, "eat up. I'm going to take my dogs and leave as soon as I finish my coffee. I'm taking the truck. I want you to promise not to light a fire in the stove until dark. But before I go looking for Gary, do either of you know where he is?"

Tim glanced up almost furtively. "I called him and called him, Ben, like you asked. Friday night. But I never got him. And then I lost my phone in the dark. What happened is Artie's story."

Artie drew in a deep breath and set down her coffee mug. Why couldn't Tim have said it? "Gary is dead, Ben."

"What? What do you mean? How can you know that?" he demanded, leaning over the table toward her, sparks of light in his gray eyes.

She dug in a back pocket and pulled out the ball chain. Gary's three dogtags rang together sweetly, clinking like tiny wind chimes. She laid them gently on the table, the chain coiling gracefully on the oilcloth.

Ben whirled away from them, and Artie gasped; she thought he was angry. But a moment later he held a lighted match to the wick of an oil lamp there in the center of the table. The little flame leaped up and brightened.

Ben held the dogtags to the light. All three showed smears of dark blood, but the die-stamped letters and numbers were clear in the light of the small flame. Ben lowered himself heavily into his wooden chair. "These are Gary's, all right. Two of these were his grandfather's, from Viet Nam. See that? Connor Lawrence Scott. And the third one his grandfather had made for Gary: Gareth Lawrence Scott. Gary always wore these. So what happened, Artie? How did you get these? Where is Gary now? How did you get here, to the Place? Did you and Tim come from Hailey together?"

She drew out Gary's wallet and slid it onto the table beside the dogtags, and then his map and pocket knife. "Gary was shot in the back," she said. "By a soldier, he said. I found him yesterday morning south of Bellevue, just before he died. We have some

things to tell you about what happened in Hailey and Bellevue."
She took a bite of her sandwich and chewed without tasting it.

"Your grandfather," Tim began, hesitating. "Your gramps
is—"

"I know about Gramps," Ben said, stony-eyed. "Go on."

Artie closed her eyes and tried to remember just how Gary
had worded his message. The dogs crunched on, the only noise
in the silence that stretched out, and Tim wasn't saying anything
to fill it.

Finally, Artie said, "Gary was shot in the back, and I found
him along the river. He gave me his map to this place. I tried to
help him, but it was too late. Gary said he wanted me to come
here. He said I had to find you and tell you—to tell you how
he died. And to tell you that he hadn't acted right, he said. He
wanted you to know that he was sorry about that. He told me to
tell you that you were, you *are* his best friend, his very best friend,
have always been his best friend, since you were little kids." Artie
opened her eyes, met Ben's gray ones. "Gary told me I had to
make it here so I could tell you."

Ben covered his eyes with his hands. "First Gramps, then
Gary," he said.

"My mom, too." Tim spoke softly. "And Artie's whole family.
All dead."

Ben dropped his hands and stared intently, first at Tim and
then at Artie. "Gramps," he said, as if to himself, then added,
"Gramps was right. Your families? Holy crap. You have to tell me
everything."

So they did.

Sitting around the table, Tim and Artie told their stories yet
again: the deaths, the water, the soldiers, the white buses, the

white Humvees, the shots, their escapes, the rain. Then Artie told about the Hailey night fires and finding Gary—and then how she had stumbled upon Tim and Smoke last night.

Suddenly, Artie looked over at Tim, who had been silent for some time. He had been holding his head in his hands, propped on his elbows. He still held that position, but he was fast asleep. "Got a bed?" said Artie softly.

"Sure." Ben shook Tim's shoulder, but he didn't respond.

"That's how he was before," said Artie.

"Let's carry him, then," Ben said. "But first, let's take off his muddy shoes and socks, and pants. It won't be good if he gets the sleeping bag all dirty." Quickly Ben stripped off Tim's muddy clothing and left it on the kitchen floor. He disappeared into an adjoining room for a minute and then returned. "I've fixed a bed," he said. "You take his feet and I'll take his shoulders."

They carried Tim around a corner and through a doorway, into a small room with two single beds separated by a small nightstand. One bed was where Ben had obviously been sleeping; it was covered with a blue sleeping bag and sported a paperback book and a pillow. On the other lay a green sleeping bag, unzipped and folded down on one side, plus a large pillow. They laid Tim on his back, positioned the pillow under his head, and pulled over the wing of the sleeping bag, zipping the green bag up to his chin. "That should warm him up," Artie said. "I think he is just exhausted from trying to keep himself warm all this time."

Ben nodded.

Back in the kitchen, Artie picked up Tim's muddy things and asked, "Do you have a way to wash clothes here?"

Ben looked at her sharply and then barked a short laugh. "Sure do! Gramps got us a Rollowash. I'll show you." He led her out onto the covered porch.

Artie followed, puzzled.

Most of the deep porch was crammed with split and stacked pine. Ben took Tim's soiled clothes from her and rolled them into a bundle, which he placed on the woodpile. Then he reached into a cavity in the stacked wood and pulled out a thing of molded red plastic that looked like an odd wastebasket with a lid. "Here you go," he said. "The Rollowash." He presented it to Artie with a shy flourish. She held out her hands and took the Rollowash.

Artie turned the thing over and unscrewed the lid. Inside were molded bulges, like the vanes in an old washing machine. "Oh!" she exclaimed in sudden understanding. "I get it! You put in warm water and soap, screw the lid down, and roll it back and forth. Then you dump out the soapy water and do the same with clear water for a rinse, right?"

"I guess," Ben said. "We never used it."

"It looks big enough to do Tim's stuff and maybe some of mine, too." Artie looked at Ben, trying to read him. He slung an arm around one of the wooden porch columns and looked west into the distance.

"It's now or never, I guess," she thought. Her hands began to shake and she held the Rollowash tightly to her body as if holding in her courage. "Ben," she said. "Ben, can I stay here? With you and Mothy?" Artie held her breath.

"What?" he turned to face her. She was caught in the tiny swirls of pale and dark gray in the irises of his eyes, in the texture of his skin, in the curve of his lips. She had known all these so well for so long, but had rarely been this close to him.

"I—I wasn't invited here, like Gary and Tim were," she continued, holding the red plastic cylinder even tighter. She had compressed the plastic into a narrow oval. She wondered if it would crack and fall to pieces on the porch floorboards between her shoes. "I just—came." She looked away, terrified.

Ben took a step toward Artie, and stopped, closer.

What have you been thinking? Of *course* you are staying, Artie," he said. "Of *course* you can stay here. That's what the Place is for. And you're—you are one of us."

Artie could breathe again. She could stay!

CHAPTER 13

BEN'S PLACE

"Come on, Artie, let's go get the washtub so we can heat washing water on the stove tonight," Ben said, thinking, "Maybe it's going to be all right having Artie and Mothy here." He knew he hadn't yet felt the full impact of Gary's death—or even that of losing Gramps. Ben gritted his teeth. He'd try for cheerful, and if he couldn't manage cheerful, he'd try for ordinary. "The washtub is down here in the loafing shed." Letting go the porch column, he swung himself onto the path through the back yard.

Artie followed Ben down the slight slope to the loafing shed, a long, partly-open metal building with three and a half corrugated metal sides, a timber frame, and a gravel floor scarcely to be seen beneath hundreds of barrels, stacked two deep, neatly covered by brown tarps held down by large rocks. Ben lifted a corner of a tarp and revealed some of the barrels, rank upon rank, each labeled in marker. In the third row back, Ben found the washtub upended over a barrel like an oversized gray metal hat. He lifted the washtub off the barrel and passed it to Artie. "There's a jar of detergent in the house, in the pantry." He had a sudden thought. "You like carrots?"

"What?" Artie seemed startled by the nonsequitur, as if her thoughts had been miles away. "Sure, I like carrots," she said. "Why?"

"Well, I want to bring everything we need for dinner inside before dark," Ben said, "and we're close to the old bunker now, and that's where the carrots are kept. So let's get some. I can show you the bunker, anyway." This would be good, Ben told himself. Inside the old bunker, he'd felt alone and cold with his grief for Gramps. Having someone with him would help, though he didn't know why. It was just Artie, the Artie he had known nearly all his life.

"OK," Artie said, trotting along.

Once inside the bunker, Ben opened one of the sawdust barrels and pulled out six fat carrots, replacing the lid with care. "This is amazing," Artie commented, wide-eyed, looking around at everything stored in the bunker.

Ben couldn't meet her eyes to take the praise. "It's not me who made all this happen. It was Gramps. Gramps, not me."

"Nevertheless," Artie said. "You are a big part of this. And it is amazing, amazing. And—" she added as an afterthought. "We won't ever forget your gramps. How could we? He has saved us."

Ben didn't know what to say, and he thought, "So what's new about that? I never know what to say." But he smiled at the thought of Gramps being unforgotten. Gramps would like that. He shut the heavy wooden door to the bunker but left the padlock open. Somehow, he felt better about the bunker now. After a couple of breaths, words came to him and he said, "Let's go back and see how Mothy is doing."

Carrying the washtub, Artie started up the dirt path to the house ahead of him. Ben suddenly realized that she seemed unsteady on her feet. He hurried to catch up. "You're not thinking," he told himself. "You're not used to thinking about other people. You have no idea how far Artie has walked today."

⊨⟨⊢ ⊣⟩⊨

Suddenly, the washtub felt heavy. It felt so heavy that she had to stop for a moment and put it down. She felt her cheeks start to redden. She did not want Ben to think she was weak and incapable. "Sorry," she said. "Tim and I were supposed to trade watches last night, but he was so tired that I just let him sleep. I've been up a long time."

Ben was behind her on the path. He put the carrots in the washtub and took it from her. "I'll take this. You are done in and don't know it," he said, continuing along the path to the house. Artie followed him on feet heavy as lead.

In the house, they checked on Timothy. He was lying in exactly the same position in which they had left him, snoring softly. Smoke was curled up behind the bulge in the sleeping bag that marked Timothy's knees.

"Next door," Ben said, withdrawing from the room. Instead of two single beds, the second bedroom had a double bed and a single bed, separated by a nightstand. Slightly larger, this room also sported an old highboy dresser topped with a small oak-framed oval mirror. In this bedroom, too, a rolled-up sleeping bag and large pillow had been placed on each bed. Ben untied the bag on the single bed and shook it out. "Here," he said. "Why don't you get some sleep? I'm going to take the dogs for a walk."

Artie didn't have to be asked twice. She found that she couldn't even wait to unzip the bag, but kicked off her shoes, crawled under the bag, and was asleep before she had time to have another thought.

⊨⟨⊢ ⊣⟩⊨

Ben stood in the doorway for a long moment. Already Artie was just an irregular lump under the dark-red sleeping bag. The only part of her still visible was the end of her honey-colored ponytail hanging down off the striped mattress. "Very odd to have a girl at the Place," he thought. "There hasn't been a girl here since— since Grandma."

Ben called the Shelties to him, and Smoke came as well. "You might as well get used to the routine," Ben said to the Poodle. "Come on, Smoke. Sunset will be here before we know it. Let's do our last walk of the day. We'll make it a long one."

Ben took the dogs upstream, following the creek. He led them into the aspen grove, and upstream as far as the place he called "the Narrows," where the road was a hundred yards above the stream and barely visible as a pale line in the sage. Here the meadow pinched itself down to a few feet of grass on either side of the creek in an aspen-grove corridor where the water flowed rapidly through a tumble of granite boulders. He was glad to see that Smoke was staying with the Shelties, and was biddable, coming when he was called.

Ben had a favorite place to read and sketch at the Narrows, a pale gray slab of granite, almost flat, only slightly tilted and jutting out an arm's length over Spear Creek, shaded most of the day by the aspens on both sides of the stream. In summers past, Ben would often bring a book here, or his sketchpad, and laze away the long afternoons reading or sketching, and watching the dragonflies and minnows.

Today the water in the creek was low, as it always was in the fall, crystalline and dappled with leaf shadows. On the slab of rock, Ben lay full-length, trailing one finger in the cold, clear water.

"Gary, shot and killed," he thought, as the dogs surrounded him and flopped down on the big flat rock to be near him. "It's going to take me a while to realize that Gary is gone, that he won't be coming, because I had planned so many things for us to do. Can he really be dead?" Ben's breath caught in his throat and he drew Bear close to his side. "I thought we'd carve a few of the pumpkins on Halloween and tell ghost stories like we have always done," he thought. "And Gary would sit for me so I could draw him, if I could get him to hold still. We would do marshmallows in the fireplace. Gramps got a bunch of marshmallows. He said they would keep next to forever. We'd take that big toboggan out of the barn, the one Gramps got for hauling things in the winter, and try it out on the hill down from the Hand, once the snow was deep enough. We'd—" Ben's throat closed. He worked his fingers into the thick black fur on Bear's neck until he felt the warmth of the skin beneath, and Bear turned to lick his arm.

The shallow water raced over a lip of smooth granite and broke into silver ripples a foot below where he lay, over and over. An amber-bodied dragonfly lit on a rock close by, and an oval snail, darkly shining as a bead of tar, glided slowly down a submerged stick an inch below the water's surface. Close to the stick, a tiny trout fingerling held its place in the current, transparent fins beating. "Things change," Ben said to Bear. "And if I am truly honest with myself, I *thought*, I figured, I *knew* that Gary wasn't going to come, that all these things I hoped we'd do were just--what? Castles in the air, I guess. Dust. Dreams."

Bear watched Ben's face. The other dogs had fallen asleep on the shady rock, and Ben moved to sit, his back against an aspen that crowded nearby. The water below rippled around the rocks the way it had always done. "But," Ben said aloud after several minutes had passed. "But now at least I know that Gary *was* coming. He *really was* coming after all." Ben pulled Bear closer. "And we would have done—all those things together. And more."

He sat a long time with Bear awake beside him and watched the golden aspen leaves flutter and sway as the shadows lengthened in the meadow grass. He saw occasional bright leaves float by on the rushing water: willow leaves long and pale and narrow, golden aspen leaves round and vivid and spotted here and there with chocolate brown, and once a ragged leaf of wild geranium, still green but rimmed with deep scarlet. This was the Place he had loved for so long, and it was still a good place, his place. But the Place felt different now.

"Time to go back," he said at last. "Come on, lazy dogs!" The Shelties knew about go-back time, and they ran ahead with Smoke trailing, galloping through the long, narrow aspen grove all the way back to the wide meadow.

Smoke followed the Shelties tentatively as they frolicked and rolled in the brittle grasses and sedge. Ben thought he would give them a few minutes to get down to doing their business before going in, so he wandered over to the waterwheel and leaned against its concrete support to watch them playing. "It doesn't take much to show a dog a good time," he thought with a smile.

The Shelties were his family now, the last three remaining of Gramps' breeding and showing line, Spiderweb Shelties, famous for their intelligence, good structure, and tireless, correct gait. "You'd never know," Ben thought, "that Bear is Grand Champion Spiderweb Infinity and Moonie is Champion Spiderweb Silverdust. Molly would have been a champion, too, if things hadn't fallen apart: Spiderweb Dark Lady of the Sonnets. And I will continue Spiderweb someday," he said, "whatever it takes."

A raft of narrow clouds barred the sky just above the hills and blocked the rays from the descending sun. The dogs took no notice when the shadow swept across the grasses, but Ben felt as if a great hand had wiped the joy from the meadow. "Gary is dead," Ben said aloud, very softly. "My one friend, my only friend." He said aloud what he had been trying not to think all afternoon. "I couldn't get him to believe me, not until it was too late for him to get away, and it got him killed."

He stared into the clear, cold water spilling and spilling from the wooden wheel. "This morning I was all excited about going to look for Gary between here and Hailey," Ben whispered. "I never would have found him, not in a million years, because I would have searched along the roads. And maybe, *probably* I would have been caught by the soldiers in the white Humvees. I am such an idiot. How many thousand times did Gramps tell me to think outside the box? But I guess it doesn't matter where I would have looked for him; this morning Gary was already dead."

On the ridge to the east, the blunt granite columns of the Hand thrust into the sky, and Ben remembered how he had felt this morning when he'd climbed there and had seen Artie and Mothy on the road downcanyon, when he had thought that Artie was Gary. It had been such a punch to the gut when Artie had told him that Gary was dead. He still had a difficult time wrapping his head around that. But he'd known Artie for years. Artie had no reason to lie about Gary, and it wouldn't be like Artie to lie, anyway. And the dried blood on those familiar dogtags, the wallet . . .

He clenched his fists. Without Artie, he'd never have known that Gary was gone. How long would he have searched for Gary? The real name of that question was "How deep was the friendship?" And he knew, had to admit that Gary had been letting go, letting go of their friendship, until last night, until he began running so desperately to get to the Place after all. So how deep *was* the friendship? "On my side, the friendship was still as deep as it had ever been," Ben thought. "I'd have searched for him until the snows came, and then I'd have searched for him in the spring, years even, until I found him."

He held his head in both hands, fingers gripping his hair, and spoke softly into the sound of water falling from the wheel. "I couldn't get him to come here while it was still safe to get away. Didn't I try hard enough? Did I not try hard enough because I didn't want to look stupid? Was Gary not convinced because I didn't believe Gramps a hundred percent myself and Gary could sense that? Or *did* I believe Gramps a hundred percent, so that made it seem too weird to Gary, until he saw things falling apart? *God.*" The pain of it burned. Ben took some deep breaths. He needed to talk to Gramps, that was what he needed.

"Didn't try hard enough," Ben said aloud, pushing away from the waterwheel. In his heart, he knew it was true. Even as he had been trying to persuade Gary to come, hadn't Ben been just a little cocky, feeling that he was in on an important secret that Gary didn't share? Ben felt warmth creeping up his neck, the warmth of guilt. *Too late, too late.* "Got to make sure that doesn't happen again. Only thing I can do, now."

"Well, Gramps," Ben said more strongly, feeling like a fool. The dogs stopped their play and turned to look him. "Well, Gramps, I didn't get Gary here, but somehow I got Mothy and Artie instead. I'll take care of them. That's what you would do. That's what you always said the Place was for."

The sun was sinking in the west, and dropped below the level of the clouds. A wash of fallow gold fanned across the meadow, turning the willow leaves to chips of light and the grass to golden wires. After a few minutes, the dogs finished their business and came one by one to lie in the tall grass at Ben's feet.

He saw movement to the east, and turned his head slowly, knowing what he would be likely to see. A big mule deer buck and three does walked slowly from behind the loafing shed, through a narrow band of sagebrush, and down to the creek about fifty yards from where Ben stood. The deer were screened from the dogs' view by the tall grass. They were deep-bodied and glossy, going into winter in good condition, Ben was happy to see. One doe was quite large, one was medium-sized, and the third doe was noticeably smaller than the others, obviously last spring's fawn.

At the creek, the buck stood motionless for some time. He was a five-pointer, all velvet gone. The tines of his antlers glinted sharp and bright in the sun's last light. Then he dipped his head and drank, along with the two smaller does. The large doe stood behind the others and waited until the others had drunk their fill. Only then did she step forward and lower her head.

When at last she lifted it, droplets of shining gold fell from her graying muzzle into the grass, and she seemed to look straight into Ben's eyes. "But the best thing, the *only* thing that matters, is what Artie said," Ben told himself. For a fleeting moment he could see Gary's thin cheeks, his bright blue eyes in the long face, the one-of-a-kind flaming hair. "Gary wanted me to know that I was still his friend. He was sorry he had pulled back from our friendship and wanted me to know that he was still my best friend. Damn it to hell." Ben blinked back tears. "That's what Gramps used to say," he thought.

"Hello, Jane," he said softly to the doe. "Nice to see you and your family again. That's what Gramps always called you. Jane Doe." The old doe held her pose for a long minute, then lifted herself gracefully and jumped the creek, heading across the far side of the meadow at a brisk trot, followed by her three companions. Before long the four of them had disappeared into the aspen grove upstream. "See you soon," Ben whispered. The golden light was gone from the grass. Sundown.

Far to the east, the first coyotes of the evening began tuning up, with a faint run of yelps and screams up and down the scales. Ben whistled to the dogs and took them back to the house, Smoke in the middle of the bunch now, he noticed, accepted by the Shelties. That was good.

When Ben returned to the kitchen with the dogs, he found Timothy and Artie up and sitting at the kitchen table. Tim was wearing the red plaid throw blanket wrapped around his waist, like an ill-fitting kilt, above pale and spindly legs. He was bristling with outrage. "So whose idea was it to take off my pants?" he demanded as Ben came in through the back door.

"Chill, Mothy," Ben said, letting a wash of cool air and the four dogs into the house. "Just fade back. It was my idea. I didn't want all that mud to fall off in a clean sleeping bag. And you were dead out. You didn't even open your eyes when we moved you to the bedroom."

"Well. . ." Tim said. He stabbed a glance at Artie.

"It's OK," she said mildly. "I'd expect you to do the same for me. Let it go."

"Hey, what's for dinner?" Tim changed the subject. "Got stuff for dinner?"

"I've got a whole canned chicken in the pantry," Ben said. "And carrots. And there's powdered mashed potatoes."

"How about cornstarch, or some flour and oil?" Artie said. "I can make gravy."

"Gravy?" Ben hadn't thought of gravy. He loved gravy, but had no concrete idea of how to make it. Gramps had always done that. Gravy was in a frying pan, and that was *it*; gravy had *appeared* in a frying pan, every time it was needed--just one more thing Gramps had always done for them. This winter Gramps had planned to teach Ben how to cook. "We'll have all winter for that," Gramps had said several times during the past week.

"Uh—we have cornstarch here in the pantry, I think," Ben said, interrupting his own painful thought. He felt his mouth watering, and swallowed. "Gravy would be great."

Ben peeled the carrots, gave the peelings and the ends to the dogs, and got out a saucepan. Artie found the cast-iron frying pan and assembled the things needed to make gravy. As soon as the light outside turned to deep indigo, Ben lit a fire in the stove, refilled the oil in the oil lamp, and lit it as well.

Twenty minutes later, the carrots were bubbling away, Artie was whisking potato flakes into a small saucepan of steaming water, the coffeepot was on, and Artie had chicken in gravy simmering in the frying pan, from which rose an achingly familiar aroma. *Gramps had made chicken gravy.* Ben got out the plates, cups, and silver, laid the table, and fed the dogs their kibble.

Ben sat at the table and watched as Artie filled their plates, then set the galvanized tin washtub on the stove and used a pot to half-fill it with water from the tap. It was odd, being waited on, but it felt warm.

They dug in. "This is great," Tim mumbled, his mouth full. "Real food. I'm absolutely starved."

Artie met Ben's eyes over Tim's head, and they both smiled. Ben held his breath for a moment. This felt extraordinary but oddly, almost normal: three friends having dinner together. His eyes filled suddenly and he looked down at his plate: carrots on the side, and chicken on top of mashed potatoes, all smothered in rich, hot gravy with salt and pepper in it. When was the last time he'd had a meal with friends, with more than just Gary (and Gramps)? Fourth grade? Fifth? Ben lifted a forkful of chicken, dripping with gravy. Would Artie and Timothy be his friends?

"Service with a smirk from the slaves to your mouth, Tim," Artie was saying with a wink at Timothy. "Tomorrow night, you can cook."

Tim looked at Artie, something like mild panic on his face. "Cook? Me? I can't cook. At all. Mom cooked, everything. Only thing I can cook in is a microwave. You know: Stouffer's. Di Giorno. Tombstone. Hot Pockets. Eggo. Marie Callender pot pies. Popcorn. Punch the buttons to what it says on the package. And I mean, this isn't even a real stove. This is a *wood* stove. *Wood*."

"Looks like a real stove to me," Artie said, forking a chunk of carrot, which Ben had already found blissfully tender and succulent. He saw her shut her eyes for a moment of what looked like sheer enjoyment. "You can learn, Tim. And anybody can help, and wash dishes," she added.

"Urgh," Tim said, again with his mouth full. Artie rolled her eyes.

"Normal; they sound almost normal," Ben thought. "Almost. This might be a good time for the rules." Ben got up for a moment and took down a single sheet of paper that had been tacked to the wall between the two kitchen windows. He laid it on the table, smoothing it with one hand. "I feel kind of funny bringing these up," he began, "but this is Gramps' Place, and these are his rules. We've always kept the Gramps Rules at the Place."

Tim and Artie bent their heads over the paper and Ben watched them read the rules silently.

"1. Never have the dogs outside when it's dark unless you stand right with them, because of the coyotes.
"2. Don't put paper or anything but human waste down the privy hole. Put everything else, including toilet paper, in a covered bucket and bury or burn the contents when full. If you burn this stuff, bury the ashes. Don't bury this stuff in the meadow. Dig on a hill and put rocks on top so the coyotes won't dig it up.
"3. Keep the Place clean and tidy.
"4. Never have a fire in the stove or anywhere else unless it is dark.
"5. Don't waste resources. Re-use, recycle, and use only what is needed.
"6. Never take off without telling someone where you are going and when you will be back.
"7. Don't tell anyone the location of the Place. Ever.
"8. Keep the Place in good repair. Fix what you break; mend things as needed.
"9. Do your share of the work, and more.

"10. Don't use foul language.

"11. Give everyone respect and privacy.

"12. Don't pollute the creek.

"13. Leave the wildlife alone."

After a minute or two, Tim raised his head. "That's pretty straightforward," he said. "But why no foul language? I mean, your gramps was a guy. He'd been around the block a few times."

"Sexist," Artie put in.

"Gramps said he heard enough verbal garbage while he was in Viet Nam to last him a lifetime," Ben replied. He found that he didn't want the Gramps rules to change; that was part of being Frank Elliott's grandson and being at the Place. "That's Gramps, the way he—was."

"OK," said Artie. "No problem."

"No problem," echoed Tim. He took a deep breath. "Do you think they'll come for us?" The question hung in the air for a long moment.

"Who?" Ben countered, finally. But he knew.

"The soldiers in the whitish uniforms. The guys with the white buses and the white Humvees. The guys who killed Gary. *You* know," said Tim. "Where's your TV? This stuff will be on TV."

"There isn't a TV here," Ben said flatly, seeing at once the shock and dismay in Tim's eyes. "There's no electricity at the Place. The only thing I have like that is a hand-crank emergency radio, and the National Emergency Channel has been repeating a two-sentence message that sunspot activity has knocked out most communications. That's the only channel I can get now." He added with a wry smile, "We're all supposed to stay home and not panic until the sunspots are over, or something like that." He shook his head. "I don't believe that's what happened. But I don't know anything about soldiers or white buses." He put both elbows on the table and leaned on them.

"What *do* you know, Ben?" asked Artie, and her words came softly. "Your gramps must have had some idea of what was going to happen. This place is proof of that. And you yourself got out of town just in time, just barely in time. You weren't in school for half of last week. You knew something was up. You have to know more than we do."

Ben sighed. He did know more; it didn't make sense to hold it back now. "OK. I'll tell you what I know, but it's not as much as you might think," he said, getting up to pour himself a second cup of coffee. "I wasn't in school on Thursday and Friday because I was in Twin Falls buying stuff for the Place and hauling it out here. The last stuff. Gramps told me that Friday at four was our deadline to get out of Hailey, and everything, including us, had to be here before dark on Friday night. Gramps said he didn't have enough energy to go to Twin and do the last buying with me, so I drove the pickup down to Twin and spent all the money by myself. It was Gramps's whole savings, what was left of it, anyway--almost fifty thousand dollars, and I spent it all in two days."

"Wow," said Tim. "That must have been fun."

"I guess it was fun, in a way," Ben said, considering, "but it was work. I was supposed to get it all spent and most of the new stuff stashed here by Friday afternoon. Then I was supposed to pick up Gramps, the dogs, and a few last things from the house, so we could be out of Hailey before dark on Friday." Here Ben paused and steadied his breathing. "But when I got back from Twin Friday afternoon, Gramps was . . ."

Ben decided the only way to tell it was to let it come out in a rush. "He was sitting in his favorite chair and he was dead. I thought he'd had a heart attack, but—now I don't know. What if it was the water, like with your families?" Ben took a sip of coffee. "Gramps knew something was bad wrong with him all of a sudden, because he wrote me a note not to call anybody if he was dead by the time I got home. His note said to leave instantly and come here. So I took his suitcases and my things that were sitting there already packed, filled up a couple of pillowcases with some food and stuff, got the dogs and the shotgun, and took off. I hated leaving him." He looked at Tim over the rim of his coffee mug. "And I didn't know for sure until you called me that same night if I had escaped a bad scene, or if I was an idiot running from nothing."

"I hated leaving my mom there, too," Tim said quietly, his fingers twisting the fringe of the red wool throw. "At the time I didn't consider at all, I ran--but I hate to think of her still there in the kitchen. I'm trying not to think about it. She told me once she wanted to be cremated, but that was supposed to be a long time in the future. It's not right for her to be just, just left there to—" His face began to crumple.

"When I was hiding close to the river on Sunday night," Artie interrupted, "someone was going around setting houses on fire. There was a huge fire glow over Hailey all night, just like the glow from the Beaver Creek fire that time, remember? Maybe your mom got that one wish, after all."

"Maybe. It's not a very good thought, but it's a better thought than her just lying there--sitting there, I mean. But, finish telling us what you know, Ben," Tim said.

"Here goes," said Ben. He let out a long breath. "I know Gramps didn't tell me everything, but here's the gist of it, and it goes back a good while." He drank coffee and held the mug in both hands. "When Gramps was young, he came out of Viet Nam with four good buddies: Simon, Beezer, Cuda, and Rob."

"'Cuda' is an odd name for a guy," Tim put in.

"*Barra*cuda, they called him," Ben said. "His name is really Mario Cipriano, and he's from New Jersey. The four of them kept in touch through the years. Cuda stayed in the Army and ended up being a general, so he knew things. These last few years, he's been in Washington, D.C. He's retired now and is a consultant for the Army, whatever that means. And Beezer worked for the airlines, got to be an executive, and he knew things. He's in Houston, or was. And Simon is from California. He got together with Phil later on. Simon and Phil work—worked—for a TV station in San Francisco doing some kind of important stuff, so they knew things. And Rob lived in Montana and ran his family's ranch, and he married Lucy, and she had her special info, so they knew things. When I was just a kid, Rob and Lucy called a meeting of the old buddies, a reunion, and they had it here at the Place. I think the reunion was actually Lucy's idea. All of them came, Simon and Phil, too. And they got to talking and they put some things together. Dr. Lucy was working on a government grant. She found out that some big geology disaster was very close."

"Dr. Lucy?" Tim interrupted. "She's a doctor? And what special info?"

"She's a geologist, not a medical doctor. She's at Montana School of Mines. A professor. OK," Ben picked up the thread of his story. "And Cuda knew that the Pentagon was worried about this geology disaster that was coming, that Lucy had been studying for years. And that the economy was going toes up. Gramps saw that one, too. And Beezer had seen some document that put all the planes in the country under government control if a big disaster happened; that's common knowledge now, but it wasn't back then. So they set themselves to look for more information on what was coming, and to share it. After that, they met every two years or so, and a couple of the meetings were here at the Place. Gramps said that every time she came here, Lucy spent a lot of her time walking all around taking photos and drawing maps of the rock formations, collecting GPS points, and that sort of thing."

Restless, Ben got up to tack the Gramps Rules paper back onto the kitchen wall. "And sometime along the way, Simon and

Phil said that they had intercepted some kind of coded TV transmission, but they couldn't break the code. But the transmission had a map with it, and they downloaded the map image and sent it to the other buddies. Dr. Lucy understood the map, she said. But by that time her husband Rob was really sick, and not too long after that Rob died, and Gramps and Cuda and Beezer, and Simon and Phil-- the buddies went to Rob's funeral in Montana. That was three years ago.

"No," Ben said in response to Tim's sharp glance, "no, I didn't get to go. I had to stay in Hailey with Uncle George and Aunt Cora while Gramps was gone. But—they had another meeting later in California and got some plans going. Dr. Lucy said that she wasn't 100% sure, but she thought the Place would be safe. She studies volcanoes, so you can guess what she thinks is going to happen. She worked out some safe areas for the others, too. And they all met here another time, two years ago. The plan was for everybody to work on their Places and get ready for everything to fall apart, and everybody was to stay in touch until then, and when the time came, they would all bug out to their Places, and wait until things were stable to make contact again. Gramps said that could take years."

"But—what about the soldiers, and the poisoned water and the white buses?" Artie said. "What about shooting people?"

"I don't know anything about that," Ben said. "At all. Gramps didn't tell me much about what he thought the government was going to do. And I really don't know if he actually knew much about that, just that he didn't trust them." He took a gulp of cooling coffee. "I wish now that I had asked more questions. I just know that he took it very seriously that we should be out of the way. Hidden in plain sight, he would say. Under the radar." Ben thought for a moment.

"Just a few days ago, Gramps did say that Cuda had seen some plans for the 'population to be consolidated,' as he put it. That guys who weren't in some important industry were 'excess.' They could be put to work in more populated areas, some of them. Or 'it would be easier to feed and house them if they were consolidated,' is the way Gramps told me that Cuda had said it."

"That might very well be Hailey, Ketchum, and Bellevue," Tim said. "Excess. There aren't any real industries, not good-sized ones. Recreation—tourist stuff--is the big business here, but it isn't exactly an industry that produces anything, at least not at our end."

"One more thing," Ben said. "Dr. Lucy is coming here." Tim and Artie turned to him in surprise. "Yes. She's driving a pickup and pulling a travel trailer. She was supposed to get here Saturday night. But she doesn't answer her phone. I'm worried about her. I don't know her all that well, but Gramps trusted her."

"And she's sure to know more about what's happening than we do," added Artie. "I hope she makes it. Do you have enough food here for all of us?"

"Gramps's goal was enough food for 20 people for 20 years," Ben said. "I don't know if there's that much here or how long it will stay good, but there's a bunch, for sure. We'll be fine over the winter." *And Gramps and Gary aren't coming,* his brain said silently.

"Is anyone else coming?" Tim asked.

"Not that I know of," Ben said, thinking about the map he'd sent from Shoshone. He hesitated, but decided to come clean. "I sent a map to Mrs. Phillips, but I don't know if she got it before things in Hailey fell apart. Gramps invited my Uncle George and Aunt Cora, and my cousin Neil. This was back last year sometime. They thought Gramps was nuts and turned down the offer. Made him feel terrible about it, too. And no, even during all the years he's owned it, he never told them where the Place actually is, so they won't be coming. But—" Ben paused so he could get it just right. "But, Gramps said that others, other people, were bound to show up at some point, or that we would run into them

if we left the Place to do some recon. And if they weren't dangerous, and if there weren't too many, we would take them in. So I
guess that still goes."

"As long as they are real people and not the guys who seem to
be the enemy," Artie said into the drawn-out silence. Ben stared
at her for a moment. Artie wasn't—had never been--stupid.

Tim got up and took his mug to the sink. "Look, Artie, the water
in the washtub is starting to steam," he observed. "You might say
that I'm fairly anxious to get my pants back."

"I'm doing it for you just this once," Artie said, "because I
want to see how it works. But after this, you're on your own."
Artie stuffed Tim's jeans, t-shirt, and socks into the Rollowash,
and using a saucepan, added hot water from the washtub on
the stove and a measure of soap powder from a jar in the pantry. She got down on her knees and rolled the thing on the
wooden floor for a while, repeating twice with clean, cold water.
She did a second load consisting of her own sourly wet clothing that she had taken off at her grandparents' house. By the
time the washed things had been taken outside onto the porch
and wrung over the grass, then draped across chair backs in the
kitchen near the stove, Artie felt worn out. Nevertheless, it was
comforting to know that it was going to be possible to keep their
clothing clean. But she certainly wasn't going to do Tim's washing from now on.

Tim, however, hadn't let go of the evening's discussion.
"But Ben, if someone hostile does come after us—do you have
weapons?"

"Sure," he said. "Here, I'll show you." Ben took up the oil
lamp and they followed him into the smaller of the two bedrooms. Ben opened the closet door to reveal a large black gun

safe. "In here." He handed the lamp to Tim and twirled the dial on the door, then grabbed the handle and pulled the thick door open. "It's not an arsenal or anything--mainly our family guns and some ammo for them."

Tim bent forward and held the lamp so they could see inside the safe, where rifle and shotgun barrels gleamed darkly, and columns of small ammunition boxes were stacked between them. The clean scent of gun oil filled the room. "Can you shoot, Ben?"

"Sure," Ben replied. "You?"

"Nope. Mom wouldn't have a gun around."

"How about you, Artie?"

"Yes. I'm not super good or anything, though," she said.

"OK," Ben commented. "No big, Tim. I can teach you," he said, preparing to swing the door shut.

"Wait!" Artie said. "Isn't that a photo album on the top shelf?"

"Yes. Two of them, in fact. I put them up there with the handguns."

She went on, "I brought my scrapbook. Could it go in here, too? To be safe?"

"Sure," Ben said again.

Artie ran to extricate the scrapbook from her pack, unwrapping it from its black plastic cocoon. "Here." She held it out. "I'm glad I have some pictures of my family."

Tim said, "Wish I had a photo of Mom."

"Oh, Tim, I'm so sorry," Artie began, and then a sudden thought struck her. "I have a picture of your mother! It's here in my scrapbook. Remember the fifth grade, when you had to go to the other 5th grade class because they wouldn't let you have your own mom as your teacher? That was the only year you and I were in different classes. Well, I was in her class and I have the class picture." She opened the scrapbook, which was a little crunched at the corners from being inside her pack for so many miles. She turned a few pages. "See?"

And there in a glossy, yellowing five by seven print were four rows of children seated on bleachers. Artie was on the bottom row in pigtails and geometrically correct bangs, wearing her then-favorite Triceratops t shirt, next to Rosa, whose tanned ankles and feet showed trim below her red capris and through her white sandals—the wheelchair was still a year in the future. At the very top on the right sat Ben in a plaid flannel shirt, looking off-camera to some far place none of them could see. And leaning against Ben was Gary, with his stand-up red hair and goofy grin, arms crossed on his chest, mugging for the camera, with his tongue licking at one side of his mouth. Standing on the left, straight and slim, was Mrs. Rich, Mrs. Teresa Rich, in a simple maroon skirt topped by a cream-colored blouse with ruffles at the neck and wrists, wearing sensible black shoes. Artie held her breath. Inside the photo everything looked so safe, so—ordinary.

Tim leaned forward. "Sure enough," he said, barely audible, tracing the bottom edge of the photograph with a finger. "That's great." He closed the scrapbook with care and handed it to Ben.

Ben placed Artie's scrapbook on the top shelf with Gramps' two albums and swung the thick door shut. He twirled the dial. "The salesman at Cabela's wanted to sell Gramps one of the digital gun safes, you know, with the keypad, but Gramps said no, he liked the dial. And then they wanted to deliver it, but Gramps wouldn't allow that, either. He went and picked it up in a rental trailer the last time all the buddies were here. They had to take out part of this wall on the west side of the house to get it in," Ben continued, pointing. "And they used rollers to move it. Gramps and I could never have gotten it in here by ourselves."

"I like the gun safe," Artie said, feeling the cool, smooth enamel of the door with one hand. "Even after we are gone, if the house is only sticks and ashes, the pictures of our families will be here in the gun safe. Maybe some archaeologists will come find them and wonder what happened to the world."

"How would they know?" Timothy retorted. "The pictures in the albums just show normal things happening. Everything would look normal."

"Oh, I'm going to write about it," Artie said with conviction. "There should be a record."

Tim fell back onto the nearest bed and looked up at the ceiling, an expanse of wide boards painted white. "All the kids in our school," he said. "What if we are the only ones left? What if all of them are dead now? Carl Myers, John Lopez, and Andy and Shandy Johnson, and Ridge Lafferty and Millie Salmon and Kelsey Joiner and Rosa--" Tim broke off suddenly and looked down.

"Gary told me that people were being rounded up and put on the white buses," Artie said. She felt miserable thinking about it. "You saw that, too, Tim. Gary said that there was a white bus on Rosa's street. He begged me not to go back to Hailey, and I felt that he was right. And I saw for myself that somebody was setting fire to the houses. The whole sky above Hailey was lit up with fire on Sunday night." She hugged her own ribcage and thought of Rosa; a formless blackness filled her mind where once there had been the image of Rosa's shining dark hair and sunny smile. Rosa couldn't be dead. Could she?

Ben looked thoughtful. "I left town Friday late in the afternoon. I drove down Main Street on my way out of town, and everything was as normal as pie. Apple-pie normal, Gramps used to say. I saw the school bus with the football team and cheerleaders turn south just ahead of me, on their way to the game in Filer. Wonder what happened to them."

"Who knows?" Artie said almost in a whisper. "While I was hiding in the culvert Saturday night, a bunch of vehicles went over me. In the dark, in the rain. They came from the south, though, and Gary said that the white Humvees and buses he saw came from the south and then drove north out of Hailey, after the people were loaded in. So who knows?"

"Doesn't make sense that they would send buses for people if they were going to kill them," Ben said. He shook his head. "I never heard Gramps say anything about buses or soldiers in white Humvees."

"But a bunch of people were already dead because of the water," Artie protested. She couldn't figure out why the water had been poisoned.

"Fewer buses needed," Tim commented.

Ben shook his head in silence.

"What if everyone else has died?" Artie said slowly. "What if the three of us are the only ones left alive?" Ben felt a sudden shiver down his spine.

CHAPTER 14

NIGHT AND DAYS

Outside, the coyotes screamed. They were close, and Artie found herself shivering, though the house was actually too warm for comfort: the kitchen stove's fire had been built up for a long time to keep the water hot for her clothes-washing effort.

"I'm tired, "Ben said abruptly. "Let's turn in. Leave the bedroom doors open so the heat can circulate. It's hot in here now, but it will cool off before morning."

Holding the lamp, he showed Artie to her room and from his lamp lit a smaller lamp on the dresser there for her. Once he had gone, she unzipped the sleeping bag this time, shucked off her jeans, and climbed in. It was cooler in this bedroom, farther from the wood stove. She had found a second pillow in the narrow closet and a flannel pillowcase in a drawer of the dresser. The sleeping bag was brand-new, and the soft flannel lining felt delicious on her bare legs and smelled fresh and clean. She blew out her lamp.

"This oil lamp is fairly dim," she heard Tim saying in the next room. "Don't you have any battery lanterns?"

"Yes," Ben answered. "There's a bunch of LED lamps somewhere. I just have to find them. But you know that batteries don't last forever."

"I know," Tim said. "But either does oil. Still . . ."

A few moments later the faint glow from the lamp in the other bedroom went out and she heard settling noises as the boys got into their bags. Artie lowered her head onto the sweet-smelling pillows and hoped she could sleep. "Even if I can't sleep, it's better than the night in the logjam," she thought, "and better than last night out in the sage. So much better."

After all the grief, worry, and confusion of the past two days, it was difficult to believe that she was full of warm food in a soft, clean bed. And at Ben's place. *Ben's.* Of all people in the world, she had found *Ben*, thanks to Gary and the map. "Life is stranger than strange," she thought. "And last night at this time I was sitting in the dirt next to my fire hoping that Mothy was going to wake up, hoping that I could find this place, and hoping that if I did, I could stay." She squeezed her eyes shut and tried not to think of her comfortable, familiar bedroom at home, the place she had once thought the safest place in all the world.

A new chorus of coyote screams brought Artie bolt upright; the coyotes sounded like they were gathered right under her window. Then she saw a faint blur of movement near her bed and nearly cried out, but at the last second realized that it was one of the Shelties. The dog jumped on the bed, turned around, and settled at Artie's side. Another series of cries came through the windowpane, and the Sheltie lifted its head. By the faint starshine Artie could just make out that her companion was the gray female, Moonie. "Good girl," she said in a whisper. "The coyotes are a little too close for comfort, aren't they? No wonder Ben's Gramps said we can't have you dogs outside after dark unless we are right with you."

Artie eased herself into the sleeping bag once more and cradled Moonie's head against her shoulder. The dog's warmth and gentle breathing were comforting. She had always wanted a dog, but Dad and Turner were, *had been*, allergic. Artie found herself thinking again of her little brother dead on the kitchen floor, of her mother's hair jeweled with sparkling fragments of glass, and of those dry, cloudy eyes. And into her mind came her father's feet, looking so strange and vulnerable as he lay rigid on the bathroom floor. Tears pricked her eyes now that no one could see her, and she cuddled Moonie closer. "When I find out who poisoned the water," she thought, a thread of steel, "I will hunt them down. And I will write it for everyone to know. Everyone." She lay still in the dark for a long time while the snaps and crackles of wood in the stove became less and less frequent. But sleep would not come.

Suddenly, a harsh scream split the air.

Terrified, Artie heard Moonie hit the floor with a thump. She stood up in the darkness and frantically pulled on her jeans, wondering what she could use as a weapon. Where was her knife? She felt stupid that she hadn't taken the knife out of her pack and put it on the nightstand. Then she heard Ben's voice.

"It's all right. Everything is all right. Tim had a nightmare."

Artie stood in her doorframe, shaking. The coyotes under the window shrieked and howled. "That does it," she said aloud. Louder, she continued, "Can I come in there?"

Ben's voice reached her in the dark after a long moment. "OK," he said. "Sure."

Artie grabbed the sleeping bag and pillow from her bed and made her way to the other bedroom. Ben had lit the oil lamp again, and she shoved the night stand to the foot of Ben's bed, laid the sleeping bag on the floor between the beds, and climbed in, pulling the bag up around her shoulders and sitting up, shoving the pillow behind her back as she leaned against the wall at the head of the beds, between Tim's bed and the nightstand. "Thanks," she said. "Maybe after a while I'll be able to sleep."

"No worries." Ben blew out the lamp.

This was better. Moonie curled up near her feet. Somehow, Artie felt calmer, listening to the quiet breathing of the dogs and the boys nearby. She slumped back against the wall, telling herself to relax.

Then she heard Timothy's breathing turn irregular, gulping, and felt his hand come down to touch her shoulder. "We have all lost our families," she thought, and half unwilling, she took his small hand in one of hers. His hand was cool and soft. She felt the slender fingers tighten around her own.

Suddenly she heard the smooth swish of fabric on the other bed, and Ben's voice came softly. "Nothing bad," he said. "I don't mean anything bad." Still inside his sleeping bag, he slid from his bed and came to rest next to her in the narrow space between the beds. Ben's head was in her lap, on top of her sleeping bag. One of his arms stole half around her waist. Stunned, she froze.

Ben took her free hand and brought it to his face, and she felt the slight roughness of his cheek--and to her surprise, she felt tears there. Astonished, she thought, "He isn't ashamed for me to know he is crying."

Artie felt emotions she couldn't name wash through her. "I have loved Ben as long as I can remember," she thought, cupping his cheek. "But this is different." Though the boys couldn't see her face, she blinked back hot tears and controlled her breathing. "They need me to be the strong one," she thought, amazed. She longed to throw herself down as well, and cry herself to sleep. But tonight, she knew, that would not do. "I can be strong. I can be strong," she told herself.

Outside, the coyotes shrieked and shrieked in the dark. Eventually a wind came from nowhere and took their cries away, fading, far down the gulch. Artie sat motionless in the blackness for so long that she felt cramped, but she wouldn't move and break the spell.

After a long time, Tim released her hand, turned over, and began to breathe the deep, measured breaths of sleep. A few minutes later, Ben's arm around her waist went slack, and he, too, fell asleep. The coyotes were silent.

The strong wind rose and moaned around the eaves. "Dark of the moon," Artie thought. Very slowly, the room began to cool, and her legs felt comfortably warm inside the sleeping bag. Ben turned his face and her hand trailed across the back of his neck and came to rest in his hair. "If I go my whole life and have only this night to hold him . . ." she thought.

She held Ben for hours, until the wind had died away once more. Finally she could keep sleep at bay no longer, turned to one side, and went out like the lamp.

⊨⊣ ⊢⊨

Artie rolled out of bed when she heard barking. The windows were still black, but light from the kitchen fell across the bedroom doorway. She heard movement there. She remembered that she was already dressed, and took her sleeping bag into the other bedroom, smoothing it out onto the bed she had vacated so hastily the night before.

In the kitchen, Ben was feeding the fire in the stove, and the dogs were dancing around the table, even Smoke, playing keep-away with a knotted rope.

Timothy was sitting at the table, wearing his newly washed pants. They looked rather stiff, but they did look clean, Artie noted. "What's for breakfast?" he said when he saw her in the doorway, rubbing his hands together.

Artie had wondered if this morning would be awkward, given last night's strange closeness, but it seemed that the boys had decided not to speak of it. Artie stifled her sigh of relief. She wouldn't have known what to say.

"How about bacon and eggs?" Tim continued. Artie could see that the coffee pot was on and already steaming.

"No fridge, no freezer," Ben said. "No bacon, no eggs. Sorry. And no toast. I used the last of the bread I brought from town for those Spamwiches yesterday."

Artie pulled out a chair and sat at the table.

"I don't mean to be ungrateful," Tim said. "But somehow, I don't feel much like having carrots early in the morning."

Artie thought a minute. "Ben, do you have flour and baking powder? Or maybe Bisquick?"

"Yeah," Ben replied slowly. "There is a gallon jar labeled 'Bisquick' in the pantry, and there's more of it out in the barrels. I know Bisquick has directions printed on the package, but there's no package. Gramps put a lot of things into glass jars so that bugs wouldn't get into them." He spread his hands wide, looking uncomfortable. "I don't know how to deal with it."

"I do," said Artie. She was pleased. Here was another thing she could do to earn her keep at the Place. She looked from face to face. Ben's dark hair stuck straight up in back, and his cheeks showed a slight, dark stubble, while Tim's light brown hair flopped down over one eye. His cheeks were as smooth as they had always been. "Pancakes or biscuits?" she added.

"Huh?" Ben looked lost for a moment.

Artie grinned. "Got jam or syrup? Got a griddle—or a baking sheet?"

"Yes," Ben seemed to come to himself. "Sure. All of the above. But no butter."

"Dang. Now, I am completely not sure how to cook this stuff on a wood stove, but I can try. So." She repeated, "Pancakes or biscuits?"

"Biscuits!" Both boys said at once, and Artie laughed.

"We could have Spam in biscuits," Ben said, brightening. "And put jam on some more."

"OK," Artie said, hoping it wouldn't lead to disaster. She had made biscuits many times at home, and even in a Dutch oven nestled in the coals of a campfire, but never in a wood stove. "I'll try. Bisquick, a bowl, a baking sheet, a drinking glass, and some grease—oil or lard, either one. Got that?" Ben nodded. "And a frying pan for the Spam," she continued. "I have no clue how to tell if the oven is the right temperature, but—nothing ventured."

"I can fry Spam," Ben said. "I'll do that. And Tim, pay attention, because believe me, it's going to be your turn to cook at some point. And get the metal dishpan from the pantry. You can fill it with wash water and stick it on the stove."

Silently, Tim obeyed. Ben found Artie what she needed, then took the dogs outside.

Tim picked up the can of Spam on the table, his expression gloomy. "I'm useless," he said.

Artie decided she wasn't having any of that this morning. "Yes, you're just a slug, a little ball of slime, a tool with no purpose," she said, dumping a generous pile of Bisquick into the stainless steel bowl Ben had taken from one of the lower cupboards.

She had a sudden vision of a family camping trip high on the East Fork of the Big Lost River in August, only two months ago. She remembered the crisp, pine-scented air as she had crawled from her sleeping bag into the first light of dawn. Turner, still heavily asleep in his bag four feet away, didn't even stir, nor did her parents, zipped into their green tent nearby. Artie had built up the fire, gone down to the creek for water, grabbed a bowl and the Bisquick, and had made biscuits in the Dutch oven. She'd made coffee as well, and had been taking her first scalding sips while tending the big skillet, turning over the brook trout frying gently in butter, when the others woke up. That had been a good morning and was a good memory still, but it hurt.

Artie clenched her teeth on a smile and poured cold water into the Bisquick, stirring vigorously. "Hurts, hurts," she thought, "with no way to make it stop." She found a red quilted pot holder hanging on the wall and used it to open the oven door. Carefully she stuck in a hand, trying to gauge the heat. "Listen," she said under her breath. "Listen to me, you old black stove. I'm going to make these freaking biscuits, and if you know what's good for you, you had better cooperate."

Artie plunged both hands into the ball of dough and punched it into submission. She dusted a handful of Bisquick onto the table's oilcloth and used the side of the drinking glass to roll out the dough. Having smeared some Crisco onto the baking sheet with her fingers, she proceeded to use the glass to cut out biscuits. "Paper towels," she wailed soundlessly, wiping her fingers on the rag draped over the faucet. "What's it going to be like living without paper towels?" She had made more than two dozen biscuits, she realized, but boys ate a lot, didn't they? And biscuits would keep for several days. Gingerly, she placed the biscuits on the baking sheet. They looked like biscuits; she hoped fervently that they would turn out to *be* biscuits.

Ben and the dogs came back inside, the dogs' wet muzzles showing that they had been down at the creek. "Hey," he said. "Can you guys find the outhouse in the dark? Need to go? I put new paper in it, and there's a bucket with a lid for the used paper."

"Yep," Artie said, wiping her hands on the back of her sweatshirt. "I'll go next." She extricated Grandpa's flashlight from her pack and took off into the cold early morning darkness. "Sitting on the privy hole is going to be something else when it's below zero," she thought, wondering how long she might be living at the Place. She ran back to the house as soon as she could.

Ben was cutting Spam into slices by the time Artie returned, and he slid a lump of Crisco into the frying pan on the stove. She handed the flashlight to Tim and he took himself off.

Artie opened the oven door once more and felt the hot air inside. On the table, the cut-out biscuits, sitting on the baking sheet, had risen and looked puffy, the way they were supposed to look. "I'm going to put these biscuits in, and then it will be ten minutes before I check. Or maybe I had better check after five minutes. I have no idea how hot this oven is."

"Me either," said Ben, sliding the Spam-filled skillet onto a stove lid and standing over it with a spatula.

"It occurs to me that I have no idea how long ten minutes actually is," Artie said suddenly. "Seriously, no idea."

"I do." Ben dived into the living area and came back with the wound-up alarm clock. He pulled out the key on the back and wound it until it was tight.

"Great!" So at five to seven, we'll look," she said, relieved. Maybe the biscuit-cutouts would actually be biscuits.

Tim soon came stamping back into the kitchen. "Brr," he said shortly. "Coffee ready yet?"

"Yes," said Ben. "The mugs are above the sink."

After some hesitation, Tim grabbed three mugs and plunked them onto the table, then poured all three full of coffee. "Used to being waited on," Artie thought, trying not to feel smug. "Well, that will change."

Those first biscuits were an unqualified success, except for the row unlucky enough to be in the back of the oven on the baking sheet. Those were black on the bottom, brown on top, and had the texture of cement. The dogs loved their biscuits, though they took some time to eat. Artie was pleased.

Artie was to remember the next ten days as a dream time, a time to hold in her heart and remember—because after those ten days, the Others came to the Place, and it was not the same, would never be the same.

Ben took Tim and Artie on a long tour of the Place on the morning of Artie's first biscuits: the basement, both bunkers, the woodshed and the dog run, the chicken house, the loafing shed, the barn, the waterwheel, and the tiny spring.

That afternoon, they began cataloguing. Ben had some lists, but they weren't very detailed, particularly regarding the new things he had bought himself. Artie started a map of barrels and other storage containers and shelves, listing their contents. Tim drew columns in a notebook to record all the quantities.

They spent the first of several evenings huddled around the table over lists, swilling coffee, and at last coming up with another list, a list of those things they would want in or close to the house during the fast-approaching winter.

Most of the items in the old bunker could stay there for the winter, they decided, since Ben told Artie and Tim that the bunkers would not freeze. Artie realized that during the winter they would be shoveling a path from the house to the old bunker to get at the fresh food stored there. But things like dog food, flour, Crisco, aspirin, soap, rice, oatmeal, candles, blankets, snow shovels, and toilet paper they shuffled about and moved closer to the house, while other items, including screen, certain tools, fenceposts, sheets of plastic, nails, glass jars, and chicken wire were moved to less-accessible locations. Artie was relieved to find several barrels labeled "Female Supplies," and moved one of these barrels to the front row in the chicken house. "Frank Elliott was a saint," she told herself silently. "I will never think of him as Crazy Frank again."

That evening, after a dinner of canned chunky beef soup and crackers, Artie wondered where she should go to sleep. She had been wondering all day, or trying not to wonder. The night before had been strange and almost eerie, a space out of time, a strange dream of love and loss and darkness. She wondered if she should put her sleeping bag back in the boys' bedroom, leave it where it was—or what. She dithered at tidying the kitchen and tried not to think of it, but finally the moment came when Ben carried the oil lamp from the kitchen into the bedroom. The small flame wavered and held as Artie stood in the doorway.

The nightstand had been moved to one side and the two beds pushed together. Three sleeping bags, spread out carefully and zipped closed, lay side by side, Artie's dark-red one in the middle. She turned to Ben, couldn't help herself, was about to say something, but she had no idea what to say.

"Nothing bad," he said, reaching past her to place the lamp on the nightstand.

"Family," said Tim, so softly that she wondered if she had heard him at all.

And that's the way it was at the Place until the Others came; three in a row, and, randomly positioned on and around them, four dogs. Sometimes in the coyote-haunted darkness, Tim would sob and put out a hand to touch her shoulder. Sometimes he would cry out in his sleep, startling them all and causing the dogs to reshuffle. Sometimes Artie would sing a little tune to get him back to sleep.

And sometimes she could feel Ben's breath on her arm when he was fast asleep in the long deepness of the October night. He didn't reach out to her again, but she felt comforted in the darkness so close to him. "Damaged goods," she would think every night. "We are damaged goods." Often, when the boys and the dogs were asleep and Artie lay awake listening to their breathing, she wondered if she could have borne losing her family if she had not had Ben and Timothy.

"Nothing bad," Artie told herself at times when she was the only one awake, which happened nearly every night. In the sleeping bag, in the darkness, she would distract herself a hundred ways, trying to avoid thinking of what she wanted and of what she had lost. She wasn't like Tim. Thinking of her lost family had to, *had to* wait until the light of day, so she could stand to remember that they were gone.

⊫+ +⊨

After days at the Place, life began to fall into something of a routine, Artie thought.

Artie had found herself a blank notebook and some pencils, and every afternoon when the boys would settle for an hour or more with either books or a card game, Artie would write in her new journal. She hadn't expected it, but there was much to record.

The days sped by rapidly before the Others came.

One morning, after Ben had climbed to the Hand for a long look down the gulch, they drove the pickup farther up Spear Creek Road to where stands of lodgepole pine grew on the east and north faces of Cat Mountain. Three times that day they heaped the pickup with small deadfall trees and stout fallen branches broken from dead trunks, ferrying them down the mountain and piling the wood near the woodshed for later cutting and splitting.

Then Artie watched Ben park the pickup for the winter, not inside the barn, but inside the new bunker, where he positioned it under the 60s half-pickup above it on the earthen roof. Ben explained to Artie and Tim about ground-imaging radar. They did not explore the new bunker, which was largely empty, but simply drove the pickup into its chill darkness and left it there.

Artie thought of the bunker as a tomb for the pickup; it was depressing. She wondered if she would ever again wake up in the morning excited to be going on a picnic, or on a week's trip to the Oregon beaches, or to Redfish Lake on a camping trip, or simply to Twin Falls to do some shopping.

Ben's and Gramps' cell phones went dead, as dead as Artie's phone had been for days, their batteries exhausted. They placed the phones in a small steel cookie tin in the old bunker. To Artie, it felt almost like a burial. The night that the last phone, Gramps', went dead, Artie lay awake in the dark for a long time, trying to understand how life would be in the future, now that the final link from the Place to the outside world was gone.

Dr. Lucy still had not come. They kept searching and found several LED lanterns and a box of standard batteries, but the solar battery charger eluded them, so the phones stayed silent. The message on the hand-crank radio remained the same.

⇒⟨+ +⟩⇐

Five days after Artie and Tim came to the Place, Artie went out at dawn and found the meadow grasses heavy with frost. She recorded that in her journal.

Spear Creek itself began to freeze, the first ice creeping out from the banks a little more each morning, then gradually forming a shining skin over all but the fast-moving center of the stream. Ben took out the penstock, leaving the box and its pipe high and dry in the meadow for the winter. Tim had the idea of bringing two of Gramps' scavenged wooden pallets down to the stream's edge not far from the house and using their wood to make a platform where they could stand each time they came to break the ice with a shovel and scoop up water in buckets, so the bank there wouldn't become a trampled mess, at least until the soil froze solid.

Artie felt happy to do much of the cooking; it was something she could do for Ben, for letting her stay. But Ben did some cooking, and Timothy was learning. Artie had to smile. *Trying* was a better word for what Tim was doing. All of his biscuits were dog biscuits, and it took two days after Tim's green bean adventure for the house to stop smelling like burned green beans. "I'm hiding

237

the cans of green beans for a while," Ben had said. Neither Artie nor Tim had protested.

One morning Artie saw a bobcat crossing the meadow just upstream from the waterwheel. She watched the deer come to drink nearly every evening, and the coyotes howled every night. Artie found that several cottontail rabbits were living among the big boulders near the east side of the barn, and once she saw a snowshoe hare in the meadow.

Artie took to climbing the east ridge in the late afternoons. She would sit on the Hand singing and writing until cold blue twilight drifted up the gulch and drove her back to the house. She had always gone out to the hills to sing, summer and winter, ever since she could remember. She thought of her family, and sang and sang. And she wrote descriptions of her family, and of Rosa, and of Hailey in general, and of what had happened in Hailey, and of what was happening at the Place every day.

⊶ ⊷

A task that occupied all three of them for nearly a week was Artie's idea.

The idea came to Artie with a warm, honey-dripping mouthful from a specimen of her third and most successful batch of breakfast biscuits, as she looked out the kitchen window into the pre-dawn blackness. "Ben," she said, "what if someone flies over us?'

Ben sighed, then began once more to explain about the ground-imaging radar.

"No, no," Artie said, excited by her sudden idea, "that's not what I mean. The wood on all the buildings is unpainted. It's weathered, and it looks old. But if someone flies over, they will see good gray roofs. All the roofs here are metal, the same color. They are all in perfect condition. I can see them when I'm up at the Hand."

Ben set down his coffee cup. "The roofs are only two years old. Your point being?"

Artie was starting to warm to her idea. "Do you have any paint here, outdoor-type paint? And brushes?"

"Yeeess," he said slowly. "Gramps and I would pick up a gallon here and there when paint was on sale. The cans of paint are stacked by the north wall of the new bunker so they won't freeze."

Artie let her idea burst forth. "You can paint, Ben. You have always been good in art class. So what if the guys who flew over saw buildings with holes in the roofs? You know, black holes? And open rafters, and beams that were falling down? And rust?"

Ben looked at her, silent. Then his lips curved in a slight smile. "You mean paint the roofs to look like they have holes? Paint fallen rafters that look like they're inside? Paint rust and loose boards and light coming in?"

By then Tim was chiming in, "Yes! So their eyes would see an old ramshackle place, just like their ground-imaging radar will. Whoever they are."

"Holy crap," Ben muttered. "Let me think. Let me think. I know we've got white paint, and black, and some brown and some red. Got some brushes. I've never painted anything that big except a wall. But." He was silent for a moment. "I can draw it out on paper first, for each roof. And there's a tall ladder in the barn."

"We could even lean some boards or logs against the walls here and there, to make it look like the walls were falling down," Artie added.

"But when you fly over something, the light reflects off it," Ben said. "Paint is shiny. Even matte paint is fairly shiny."

Artie had a thought that took her back to her geography project in the fourth grade: Little Manolo's house in Saltillo, Mexico, made from a cardboard box and painted tan with sand in the paint so that it looked like adobe. "Have you ever put sand in paint? That gets rid of the shine and makes the paint look rough," she said. "There's lots of sand in the creekbed. We could dig up some sand. We could dry it on a pan on the stove."

"Let's do it!" Ben cried. "I'll get some paper and start making the drawings. We have to do it now, before it gets too cold for the paint to work. I'll start on it right this minute." Then he added soberly, "Gramps would have been thrilled."

And so Artie's Brilliant Idea as Tim called it, took five days to execute--and transformed the Place, aerial view, into a run-down, abandoned, early 20th-Century ranch.

Artie wrote it up in her journal. The house, thanks to a can of black paint and some careful mixing of red and brown, now had a rusty stovepipe with two small holes on one side, and a stovepipe roof plate that was both rusty and bent. Next to it, an irregular "hole" pierced the roof over one bedroom, with "fallen rafters" seen dimly below. The outhouse soon sported a vertical "gap" between the boards of its siding, about a foot wide and three feet long, plus a door that "stayed ajar" permanently. The loafing shed roof was left as it was, the roof being too flimsy for Ben to climb on to paint, but he nailed two pieces of metal roof-ing to one end of its roof and painted below them a square black shadow, so that from the Fingers, it looked like someone had tried to repair the roof a long time in the past, and the patch had come partly undone, revealing a hole beneath it.

The barn got several "holes" near the edges of its roof, and a black "hole" large enough for a horse to walk through, painted into the east wall and supplemented with old, leaning boards. The chicken house had a few logs, gray and weathered, braced onto two sides, as if the building had tried to fall over, plus jag-gedly "broken" windows, a black-painted "missing" door, and yet another hole in the roof.

Those days were busy. Ben painted, Artie cooked and washed up, Tim did fetch and carry, and all three of them would climb to the Hand several times a day to check on the relative realism of each of the effects from the height of the east ridge.

Artie's Brilliant Idea, ABI, or Abbie, as Ben decided to call it for short, made Artie feel good down to her toes. "I belong to the Place now," she wrote in the journal the night they finished Abbie. "This is now my Place, too, a little." After Artie finished writing about Abbie, she slipped Ben's working drawings between the pages. "History," she thought, placing the journal back into the living room bookcase that night. "This is the history of the world after the end."

CHAPTER 15

THE OTHERS

A rtie had begun to lose track of the days. Her last few journal entries had been undated. "Friday," Artie told herself late that afternoon as she sat in the Hand looking down at the Place from the east ridge. A glint of ice gleamed from Spear Creek, and above the squatty willows a kestrel hung in the air, searching for prey in the tall, frost-bent grass of the narrow meadow.

Artie held her journal on her lap and bit at her pencil. She had nearly finished writing for the day. Her fingers stung and were beginning to feel numb. It was getting too cold for outdoor writing. "It's another Friday. I need to put dates in my journal every day, not that it matters right now." She considered. "But it might matter someday, when the journal is history."

Today had been a busy day. "Book Day," Ben had called it, a day when they had searched the barrels of stored books that over the years Ben and Frank Elliott had bought, brought from Hailey, or salvaged for the Place. Ben, Artie, and Tim had spent the day making their choices for winter reading.

Today had been a crisp, sunny day with a light breeze, a perfect autumn day in Spear Creek Gulch: deep blue skies, a cool breeze blowing, dogs rolling in the yellowed grass, and a golden eagle circling very high above the east ridge. After Artie spotted the eagle, she kept a close eye on the dogs.

Ben had brought the garden cart from the barn, and they spent hours book-sorting and book-choosing.

Artie had been delighted to discover several thick books, stuffed with photos, about vegetable gardening. Another that looked promising was *Gathering and Saving Seeds.* Gramps had even acquired a key to identifying Idaho native plants, identical to the one her mother had always used, which she also pounced upon.

In one barrel she found a trilogy tied together with torn strips of frayed and faded red and white gingham fabric, three books by Alexandre Dumas: *Louise de la Valliere, The Viscomte de Bragelonne,* and *The Man in the Iron Mask.* Artie found herself captivated by the delicacy of the illustration that was the frontispiece of the *Louise,* which had been printed in the 1920s. "Well, Dumas wrote *The Three Musketeers,* so it might be fun to read these," she thought, and added them to her pile, along with several slim books of poetry, *The Lord of the Rings* trilogy, *Easy Breadmaking, The Complete Sherlock Holmes, Riders of the Purple Sage* (which sounded very romantic), *Stories and Poems by Edgar Allan Poe, A History of Pioneer Idaho in Pictures,* and a number of mystery paperbacks.

All day in the back of her mind, Artie had thought about school, the school she was missing, the schooling she might possibly never have again, so as well as books to read for pleasure, she chose books to study during the winter, when they would likely be snowbound—geology texts; classics of literature; biographies of significant scientists; several books of natural history, including a field guide to the birds and *Carnivores of the World;* more history, topped with a biography of Alexander the Great; and even an old mathematics textbook printed in the 1960s, which had "Frank Elliott" scrawled on the flyleaf. She hoped she could bring herself to open that one.

Tim and Ben chose dozens of books as well. Artie had seen Ben putting into the garden cart a book on dinosaurs, several art books, two books on volcanoes, some science fiction, *Fish Families of the World, Lad: a Dog, The Ship,* a few westerns; some floppy paperback books of crossword puzzles, and a copy of *King Solomon's Mines*—while Tim piled up an untidy stack of used graphic novels, a battered copy of *Tarzan of the Apes,* several how-to books, and a manual for a generator. Artie had to smile at the picture forming in her mind—technophage Timothy Rich with his nose buried in *Tarzan of the Apes.* That would be delicious.

A garden cart full of books went out to the barrels from the livingroom and bedroom bookcases to make space, and three garden carts full of books came inside from the barrels and re-populated the living room and bedroom bookcases, as well as filling the remaining spaces under the beds, with the choices they had made. "Hunkering down," Tim had commented to Artie and Ben. "That's what we're doing. Getting ready to hunker down. Wonder when it's going to get really cold. Good thing that Gramps got us all winter coats and boots."

"We are all calling Frank Elliott 'Gramps' now," Artie thought. "He seems to belong to all of us." She hoped that Ben's grandfather would have liked that. Ben didn't seem to mind.

October was wearing on. Each night was a little colder, each day a little shorter. Artie had noticed that the Shelties and even Smoke were putting on winter coats. The aspens in the upstream grove had lost nearly all their leaves, and so had the small willows of the meadow.

The waterwheel stood unmoving, sheathed and gleaming in ice from the last water it had carried. Spear Creek was frozen, too frozen now to dip a bucket first thing in the morning without first breaking ice with a shovel. Ben spent at least an hour a day splitting wood and sawing it to length with the big bow saw, and Artie was learning to use the axe and wedges. She had been more successful in breaking smaller branches into lengths sized for the stove. Artie hadn't made much of a dent in the big piles of dead wood they had brought down from the mountain, but at least she hadn't made a dent in herself or anyone else—so far.

Ben and Timothy and Artie were getting along. Artie felt good about that. Sometimes they had small, scratchy disagreements, but these felt more and more like family arguments, and no one had become mean or selfish, nor did anyone seem to hold a grudge. Artie felt comfortable with them.

Artie knew she would always miss her family, but this was so much better than having no one. And in a way, now she had Ben—not in the way she had dreamed, but here he was, in her life every day. "Ben is safe," she thought often. "The important thing is that whatever has happened out there, whatever might someday happen between us, Ben is safe." The thought always made her smile.

The wind pressed the scent of sage against her face; something was different about this evening, but she couldn't put a name to how she felt and why the end of this day seemed strange. She pulled Gram's scarf up around her ears.

On the top of a higher hill two draws to the east, so far away that he was barely visible, a lone coyote trotted downhill through the sage and tall wild rye, gray against gray, intent on some hidden purpose.

Artie watched him and thought of Rosa and of her own grandparents. She wondered where the white buses had gone, who had been taken, what was left of Hailey now, and who, if anyone, still lived there. She imagined furtive, skeletal figures darting about the burned shells of buildings in the dying light, shivering and starving in the snow to come. Would there be wolves?

She pulled up the chain she wore around her neck, held the cooling dogtags against her cheek, and remembered Gary on that last day, the clear blue eyes in his white face, his bloody hand lying in the fallen leaves, and how she had heaped the leaves over his body and walked away. How she had trotted through the river cottonwoods afterward, trying not to cry. *Would there be wolves?*

Artie resettled herself on the gray granite Hand and rearranged Gran's scarf around her ears. She leaned back against one of the Fingers and wrote a few last lines about the day's activities. Though her hands were cold and getting colder, she wanted to to write about the books each of them had chosen for the winter.

Artie looked up, suddenly disturbed by something she couldn't name. The air now felt oddly still, heavy, without a breath of wind. The light was fading fast, the way it did after sundown in October.

The west looked darker than it should, with indigo clouds moving rapidly toward the Place, so low they clipped the summits of the Castle Hills. Artie wondered suddenly if it would snow tonight.

Living in a winter resort area, like everyone she knew, Artie hoped for snow all winter, every winter—hoped it would be early, hoped it would be powdery, hoped it would be deep, hoped it would come often, hoped the snow would last. Good snow on the ski mountains, on the remote heights loved by adventure-skiers, on the ski trails below—that meant money, jobs, security. Some years it snowed before Halloween; some years it waited until after Thanksgiving. It was worrying to everyone when ski-able snow hadn't come by Christmas, even though the ski mountains had snowmaking machines. Artie bit her yellow pencil. What kind of year was this going to be? And what did she want it to be?

What *could* she want now? The old life, *her* old life? That couldn't be recovered, ever, because her family was beyond reach. The new life Artie had been taking day by day; the future was hidden behind a black blanket, invisible.

She looked down the narrow valley, where the frost-killed grass, already yellowed from the usual end-of-summer drought, had turned silvery in the twilight, the round willows darker puffs along the creek. The roofs below, so artfully painted to look old and damaged, darkened with the fading light. She saw an owl take off from the cottonwood on the far side of the barn and skim soundlessly over the meadow on the first hunt of the evening.

Tonight was Ben's turn to cook dinner, so Artie stayed a few more minutes on the ridge. She saw the buck and his three does walk across the lower meadow, trail upstream to the aspens, and pass through the aspen grove and over the west hill out of sight. Somewhere to the south, the coyotes tuned up.

The air was thickening now. Soon Ben would light the lamp and the stove, and the ranch house's windows would glow faintly golden; the stovepipe would puff invisible smoke into the night, and she, Tim, and Ben would be warm in the kitchen with the dogs. She had no idea what Ben was going to cook, but she didn't care. There would be something hot to eat, and coffee with it, a wonder in itself in these strange times. "I have a Place." She said the words aloud, hugged them to herself.

Artie stood and slowly turned in a circle, taking in 360 degrees of the horizon. Time to go down, while the bare, narrow path she had already worn into the hillside was still visible. There would be no moon tonight; the moving clouds were thick over the darkening hills. Soon those clouds would be overhead.

Suddenly she froze, her attention arrested by movement far to the south. "It's a light," she whispered, caught between amazement and fear. "I can see a light down there." After a time, she realized that the light was moving, moving east very slowly. "Oh, my God," she breathed. Her legs felt like concrete; her arms weighed fifty pounds each. "Are we going to be discovered?" She stared at the tiny light, breathing in great gasps. The light went out.

Then Artie was running, bounding down her self-made trail, sprinting toward the house, jumping over rocks, scraping through sage, sliding on a little patch of ice where a tiny spring oozed across her path. She cleared the road and had another look toward the south; nothing.

Artie swung the door back and burst into the kitchen, startling the dogs into barking. "There's someone out there," she said, breathless.

Ben dropped the match he had been holding and stepped on it. "What? What?"

"I was up at the Hand," she said, trying to make herself understood. "I was about to come in and I saw a light way down the road, maybe two or three miles away."

Tim stood up and gripped the back of a chair so tightly that his knuckles turned white. "A car? Was it car lights?"

"No," Artie said. "The light was small, tiny. One light. It was moving, moving east on the hillside. Not fast at all. And then it went out. It went out just about where the road disappears behind the hill downcanyon."

The three of them looked at one another for a long moment without speaking. Then Ben ran to the gun safe and pulled out a heavy handgun and a speed-load cylinder already chinked with six bullets. He rummaged in the closet. "Here." He tossed something puffy at Artie. "Put this on and let's go. Get your flashlight." She struggled into the too-large dark blue parka and turned back the sleeves.

"Tim," Ben was saying as he shrugged into a parka, "Lock the dogs in the bedroom. Blow out the lamp. Bolt the doors from the inside. I've got my headlamp." He put it on, centering the LED module on his forehead. "I'll flash it four times from the road when we come back, so you'll know it's us. No lights inside, and don't light the stove. Keep the dogs quiet. Hang tight and watch."

Tim nodded, his face drained of color.

"Come on, Artie," Ben said, and went out the kitchen door without waiting to see if she was following. Tim leaned forward and blew out the lamp.

⊨═◄╫ ╫►═⊨

Ben shoved the .38 Smith and Wesson revolver into the front pocket of his parka and the speed loader into the pocket on the other side. He zipped his parka to the chin against the rising wind and kept walking, fast, out to Spear Creek Road.

He could hear Artie's steps on the gravelly dirt behind him and hoped she would be able to keep up. *Ohgodohgod,* his mind kept saying. *What if they come to the Place, what if it's those white soldiers and what if they come to the Place? What would Gramps do? What?* With every step, he could feel the gun dragging down his coat on one side.

They reached the roadway, and Ben turned to Artie. "Where? Where did you see it?"

She pointed south. Ben could just see her hand in the gloom. "Down there," she said, "where the shoulder of that ridge comes down to the road, beyond that, from down in that little valley. The light moved east, a little. Then it was gone."

He stopped for a moment and dug the revolver from his pocket, snapped open the cylinder, fished the speed-loader from his other pocket, and loaded the gun.

"What kind of light do you think it was?" he asked. The Smith & Wesson was even heavier now.

She answered at once, with positive emphasis, which he hadn't expected. "I think it was a flashlight. A big flashlight."

They looked at each other in the near-darkness, and Ben said it, what they were both thinking. "People."

He could hear Artie's teeth begin to chatter. "Friend or foe, that's the question," she said.

249

"OK," Ben said, walking again, striding down the road. "We're going to go down the road here and we'll stop now and then to look and listen. Stop me if you see or hear anything, anything at all."

"OK," Artie whispered.

They walked fast, jogging at times, on the pale surface of the granite-sand road, in the deep twilight a ribbon of pearl gray between stands of dark sage. A mile went by, then another, and then Ben stopped, breathing hard, at the place where the road took a sharp bend and turned southwest near the summit of a little hill. He knew that in a few dozen yards more, the road made a steep downhill run with a shoulder of sage hill close on either side. It was nearly dark now, with clouds pressing close overhead and moving, flowing with the wind.

"I figure that on the other side of this hill is about where the light was when you saw it go out," he said softly, trying to think logically. He took some deep breaths: his heart seemed to be banging against his ribs. "Whoever it was might have been down in this next little valley and flashed the light on the slope to the south just long enough for you to notice it. Let's stand here for a minute and get our breathing back under control before we go any further."

Ben held himself rigid as he tried to plan. His thoughts whirled away with the strong wind, but he knew. He knew what they should do. He wished he could send Artie back now, but he needed her, might need her for a number of reasons.

⚔ ⚔

Artie was glad for the rest. Ben was in better condition than she had thought, and she had been gasping as she struggled to keep up with him. They stood in the road, in the deep blue at the end of twilight, simply breathing. A tribe of coyotes howled from the east hill and goosebumps prickled up Artie's arms.

"I'm hoping it isn't the bad guys," she said very softly. "Don't you think the bad guys would come in vehicles, in a bunch of vehicles, and not just with one flashlight?"

"Probably," Ben answered. "But." He came to a full stop. "But we don't know." He was close. Artie imagined that she could feel the heat of his breath on her cheek, wondered if she would ever have the courage—or the stupidity--to tell him how she felt.

"Do you feel it?" he asked, a whisper.

Artie was startled. Had Ben read her mind?

"The air," he went on. "The wind has been getting stronger. It's warmer. It feels damp. You know what that means."

"The air," she thought, taking a ragged breath. "That's what he means. He means the air." Ben hadn't read her mind after all. Artie let out her breath in a silent sigh. She did know. *Of course*; this was partly why the evening had seemed strange. She said it aloud. "It's going to snow."

She could breathe now without gasping and her heartbeat had slowed to normal. "What next?"

"We're going to do some recon now," he said slowly. "We'll have to be sparing with my headlamp, so we'll have to be careful we don't fall, but I would bet that he or she would be stopping for the night soon, if he hasn't already done that, or if he hasn't already gone. You and Mothy came this way the day you got to the Place. Remember what's at the bottom of this hill?"

Artie swallowed. "A meadow?" she said. "A little flat? And there's a trail, maybe an old road, that takes off to the west, isn't there?"

"Yes," he said. "I would be very surprised if whoever it is would continue cross-country in the dark unless they are in an ATV or something. He—or they--would stay on the roads, or else stop for the night right away. He would go to the southeast and down to Gray Creek, Horner Ranch Road, and the highway—or better, he would turn west onto that little road. I'd think he might do that."

"Why?" Artie asked.

"Because there's an old shed a hundred yards down that road," he answered. "Used to be an old ranch house there, and a barn, too, Gramps told me, but the shed is the only thing left standing. The other buildings are just scattered boards now. When I was a kid, I used to go down there looking for square nails. I found a gray marble there once, made out of real flint. I still have it." Ben paused for a moment, as if surprised by the memory. Artie could sense him hauling his mind back to the present. "With a flashlight, whoever it is might be able to see the shed from the intersection. It's not that dark yet."

"I remember that shed," Artie said, suddenly seeing it in her mind's eye. "Tim and I noticed it the morning we came to the Place. Tim said if we couldn't find the Place, we could come back and spend the night there."

"Good. Here's the plan," Ben said, starting to move again. "Follow me, Artie. Slowly. No lights. No sound. Touch my shoulder if you need to talk or if you want me to stop. We're going to find whoever it is, and watch him. If he goes into that shed, well, that will make him pretty much blind on three sides. It has three walls and is open to the east. If it was me out here tonight, I'd go in there before it got pitch dark and pick up some of the old wood lying around. I'd build a fire in the open side of the shed."

He stopped walking for a moment and said, "When we get even with the shoulder of that hill on the west, we're going to leave the road and walk up there, below the crest, and then we'll crawl to the top and look down into the meadow. We'll see if there are any lights down below, or if there's any light coming from that shed. If there's light in the shed, I can go downhill and sneak around behind the willows in the meadow and see if I can tell who it is. The person could be armed. If I don't see anything, I'll flash my light and come back up. If whoever it is didn't stop at the shed, he has probably kept going in the same direction that you saw the light moving. So we'll go to the east a little ways, and if we don't see anything, he has probably gone on down to the state highway and we can go home. I'd bet that whoever it is won't be up on the hills in the dark. My bet is that he'll stay with the roads."

Artie sucked in a breath. She hadn't been thinking. If the white-garbed soldiers were down there, of course they would be armed.

"Come on," Ben said, turning abruptly off the road. "Up the ridge." She followed him.

⊶⊷

Ben kept a slow, steady pace. It wouldn't do, he thought, to huff and puff and block out sounds they needed to hear. The ground was dry and soft; that was good. He pushed through the sage, taking care not to fall in the near-darkness. Finally he stopped, figuring he was far enough west that the old shed would be just below, and might even be visible in the early darkness as a black block in the meadow of pale grass. He touched Artie on the shoulder and put his mouth to her ear, whispering. "I'm going to look down into the meadow now."

On all fours, Ben crawled the few remaining feet to the top of the low ridge and raised his head. He froze in place, then whispered for Artie to join him. "There's the old shed," he breathed. "And there's a light. Some one *is* there." He turned to her, deciding instantly what he should do. He wondered whether or not he felt afraid, but his mind wouldn't focus on that. What he knew was that he had to get down there and see what was happening. "Stay here," he whispered. "I'm going down."

"But Ben," she protested. "I want to go with you."

Ben blinked; he hadn't expected Artie to want to go with him. He said, "I need you to stay here and watch, Artie. All right?

I'm going to crawl down there to the back of the shed, and hope to hell there isn't a dog in the shed, or a guard posted outside. It's going to take me a while, maybe even a couple of hours. I figure that there are plenty of cracks and knotholes in the back wall of that shed. Can you see the light coming out a little? So I will spy for a while, and that will decide me what to do next. I don't expect anybody else to be around, but if you see something, someone—flash your light just once, to the southwest." Ben took Artie's sleeve and moved in the direction he wanted her light to point—away from the back of the shed.

He continued, "You saw the light disappear, and now that we've found someone here, we know he was going southeast, so chances are that he, or they, will never come near the Place, but will keep going in the same direction tomorrow until they hit the state highway. We'll be fine. But I have to know who it is. OK? I mean," he paused for a moment, "I mean, what if it's Dr. Lucy?"

Finally Artie nodded; Ben could just make out the pale oval of her face in the gloom. "Then what, Ben?"

"Then I will come back. If I think it's safe to do it, I'll flash my light a couple of times when I start up the hill to let you know it's me. Wait here for me. I'll tell you what I found and we'll decide what to do."

"OK," Artie whispered.

He could hear her teeth chattering again. His nose felt a fleck of ice. He looked at Artie, and between them fell a snowflake, white against her dark parka, soft, spiraling down with timeless grace.

━━ ━━

Ben smiled, and whispered back, "Snow is good." Artie saw the gleam of his white teeth in the dark, and then he was gone, lost to the night.

Artie tightened her scarf around her neck, sealing out the cold wind that had been diving down her spine. She lay on the bare ground and inched forward on the dry dirt until she could see the small gleams of light bleeding from the little shed down in the meadow. Sparse snowflakes fell; she could hear their whispering swishes in the dark.

Suddenly, the light at the shed flared and vanished. At once, the light flickered again, less dramatically. She could hear small scrapes and rustles as Ben made his way cautiously down from the ridge; then the noises faded in the wind. Artie clenched her fists, already wishing she could seize Ben somehow and drag him back up to the ridgetop.

The wind changed, veering this way and that, beginning to rise even more. A blast filled with snowflakes gusted right into her face, bringing with it the strong smell of wood smoke. The smoke, the changing light—yes, that was a fire down at the shed now. The fire meant that whoever was down there had stopped for the night. That was good, too. "He will be tired," Artie thought, hoped. "He will stay in the shed while Ben is down there."

The wind stabilized, blowing steadily now from the west. Artie pulled on the hood of the parka, tugging it as far forward as she could, and hugged herself as she lay under the sage. This was a storm, all right. The light from the shed was dimmed now, barely visible through the falling snow. Snowflakes thickened on her eyelashes, and she could feel that her face was wet.

"People get lost in storms," Artie thought, shivering. "They wander all around and their tracks get covered up, and they freeze to death." But she had the hill and the road to guide her back to the Place. The road, even in the dark, even if covered with snow, would be a blank strand of sameness between masses of sage, going uphill all the way to the Place once she climbed down from this ridge. And besides, she told herself, she had always had a built-in compass, just like Gran.

She focused on the shed below and the faint, inconstant light, now dimmed by the gusts of snow, now obliterated entirely for several heartbeats at a time, leaving her in complete darkness. She saw no sign of Ben. The world was a chaos of keening wind and blowing flakes.

But Ben would be all right. She could feel it. And she knew that these hills, the meadows and gulches around the place, were his back yard, and he knew them. "With this wind, it'll drift later on if it keeps snowing," she thought. "I'm glad it's only a couple of miles back to the Place."

Artie turned her back to the penetrating wind and wondered what Hailey was like tonight. At home, were snowflakes sifting down on the front porch to cover what was left of little white Sally? Was the dead body of the man shot on Main Street still there, bloated and rotten by now? Was Rosa's house cold and empty, or were there bodies on the floor in the dark and an empty wheelchair beside a certain bed? Or had Rosa's house burned?

Was her own house with its awful contents even *still there*, or had it gone up in flames? An image of her bedroom with its bedspread and curtains the color of rich chocolate, the books crammed into the bookcase and stacked on the floor, the funny frog pillow that Gran had made, the desk with the little ceramic frog pencil holder . . . Dark now, it would be *dark* in her room, all the colors gone. And the stench? "Evil thoughts for a black night," Artie told herself sternly, swallowing down bile. "Stay in the present. Focus."

Artie began to move her arms and legs back and forth; they were going numb. Finally, she slithered a few feet backward so she could stand with just her head above the level of the ridgeline. She wondered if Ben had reached the meadow, but she could no longer catch even glimpses of the firelight; it was snowing too hard. Now all was black, and the wind sliced over the ridge like a knife, howling.

She jogged in place, swinging her arms, until she was out of breath, wondering how long she would have to stay on the ridge, waiting. *What if Ben doesn't come back?* "Now, Artie, you stop that right now," she told herself. "You know he will be all right. You know this. Nothing is wrong."

Artie stopped moving and took some deep breaths. *What if Ben doesn't come back?*

She should let her mind open to the storm and see what she could feel now, to be certain. Was something bad coming? Could she tell? The snow eddied into her hood and plastered her right cheek with sodden flakes. Wind raced along the ridge, carrying more snow.

Her head filled with wind and snow and blackness, but that was all. "Remember this later, and learn," she told herself silently. "Tonight I didn't feel evil coming." But somewhere in her gut, she felt a small tremor and clenched her teeth against it. She felt *something. Who was down there? What would happen now?*

She began to feel very tired and seriously cold, because the falling snow was wet and had already soaked through the backs of her pantlegs when she lay on the ground.

Suddenly she saw two faint flashes of light below on the meadow near where the base of the hill would be. Artie almost cried out in relief. Ben. Ben was coming back.

"Ben must have an inner compass like I do," Artie thought a few minutes later, when she heard him crest the ridge not six feet from where she was standing. "Here," she said quietly.

He reached out a hand in the dark and connected with her arm. She hoped he wouldn't notice that she was shaking. "Come on," he said under his breath. "It's not the bad guys. Let's get back down the hill and back on the road. Then we can talk."

Artie followed Ben down the hill, curiosity burning in her throat. He went slowly, methodically, stopping at times to listen, using his light now that they were hidden from the shed by the ridge. Artie could feel underfoot that nearly half an inch of snow had fallen already, making the hillside slippery, but they were careful, and neither of them fell. When they reached the bottom of the hill, Ben made for the road.

He kept walking, walking fast, until they were far enough away from the downward slope that there was no possibility that they could be heard from the meadow.

They began to walk faster. "Artie," he said, "This is the weirdest thing. No, don't stop. Keep on walking. The snow will cover our tracks fast, and we have to get a move on. Listen," he said, turning his face toward her and shortening his strides a little to match hers, "As far as I could tell, there are seven people there in the shed—and—Artie, we know them!"

She slipped on a small rock and almost fell. "We know them?" That didn't seem real.

"It's Mose Twohorses, and Andy and Shandy Johnson," Ben said, the names tumbling out rapidly. "And Carlos Aguirre, Lainey Adams, Kaylee Field, and, and—Turk Thomas."

Artie couldn't help herself. She clutched at Ben's arm. "Turk? Turk is there?"

Ben stopped in his tracks. "I know," he said. "Turk is the last person, the very last person, I would want to see on a dark and stormy night. Or any other time."

"Dark and stormy night, dark and stormy night," Artie repeated to herself, her thoughts pinwheeling toward silly laughter, "Very witty." And then a sudden realization sparked. "Of course," she said aloud. "They must be from the football bus that was going to Filer, to the away game on that last Friday night. Football players and cheerleaders. Ha." Artie tried to laugh; she could tell it sounded false. It was a strangled little bleat, not a laugh at all.

"But—" Ben continued, walking again, "there seems to be something wrong with Turk, Artie. He wasn't asleep. He was sitting on the ground next to Lainey, but all the time I listened, everyone else was chattering away, but Turk didn't say a thing. He didn't move. He didn't even turn his head, but I could see that his head was bandaged. I wonder what happened to him."

"Did they see you? Did you show yourself?" Artie had to ask.

"No," he said, shaking his head. "No, I didn't want to—" here he hesitated, then finally went on. "No, I felt, I felt—outnumbered, that was it. I felt outnumbered, and I wanted to talk to you first, and to have a plan."

Ben wanted to talk to me first. Artie hugged the thought to herself. But still, this was an odd turn of events, strange, frightening. *Outnumbered*, he had said. Yes, that was the perfect way to think of them. All through school, Artie had always felt outnumbered.

Ben was striding away with his hands jammed deep into his pockets, and Artie could tell he was worried. "Ben, what are we going to do?" Artie asked, trying to keep up with Ben's long strides. She knew, but was hoping against hope that Ben wouldn't say what she knew he was going to say.

"I'm not thrilled with this, Artie, but—Shandy isn't doing too well, either. I couldn't see her from where I was, but I heard Andy talking to her a couple of times, and Andy sounded really stressed about her. He kept asking her how she felt. We have to take them in. We have to get them. Right?"

Artie sighed. She knew he was right. "Even Turk," she said with a shudder.

"Even Turk," Ben replied. "I hoped you would feel the same way, but I don't like it, either. We're not going to be stupid about it. I started thinking as soon as I saw who it was, and here's how we can do it. We'll get home and take the pickup. I know these little roads, even in the snow, even in the dark. I'll get them all in the pickup shell, and I'll drive around for a while on some of the dirt roads, and then I'll bring them in. I'll do some doubling back, too. I don't think they will be in much shape to have a clue what I'm doing. And there's the storm."

"You don't want them to know exactly where the Place is," Artie said, with a flash of understanding. "And in this storm, the pickup tracks will be gone in minutes."

"Got that right," Ben said, in a harsh tone Artie hadn't heard him use before. "I want you to come with me when I go back for them, to keep an eye on them when we pick them up. OK?"

"OK," she said, and felt a little warmth around her heart. Of *course* she would go with him.

"OK," he echoed. "Let's get back to the Place and tell Tim what's going on. He can get the house warmed up and put on the coffee pot, maybe two coffee pots." Ben walked faster, and Artie began to jog beside him.

Artie found that her nails were digging into the palms of her hands and was glad Ben couldn't see that. *Lainey. Kaylee. Andy and Shandy. Mose. Carlos.* And *Turk.* Her racing pulse beat out the names, and the snowflakes, growing drier now that the storm had fully arrived, ticked them against the fabric of her parka and feathered them into her face, over and over.

So much for the cosy sanctuary that the Place had become. So much for having Ben almost all to herself. So much for, for-- Gary, gone. Rosa? Who knew where? But Lainey, Carlos, and Turk, Turk especially—it wasn't fair that they had made it.

Artie remembered her mother saying, "You can't expect life to be fair. Life isn't fair, Artie. You just have to accept and deal."

Artie had learned that there were certain memories that would not be suppressed, were too painful to die. Lainey in the hall outside the school library, pointing and saying, "And you call that a hat? Seriously? And that skirt. Why would anybody wear a color that looks like a crotch stain?" Carlos, leaning back against the wall near the Liberty Theater, standing there with Turk, watching people pass on the sidewalk. "Not worth a look," he'd said as Artie passed, and Turk's laugh, a sharp, sly bark, seeming to bounce off the wall and follow her halfway home.

Lainey, Kaylee, and Lenny together, and Kaylee whispering, "Ames as a lab partner would just be *dire*. Help me find a way to not have her."

Artie clenched her teeth and tucked her head as she trotted after Ben up the long, now-snowy grade toward the Place. "Breathe," she kept saying to herself. "Just breathe." In her heart, she hated this. But in her heart, she knew it was the right thing to do.

The last mile went quickly, and soon Ben was flashing his headlamp at the Place's dark windows.

Two minutes later, Ben and Artie, stiff with cold and dusted with snow, almost fell into the black kitchen. Tim was sitting at the table in the dark, wearing a coat and gloves. The kitchen was cool, almost cold. Ben felt along the wall and came up with a match from the holder. He lit the oil lamp.

"Well?" Tim said irritably. To Artie he sounded a little scared. "Well? You two were gone long enough."

Ben got another match and opened the fuel box door of the stove. He lit the stack of piled kindling with care and adjusted the damper on the stovepipe. "We found them," he said to Tim over his shoulder. "It's seven people from our high school. They're in an old shed about three miles down the road." The match caught wood and the flame held. Ben closed the small iron door.

Tim looked up. "What? Who is it?"

Artie listed the names this time. "Andy and Shandy Johnson, Mose Twohorses, Lainey Adams and Kaylee Field, Carlos Aguirre, and Turk Thomas."

"Carlos and Turk." Tim's reaction was predictable. "Lainey and Kaylee," he added. It seemed to Artie that he was spitting out the names. "Did they see you?"

Ben shut the stove door and sighed. "No. We're going to take the pickup and go get them," he said, and his voice was colorless and heavy.

"What?" Tim was almost shouting. Muffled barks issued from behind the door to their bedroom in response. "You are going to bring them here? Carlos, and Turk, and—"

"Yes," Ben said. "I'm not sure, but I don't think they're in very good shape, some of them." He sat at the table then and said. "It's going to take a while to get them here. I'm going to give them what I hope is a confusing, loopy ride to the Place, so they don't get an idea exactly where it is or how far away."

"But they are going to come *here*. Carlos. And Turk. And those girls," Tim said, hunching his shoulders inside the thick parka.

"It's what we have to do, Tim. You know that," Ben said.

"But—it's snowing. It's a snowstorm out there," Tim said.

Artie sat at the table and wiped her wet cheeks with one hand. "As if we hadn't noticed, Tim. Come on. We really don't have any choice." Artie's head began throbbing suddenly, in a tight band around her forehead. *Was* this the right thing?

Tim searched her face, then Ben's. "Urg," he grunted after a long pause. "I guess you're right. Sure doesn't bing my thrill meter. Carlos is a tool. Turk is, Turk is . . ." his voice trailed off.

"We'd better get moving," Ben said, getting up. "We'll probably need two pots of coffee, Tim. It's cold out there; it's going to be freezing in the back of the pickup. The other coffee pots are in the cellar, behind the stairs. Gramps got about six of them for trade goods. Two scoops per pot, and keep the fire in the stove built up, OK? And keep the dogs in the bedroom. Give us about an hour."

Artie stood up and zipped her parka to the chin. Tim stood, too. Then Ben did something Artie never forgot. He put out a hand and looked at them each in turn. Artie put her hand in his, and, slowly, Tim laid his hand on hers. Ben's other hand came down to hold them all fast. "Whatever happens," he said, "they are them and we are us. Family. We're family. The three of us and the dogs, the family of the Place. And if they treat us like crap, we kick them out."

"Family," Artie echoed, curling her cold fingers tightly around his. The tension in her head eased.

"Family," Tim said at last. "Kick them out," he added cheerfully, with a faint smile.

Ben took the pickup keys from the hook beside the door, and Artie followed him out into the storm.

END BOOK 1

BOOK 2

The Others

CHAPTER 1

RESCUE

B en turned the windshield wipers and the heat to high as they drove Spear Creek Road downcanyon toward the shed in the long meadow. Snow clotted the windshield, the flakes almost covering it between swipes of the wipers. Visibility was down to about twenty yards, even with the headlamps on low.

"I'm going to turn my lights off before we get to the top of the hill above the meadow," Ben said. He had pulled on a black watch cap and was bowed over the wheel of the pickup. "So don't be freaked by that, Artie. Then we'll coast down the hill and past the intersection with that little spur road. It's a straight shot. I don't want us to be seen yet. If I can, I'll turn around before I put my lights back on. With any luck, they'll think we came from the southeast instead of the northwest. Their fire won't help their night vision, and the snow won't, either."

"And the wind won't help their hearing," Artie added. "I get it." She grabbed the door handle, needing something to steady herself. Freewheeling down a hill in the dark on snow wasn't something she would do, but Ben seemed confident. "I hope he's done this before," she thought as she felt the truck starting up the north side of the hill where she had waited for Ben less than an hour ago.

Ben turned off the truck lights, leaving the LEDs embedded in the dash as the only glow, and he dimmed them so that they were barely visible. Then he punched the button to open the driver's side window, and stuck his head out as far as he could. "So I can hear the door hitting the sage at the edge of the road," he said.

Artie held her breath as the pickup began its gentle roll down the hill. The roll became a slide as the truck picked up speed, but Ben's hands were sure on the wheel. Artie felt a bubble of panic gathering in her throat. The world was nearly black; she could see absolutely nothing beyond the glow from the dashboard. She could feel the truck shaking as gusts of snow-laden wind pummeled her door.

Eventually, the truck rolled gently to a stop on flat ground. Ben turned off the switch for the ceiling light, then jumped out of the truck with his headlamp in one hand and turned it on, close to the ground, for a quick look at the road edges at the place where they were stopped. A swirl of snowflakes curled into the cab and melted on the seat.

"OK," he said, hopping back inside and sending the window up. "That carried us past the meadow and the spur road. I can turn around easily here. There's a good three feet of room each way."

Even so, he was cautious in the blackness, and it took him three back-and forth maneuvers before the truck was facing in the direction from which they had come. "Nothing ventured," he said, and, turning on the headlights, began to drive the road northwest back to the long meadow.

Artie found that she was clutching the door handle so tightly that her whole hand felt numb. She made her fingers open and thrust them into her pocket. She stole a glance at Ben in the dashboard's glow. Large, cottony snowflakes were melting on his eyelashes and on his cap.

"More than an inch of snow," Ben was saying, "already. It's coming down really fast. When we get to the intersection, I'm going to stop and hit the horn. Then I'm going to shout out. I don't want to drive right up to them, and there's a fence, so I probably couldn't drive to the shed anyway. Crouch down below the dash until we see what they do, but from what I could see earlier through the cracks in the shed, I don't think they have any weapons."

Weapons. Again, she had forgotten about the possibility of weapons, and was glad that Ben had remembered. Frank Elliott must have trained him to think that way. "I hope they're glad to see us, Ben," Artie said, fiercely. "They had better be glad to see us."

His teeth showed white in the faint light from the dashboard. He said, "They had better be."

Within a minute or two, Ben came to the intersection and put on the brakes. The headlights showed a broken gate half-down across the little spur road, two posts side-plastered with new snow amid tangles of barbed wire showing dark, irregular loops against the background of white.

Artie clutched the door handle again and admitted to herself that she didn't want these people, these people in particular, to invade the Place and change everything. Macroprincesses Lainey and Kaylee, of all people. Artie wondered why Lenore, Lenny, the third member of the royal court, wasn't with them. And also, where was Paige, the fifth cheerleader? But with them Ben had seen huge Mose Twohorses, who hung with Turk Thomas and Carlos Aguirre, her least favorite classmates; he had also seen Carlos and Turk there. Andy and Shandy Johnson might not be so bad, but *still*. Seven more people at the Place. *These* people. God, Carlos and Turk. She found herself wishing that she hadn't seen the flash of their light, or hadn't reported it to Ben.

And, she mentally kicked herself into admitting, she wanted Ben all to herself, even if . . . But--Ben was better than that, better than she was. Artie felt a little ashamed of her thoughts. The reason she had fallen for Ben in the first place so long ago was the sense of honor that showed in everything he did. But still, *still*. She had seen Kaylee and Lainey humiliate Timothy many times, and had seen these boys bully him. And they had been unkind to Ben as well, almost every school day for years, as a matter of course for them. *Scavenger.*

Artie, for the most part, had been invisible to them, though she did bear a few still-painful scars from their deft little scalpels. Invisibility had been a good thing for Artie, in the world of *before*. "Invisible no more," she said to herself, a promise. Things were different now. Artie had been through fire and rain, death and darkness since she had last encountered these people. Turk, Carlos, Lainey, and Kaylee? Mose? The Johnson twins? "Piece of cake," she told herself, half-believing. Well, half was better than none.

"Got to do it," she thought, made herself think as she bit her index finger lightly. "Right thing." Once, the right thing to do was to give back a five-dollar bill someone had dropped on the sidewalk, or not to cheat on a test. Now the right thing to do was the most undesirable of choices. Maybe this group could have trekked to Hailey on their own and holed up for the winter in whatever buildings hadn't been completely destroyed by the fires. Maybe they would have been captured by the soldiers, herded into white buses, and taken somewhere to spend the winter in comfort. Maybe that would have been better. Artie realized that she wasn't convincing herself and gave it up.

She glanced at Ben; his mouth was set in a hard line. She wanted to put out a hand to touch him, but this wasn't the time. She knew what time it was. "Showtime," she whispered.

"Showtime," he echoed.

Ben flashed the headlamps and honked the horn several times, then got out of the pickup and stood behind it for a minute. Dimly, through the swirling snow, Artie could see fire leaping in the open side of the shed, and some movement beyond. The flames flattened, shot upward in a shower of sparks, then flattened once more as the snow-laden wind veered wildly. "Blizzard now," she thought. She bent at the waist and crouched in the footwell as Ben had told her to do.

"Hey!" Ben shouted. "Hey, you with the fire! Hey!"

Artie heard some answer, but she couldn't make out the words.

Ben yelled again. "Hey! You OK? My name is Ben Elliott. Come on!"

"Ben Elliott?" came a bellow from the direction of the shed. "What the--?"

"Come on!" Ben cried once more. "Come on out here!"

Artie opened her door and stuck her head into the storm. In front of the fire, she could see a tall, hulking form standing on two legs planted well apart, a figure thick-necked and broad-shouldered, a Frankenstein silhouette. That had to be Moses Twohorses, Wood River High School starting fullback. Behind him, behind the fire, she could see the faint, firelit outline of another person standing motionless. Artie decided to add her voice to Ben's. "Hey, come on!"

The oversized figure took some steps, stopped a moment, looked back, and took some more steps. It was Mose, all right. Artie could see that the truck's headlights were blinding him, but at the moment, she didn't care. She needed to see.

Mose blundered up to the truck, tripping and almost falling when he walked through the wire of the downed gate, and Ben went to meet him. Artie could see that Mose was wearing a jacket much too small for him—the sleeves came only halfway down his thick forearms, and the front panels couldn't possibly meet across his chest.

Mose swore, brushing snow from his eyes. "It's you, all right," he said to Ben as they walked toward the truck. "Elliott. What the crap are you doing out here in the middle of nowhere?" His large head swiveled as they reached the pickup, and he seemed to see Artie for the first time. "Artie Ames?"

"That's me," she had to say.

"Well, what's your deal?" Mose said then, and turned back to Ben before she could answer. "We're holed up in this stupid shed for the night, trying not to freeze to death, and—"

"All right, Mose," Ben said, impressing Artie with his calm. "All right. Go tell the others that it's OK. Get them over here, and we'll take you all back to the house. Unless you want to stay here."

Mose straightened, towering over Ben. "A house? You bet we'll come," he said, shaking his head. "Holy—" And he turned at once and marched away into the headlight-defined veils of falling snow, without saying another word.

Artie drew closer to Ben. "I'm kind of afraid of Mose," she said.

"Don't be," Ben said. "You might be surprised. He hangs with those assholes mostly because he lives for football. Mose has his off moments, but down deep I think he is good people."

"Down pretty freaking deep," she couldn't resist saying. Artie bit her lip again. She knew Mose; she had gone to school with Mose all those years, too, as she had with Ben and Tim and Gary, and the big guy had been one of the typical first-string-jock bullies, at least most of the time.

Presently, Mose reappeared from the tunnel of snowflakes, followed by Carlos and Kaylee, and then the twins Andy and Shandy; Shandy seemed to be faltering, and Andy held his sister tightly around the shoulders. Bringing up the rear were Lainey and Turk. Lainey was clutching one of Turk's arms, and he looked straight ahead without saying a word, though the others were chattering nonstop.

"Scavenger," Carlos said when he came up to the truck. "What?"

"My name is not 'Scavenger,' Carlos," Ben said coolly. "We saw the fire and stopped to see what was going on here, if anyone needed help."

"My god, yes!" said Lainey, pulling Turk close to the truck. Artie saw that her hair was hanging in strings, and that she was wearing what looked like a wool blanket wrapped around her shoulders like a heavy shawl. "Take us out of here! I want to go home. Can you take us home?"

"Not tonight, Lainey," Ben said, still seeming imperturbable. "First things first. You can spend the night at our Place."

"Is your place warm?" Andy was asking. "Do you have food? Shandy isn't doing too well."

"Yes and yes," Ben told Andy. Ben led them to the back of the truck and opened the hatch to the shell. "Get in. It's going to take a while to get to the house. It'll be a bumpy ride."

Lainey turned at the last minute and said, "My bag. I left my bag in the shed."

"I'll get it," Artie said, and followed the headlight beams until she had reached the dying fire. Though she was sure no one else would be out in this storm to see the fire, and that it couldn't possible spread in this storm of wet snow, it was stupid to leave a fire burning. Sure enough, there on the dirt floor lay a blue messenger bag glittering with metal studs. She slung the bag over one shoulder, and stopped to kick snow and dirt into the fire until she could stomp it out.

She headed back toward the truck, and then she saw that Ben was coming to meet her.

"OK," he said, "I've got them all in the back. Something is wrong with Turk, just as I thought, but I don't know what it is.

And Shandy seems to be sick or hurt in some way. At least she can walk. Even so, we might freeze them a little taking the detour home, but I'm determined to do it. Come on."

Just then Artie saw a white flutter of fabric near the front of the pickup. Ben saw it at the same moment and ran to the truck.

Next to the front tire on the passenger side, crouched a young girl. She was wearing only light sneakers and a long, pale flannel nightgown. She seemed to be made of snow. Her wet hair was ivory-white and her arms and ankles were even whiter.

Artie bent to her and was surprised when the girl jerked away. "Come on, I won't hurt you," Artie said, mystified. Where had this unknown girl come from? The girl turned frightened eyes toward Ben and Artie added, "He won't hurt you, I promise. Come on—you'll be safe with us. I'm Artie Ames. What's your name?" The girl was silent.

Artie heard a noise and Mose appeared beside her. "That's Paleface, Artie," he said. The girl edged away from him. "She's been following us almost from the beginning. She doesn't speak and she runs away when we try to catch her. Maybe you can have her get a move on, because, by the way, we are freezing here. Just so you'd know." He lumbered to the back of the pickup and Artie saw it rock as he got back into the shell and pulled the hatch shut.

"We have to go," Artie said to Paleface. "You can't stay out here in this storm. We have food and a nice, warm house. And you can ride up front with me. And it will be fine. We even have dogs there, and a big stove." Artie heard herself babbling non-sense, but the girl reached out tentative fingers and Artie took the white hand. The small fingers were ice-cold and wet. "Come on, come on," Artie said, coaxing. She opened the door and eased the girl into the pickup beside Ben. "It's OK. You're OK," she said. She heard the faint click when Ben locked the doors and felt the girl lean into her side.

Ben started the pickup, reversed, and headed back down their
false trail, south, away from the Place. The tracks they had left
in the snow only minutes before were virtually gone. He drove
south down the road, up out of the long meadow, and into low
sagebrush hills.

At some point, he turned east, then south again, then west,
and Artie eventually realized that, though the current roadway
was as white and featureless as the small dirt roads, suddenly the
pickup was gliding smoothly instead of bouncing, and they were
passing green mile markers--so they were now on the state highway. She felt that they were heading west toward Fairfield.

After a time Ben turned what might have been north onto a
smaller road, then turned again, and then once more. Then he
turned north again. She thought it was north, from the angle of
the snowflakes. She was almost sure.

By this time Artie was somewhat disoriented. She began to
feel a little panicked as the snow whirled by and deepened under
the wheels. She couldn't see anything but whiteness below and in
the air, and blackness beyond the reach of the headlamps--and
didn't see how Ben could tell where the road was, let alone which
road they were taking.

Ben said little, but leaned forward in his seat and gave his full
attention to the driving. "Drifting already," he said once, and
indeed, every few minutes Artie could feel the truck lurch as it
tackled a small drift and punched through.

After considerably more than half an hour, the windshield
wipers were struggling harder to keep up with the windblown
snow, the drifts were deeper, and visibility even in the limited
reach of the headlamps was almost nil.

Artie wanted desperately to ask Ben where they were, but
didn't want to say anything in front of the unknown girl. Artie
told herself, "Ben knows these roads. I have to trust him. I have
to trust him." She could feel a dampness seeping into the left

thigh of her jeans from the girl's wet nightgown. Artie bit her lip once more and held her peace.

Ben stopped suddenly in the middle of the road. He said, "Get the gate, Artie?" and waited for her to get out.

"Gate," she repeated, feeling stupid.

"On the left," Ben said, and she could hear confidence in his voice. She took a deep breath and let go of her fears that they had become lost in the blizzard. Artie looked closely at the blowing snow illuminated by the headlights—and there was a barbed-wire fence, barely visible.

Paleface wouldn't release her grip on Artie's arm, so Artie pulled her from the cab and dealt with the gate. Snow had blown against the weeds at the bottom of the wire-strung gate, and the little drift there reached above her ankles. Close, she recognized the odd, offset gate--it was the gate to the Place. They were home!

Ben drove through and Artie shut the gate behind the truck and put herself and Paleface back in. He drove on to the barn, where Artie hopped out again to swing the big doors back while he drove inside and turned off the engine.

Artie opened the back of the shell and let down the tailgate. Everyone scrambled out into the dark barn. The dry, sweet smell of hay engulfed them.

"This is your *house?*" Lainey asked, a little sarcastically.

Artie sighed and thought, "So it begins. But," she told herself, "Lainey probably couldn't see the house at all in the dark with all the snow, and the windows on the west side are nearly covered by the stove wood stacked against the wall." She said aloud in a voice as neutral as she could make it, "No, this is the *barn*. Let's get up to the house."

Following Ben and his headlamp, they trooped through three inches of snow up to the house, and then through a two-foot drift near the porch, Lainey still holding Turk's arm. The wind came shrieking around the eves, and in the glow of Ben's headlamp, Artie saw that the ends of the stacked wood on the back porch were wind-plastered with snow all the way up to the porch ceiling.

Tim held the door to let them in. He had kept the dogs penned up: Artie heard faint barking coming from the bedroom they had been using. But he had kept the stove going.

She settled her damp parka on a chair back not far from the stove and spread her hands to catch the heat. Ben led the new people into the living room, where they flung themselves down on the chairs, sofa, and the braided rug. Paleface stayed in the kitchen, close to Artie.

The house was very warm, almost too warm, and for the first time, Artie saw a fire burning in the living room fireplace. Tim had done that, and he must have figured out how to use the damper in the chimney, because there was no smell of smoke, just the clean scent of burning pine—and something else, a delicious, rich smell. Artie pulled out two kitchen chairs and, tired of coaxing, pushed Paleface into one of them and made her sit. She looked around, glad of the oil lamp on the kitchen table. Tim must have lit that, too.

The old black stove was giving off great, comforting waves of heat, and on it two coffee pots steamed, but there was more. A large, two-handled stainless steel kettle steamed there as well, the source of the delicious smell. Artie got up and leaned over it. Soup. Then she noticed a group of red and white soup cans on the floor nearby, neatly arranged around a much larger can. She looked at Tim, who was standing warily in a corner, all but rolling his eyes like a nervous horse. "You made soup?" she said. "It's minestrone, isn't it?"

Tim nodded. "I put a whole canned chicken in it," he said, "Is that—"

"That's excellent," Artie told him, and then saw that the newcomers had found a few towels in the living room that Tim must have put there, and were drying their faces, arms, and hair. Some were taking off wet shoes.

Ben, who had gone into the living room ahead of the others, strode back to the kitchen and hit Tim on the shoulder. Tim stepped back, looking worried.

"Artie," Ben said very softly, his face turned away from Paleface, "we went to all that trouble trying to make sure these guys don't know exactly where the Place is, but I forgot about the map on the wall."

"Oh, no," she whispered. "I didn't even think."

"But Tim didn't forget the map," Ben said. "I ran to take it down the second I got into the house, but it was already gone. Good going, Tim."

Tim looked down at the table.

"I mean it," Ben said. "Good thinking. What did you do with it?"

"The map, it—it's locked in the gun safe," Tim stammered. "I thought you wouldn't mind. You did show us the combination."

"That's perfect." Ben adjusted his headlamp. "We've got to get some sleeping bags from the barrels in the barn." He said, "Come on, Tim."

Forgetting a coat, Tim turned to follow Ben out the door into the storm. Artie handed him her parka and realized that Tim, who hated the dark and hated going to the outhouse in the dark even with a flashlight, must have gone down to the creek while they were gone, had broken the ice, and had brought up enough water to make the soup and two pots of coffee—and then had made a trip to the barn for towels. "Family," she thought, and enveloped Tim in a quick, tight bear hug. He gaped at her as if astonished, and then ran out into the night.

Artie looked at Paleface sitting across the kitchen table, her narrow face lit warmly by the oil lamp. "Why, she's as old as I am," Artie realized suddenly. "I thought she was a child. She's just very small and thin." Artie wondered if Paleface could be a mute, or had some mental or emotional challenge. The flannel night-gown was wet and filthy; its hem was torn and tattered. Paleface must have been wearing it for some time. "Your name can't be Paleface," she said. "Can you tell me your name?" The girl looked at Artie, a level gaze from very light blue eyes, but said nothing.

"OK." Artie decided to treat Paleface as if she had ordinary intelligence. "I'm going to pass around the coffee. Do you drink coffee? Do you want some soup?" The girl nodded twice. "That's good news," Artie thought. "She can understand me."

Artie continued. "I'm going to see if I can find some more mugs in the basement. And then I'm going to get you some dry clothes. Clean clothes. We have lots of clothes here." Artie was glad she had spent so much time recording what was in all the bar-rels. The girl nodded vigorously, then shrank back and crossed her hands protectively over her chest. Artie looked up. There was Mose, taking up the entire kitchen-living room doorway.

"Smells like there's something on the stove," he said.

"Soup," Artie said. "And coffee. Here, want to help?" Artie rummaged in the pantry and came out with a box of lump sugar and a can of evaporated milk, which, taking Gary's pocketknife from her jeans, she punched with the requisite two holes. Mose held out his huge hands and she gave him the things to take into the living room. There were only five mugs in the pantry, and Artie set them all on the table.

Then she took the oil lamp and dived down the wooden stairs into the cellar, where she had seen a box full of mismatched cups and mugs, some ceramic, some glass, some plastic. She managed to fish out six more mugs, and holding the mugs by the handles in one hand and the lamp in the other, made her way up the dark stairs.

Back in the kitchen, Mose was pouring coffee into the mugs on the table, and Paleface had shoved her chair so far back that it was touching the wall, as if she would shrink right through the wall if she could.

Artie plonked the additional mugs down on the table and said to Mose, "I don't think there are extra bowls in the house, so people can have coffee first, or soup first. Tonight we can just rinse out the mugs and re-use them." He nodded and carried four mugs into the living room.

Ben and Tim came in with a cold blast of wind and snow, and behind them on the porch Artie saw the garden cart piled full of sleeping bags already sprinkled with white. Artie helped ferry them inside. "Up to the loft," was all Ben said.

"Going back for clothes," Tim added. The kitchen door shut, and for a moment Artie could hear the cart's wheels rumbling across the planks of the porch, and then nothing but the wind.

Artie found a big spoon and ladled a mugful of soup for Paleface, who scraped her chair up to the table and took it in both hands. Andy Johnson was helping Mose distribute the mugs of soup and coffee, so Artie pulled down the cord for the stairs to the half-loft, and after lighting a spare oil lamp she had seen in the basement on her foray for mugs, began trudging up the ladder-stairs with the sleeping bags.

She had seen the loft from the ladder, but hadn't actually been in the loft before, and she took a moment to glance around before setting the spare oil lamp on the dresser. The loft was a bare wooden floor with an old six-drawer dresser standing against one wall, a fly rod cabinet upright against another, and two wide mattresses pushed together on the floor and shoved to the north wall, centered with a pile of pillows.

Rows of canned food five deep and four high lined the walls and gleamed from beneath the dresser. "I hope there's as much food at the Place as Ben says there is," Artie muttered under her breath, thinking of all the empty cans on the kitchen floor for just one meal.

The loft was surprisingly warm, but, of course, the half-wall opened above the living room. "Heat rises," Artie thought, and noticed that, encased in a square pillar of brick, the stovepipe ran up against one wall. That would bring warmth as well. When she had carried several sleeping bags to the loft, Artie stopped to wonder how the sleeping arrangements should go. Boys up, girls in the unused bedroom below? Or?

She looked down on the group gathered around the fireplace, drinking from their mugs, and decided that she wouldn't say anything. They could decide for themselves, as long as they stayed out of the small bedroom. Or Ben could tell them what to do.

Turk seemed to be staring into a corner without speaking, Lainey still with a hand on his arm, now holding a mug to his lips. Sleeping in the same house with Turk Thomas was not a pleasing prospect. "I'd almost rather sleep out in the barn," Artie thought. But the wind was louder up here next to the eaves, and it was so snowy and so dark tonight . . . She heard the kitchen door open and slid down the rungs.

Tim staggered into the kitchen under a load of folded t shirts and sweatshirts, and Ben flopped a pile of jeans onto the table. He went back to the cart and came in with a cotton drawstring bag that turned out to be full of socks. "That's it for now," he said to Artie. "I'm going to run the cart back to the barn so it doesn't fill up with snow overnight." He went out; Artie caught a glimpse of what looked like almost horizontal waves of snowflakes in his headlamp beam before he shut the door.

Tim shook snow off the parka and draped it over a chair. He looked across the table at Paleface. "Who are you?" he asked "I don't know you." Then as if remembering his manners, he added, "Hi, I'm Tim Rich."

Paleface stared at Tim but said nothing.

"She doesn't talk, Tim," Artie said, "Do you want coffee first, or soup?"

"Oh," he said, still staring at Paleface, "I've had coffee, before you got back. Soup."

She filled a mug and handed it to him, then turned to Paleface. "Here, girl, let's look through this stuff before the other guys and see if we can find something that fits you. You must be cold; your nightgown is soaked. Ben said his Gramps insisted on stockpiling a bunch of different sizes, that he'd gotten clothes from nearly every sale he came across for the last five years." Artie rummaged through the pile of jeans and held up a small pair by the waistband. "How about these?"

Paleface stood to reach across the table and grab them. She held them up to her own waist and nodded.

"OK. Next, a top. You do the looking."

Skirting the table opposite from where Tim was sitting, Paleface began to dig through the pile of t shirts, and chose a plain peach-colored one, then found a small gray sweatshirt as well. She looked at Artie, a question. "Let's go in the bedroom," Artie said, grabbing a pair of socks and stuffing them into a pocket. "You like dogs?"

Paleface nodded.

"Good." Artie scooped the oil lamp from the table.

It took an interesting set of maneuvers to get herself and the lamp, the clothing, and Paleface, inside the small bedroom without letting the dogs out, but Artie accomplished it, and sat on a bed while Paleface turned away, and fending off the four curious dogs, stepped out of her soggy, muddy nightgown and put on the new clothes. Artie marveled at the girl's long, wavy hair, thick and almost white—yet Artie saw no sign of dark roots. Paleface's face was indeed pale, and her eyebrows and eyelashes were lovely but nearly as colorless as her hair. "Why, she's almost an albino," Artie thought.

Aloud she said, "I'm going to help get the other guys settled for the night. Do you want to come out, or would you like to stay in here with the dogs until I come back? I have to take the lamp." Paleface leaned away from the door with a movement that was becoming all too familiar, so Artie retrieved one of the new sleeping bags from the kitchen, passed it in to Paleface, lit the oil lamp on the night stand, and left her there, shut in with the Shelties and Smoke.

Artie saw that Ben had taken a mug of soup into the living room and was sitting on the floor near the fireplace. She ladled out some soup for herself and joined him in the ruddy dimness; the fire was the only light in the room. Tim followed and sat himself next to Artie, his back against the stone wall of the fireplace itself.

"Oh, good," Ben said as Artie and Tim sat down. "I want you to hear this, too. OK," he said, glancing from face to face. "Who's going to start? What happened to you guys and how did you get to that shed?"

Carlos leaned forward into the firelight. "What I want to know, is where's Crazy Frank? This must be the Elliott place."

CHAPTER 2

THE OTHERS' TALE

B en set his cup of soup on the floor and looked steadily at Carlos. "My grandfather is dead, Carlos. And yes, as a matter of fact, this *is* the Elliott Place. My Place."

Carlos subsided at once. "Sorry," he muttered.

"I'll start," said Kaylee a little timidly, pushing a tangled curl behind one ear. "Because I think I was the only one of us awake when the white Humvees started chasing our bus. We won the game with Filer," she went on, "and Coach let us stop for some food in Shoshone, so it was pretty late when we left, and everybody on the bus was pretty much out by the time we went past the Ice Caves road."

"White Humvees," Artie thought, with a little shock. She looked around at the new faces. Lainey, Turk, Shandy, and Kaylee sat crowded together on the sofa. Lainey's exquisite, clear profile showed firelit and crisply defined against the darkness of the room behind her. With her hair pulled back now and her lips parted, Lainey was beautiful as always. Artie saw Ben glance at her, and thought ungenerously, "How very, very much I don't want Lainey here."

Shandy was hunched inside the dirty blanket Lainey had been wearing, staring into her mug of soup and taking occasional sips; Andy sat at her feet, leaning against her knees. Mose, too, sat on the floor near the sofa, as did Carlos.

There *was* something wrong with Turk, Artie decided, something wrong in a way different from how he usually was. His face looked, looked--*blank*, that was the word, like no one was home. He had no focus, no expression. Artie felt a chill run down her spine. Something was off with him, way off.

Kaylee went on. "I was bored, so I decided to move up front in the bus so I could talk to the driver and keep him company. Oliver is only 26, did you know? It must have been after midnight by then. We didn't meet a car for a while. And a few minutes after we left Shoshone, I saw lights behind us, and then a white flashing light came up beside us, and a Humvee tried to make us pull over. But Oliver wouldn't, and he put on the speed, and pretty soon there were two more Humvees behind us, at least two more. And you're supposed to pull over for red and blue flashing lights, not white ones, right? Maybe that's why Oliver didn't stop.

"Then one of the Humvees started bumping us, just a little at first," Kaylee went on. "I wanted Oliver to stop, but he wouldn't. Oliver said, 'Hang on, honey,' and kept right on going. I don't know why he wouldn't stop." Kaylee pushed back her hair again. "People were waking up then, shouting, 'What's going on?' and like that. And then we came to a curve, and one of the Humvees hit us hard, and the bus—" Kaylee stopped for a moment, gulped, and went on, "the bus fell over. It fell over on its side and spun around—it spun across the road—and I went out, went black."

Carlos took up the story. "All hell broke loose. I woke up when the bus went flat sideways, and people fell out of their seats and were thrashing around screaming like pigs, and then it started to spin. I was right at the back, you know, where the emergency door is. It was black in the bus and as soon as the bus stopped moving I could hear some pounding up front, and glass breaking. Well, I did that thing where you shove the emergency door open with that bar, and I rolled out in the dark. I could smell gas. There were headlights across the front of the bus as well as the flashing lights—probably from one of the Humvees that Kaylee saw—and I could see a couple of guys hammering on the front door and breaking windows to get into the bus, so I took off. Turk came right after me, and Andy. We were where the road crosses that big lava place, you know? And we got into the rocks and kept falling in the dark, but the rocks were good, because they gave us a place to hide. And the three of us just kind of crouched there in the rocks and stared for a minute, and then Andy here took off to get Shandy."

"I went in through the emergency door," Andy said, "and I got back on the bus. People were screaming and falling around in the dark. I stepped on somebody, and I yelled out for Shandy, but Kaylee was standing there all of a sudden and grabbed my arm, and I turned around to see who was grabbing me and ran right into Mose with Shandy, and told them to come with us. Lainey came out with us, too. Shandy was out of it, totally. Mose had Shandy by both arms and dragged her out the back door and then picked her up, and we ran to the rocks."

"Yeah, we hid there," Carlos said. "It was the weirdest thing. We went to the rocks in the first place just to get away if the bus exploded, you know? We thought it would be good to have the rocks between us and the bus if it went ka-pow. But things kind of went creepy right away. A bunch of white Humvees and some guys that looked like soldiers were there. They had flashlights. But their uniforms were almost white—weird. You know, like digicamo, but almost white. And then a white bus pulled up behind our bus and kind of blocked the scene. We couldn't see much after that. But then there was a little explosion, a little puff-*pow!*, and our bus started to burn."

"The screams," Lainey said, making Artie jump. For a moment she had forgotten Lainey was there, so close. "People were screaming and screaming, and there were two gunshots. We saw a guy fall down on the road and not get up. I think it was Charlie Evans. I remember asking Turk, 'Who is shooting? Why are they shooting?' It didn't seem like a good idea to go back there."

"Especially after we saw that one guy go down," Carlos added. "And after he fell over, you could hear more screaming, serious screaming."

Lainey continued, "I had my bag on. It's one of these cross-body bags, and I was wearing it when this all came down. So I felt around and got out my penlight, one of those little LED lights on your keychain, and we crouched down behind the rocks and used that light and Andy's phone to help us move away from the road, behind the rocks, so we wouldn't fall any more and make noise. And we kept going away from the road, way back in the rocks. All night, we kept moving and moving away from the road. Shandy was unconscious, like a rag doll. Mose had to carry her."

"We were heading west to get as far from the road as we could," Mose said. "I was glad we were mostly on rock because they wouldn't find our tracks. We stuck to the lava rocks for a good while. Andy tried calling his parents a few times when we stopped to rest, plus 911, and so did Kaylee and Lainey, but they didn't get any bars." Mose wagged his big head. "The sky was going gray, and we were still in the lava when Turk fell over. He fell over into a bush and wouldn't wake up. We were all worn out and freaked out by then and just kind of piled on each other and went to sleep. If anybody came looking for us, we never saw them."

"We woke up sometime in the morning and saw that we were at the edge of a field," Carlos said. "Shandy was awake then, too.

We could see what we were doing by then, and Shandy had a goose egg at the back of her head and a big rip down the middle of one arm. But she was awake, and she could walk. Turk woke up, too. He had, has this big old bump on the side of his head above his ear, all bloody. But he seemed OK. And then we saw the farmhouse back in some trees on the far side of the field."

"We went over there and there was no one home. The doors weren't locked. There was no car in the garage, only an old truck and a tractor in the barn," Mose said. "The next day I tried to hotwire both of them, but no go. Anyway, it was just someone's house, only without the someones. We went in there and turned up the heat, and drank a bunch of Coke and beer, and fell on the beds and slept until dark. We kept calling."

Artie thought back. That would have been that first Saturday, when she had spent most of the day hiding behind the potted trees next to the bank, when she saw the man get killed in the middle of Main Street.

"There was food in the kitchen, and the place had a gas stove and gas heat, so we were good even though the electricity was off," Mose continued. He finished his soup and put his mug on the floor. "We had some stew and a pie, and made melted cheese sandwiches, and ate some peanuts and some other stuff, and—"

"And we used our cells and called and called," Kaylee said. "At least, Lainey had hers, I had mine, and Andy and Carlos still had theirs. But nobody would answer. Not 911. The phones had bars there. But our families didn't answer, either." Tears stood in Kaylee's eyes. She appealed to Ben. "Do you know what's going on in Hailey? Nobody answers!"

"When you're done, then we'll tell," Ben said. "Go on."

"Not a lot more to tell," Andy said. "We decided to stay there that night, at that farmhouse, and before it got dark, it started to rain. Big time. Kept raining. So we just stayed there. For two days. Who wants to walk in the rain? And then we were running out of decent food--I mean, these guys had cans and cans of hominy. Who eats hominy? But there was a map of Idaho in a desk drawer there and we figured out about where that farmhouse was, where we were. So when it stopped raining, we got ready to go in the direction of Hailey and maybe find ourselves another farmhouse on the way, or a car, only. Only that's when we found *her*," Andy said, with a toss of his head in the direction of the closed bedroom door. "Miss Paleface."

Lainey said, "We took some snack food and some coats from there, and were heading out, when all of a sudden we spotted her. She was watching us from the door of the barn. Turk took off after her, and she ran into the barn. I told him to leave her and come on," Lainey added. "But he didn't come out. We waited."

"Finally I went in after him," Mose said, "And he was passed out on the floor next to a tractor. That head lump of his was bleeding. So I carried him and we went back into the house. We stayed another night. Turk didn't wake up until the next morning, and when he did, he was—like this."

"He doesn't look at anything," Lainey said, and her voice was tight, grating. "He will eat and drink if you hold whatever it is right up to his face, and he will walk if you hold onto him and pull a little. He's even housebroken," she said, "if you help him a little. But that's all. He won't say anything."

"Hematoma," Ben said as if to himself. "Maybe bleeding in there. Pressure."

"Well, listen to Doctor Who," Carlos said.

"Gramps was a vet," Ben said, stonily calm. "I went with him on calls." Ben got his headlamp and looked closely at the swollen side of Turk's head. The whole area was crusted with dried blood; Artie saw the others turn away. "He seems stable and it's not bleeding now," Ben said after a minute. "Looks like it hasn't bled for at least a couple of days." Ben took Turk's stubbly chin and moved Turk's head from side to side. "Look. One of his pupils responds to the changes in the light, but the other one doesn't. I'll have a better look tomorrow." Ben looked at the others. "Unless anyone else wants to take over."

"Please," Lainey said, lifting a hand to plead harmony. "Please."

"So there isn't much to tell after that. When Turk passed out in the barn and Mose dragged him back into the house," said Andy, "we decided not to leave that day. We stayed in that house until Turk woke up the next morning. It stopped raining. Then we were more than ready to go home.

We knew we were west of Highway 75, so we knew if we went far enough north, we'd come to the highway to Fairfield, the state highway. Then we'd go east on it to Timmerman and then north to Hailey. But we figured that we wouldn't have to walk the whole way. We thought that when we got to the state highway or even before, somebody would come along and pick us up.

"It couldn't have been more than 60 miles home from that first farmhouse, even if we didn't get picked up. We figured we could walk it in a couple or three days, easy. And we'd find a car or some people at a farmhouse, we thought. So we kept going north, and we found three more farmhouses--no people, no cars. No cars that would run, anyway. We'd eat what food was there, sleep, carry some food with us, try their landlines to call, put on clean clothes if we found any, and go on. 911 didn't work; it would just ring and ring. None of the numbers we called answered. One of the farmhouses had electricity from a backup generator. That TV just showed static, and once an hour it showed the message to stay tuned to the emergency network, but the emergency network just said a stupid thing about sunspots, over and over. There weren't any computers at those farmhouses."

Andy stopped for a moment to take her empty mug from Shandy and set it on the floor. "Paleface followed us," he continued. "I think she went into the houses for a little while after we were gone, each time we moved on. Sometimes we wouldn't see her for a whole day. But then she'd be there—not close, but almost out of sight. We tried to catch her a couple of times, but she's fast.

"We went over a bunch of rocky hills on a paved road, and found one more farmhouse. Then we didn't find any more houses, and Shandy and Turk started to slow us down. Way, way. Especially Shandy. Her arm started to go bad. That was two days ago. Then this afternoon we got off the paved road to see if we could find a house for the night. We went a few miles up this dirt road. But when the sun went down, there was just that shed, no more farmhouses. Carlos has a lighter on him, so we built a fire. And then it started to snow." Andy nodded sharply and held his hands out to the fire. "That's it."

"So that's our story," Carlos said, easing himself from a sitting position to lie on the floor, propping his head on one hand. He scratched at the dark stubble on his chin. "What's with town, then, and what are the three of you doing here?"

Both Ben and Tim looked at Artie, so she told a shortened version of their various experiences. "So our families are dead," Artie finished. "And Tim and Gary both saw the white Humvees and the soldiers in the pale uniforms, and people being forced into the white buses. And people being shot. I saw that happen myself. On Main Street. And I have no idea who might be left in town, if anybody--or how many buildings were burned." Artie looked from face to face, realizing that each person was thinking about his or her own family and hoping against hope that they were not dead.

"Turk's dad isn't dead," said Lainey suddenly. "He's in Vancouver filming an action flick. He'll be all right."

Tim made the only comment he'd ventured so far. "We don't know how far this evil has spread."

"Evil," Artie thought. "Yes, that's what it is." The word had sounded very formal coming from Timothy.

No one said anything more, and finally Ben rose and said, "We brought in some clothes from the barn. They're on the table. You can put on dry clothes and then we can all get to bed. If anybody needs to go out, there's a flashlight hanging on the wall by the kitchen door. I'll show you where the outhouse is. I've got to take the dogs out to potty, anyway."

Ben added, "There are sleeping bags, too. Artie took some up to the loft, and there's an empty bedroom down here as well. Or you can sleep on the floor here. Choose your poison. We're in the bedroom next to the kitchen, with the dogs."

Artie saw Carlos raise an eyebrow, but she decided she wasn't in the mood to explain. She stared him down and he made no comment.

The new people, Turk led by Lainey, made their way into the kitchen to sort out the clothing. Shandy stayed on the couch, clutching the dirty blanket.

Ben knelt beside her. "Andy said you were hurt. Let me see your arm, Shandy."

Slowly she drew the blanket back. Brown-stained strips of cloth wrapped her left arm, and it stank. Shandy's shirt and jeans were wet with dark mud. She was shivering. Artie realized that on today's part of their journey, Shandy must have fallen more than once.

Ben looked at Artie and Tim and said softly, "What I wouldn't give to have Gramps here now!" He took some deep breaths and said, "We've got to take care of this tonight; it's infected. I'll get a sleeping bag for Shandy and she can sleep here on the sofa, right by the fire. Artie, would you pick out some clean clothes for her, while I take her into the second bedroom? Then you can help her get into them. Short sleeves. Tim, we've got to have a bucket full, and I mean full, of hot water. And more clean towels from the barn, and a new pillowcase, if you can find one. My head-lamp is on the table. I'll get the first aid kit from the cellar. I'll wait to take the dogs out after we are done here."

Without a word, Tim got up and went out.

Artie stared at Ben. The Ben she knew was quiet, unassuming. This Ben gave orders, orders that people just—they just—followed them. She found herself in the kitchen before she knew it, sorting through the clothing, choosing things for Shandy to wear. Ben got Shandy up and moved into the larger bedroom, and Artie found the small oil lamp she had placed on the night-stand there a couple of days ago and lit it with a match from the kitchen, then closed the door.

She looked at Shandy sitting motionless on the edge of a bed, and said, "Come on, let's get you out of those wet things." She pulled off soaking socks and shoes, Shandy's dirty jeans shed-ding blobs of dried mud as they came off. Then with great care, Artie helped Shandy pull off her shirt. Sandy needed help put-ting on the jeans and socks, but somehow managed the new blue t shirt on her own.

"Artie," Shandy said, "What *is* this place? Why do you guys have food and clothes for everyone? And sleeping bags, even?"

"Because of those guys known as Crazy Frank Elliott and the Scavenger," Artie couldn't help saying. "Because they begged, bought, made, found, and grabbed everything they could, for years, and brought it all here."

Shandy didn't comment, but got up and wobbled toward the door in stocking feet. Artie took the lamp and followed.

Mose was climbing the ladder to the loft; it creaked but held his weight. Carlos peered down from above, and so did Kaylee. Lainey and Turk were nowhere to be seen, so Artie guessed that they had managed to get up into the loft as well.

Shandy went to the leather couch and looked around for a moment. The dirty blanket had disappeared. She sat and hugged herself, rocking back and forth. Ben returned with the industrial-sized first aid kit that Artie had seen on a shelf with canned goods in the basement, and at that moment, Tim came in from the storm, hair and face wet and whitened, with a bucket, a towel, a plastic packet, and a package of cloth diapers. He set the bucket on the stove.

"The diapers, of course!" Ben said, and Artie heard a little murmur of voices from the loft. "I'm beginning to understand why you and Gary were friends, Tim." Ben continued, "Shandy, we're going to boil that water, cool it down with clean snow, and soak off your bandage. Have you taken anything for the pain?"

She nodded. "Four aspirin, at noon, the last ones." Her teeth were chattering. "Worn off now."

"Aspirin," Ben said, and a moment later Artie caught his meaning and made for the pantry. After some searching among the boxes and cans on the shelves, Artie brought back the large bottle of aspirin and a plastic cup of cooling coffee. "Three," said Ben, and Shandy gulped them down.

"Water's boiling," Tim called from the kitchen.

"Get a big steel bowl and fill it halfway, " Ben told him, "Leave the bucket on the stove, but move it to the side so the water doesn't all boil away. Take the bowl of hot water out in the yard and set it in the snow, and take a clean spoon and drop in some snow until the sides of the bowl feel luke."

"OK." Tim ducked outside yet again. Eventually, whitened once more, he tramped back into the kitchen and declared that the water in the bowl was "luke." He carried the bowl to the sofa.

"This is what's happening," Ben said to Shandy, his face close to hers. "I'm putting the bowl on your lap, and I want you to hold as much of your arm under water as you can manage. Go slow. Keep it under."

Shandy gasped when the tepid water closed over most of her forearm, but obeyed Ben without question. "Five or ten minutes," he said. "Are you allergic to antibiotics?"

"No, I'm OK with them," she said. "I was on antibiotics after that spider bite last summer."

"Which one? Which antibiotic?" he persisted.

"Don't remember," she replied. Parts of her bandage were coming unstuck, floating in the water like large brown-blotched tapeworms. Ben got a fork from the kitchen drawer, dropped it into the bucket of steaming water on the stove, then fished it out with the tongs he'd told Artie he had picked up on impulse at Ace Hardware in Twin Falls, a lifetime ago.

"Time to get the bandages off," he said, and went to work with the fork, very deliberately.   Artie saw Shandy squeeze her eyes shut.

At last the bandages were pulled away, and Artie could see the stinking wound, capped with yellow pus and surrounded by angry reddened skin, a gash almost six inches long, and deep. The entire arm was swollen. "What's this from? What cut you? Do you know?" Ben asked.

"I hit the back of my head when the bus went over," Shandy said. "I was next to the window. I blacked out. I guess Mose dragged me out of the bus, and he said there was a big piece of glass in my arm and he pulled it out after he got me to the rocks. I never saw it."

"Glass," Ben repeated. "I hope he got it all out. I'm going to poke this and then press out the pus and wash your arm," Ben said. "Tim, more luke." He handed Tim the bowl of filthy water and bandages. "Toss this where the dogs won't get to it in the morning, and rinse the bowl out with boiling water before you make the luke." Tim took the bowl and disappeared. "Artie," Ben continued, "Amoxycillin and hydrogen peroxide, top shelf of pantry."

She ran to get them; she had found them while searching for the aspirin. Ben had Sandy take three capsules of Amoxycillin. "Three?" Artie had to ask. She had taken antibiotic capsules that looked like these, but never three at a time. "These capsules are supposed to be given to dogs," Ben explained.

"Oh," was all Artie could say; of course. Frank Elliott had been a vet. These were veterinary antibiotics, sized for pets.

"Well, look at this," Ben said, speaking as if to himself while he used a folded diaper to clean Shandy's arm with hydrogen peroxide, carefully avoiding the gash itself, "This is just like the Jersey calf that time, two years ago. She was in a car wreck, or a trailer wreck, I guess you could call it. Some idiot t-boned the trailer she was riding in, and the calf had a big metal cut in the top of her front leg, like this cut Shandy has, and the guy who owned her didn't call Gramps for several days, and it got infected. I went with Gramps to help hold the calf, and I'm trying to do pretty much what he did then. Have you ever seen a Jersey calf? They have beautiful brown eyes and long eyelashes. And I saw Gramps fix up a black Lab one time that had an infected cut like this, too. Only I don't think we're going to have to put Shandy's head in a big plastic cone of shame." He flashed a smile and Artie's heart turned over. "Your arm is swollen and too warm, but I don't see any red streaks, so that's good," he said to Shandy.

Tim offered the bowl again. "Look," Ben said. "Another bowl for your lap, Shandy. Almost done."

Artie and Tim watched while Ben broke the seal of the pus with the kitchen fork, and with the blunt handle, pressed the wound over and over, rinsing and rinsing as well, driving out the pus and washing it into the bowl. He asked for and got another bowl of luke, and rinsed the wound again. He wiped her arm once more with the peroxide, staying well away from the open gash. "It's too swollen to use the butterfly bandages yet," he said to Shandy, "and it has to drain." He tore two diapers into strips and wound them loosely around her arm. In triumph, Tim produced a package of jumbo safety pins from his pocket. Artie watched Ben dunk them into the bucket of boiling water, pull them out with the tongs, and secure the bandage.

"Now, stand up, Shandy, that's the girl," Ben said, and spread a sleeping bag on the sofa. "Sit down or lie down." Shandy obeyed like a robot, and lay on the couch. Ben took the new pillowcase Tim had brought from the barn and slipped it from its plastic wrapping. He shook out the pillowcase and put it on Shandy's bandaged arm like a great wide bag. "For leaks," he said to Sandy, "to keep it clean, and so your bandage doesn't stick to the sleeping bag or to your clothes." He safety-pinned the pillowcase loosely to the hem of her t-shirt's sleeve. Then he folded the top half of the sleeping bag over her very gently and stepped back. "If you have a problem, yell for me," he said. "And if you have to go pee or anything like that, yell for Artie. OK?" Shandy nodded and closed her eyes.

"I'm going to take the dogs out now," Ben said, taking up the bowl, "and get rid of this water." He looked at Artie and Tim. "Come on."

The three of them went out with the dogs, took turns at the outhouse, and, with the headlamp, watched the dogs do their business, which they were reluctant to do in the driving snow. The snow was still coming down in force, blowing into their eyes. Finally Ben, the last one to take a turn, came out of the outhouse. They stood huddled together against the wind, waiting for the dogs to finish. "It's not going to be easy from now on," Ben said.

Tim nodded, his arms in the puffy parka wrapped around his middle and a knit cap pulled down over his eyebrows. "I'm afraid of some of these guys, Ben," he said, so softly that it was difficult for Artie to hear him over the wind. "I guess you had to take them in, but *still*." He brushed a hand over his face. "Do you know what some of them have done to me at school, what they say about me, what they say *to* me? What they have said and done for years and years?"

"To me, too, Tim," Ben said. "Been there. How could I not know?"

"Guess things always stay the same. Come on, Smoke," he said to the poodle. "You're done. Let's go to bed."

"Wait." Ben put out a hand. "Wait." He said. "It's still my Place--that is, if the laws of the USA still work at all. And I can make them go if they get too weird. Me and what's in the gun safe," he added as Tim was about to speak.

"Turk," Artie put in. She shifted from foot to foot. "Hurry up, Moonie, and get it done," she said to the gray Sheltie.

"Yes," Ben said. "Turk. There is something wrong with that guy. There was something wrong from the first day he moved to Hailey two years ago. Maybe he will never wake up and be the old Turk again. That's OK with me. But for now, he seems to be handled. By Lainey. Kind of strange, but she seems to be taking care of him. I wouldn't want to."

"Lainey," Artie repeated. "Kaylee. And Carlos isn't the world's shiniest person, either. But we have to get Shandy fixed up. You made a good start."

"Yes," said Ben. "We do have to take care of her. I hope we can. Look," he said, the light from his headlamp a puddle of sparkling silver on the blowing snowflakes between his feet. "Like I said before, whatever happens from now on, it's us. This is our home, the three of us—our Place. Not theirs, at least not until–or if ever--they prove themselves. We'll do the best we can. And you were good tonight, Tim. I wasn't sure about you at first, but you did exactly right."

Artie nodded. "He sure did." She looked up hopefully, but Ben was silent. She sighed. Well, she had to admit to herself, pretty much everything she had done today, she had done as directed by Ben.

"Let's go in and get some sleep," Ben continued. "Come on, Moonie, you slowpoke. You're finished."

Artie thought, "It's going to be weird, us sleeping in the same room, with all the others here. But I'm so tired that the others can just stuff it if they don't like it. Too freaking bad." She turned her back to the wind and followed Ben and Tim up the path to the house.

They reached the porch and stamped snow off their feet, the dogs leaping around the three of them in excitement.

"And Artie," Ben said with a light touch on her shoulder, "None of this would work without you." He opened the door and they went in.

Artie had to tell her feet to go forward. She felt a smile begin somewhere near her heart and radiate warmth even to the tips of her cold fingers.

Artie took off her parka and hung it on one of the wall hooks. The house was dim. Someone had put the larger oil lamp back on the kitchen table, but it seemed to be running out of oil and was guttering; what flame there was, was very small. The living room was dark now, except for low flickerings from the sleepy fire in the fireplace. Someone sat on the floor near where Shandy's head lay on the couch pillow, someone large, with a sleeping bag draped over his shoulders, a black bulk almost entirely in shadow. On the floor nearby, Andy lay stretched out on another sleeping bag, already asleep.

"Mose," Ben said softly, feeding the fire. "Wake us if there's any problem with Shandy. I should warn you," he continued. "We get up in the dark to cook breakfast. If you're still awake when you see it getting the faintest bit light outside, stop putting wood on the fire. We don't want to show smoke during the day."

Artie saw the black heap that was Mose give a single nod. She blew out the lamp on the table and let the dogs into the bedroom. The lamp in the small bedroom was guttering as well, but it showed her a gleam of shining hair on the floor, and Artie saw that Paleface was zipped into her sleeping bag so completely that only her hair was visible. She had chosen to put her sleeping bag in the space on the floor between the foot of the beds and the wall. The dogs stepped all over her, but she didn't seem to wake.

Ben, Artie, and Tim climbed into their bags, and the dogs distributed themselves in various spaces on the bed not already occupied. Tim blew out the lamp. Artie whispered, "There sure is a lot of breathing going on in here," and they all laughed, a little shakily.

Artie tried to hold off sleep so she could think, but she was so, so tired.

Rising and falling, the storm howled just outside the bedroom window, and Artie thought, "I'll bet the coyotes are tucked up in their dens tonight." She turned to one side and fell away into blackness almost at once.

She woke once toward dawn, and felt warmth on both sides and Ben's breathing in her hair. After a moment, she thought, "We're three spoons," and smiled to herself in the dark before she went back to sleep. She trusted them.

CHAPTER 3

SHANDY

Artie woke in the dark to an argument. She was alone in the bedroom; even the dogs had gone. Artie had fallen asleep in her clothes, and struggled out of her sleeping bag as quickly as she could. Something was wrong. She could feel it.

"Let go of me!" came Lainey's angry shout through the closed door.

"Stop it!" That was Ben's voice, raised as Artie had seldom heard it before. "Stop it, Lainey. I mean it. You are not going out there."

As Artie pulled open the bedroom door, she could see that she had slept longer than usual. The rooms were dim, almost dark, but the windows were light rosy gray. It was almost dawn. And she could hear another noise beyond the argument, a mechanical noise, very faint, diminishing. Frightening.

Carlos was climbing down from the loft. His stocking feet appeared at Artie's eye level. "What the shit are you doing, Elliott?" he said. "Let go of her."

Ben looked toward Mose in the dimness. "Mose?" he said. The big guy got to his feet and held out his arms. Ben pushed

Lainey, protesting, into them, and Mose held her. "Let's get this sorted out, Ben," Mose said, holding fast to Lainey. "What?"

"That was a helicopter," Lainey said to Ben, kicking out at him. "You ugly, lame scumsucker! Let me go, Mose; maybe I can signal it to come back."

The sound of rotors faded and an electric silence filled the room. After a moment Ben said quietly, "Oh, the helicopter will come back. I think it's a scout," he went on as Andy got to his feet and went to the window. "It's white. And I don't want whoever is piloting the thing to find us."

"Why the shit not?" Lainey had stopped struggling.

"Yeah," Carlos added, "why the shit not?"

Artie joined the fray. "Want to be shot? Want to be taken by the white soldiers? I don't."

"Shut up," Lainey said, turning to squint at Artie in the dimness. "I don't give a flying freak what you think, Artie Ames. I'm going home. *We're* going home."

"As soon as the snow is gone to the point where we can get the truck back on the road," Ben said, "I'll take you, at least to the highway. But this is my place, and you'll do nothing to attract attention to us while you are here."

Carlos took a step toward Mose. "You going to make us behave, Scavenger? And Mose, what's the matter with you?"

Ben said, "Use your brain, Aguirre. Artie saw a man shot in the back on Main Street. Tim saw at least two people shot. Artie and Tim saw their families poisoned. And you yourselves heard shots and saw one person fall." He turned to stare out the front window. "That was a white helicopter. Did you run to the white soldiers for help the night the bus crashed on the Shoshone highway? Or did you hide and run?"

Mose held Lainey by the shoulders; his hold looked casual, but though she pried at his fingers, his big hands didn't budge.

"Let's take a vote," Carlos said. "All in favor of trying to flag down the chopper—"

"The last I heard it was still the U S of A," Ben cut in. "This is my Place. If you want to go, then fine--enjoy the snow. I won't stop you, but if you go out to do that, I won't be letting you back in."

"We'll toss *you* out," Carlos began, "then—."

Andy held up a hand. "Look at the dogs," he said. "Look at them."

In the half-light of the kitchen, Bear, Molly, Smoke, and Moonie were suddenly still as statues. They sat near the kitchen door, ears up, heads cocked to the side. They were listening.

A blade of clear yellow light slashed into the room from the east windows: sunrise.

"I hear the helicopter," Lainey cried, struggling again. "It's coming back!"

Artie had a sudden thought and remembered Ben's binoculars on top of the living room bookcase. She grabbed them and headed for a window. The *whack, whack, whack* of the helicopter came louder and louder.

"East of us; it's east of us," she thought, and looked out the window toward the east ridge. "Let's see what's written on the helicopter before we do anything," she said, focusing.

"Right," said Mose. "It could be Search and Rescue. Or Homeland Security. Or National Guard."

Artie fiddled with the focus wheel on the binocs. There on the ridge were the fat granite columns of the Fingers, and above them, above them—a white helicopter swam into view.

"It's a Blackhawk," Ben said to no one in particular.

"Well?" It was Andy. Everyone downstairs but Paleface, Tim, and Shandy had crowded to the window. "What do you see, Artie? It's white, like Ben said. I can tell that there's something written on the side, but I can't read it. It's too far away."

Artie focused on the chopper as it skimmed the ridge. "17," she said. "It just says '17.' There's nothing else, not even a logo or a star." Into her field of view came the steel runners, the legs of the chopper. A long, dark bundle was lashed to one of them. The helicopter turned slightly into the wind for a moment and changing light flickered along the runners. The bundle had a face: purple, almost featureless, battered.

The bundle was a body. The jaw was wrong, and Artie realized with a shock that the lower jaw had been wrenched almost completely from the skull. The jaw hung swinging in the wind, sunlight winking on the u-shaped arc of teeth. She handed the binoculars to Andy, wanting someone else to see. "There's a dead body tied to the runner," she said.

Andy's quick intake of breath surprised her; he handed the binocs to Carlos and said, "Look. That body is wearing regular desert camo and boots, not the white stuff. Has a webbing harness, too, like in pictures of my dad in Afghanistan. No helmet, but looks to me like a dead soldier."

Mose released one of Lainey's arms and a huge hand came up to take the binocs in turn, the other dragging Lainey to the window by one wrist. "Huh," he muttered, then handed the binocs to Lainey. She lifted them to her face and gasped as the copter rocked and turned in a gust of wind. "That thing, that body is all bloody on the side," she said. "God, it's horrible. It's grotesque. But maybe they are rescuing the soldier. Or recovering his body."

"Rescuing? You want to bet our lives? They are recovering his body, all right. Probably killed him, too. Still want to run out and wave your arms?" Ben asked grimly.

"God, no," Lainey said, and with a touch of her usual confident grace, turned to him. "I'm sorry, Ben." She put her hand on his arm for a moment. "I didn't know what I was saying. I'm so worried about my family, and I want to go home."

Artie clamped her teeth shut on what she wanted to say.

Tim joined them at the window. "Anybody else want to run outside?" he asked. Carlos looked away.

"They're quartering," Tim said. "They're flying a search pattern."

The helicopter, diminishing, disappeared, heading due south. "The first time, it was so far west that I could barely hear it. It was just getting light then," Tim went on. "Next, it was over the far west hills, and I could see it, all right. And then it did a pass closer to us, maybe one gulch over. And then this pass, down the east ridge. I don't know exactly how far north and south it's going, but it's doing a pattern, flying north-south lines maybe five miles long and two miles apart." He looked at Ben and Artie with a wry smile. "We'll hear the helicopter again in a few minutes, farther east, but we won't be able to see it. It will be beyond the east ridge by then."

Artie said, "Aren't you glad it snowed, and drifted? Nobody has been out to leave any tracks yet, have they?"

"We've taken the dogs out to potty," Ben said, "Tim and I went, in the dark, before we heard the chopper the first time. But it's still blowing. It's drifting so fast that our tracks disappeared right away. And Artie," he said. "Some of the roofs have blown clear of snow. So if the chopper doesn't come back over us, Abbie has worked!"

"What's Abbie?" Andy asked.

"Oh, that's Artie's Brilliant Idea," Tim responded, "to have Ben paint black holes in the roofs and such, so that from the air, the place looks abandoned."

Then everyone fell silent, listening. *Whap, whap, whap.* As Timothy had predicted, the helicopter was flying a north-south path just east of them now, menacing but fainter, invisible. When the sound faded, Mose said, "Gone."

From the loft rose Kaylee's touseled head; she peered sleepily over the half-wall. "Did I miss something?" she asked of no one in particular. "Lainey, come up here and get Turk. And what's for breakfast?"

"Tim and I made oatmeal with raisins," Ben said, "and we mixed up some powdered milk in a pitcher. And there's coffee, and a bowl of dried apricots. The oatmeal is still fairly warm."

"Boy, am I glad we didn't have smoke coming out of the chimneys when that chopper came down the ridge," Tim said, as if to himself.

Artie saw Ben give him a tight nod. "Yes," she thought. "Gramps Rules."

Artie looked around for Paleface and found her sitting at the kitchen table, polishing off a bowl of oatmeal. When she saw Artie, she smiled. In the new sweatshirt and jeans, Paleface looked much more like an ordinary—if unusually small—teenage girl this morning. Artie smiled back, and then noticed a large pile of crumpled clothing on the floor not far from Paleface's chair. Artie sighed. Her arms and the Rollowash would get a good workout after dark this evening, when they could build a fire in the stove again. Someone had better help.

Kaylee, Lainey, and Turk trooped out the kitchen door to the outhouse. Mose and Carlos dived into the oatmeal and poured themselves some coffee as well. Artie did the same. Andy bent over Shandy, who still lay on the couch, and motioned Ben over. "Got a thermometer?" Andy said, hand on Shandy's cheek. "She's burning up."

Ben brought the first aid kit and took Shandy's temperature. "Oh, my god," he said. "It's a hundred and four. We need to get her cooled down. Maybe we could bring in some bowls of snow . . ."

Artie set down her coffee mug and went into the living room. Mose abandoned his breakfast and followed. "Or," Artie said, looking out the east window, "we could take Shandy outside and lay her in the snow, pack her arm in snow out there."

Ben smiled and said, "Another Abbie," and went to the back door even as Mose lifted Shandy from the couch. Shandy managed to put her good arm around Mose's neck but protested, "No, Mose, I'm cold. I'm cold, don't you get it? Make Mose put me down, Andy. I don't want to go outside." Mose ignored her protests and stepped off the back porch into two feet of drifted snow.

He and Andy positioned Shandy on the snow like a snow angel—on her back, with her arms and legs spread. Mose held her down while Ben heaped snow over her injured arm. "Cold," Shandy kept saying, "cold. Freaking morons! Why don't you listen to me? I'm freezing!" She struggled to get up.

Mose, his big hands on her shoulders, responded with, "Just a minute or two. Hold still. Just a minute."

Artie held Shandy's hand to keep her injured arm under its heaping pack of snow, and glanced over at Mose's face, so close: fine-textured coppery skin, prominent jaw, great slabs of cheeks, stubby lashes around small eyes so dark they looked black, large, high-bridged nose. His was a very masculine face, a strong face, but as he looked down at Shandy, Artie saw something more in Mose's intense concentration. "Why, Mose is in love with her," she thought. "Who would have thought it? I wonder if Shandy has any idea how he feels."

Mose held Shandy on the snow for fifteen minutes. Then Mose and Andy helped Artie get Shandy in and out of the outhouse and back to the sofa, where, shivering, Shandy sat herself on the end closest to the fireplace and its glowing, ashy coals. She seized the sleeping bag and pulled it around herself like a shawl, tugging it up to her ears so that she became the core of a small, puffy green teepee. Ben took her temperature. "Better," he said. "100." He removed last night's bandages, expressed a little more pus from the wound, and packed Shandy's forearm in a large bowl of clean snow. "Here's your amoxycillin," he said, handing her the capsules and a mug of water, "and you will drink a cup of water every hour. Five minutes arm in the snow bowl, fifteen minutes out, Shandy. When it melts to slush, you tell somebody and we'll get you fresh snow. No arguments." Shandy nodded and closed her eyes.

Artie found herself staring at Ben. Quiet old Ben, taking charge again. Amazing.

Ben noticed the stare. "What Gramps would do," he said, barely audible. "Training. I helped Gramps sometimes."

Artie nodded. "But it's not all Gramps," she thought.

"OK," Mose said. "I'll fetch and carry the snow. And after seeing that helicopter I agree that it's not a good idea to have a fire during the day--but I'm glad that these coals in the fireplace are still pretty warm. They should last a while."

It took some time for everyone to serve themselves oatmeal and coffee, get to the outhouse, and settle down for the day. Tim came stomping inside in midmorning, carrying the kitchen broom. "Ben, I got the tracks smoothed out the best I could do," he said, hanging his parka and knit hat on a hook beside the kitchen door. "Any coffee left?"

"Two thermoses in the sink," Ben said. "At least it's still drifting a little. That should help." Tim poured himself a mug of coffee and joined Ben in the living room.

Carlos, Turk, and Lainey had disappeared into the half-loft, from which came a soft, intermittent snoring. Andy and Kaylee had found a deck of cards in an end table drawer and were busy with a game, sitting together on the floor. Kaylee had French-braided her hair and washed her face with water from the bucket on the stove. Somehow, she managed to look lovely even in too-large jeans and a baggy sweatshirt. "But—is that eyeliner?" Artie asked herself ungenerously. Artie felt uncomfortable. She hadn't bothered much with her face and hair since she had come to the

Place. Now she was suddenly aware of her own clean but hastily gathered ponytail and bare-naked face.

Mose settled himself again on the floor near Shandy, who had fallen asleep. He had asked Ben about books, and Ben had found him a coffee-table book about different breeds of horses. Ben and Tim sprawled full-length on the rag rug near Mose, each of them with a book. Artie could hear them talking in low voices. "I tried the crank radio again this morning," Ben was saying. "Nothing's new. It's the same old recorded BS about sunspots knocking out all communications. As if."

"Huh," Mose said. "What do you think?"

"I don't know what to think," Ben replied, "but I'm really glad nobody went out and waved at that helicopter."

Mose nodded. "Huh."

Artie busied herself with cleaning up the kitchen. She wiped the bowls and spoons and stacked them, then rinsed the dish cloth and hung it to dry. Surprisingly, Paleface got up to help, but she remained silent. Artie shook her head at herself. She had slept in too long today; she would have to finish doing these breakfast dishes in the evening, after dark, when she could heat water.

Artie felt prickly and restless. She still felt as if something was wrong. "Probably the helicopter," she told herself. "That's plenty to be wrong."

Then Artie stood for some minutes in front of the bookcase in the living room and at last chose one of the books brought in from the storage barrels, one of a set of three books she had found only the day before, before the snowstorm, before the others came and everything about the Place changed: *The Vicomte de Bragelonne*. Pre-Revolutionary France was about as far removed from the current situation as she could imagine. "That's good," she thought, "escape." She came back to the kitchen with the book and saw that Paleface had already fallen asleep and was snoring softly, her head on the table cradled in her arms, the silvery-cream hair falling in rippling waves over her shoulders and down her back.

The floor under the table was lumpy with sleeping dogs. Artie moved her chair closer to the still-warm stove, eased off her shoes, tucked her stocking feet under Moonie, and began to read.

⊶⊷

Ben woke with a start, lifting his head from the *Home Medical Advisor* he had been reading. The living room was chilly, but someone had dropped a blanket over him as he slept, and he felt warm, especially where all three Shelties were pressed along his legs and ribcage. He put out a hand to Bear's black fur and was treated to a sloppy kiss. "Urrgh," he whispered as he wiped dog saliva from his cheek with the back of one hand, realizing that he had forgotten to shave this morning. What with Shandy's fever and all the commotion of the helicopter and of providing for the new people, he hadn't even thought to do shaving water. Not a crisis, he decided.

The pale blue light coming in from the east windows told him *late afternoon.* Ben pushed up on an elbow and surveyed the room. Shandy was still asleep on the couch, Andy near her on the floor, and Mose was snoring as he sat on the floor with his back to the couch, his head thrown back and pillowed on the sofa cushion. Tim lay on his stomach against the bookcase, with Smoke curled up at his feet. The red plaid throw from the couch covered him. Carlos, Kaylee, Lainey, and Turk were nowhere to be seen; they must be in the half-loft. "Sounds like everyone's asleep. I imagine that none of them has had a good rest for some time," Ben thought. "Ok." He angled his head a little and could make out the unknown girl, Paleface, sound asleep at the table in the dim kitchen, her head on her arms. Near her among the chair legs there was a stockinged foot that had to belong to Artie.

It was time to take the dogs outside and to rustle up something to cook for dinner. Since Tim had cooked last night in all the chaos and had taken Ben's turn, it was Ben's turn tonight.

Ben hoped he could get the Shelties and Smoke out the kitchen door without waking everyone up, but—he was going to take the dogs now, regardless.

He got up and the dogs, even Smoke, followed him without a command; now they knew the routine. Grabbing his hat and parka from one of the hooks beside the kitchen door, Ben stepped onto the porch, taking a moment to close the door gently. No one in the house had moved a muscle as they went out.

The dogs, joyful in the snow, frolicked and rolled. Ben surveyed the new, white world, taking a better look than he had in the morning. The sun burned low above the Castle Hills in a cloudless sky. The wind still skirled the surface of the snow, but the howling, shrieking presence of the night before was long gone. Ben surveyed the Place and concluded that almost two feet of snow had fallen during the night.

Long drifts three or four feet deep hugged the western walls of each building, and the dog kennel was drifted deep. "I'll have to break out a snow shovel to clear that," Ben thought. Timothy had done a fair job of sweeping over the morning's tracks, aided by the continuing drift, but, scanning the sky, Ben hoped fervently that no more helicopters would come. He went back for a moment to grab the broom from the kitchen.

He took the dogs past the outhouse and saw that last night's wind had scoured a portion of the meadow almost clean of snow, right down to the yellowed grasses and sedge. "That's drifting for you," he told them. This would be the best place for the dogs to go potty now. They dived into the deeper snow beyond the clear area and snowplowed with their faces, except for Smoke, who did his business rapidly and came back to lean against Ben's legs, shivering. "Your sissy hairdo is growing out," Ben said to Smoke, ruffling his fur. "Pretty soon you will have fuzz on those skinny sticks you call legs and you'll be warm like a real dog." After being confined to the house all day, the Shelties ran and ran, casting long, spider-legged shadows and making great looping sets of tracks in the meadow. "Coyotes," Ben told himself. "Coyotes do this, and Sheltie tracks look a lot like coyote tracks.

"But as we keep coming back to the same places, from the air the dog tracks won't look like coyote tracks any more. Huh," he said aloud, unconsciously echoing Mose. "Need to think about this." There were many things he should be thinking about concerning the Others, as he was coming to think of the newcomers, but Shandy's problems were the most pressing. Two hours with the *Home Medical Advisor* before he fell asleep on the floor had given him no options other than to continue what he was already doing for her.

He thought of Shandy's lovely flushed face and slender body, then the ugly, swollen arm and hand. "Last night was the first time I've even touched one of the popular girls," he thought, "the first time I have been close, really, to any girl—except Artie." Ben shook his head. Even the thought was strange. He felt odd, tense at being so close to so many others. *Others.*

"Keep on keeping on," he told himself. "Have got to get Shandy's arm fixed. Glad Mose turned out to be one of the Others." Ben shook his head slowly. The secret he shared with Mose didn't matter now, would probably never matter again, but he was glad Mose was here, especially because of Lainey and Carlos. And Turk, whatever was going on with him.

The *Home Medical Advisor* hadn't had much to say about hematomas, except "Get to a doctor at once." He'd thought much about Turk this morning, but in the end, he felt that it would be colossally stupid to try to drain the swelling on Turk's head himself.

Keeping the area clean and giving an oral antibiotic seemed wise, and—and *harmless.* Harmless. Yes, that's the word he was searching for in his mind. Ben hoped that Turk's condition wouldn't deteriorate. He sighed. The truth was that he much preferred this new, vegetable Turk to the old, cruelly arrogant, healthy Turk.

Ben let the graceful contours of the whitened hills soothe him and thought about the morning's incident with the helicopter. The house was crowded now. He had never been able to think very well when he was around people, and it felt good to be out in the open air for a while, away from them.

"The first thought the Others have is to leave, to get back to town as soon as possible," he told himself. "I don't think I have thought about actually doing that, not seriously anyway, since Gramps died. And I would bet that Tim and Artie haven't, either. But the Others are worried about their parents and grandparents. And Carlos has a little brother. *Has* or *had.* Tim, Artie, and I have no family left in Hailey. At least, I don't consider Uncle George's family as part of my family. As Gramps used to say, 'There's nothing like reality for being real.'" Ben had to smile, remembering. "Gramps also said, 'There's nothing that propinks like propinquity.' Wonder how it's going to work out with all these guys here. They're the popular crowd, except for little Paleface, and that bunch has never had any use for me. In fact, I've seen all of them be pretty cruel at times, even Mose. He knows I would never tell the secret, and besides, that's old news now. If I'm honest with myself, I really, really didn't want to go get them. I'm not sure Artie and Mothy, *Tim,* would have done it if I hadn't decided to do it, especially Tim. Hope it wasn't a mistake. Guess sometime I'm going to have to think about what divides what I would do from what Gramps would do, *would have done.* Wonder if it's the same."

Ben pulled his hat farther down over his ears. It would be cold tonight. He said to himself, "I'll have to start taking more time to saw and split wood every day, starting tomorrow. It would be stupid to use up all the split wood stacked on the porch right away, because it gives some insulation to the walls. And it's good to have a fair supply of wood done ahead for when it gets *really* cold and *really* snowy."

The Shelties didn't pause in their play when the sun slipped behind the Castle Hills and turned the world of brilliant white and sky blue to soft gray and indigo. Molly initiated a game of chase and the others followed, running and dodging in tight circles through the thin and patchy skiff of snow on the meadow. Ben took long moments to admire the great, sweeping lines of the hills made austere by the snowfall, and his fingers itched to hold a pencil or paintbrush. The Hand, stark against the dusky eastern sky, was a study for charcoals, or charcoals with light watercolor washes carefully handled, washes with grays and the tiniest floats of pure azure blue.

The three Shelties, having long since finished their business, abruptly stopped playing and started back to the house on their own, trailed by Smoke. They hadn't done that before. Ben took a step to follow them, and the world *shifted*.

The dogs ran back to Ben and gathered close, Molly standing on her hind legs, her front paws on his knees, her eyes looking up at his face. Suddenly, he realized that Molly wasn't playing. Her whiskers were extended, stiff, and the corners of her mouth sucked in. She looked terrified. Moonie and Smoke pressed against his ankles. Bear was growling.

Ben felt disoriented. "What is happening?" he said aloud. He scanned the horizon, turning in a circle. Everything looked the same: the buildings, the hills, the meadow, the Hand on the east ridge. "I must be losing my mind," he thought. "Nothing has happened." But why was Bear still growling?

Ben shook his head and headed toward the kitchen door. In front of him, Bear stopped suddenly and, turning his head back to Ben, bared his teeth. "What is with you—" Ben began to say, but the earth jerked sideways and he fell to his knees.

Over Bear's growls, Ben could hear a deep rushing, almost a grinding, and when he tried to stand, he somehow could not get his balance, and went to his knees again. The bent apple tree near the southwest corner of the house swayed like an old drunk. Moonie jumped into his face and jammed her body next to his chest, shaking. Ben gathered her into his arms and sat back in the snow while his mind tried to make sense of what was happening.

Presently the rushing noise died away and the ground stayed still. Ben found that he was able to think.

"Earthquake." The thought fell into his mind. He picked up the broom from where he had dropped it in the snow. "We've had an earthquake. I've never felt an earthquake before." Scrambling to his feet, he ran with the dogs to the house, and they tumbled inside, breathless.

Artie met him at the door, Mose close behind her. "What is happening?" she said. She looked just awakened from sleep; her bangs stuck straight out and she had one hand braced against the door frame. Further into the house, Ben could see that people were awake and just as disoriented as he had been. At the table, Paleface got up and moved closer to Artie. The dogs skirted Mose and bolted into the small bedroom.

Tim slipped into the kitchen past Mose and voiced Ben's thought. "Earthquake," he said. "Holy crap. We've had an earthquake. We'll have to make sure all the buildings are OK before it gets dark."

"Mothy can think, all right," Ben said to himself, standing the broom in a corner of the kitchen. "Yes," he said aloud to Tim. "It's going to be dark in half an hour. Let's go. Artie, keep the dogs in, OK?" He looked at her face and noticed the slightly rebellious set of her jaw. He realized that she wanted to go with them. "Please?" he added. "And check inside here for cracks and stuff—the fireplace, the stove, the stovepipe, the walls—"

"Got it," she said, handing Ben his headlamp from the wall hook.

Ben and Tim went out, followed closely by Mose. Tim stepped back into the kitchen for the broom. "Tracks," he said to Ben as the door closed behind him.

Later, in the early darkness, the three of them trooped back into the kitchen, where the oil lamp now burned on the table.

Ben felt the rumblings of hunger and suddenly remembered that it was his turn to cook. But Artie was feeding kindling to a new fire in the cookstove, upon which sat the two graniteware coffeepots. A large kettle of something brown and lumpy had been placed on the table, along with a gallon jar of what looked like yellow flour, as well as two flat rectangular pans, a can of Crisco, and one of the steel bowls.

"Find any damage?" She asked. Ben watched her dump a generous amount of the coarse yellow flour into the bowl.

Ben hung up his hat, coat, and headlamp. "Some hay bales fell down in the barn and knocked over a couple of barrels," he said. "The top came off of one of the barrels of towels. Next to the woodshed, some stacked wood came unstacked. That's all. Everything else seems OK."

"Shiny," she said, turning back to the bowl.

"What are you doing?" Ben asked.

"Chili and cornbread," she replied shortly.

"Oh," he said, feeling ashamed. "Oh. It was my turn. Sorry."

"No worries," she said with a small smile. Ben felt warmth burn his cheeks as she went on. "The chili is from cans. Coffee's on. And I found more small bowls in the basement." Artie dipped some water out of a bucket on the floor and added it to the flour, stirring. "No eggs, so it's going to be extra crumbly."

"I'm starving," Mose rumbled. "Don't care."

"I'll start a fire in the fireplace," Ben said, taking a match from the holder on the wall, "and check on Shandy." He let out a breath in relief. He had forgotten about dinner while he was checking the outbuildings with Mose and Tim, had completely forgotten. "Good old Artie," he thought. He hoped she wasn't too irritated at him for forgetting. At least there were more people now to take turns at the stove. He thought of Tim's disaster with the green beans and hoped some of the others, the Others, could cook. But now he knew that Artie would pick up the slack, and that was good. "One less thing to worry about, at least for tonight," he thought.

CHAPTER 4

EARLY WARNING

Lainey fed Turk his chili at the kitchen table; Paleface took her bowl into the small bedroom. Artie stayed at the table to eat her chili; she decided that she wasn't going to let Lainey and Turk oust her from her favorite place near the stove. And besides, she needed to keep stirring the chili so it wouldn't stick, until everyone had been served at least one bowl of hot chili and she could take the kettle off the stove. When she and Gran made chili, Gran never added the cooked beans until the last minute. "Beans make it stick," Gran always said. But this chili was pre-made, with beans already in it, so it would have to be stirred the entire time it was on the stove. Where were Gran and Grandpa? It was difficult even to think about that. "One thing at a time," Artie told herself. "Stir the chili and get these people fed." Gran would have felt the same.

Artie tried not to look at Turk across the table. Turk's empty eyes were eerie. Artie found it hard to reconcile his former air of disdainful superiority with this calm, mindless creature, docile as a kitten, opening his mouth for the spoon. Ben had looked at Turk's head injury again, probed it with his fingers, and said he thought that the skull hadn't been fractured, but couldn't be

318

sure. The bulge behind Turk's ear persisted, and Ben had given Lainey some antibiotics and some aspirin to give Turk twice a day as a precaution against infection.

It was odd to see Turk's long, heavily muscled forearms lying slack in his lap as Lainey fed him spoonful by spoonful. Artie wondered at Lainey's devotion; after all, Lainey had been a part of Artie's class from first grade on, and before Turk, Lainey had pursued and discarded boyfriends on a regular basis. "Before Turk, Lainey's record with a boyfriend was about 6 months," Artie remembered. "Guess I don't know her as well as I thought," she concluded, watching the chili-laden spoon arrive at Turk's lips a final time. "Maybe Lainey truly is in love with him."

That was just fine with Artie; she felt shuddery just thinking about having to take care of Turk. She had wished Turk dead on several occasions in the past and had almost seriously meant it. Maybe she *had* meant it. He was habitually quite cruel to those who weren't part of the in crowd, and to teachers, bus drivers, and custodians. Even the most popular treated Turk Thomas with exaggerated care. He could and would turn on anyone at a moment's notice, anyone but Lainey.

Kaylee and Andy helped Artie with the dishes and then joined Mose, Carlos, and Lainey in a card game at the kitchen table. Paleface moved her sleeping bag into the larger bedroom and coaxed Molly in as well.

Shandy was somewhat better. After Ben, Tim, and Mose had come back from checking the other buildings an hour earlier, Ben took Shandy's temperature and announced that it had fallen to 99 degrees. Her arm was considerably less red and swollen. Mose had been bringing in fresh bowls of snow for her until they had all drifted to sleep in mid-afternoon. For dinner, Shandy stayed on the couch, but seemed more alert than she had been in the morning. She had been faithful about drinking the water Mose and Andy brought her.

Everyone seemed subdued as the evening lengthened. Today's helicopter and earthquake were strange enough, but Artie figured that the others were at last realizing that going home wouldn't be easy, and that some might not have a home or even a family left in Hailey. Cards were a good thing, an occupation for minds that needed some distraction.

Artie was glad of the dishes and the cleanup work. She felt reactive, hyperalert for no reason, and needed to be doing something, anything.

Tonight the blackness outside the windows seemed oppressive; somehow she felt vulnerable. A movement near the kitchen door caught her eye as she finished washing the chili pot. Bear sat staring at the door, ears erect, moving his tail slowly back and forth on the floorboards. He turned to face her for a moment and she thought, "He isn't wagging because he's happy. He's tense." She reached down and stroked his head, but Bear didn't look at her, didn't move. Goosebumps broke out on her arms; she could feel them without even looking. She felt Bear's tension crawl into her throat, take over her breathing. "What's out there, Bear?" she whispered. "What is out there?"

Artie frowned. Maybe this feeling was caused simply by the Others; it was irritating having them crowding the Place. The heap of the Others' damp and dirty clothing still occupied one corner of the kitchen floor, and nobody had made a move to do anything about it. Artie wrinkled her nose. The clothes wouldn't smell any better tomorrow. "Wonder if I can get somebody to bring me some water and some more wood if I wash the clothes," she thought. "And I am not, *not,* going to be the only one who does any housework around here. The new guys can have today off, and then they are going to take their turns. And tonight, someone else can fetch and carry." She made a trip to the basement, where she had stashed the Rollowash and the galvanized tub for heating water, and retrieved them. It was going to be a long evening. But at least she had something to do.

⊫ ⊨

The next morning the dogs woke Ben by scratching at the bedroom door to go out. It was still midnight-dark. It had been an odd night. Sometime toward morning, movement on the bed had awakened him. At first he thought it was one of the dogs resettling, but eventually he realized that it was Artie, pulled by Paleface, gathering up her sleeping bag and leaving the bedroom. That was odd. But he had noticed that Paleface didn't like to be close to any of the boys, himself included. He hoped he hadn't made Artie angry by taking off to check the other buildings without her. Before he could think too much about it, he had fallen asleep again, and all was blank until the dogs woke him before dawn.

Quietly he let himself, and all four of the dogs, out of the bedroom. He woke up the fire in the stove with a few new sticks of split pine before he took the dogs outdoors. That way, Ben thought, he could put the coffeepots on as soon as he came back in. He threw on parka and hat, grabbed his headlamp, and went out.

Outside, the wind was howling, but the stars were clear and bright in the black sky. There shone familiar Orion near the end of his night's hunt, about to fall behind the hills before the sun came up. And higher, Ben found the Little Dipper and followed its pointer stars to Polaris, the north star.

The wind carried tiny beads of snow, picked up from the surface. They stung his face; the cold air was sharp, too, but clean and pure. Patrick or Ramona passed silently overhead, blanking the stars in the path of dark wings. From a cottonwood near the barn, one of them screamed.

Ben walked the dogs to the meadow and stood still, sweeping his headlight back and forth among them as they played and did their early morning business. The air was cold, colder than it had been so far this fall. Ben felt the cold seeping into the soles of his feet.

Downcanyon, the last of the night's coyotes tuned up with long, wavering cries. Ben took a deep breath and held it. "I love this place," he thought. Despite, or perhaps because of Gramps' death, in the cold of this dark morning Ben realized that he loved the Place with everything he had in him.

He felt rooted here, part of the meadow, the hills, even part of Cat Mountain. Though he couldn't see them in the pre-dawn darkness, he knew where the willows stood in the meadow, where Spear Creek twisted and turned, knew where the grasses and sedge ended and the stands of sage began at the bases of the slopes, knew where the wild geraniums slept near that big fallen aspen up in the grove, where the ground squirrel holes were, could find each place where the deer liked to cross the creek. "My Place," he thought, breathing deeply of the icy air. *Live for the Place, die for the Place,* something deep inside seemed to say, and that felt just right.

It felt good to be away from the house and its unusual bustle. He took another deep breath, and with it came a name. *Lucy.* The sudden thought stung him like a wasp.

Dr. Lucy had not come. He'd figured her arrival for two weeks ago, about the time Tim and Artie had arrived. What would Lucy do, in her big pickup with its trailer, now that the little dirt roads to the Place were blocked and drifted with snow? Two feet of snow might not stop a big pickup, but the drifts would. And it would not be possible for her pickup to pull the trailer up the long hills in this much snow.

Typically, he remembered, Horner Ranch Road was plowed in the winter, as far as Horner Ranch, anyway. Gramps had said that the Horner family did the plowing themselves, because Horner was a private road. Ben wondered if that would still happen. In any case, Lucy was fit enough. Even in two feet of snow with deeper drifts, she would be able to walk from the state highway to the Place in a day.

But what if nobody plowed the state highway? Ben rubbed his cold hands together and shoved them into his pockets. He had better locate the rest of the gloves today. He hadn't considered that the main roads might not be plowed. The main roads were always plowed, always. He shook his head. That would be quite a handicap for Lucy.

He needed to get his head around how different things in the outside world might be now. "Got to find that solar charger," he chided himself. "Have to call Lucy and find out where she is, how she is." The thought of actually knowing what had happened to Lucy was a little frightening; he shivered. "Come on, dogs," he called. "Time to go in and make the coffee." He sent his thoughts ahead and began planning out the day.

"I hope Shandy is better this morning," he thought. "And I hope Tim or Artie remembers where the yeast is. With this many people here, somebody is going to have to learn to bake bread." He smiled nervously at the thought. "Hope it's not me."

Artie stacked the newly washed breakfast dishes in the sink and wiped her hands on her jeans. Hot canned peaches with cinnamon, coffee, and freshly baked biscuits was a pretty fair breakfast, if she did say so herself, though she found herself longing for bacon and eggs. Tim had, under direction, prepared the peaches. She didn't trust him to make any more biscuits just yet, but now for her they were easy and getting easier. She was getting the hang of the big black stove and was glad it had come through the earthquake undamaged. "Earthquake," she thought. "Scary. Wonder what's going on down deep." But Shandy came into the kitchen to bring a forgotten coffee cup to be washed, and the thought faded.

Shandy was considerably better today. That was good. Her arm was much less hot and much less swollen. Mose was hovering around her like a bulky shadow. That was good, too.

This morning Ben had decided to make an all-out effort to find the solar charger, the yeast, and a few other things that would be good to have handy during the winter. Shandy and the dogs would stay inside, but everyone else would help look.

It was cold. The thermometer mounted outside the kitchen windows read six degrees, and there was a wind. But Artie was eager to spend some time outside the confines of the house. Everyone else seemed just as motivated: they all wanted working cell phones, and they all wanted bread. Ben had found jackets for all of them, Mose, too--though his new black Gramps-parka was tight through the shoulders. They would look for more gloves as well.

Even Paleface was getting suited up for the outdoors, brilliant in the shocking pink of a child-sized parka from one of the barrels. Artie wished for the hundredth time that she knew Paleface's real name, and why she wouldn't, or couldn't, speak.

Artie shoved the chairs back into place at the kitchen table. Then she noticed Bear, who was pacing back and forth, back and forth, in front of the door from the kitchen to the outdoors. "Bear wants to go outside, too," she thought, reaching for the blue parka Ben had given her two nights ago, when they had gone after the Others. "But what's the deal? He went out to do his business less than an hour ago. By this time, he is usually fast asleep under the table." But then she looked closely at Bear. His whiskers stood out stiffly from his muzzle, and the white-tipped plume of his black tail was carried at half-mast, also stiffly. "Bear," she said, and the dog rolled an eye at her but didn't give up his pacing. She zipped the parka thoughtfully. Why was Bear on alert? A tingle of unease lifted the hairs on the back of her neck.

Everyone but Shandy and the four dogs spilled out into the early sunshine and headed for the barn, Paleface last of all. "Barn first," Ben had said. "I seem to remember seeing the solar charger in the barn the last time I was here with Gramps. It must have been stuck into a barrel that got labeled something else."

Artie helped Ben and Tim open both barn doors, sweeping back the snow in twin arcs, to let in as much light as possible. The cold came in as well, but that was all right; it was as cold in the barn as it was outside. She felt warm in her knit hat, puffy parka, thick socks, and Gran's rubber boots. Artie had her map of the barrels in her pocket and noticed that Tim was clutching one of his lists as well.

Carlos strode to the back of the barn and pried off the lid of a barrel there. "I'll take this area," he said without looking at the others. As clearly as if Carlos had written it on his jacket, Artie read "and nobody is going to order me around today" in his posture and tone of voice. She saw Ben shrug, heard him say, "OK."

Mose and Andy began looking in barrels near Carlos. Lainey sat Turk on a hay bale and placed his hands in the pockets of his parka. She began looking in barrels close to him; Kaylee fluttered nearby. Artie decided to stay near the doors. It seemed a little colder there, but she could see better. Paleface and Tim flanked her, and the three of them began prying lids from barrels. Ben turned suddenly and went back to the house.

Faintly, Artie could hear Bear barking from the house. That was odd. Why would Bear bark? Could he be miffed that he didn't get to come to the barn with everyone? Maybe he had to do another dog-potty run. Artie stood straight and stared into the dark corner of the barn nearest her, where a dim wall of baled hay stood against the old boards, smelling sweetly of sunshine and the dry end of summer. She shivered, a little creeped out, for reasons she couldn't fathom.

Leaving Turk for the moment, Lainey sidled over to Artie and took her aside. "Artie," she began conspiratorily, as if Artie were one of her inner circle, "where is the stuff kept? *You* know. "

"What stuff?" asked Artie, trying not to sound irritated. "I don't know what you mean." Why couldn't Lainey just say what she meant?

"Feminine things, " Lainey said softly. "From what I see, Crazy Frank Elliott wasn't that crazy when it came to this prep stuff. Did he think of feminine supplies? You do know what I mean."

Artie nodded. "Oh. Yes, there's lots of that stuff, several barrels full, all kinds. I'll show you where those barrels are later on. They're in the chicken house, right at the front."

Lainey smiled, as if she had known that all along. "And the other stuff?"

"Come on, Lainey," Artie rejoined tartly. "Don't play games. What other stuff?"

"All right," Lainey said with a little more volume. "Birth control. Where's the birth control stuff?"

"I don't know of any," Artie said.

"Well, what are *you* using?" Lainey demanded softly. Her porcelain-fine skin seemed to glow in the twilight of the barn, her deep blue eyes shadowed by the long black lashes.

"Me?" Artie was taken aback. "I'm not, we're not—"

"Right," Lainey said with a tight laugh. "Little miss innocent. Well, ask Ben. Ask him."

"Ask him yourself, Lainey," Artie bristled, turning away. "You want to know, you ask him."

"Fine. I just thought, since you know him and I don't . . ." Lainey turned on her heel and stalked back to Kaylee and Turk.

Artie found herself looking into the ice-blue eyes of Paleface as she turned back to her barrel. Paleface shook her head, then made a thumbs-down gesture. Artie smiled and did the same. "I do know Ben, at least better than Lainey does," she thought.

She dived into the barrel at hand. Sugar. Bags of sugar. She lifted out the bags and stacked them all on the floor until she could see to the bottom of the barrel. "Well, what did we expect?" she said to Paleface, who grinned at her. "After all, these barrels say 'Sugar' on them." The whole barrel had been packed with five-pound bags of sugar, clear to the bottom. Paleface handed her each bag and Artie re-packed the barrel. Tim passed her the lid and she pressed it down tight.

They moved to the next barrel. Sugar. They dug out bags. More sugar. Artie fought to keep her temper under control. OK, so she *was* an innocent. So she believed in waiting for true love. So she was inexperienced. She smacked the barrel's lid back onto the barrel and hit it all around the edge with the heel of her hand to seal it. "So what? Things are different now," she thought, moving on to the next barrel and prying on the lid to loosen it. "This isn't town, it isn't school, and I'm the way I am. The Others can lump it." She wondered what Ben would say when Lainey asked him about the birth control supplies, what he would think. During their mapping of all the barrels, Artie hadn't seen any birth control pills or packets, or even condoms, but maybe they were in one of the bunkers, places she hadn't really investigated.

Suddenly she remembered something her mother had told her, almost out of the blue, several years ago when they were en route to Boise on one of their girls-only plant-shopping trips.

Her mom hadn't been big on ferreting out Artie's secrets or forcing girly talks upon her, but on this occasion, something her mother had said had burned itself into Artie's heart. She couldn't even remember what had led up to these words, but she could hear her mother's voice clearly even as she stood on the worn boards of the old barn with her fingers prying at a cold plastic barrel lid: "Artie, your body is your own. It's not mine, it's not God's, it's not society's, and it certainly doesn't belong to anyone you date, or even anyone you marry. It's *your* body, for you to live in, for you to give and for you to hold back. Yours. Just remember." And she did.

Artie smiled to herself and began to hum under her breath. Paleface seemed to relax a little and leaned forward to help pry off a stubborn lid. Artie looked inside the barrel and spent a few minutes lifting out bags and putting them back inside. Only sugar again, all the way to the bottom. Paleface and Tim handed her the bags to be fitted back in. Sighing, she tamped the lid home and moved to the next barrel.

Presently Ben came back to the barn with Bear, who looked as if he had been scolded. Bear's ears were folded back into his ruff, but his whiskers were stiff and curved forward; he was still on alert. Artie held out her hand to the dog and he came to her, sniffed her fingers, and then trotted to the back of the barn, where she lost his dark fur in the deep shadows there. Black shadows. The shadows there were very black.

"Hey, earth to Artie," Tim was saying. "You need help with the next lid?"

Artie came to herself with a start. She had been in another place, in that place she went in her mind when something wrong was on its way, when a wrongness was sliding down the minutes, to arrive in the near future at her feet. Automatically, she reached for the lid of the next barrel, let Timothy help her pry it free. "More sugar," she heard herself saying, but she knew Bear was right. Something here was wrong.

Tim hauled out five-pound paper bags of sugar and handed them to Paleface, who laid them in a row on the hay. "Look!" Tim said in triumph. "Look! Here's the solar charger! And here's its manual, too."

As if from a far distance, Artie watched Tim's upper body disappear into the bright blue barrel. Paleface stood close beside him to take the sugar bags he handed her. Artie held out her hands automatically and Paleface passed her the bags; Artie continued the row of sugar bags that Paleface had started.

Then Tim gave a grunt and pulled a long-necked plastic appliance from the barrel just as the others came to gather around him. Artie was rather surprised at its appearance; the thing was made of pale green and gray plastic and looked a little like a slim, small vacuum cleaner, except for the flat panels along one side. Under it in the barrel was a small booklet, its manual.

"Good deal," Ben said, coming over for a look. "That's great. At least Gramps was the one who labeled those sugar barrels, not me! And Mose has found a stash of gloves. Now all we have left to locate today is the yeast."

Carlos yanked the solar charger out of Tim's grasp without asking. "I'm first," he said. "I've got my phone right here in my pocket, anyway. I even have my charger cable, too. Where do you plug the phones in?"

Tim pulled down the hem of his parka and stood his ground. He held out his hand for the charger. Artie saw that the hand was trembling just a little, and she stepped forward to stand beside him.

"I said, I'm first," repeated Carlos, taking a step toward the barn door.

"Solar," Tim said. "It's a solar charger."

"Well, give you a fish," Carlos said. "So?"

Ben and Bear stepped into the circle of people standing around the charger. "So," Ben said, "it needs to be out in the sunshine for a few hours to get charged up. It's been sitting here in the barn for months."

Carlos set the charger on the floor with exaggerated care and headed for the house without looking back. Lainey and Kaylee rolled their eyes and then began chattering happily. "How long do you think it will take to charge it up, Ben?" Kaylee asked. "I can't wait to call my parents."

"Mine, too. And Lenny," Lainey added. "And Turk's dad."

"I have no idea," Ben answered Kaylee, "but Tim will know after he has a look at the manual. I'm going back to the barrels to look for the yeast."

Tim and Ben exchanged glances. Tim shoved the small booklet deep into a pocket of his parka and bent over the nearest barrel. "Sugar," read the label written on the side. Sighing, he began to pry at the lid.

"Good deal," Ben said, and returned to the place where he had been working.

Kaylee and Lainey, somewhat slowly, returned to their area as well. "Oh!" Kaylee said almost immediately. "Is yeast in little flat packages that are all connected together?"

Ben looked into her barrel. "Success!" he said. "That's great, Kaylee. We found all three things before anybody had a chance to get really cold."

Artie was surprised at how strongly she wished she could have been the one to find the yeast. "Never mind," she told herself. "I'll bet I can guess who will get to make the bread."

Kaylee, Andy, and Lainey ran back to the house, laughing, their breath fogging in the cold sunshine of midday. Lainey held Turk by the hand and he kept pace, but he moved in jerky steps like a wooden toy.

Paleface and Tim followed.

"I'll help you close the doors," Artie said to Ben as they stepped from the dim barn into the blinding world of sunlight on snow.

"That's OK," he said, "I can do it. The snow is pushed out of the way—" he reached for the edge of the nearest door. Bear stayed close to Ben's feet.

The others were well out of earshot. "Ben, there's something wrong," Artie said, had to say. "Something bad is about to happen."

"What?"

Her heart sank at the tone of his voice. "Something is wrong here. I can feel it."

"Everything is OK," Ben went on. "I know it's different with all these people here . . ."

"That's not what I mean," she said doggedly. Why had she thought he might understand? It did sound stupid, stupid and groundless, after all. "I just feel it," she said, hearing how weak that sounded.

"Come on," Ben said briskly, shutting first one big door and then the other, then chaining them together without clicking the padlock. "It's all right, Artie. Maybe you're just tired. Let's get back to the house. What are we going to do for lunch?"

Artie had a sudden thought. "Bear," she said. "Have you noticed Bear in the last day or so?"

Ben stopped in his tracks and looked down at the black and white Sheltie. "Bear? Bear is acting like—like Bear."

"Just watch Bear, that's all I ask," Artie said. "He's upset. He's disturbed by something. At night he keeps watching the kitchen door."

For a long moment Ben looked into Artie's eyes. "He was pretty disturbed by the earthquake yesterday," Ben said thoughtfully. "He growled, and I never hear him growl. He is probably still upset from that." Ben began heading for the house. Bear took a last long look at the barn and followed.

Artie realized that it was foolish to think that anyone, even Ben, would believe that she had these warnings, these unexplainable feelings, about evil to come. She would just have to stay focused, that was all, and hope that Bear would give some kind of alert when the bad whatever it was, actually came to pass. In the meantime, she would get *Breadmaking 101* from the living room bookcase and see what she could learn.

CHAPTER 5

FOLLOWED

B en found everyone but Artie, Tim, and Paleface sitting in a circle on the floor in the living room playing cards. Even Shandy had joined them, crosslegged between Andy and Mose, her arm still in its pillowcase sleeve. Tim had flopped onto the floor near the bookcase. Ben had to smile; the solar charger lay next to Tim and he was absorbed in the manual, which he held close to his face. Paleface sat alone at the kitchen table, reading.

Ben heard Artie's steps on the basement stairs. A minute later she was in the kitchen with three large boxes of saltine crackers. She made another trip to the basement and emerged with a big jar of crunchy peanut butter.

Ben felt a little guilty. "Here, Artie," he said. "Let me get some jam out of the pantry and some plates, and I can make lemonade from the mix." He lowered his voice. "Please don't be irritated," he found himself saying in a low tone. "I didn't mean to blow off what you were saying. I just don't know what to think." It was true. Ben had thought of Artie as the facts-only one of the bunch, the practical, "let's get it done" person. This strange claim she had made to foretell the future had put him off-balance. Though he had known Artie since they were five years old, had been in the same grade, the same classrooms with her all through school, maybe he didn't know her at all. The thought made him uneasy and he wished he could forget what she had said out by the barn.

Artie smiled, but it was a thin smile. "It's OK. It's all right," she said very quietly. Then her face changed and she added, "This is what I could think of for lunch without building a fire. People can do their own." She turned to the top drawer under the counter and gathered up several table knives.

"Looks fine," Ben said. Still feeling that he should make amends, he said, "I'll go out and dip some water with the chili kettle, and break some ice off the water wheel, and make some lemonade. Seems weird that we can have iced lemonade now when it's cold but won't be able to next summer." Artie smiled again, a better smile.

Ben felt a small wash of relief as he went out the door with the kettle and the broom; the last thing he wanted today was to have Artie irritated at him. Since the Others had showed up, he was feeling good that Artie and Tim, and to some extent Mose, had his back. But truly, he found himself thinking as he made his way across the frozen meadow, he didn't understand what Artie had meant when they were closing the barn doors. How could she possibly know that a bad thing was coming, that *anything* was coming, for that matter? Did Artie think she was psychic? Weird. Weirder than anything he would have thought would come from Artie.

Outside, the intense blue of the clear sky was being invaded by a solid sheet of cloud sliding slowly toward Spear Creek Gulch from the south. Ben saw movement on the west ridge as he approached the creek; a coyote was trotting along the skyline, supported by the hard crust on the snow, nose to ground, seeming almost black against the bright snow of the higher hills beyond. Gliding low over the ridge, two ravens followed, as close to the coyote as if they had been ragged black balloons tugged behind him on a string.

Ben, broom in one hand and kettle in the other, crunched through the snow down to the water wheel. "Trying to smooth over our tracks in the snow with the broom doesn't work at all after about the third time over the same paths," he thought, worried. "I hope we don't get another helicopter coming over." But the sky, for now, held no threat, and the meadow was silent except for the faint, muffled rushing of the creek under its blanket of snow and ice.

The broom handle wasn't heavy enough. Ben had to bash the ice with the bottom of the kettle to get to the water and eventually managed to get the kettle two-thirds full. "Bring the axe next time, and a little pot to dip with," he told himself. He broke some clear, stubby icicles from the waterwheel, dropped them into the kettle of water, picked it up by the handles, and glanced once more at the west ridge.

The ridge was empty. The coyote and ravens had taken their hunt to the Castle Hills side. That was good; he didn't want Bear chasing—or chased by--coyotes later on.

Ben had a sudden thought and set the kettle down on the snow.

Before him in the air, his fingers traced the line of the ridge, where he saw the remembered image of the trotting coyote, the two ravens after—and suddenly he saw it in his mind: dark coyote, black ravens, their blue shadows, the mantle of cottony cloud moving northward into the blue. "Raven and her mate are wise. Ravens follow Coyote for scraps from his hunt," Ben said softly. "*The Hunt.* What a painting that would make." He could see the sky dominating and veiled with ancient, half-seen symbols held in the approaching cloud, and below that, the small black silhouettes of the three living animals, intent upon their purpose, their shadows sharp and distinct . . .

Maybe he could merge the night sky with the daytime sky and its cloud, using a darker sky—Orion the hunter and Coyote the hunter. Ben shook his head. How could he paint now, with a house full of people, some of whom, Carlos Aguirre especially, were fairly nasty human beings?

But this image caught and held him. He resolved to make a sketch with notes when he got back to the house. "Sketch immediately and do your concept notes, composition notes, and color notes right away," Mrs. Phillips had told him more than once. "Capture the vision. When you get an idea, sketch *now*, do your notes *now*, let the idea simmer, and *then*, when you have the time, paint." Ben took in a breath, held it, let it out in a puff of fog. "She's a smart old bird," he thought. "Is? Was? *God*." He had learned so much from Mrs. Phillips in so short a time. "I hope you made it," he said into the sky. "I hope you're out there somewhere, Mrs. Phillips." Head down, he trudged back to the house. The kettle was heavy.

Ben set the kettle of water and ice on the kitchen table and stirred in the required tablespoons of pale yellow lemonade powder from the round box in the pantry. Everyone was up, even Shandy, slathering stacks of saltines with peanut butter and sticking them together with blackberry jam.

Ben went straight for his art supplies. He had stuffed the new supplies into a large box in the bottom of the bedroom closet, next to the gun safe. He pulled out one of the small, fat sketchbooks, a flat rubber eraser, and a soft pencil.

Ben sat on the floor against the wall, drew up his knees to brace the sketchbook, and began. *The ridge. The cloud front. Coyote. Coyote trotting, legs reaching diagonally, front and rear. The ravens. The shadows, the snow, the curve of a little draw trailing toward the meadow. The sky—Orion, Polaris, Bootes, stars. Prey. A snowshoe hare in the sky, barely visible. A deer mouse. A sage grouse with his tail folded to a point. Some quail, but no small ones, because it's winter.*

Vaguely, as if it were from a radio turned down to whispers, he heard the banter and laughter of the others over lunch, the clink of a knife against a plate, the chime of ice dropped into a cup, steps on the floor. *A darkness there behind. Colors: reduce, desaturated palette--gray, blue-gray, charcoal gray, near-black for the creatures, gray-gray-green of the sage, cobalt-blue shadows, the sky blue and indigo and midnight. Day and night at once. Time, all the time for hunting, told there in the sky. The stars, gold for richness and contrast. Hunters. Hunters. And now the sketch—the sky, the cloud, the star patterns, the ridge. Curves of hills above. Coyote and ravens, sharp and distinct. Their shadows. The foreground, snow-covered sage.*

There, the notations were finished. He surfaced as from deep water and saw Lainey leaning in the doorway, watching. He wondered how long she had been watching him. She took a peanut-buttered cracker from the small plate she was holding and bit neatly into it.

Ben closed the sketchbook at once and put down the pencil.

"That's not a real drawing," Lainey said. "You wrote right on it. Why did you do that?"

"It's a study for a painting to be done later," Ben said. He felt awkward. "I was doing my color and composition notes."

"Oh," she said. "Didn't you want to play cards?"

He saw that her lips were full and the curve of her cheek was smooth, creamy, and unblemished. The shadows of her lashes below those dark blue eyes were blue, too, almost like the shadows on snow he had been remembering. She would be quite a painting, too. He'd never done a portrait of a girl, but if her hair would swing down and forward to make a smoothly textured background for her profile, and—

"Taking a picture of me?" she said, laughing.

Ben felt his face flush. A conversation with one of the cheerleaders—that was new. He didn't know what to say. "Didn't mean to stare," he said at last. "I paint. I look at faces that way. To draw them later. To remember."

"Oh, really," Lainey said, as if this were the oddest thing in a zoo of odd things. "Well, yes, you should paint me sometime. I haven't been painted yet."

"Yet," Ben thought, "yet. As if she expects to be painted in the future. Certainty of future fame. Wonder what it's like to have that kind of mindset."

"We're going to play a few more hands upstairs and then take a nap," she was saying. "Nothing else to do." And she was gone. Ben heard the ladder creak, steps above, and the soft thuds of bodies hitting the mattresses in the loft. He got to his feet and stowed the sketchbook, pencil, and eraser in the drawer of the night stand, where they would be easy to reach when he next needed them.

He shook his head. Had that been an invitation? If so, it was the first of its kind in ten years of knowing Lainey Adams. "Wouldn't that be something?" he thought, "Scavenger playing cards with the school elite. *Invited* to play cards, by Lainey Adams." Overhead, Ben heard Carlos laughing. Was he really invited? The Place was his. He could go where he pleased here. But Ben wouldn't go up, didn't want that kind of laughter. And the image of Lainey, lush and provocative as she leaned against the door frame, began fading.

His mind filled with golden stars in a night sky, the only warm color in a world of whites, grays, and blues--a snowy ridge, coyote tracks, and raven wings. With that vision in his mind, he felt better without knowing why, felt more like himself, like Ben Elliott, than he had since--since the Last Friday, that Friday night when Gramps had died and everything had changed.

⊷⊱ ⊰⊶

Artie sat at the kitchen table and watched as everyone settled down to sleep the afternoon away. Tim had just come in from the front yard, where he had placed the solar charger in an area that would be away from the shadow of the house even when the sun began to dip low in the west. He had announced earlier that there might not be enough hours of sunlight left in the day to charge the thing fully, but this afternoon would be a start.

Now Tim was lying on his stomach on the floor next to the living room bookcase with a book propped against Smoke's furry back, studying something with more technical drawings than it had text. But his eyes kept closing, his head nodding over the pages. Paleface was already asleep at the table. Ben had gone into the small bedroom without having lunch and was still there. Turk, Andy, Lainey, Kaylee, and Carlos had climbed into the loft, Shandy had discovered the beds in the second bedroom, and Mose was snoring in the living room, asleep on the sofa with his large stockinged feet projecting off the end above the dead coals in the fireplace. "Only their second day here, and there is already a pattern," Artie thought.

Moonie and Molly were flat-side asleep under the kitchen table. Moonie was sound asleep and still, but Molly was dreaming. Her breath huffed in and out and her white legs twitched in sequence. In her dreams she was running. "I hope you catch that dream rabbit, Molly," Artie thought.

She collected the plates, cups, and knives and piled them in the sink, then stowed the remaining half-box of crackers under the counter. She capped the peanut butter and jelly and found places for them in the pantry. After wiping down the table and sweeping the kitchen floor as best she could without displacing the dogs, Artie pulled *Breadmaking 101* from the shelf near Tim's feet and came back to the table to read until she, too, fell asleep. The last thing she saw was Bear, sitting on alert, staring at the door to the back porch.

When Artie woke, the dogs were gone. She saw the kitchen door closing gently and knew that Ben was taking the dogs out for their end-of-day run. He had always done this by himself, and though Artie would have loved to tag along, she sensed that he needed his alone time. The house was silent except for Mose's intermittent snores. Everyone else must still be asleep, Artie thought. Paleface was. Her face was hidden by the long ivory hair as she slept at the table, her head on her book.

Artie glanced at the windows. The sun had gone down, and the gray twilight would soon turn to indigo twilight, then darkness. She felt restless and irritable, confined, almost claustrophobic. She missed her late-afternoon routine, established during the two weeks of tranquility before the Others came, of climbing up to the Hand and singing, then sitting on the flat rock writing in her journal, her right hand stinging a little from the chilly air, before she came down from the east ridge. But now, wallowing through snow up to the Hand meant making a path in the snow, meant tracks, easily visible tracks. And it was too cold now to write outdoors. Well, at least she could write in her journal here. She was getting behind and had two eventful days to record. That would be fun.

Artie got up and retrieved her journal from the living room bookcase, walking softly in stocking feet so as not to wake Tim and Mose. She had resolved not to write anything intimate or intensely personal in this journal. "Just the facts, ma'am," she told herself. "Just the facts." This was to be the history of the new times, and perhaps in the future her words would be read by many—by everyone, even. "The Journal of Artemisia Ames," she thought, "famous chronicler of deeds of the New Times. Award-winning chronicler. Skilled chronicler. Insightful chronicler. Courageous chronicler." She shrugged and shook her head. *Right, Artie.* But then she smiled. *First chronicler. Only chronicler.*

She found herself leaning against the living room wall, looking out the east window as the day faded from gray to indigo. The sky was empty, even of cloud. The Fingers of the Hand thrust darkly into the sky from the top of the ridge. Not a breath of wind stirred those branches that weren't covered by snow. The solar charger, looking like a cross between a personal robot and a cleaning appliance, sat fatly in the snow between the southwest corner of the house and one of the fir trees. Not a bird flew by, not a tree branch swayed. This would be a good time to write.

Notebook and pencil in hand, she headed for the kitchen table, when something caught her eye and she stopped in her tracks.

On the wall beside the front door hung the chalkboard, moved by Ben to the space where the map had been before Tim had taken it down and hidden it. In one corner someone had doodled a little alien with round head and wavy eyestalks. She remembered seeing that. At the top someone, probably Ben, had written, "Take the broom and brush out your tracks." But there was now a new line on the board, something printed very small at the bottom, just above the chalk tray. Artie stepped closer so she could read it.

"*Man followed us here,*" it read.

Artie read the line again and again. "Man followed us here." She felt strangled, felt suffocated, and all the strangeness of "bad thing coming" coiled and tightened around her chest and squeezed her lungs. This was it. This must be it, the bad thing she felt was coming. But who had written this on the board?

Artie heard Ben on the back porch, stomping snow off his feet. The door opened and three dogs bounded in. "Bear!" she could hear Ben calling. "Bear! Bear, get in here this minute!" Presently Bear trotted into the kitchen and Ben shut the door. He took off his hat and parka and hung them on the hooks, then bent to ruffle Bear's fur. "Jeez, Bear, you idiot. What's got into you?" he said.

Artie met his eyes across the room. "Maybe this," she said quietly. She waved a hand toward the blackboard.

Ben crossed the room and bent to read the tiny, crabbed message at the bottom of the board. His gray gaze, coldly accusing, pierced Artie's heart. "Did you write this, Artie? Did you?"

"No!" she said, louder than she had intended. "No, I didn't write it. I only just noticed it."

Mose raised his head from the sofa pillows and pushed himself upright. "What?"

Ben pointed to the board. "See for yourself, Mose."

Mose lumbered over to the wall and read the message. "'Man followed us here?' What the crap is that supposed to mean?"

"Unknown to me," Ben said. He looked at Artie.

"Unknown to me, too," she replied to his look, and took herself back to the kitchen. She felt crushed. Did Ben think she had written the message so that he would believe her claim that something bad was on its way? "Damn," she thought, "I shouldn't have pointed it out. I should have let him find it on his own." But then her curiosity took over and she began to wonder in earnest. Who *would* write this on the board? And why? Underneath the question she still felt a kind of heaviness, a dark oppression. Something was going to happen, and soon.

She felt almost sick, but there was no time to be sick. Though she had taken Ben's turn last night, it was her turn to cook dinner tonight, since none of the Others had stepped forward. She had better think of something to make.

The windows were dark now, and the light in the rooms was dim and fading. Shadows gathered in the corners.

Tim yawned and stretched, then stuffed the technical manual back into the bookcase. "I'm just going to run out and bring in the solar charger," he said. "I'll see if it's charged enough to do anything." He went out the front door, banging it behind him.

Carlos came sliding down the ladder. "Hey, I'm first with the phone," he said, looking pointedly at Ben.

Ben said mildly, "Fine. Let's see if the charger works."

Tim came in, carrying the solar charger. He said, "Need to light a lamp or use the headlamp so I can see the gauge."

Ben brought the lamp from the small bedroom, lit it in the kitchen, and brought it out to Tim. The others, awakened by the commotion, climbed down from the loft.

"Two-thirds charged," Tim said with a thoughtful grin. "That's good. It's working! Maybe it would charge one phone tonight. I'll put it back out in the sun tomorrow. Too bad it's not summer. Things charge slower when it's cold."

"Here," Kaylee held out her phone. "Do mine."

Carlos pushed her hand away. "I'm first, honey. My phone is first."

Tim scrunched up his face as if he smelled something foul. "Fine," he said. "Hand it over and let me look at the connectors. Got your charger?"

"Yeah." Carlos dug it from a jeans pocket and handed the thin wire and its connectors to Tim.

Ben held the lamp while Tim examined the connectors and the sockets on the solar charger. "OK," he said finally. "It will plug in."

"Great," Carlos said, "just connect it and then I'll call—"

"It doesn't work quite that way," Tim said, fussing with the connectors. "I'm just guessing that there's enough power in the unit to charge a phone. It will probably take maybe twenty minutes for your phone to get to the point where it will actually work, since your phone hasn't been charged for a long time." He plugged Carlos' phone into its charger, and the charger into the solar unit. The phone's surface, black, stayed black, blank even of the usual battery image. "Let's just leave this to charge for a while and keep checking on it."

"Yeah." Carlos threw up his hands and turned away.

"Come on, Carlos, don't be a, a—" Kaylee paused as if she couldn't think of what to call him.

"I'm next," Lainey was saying.

"And then me and Shandy," Andy put in.

"I don't know if there will be enough power for everybody tonight," Tim said, "but we'll find out."

Artie's phone had been dropped into the steel dog food bin the day she and Tim had arrived at the Place, and there it remained. She didn't care if she was the last to have her phone charged. At least the Others thought they still had family. And maybe they actually *did* have surviving parents, grandparents, sisters, brothers. She couldn't call her family, and closed her eyes at the picture her mind had suddenly flashed of them lying, rotted now, on the floor of her home. Of Sally, her white-furred head now bloated and stinking in the bowl on the porch that once had held clean water. But no, the water might be gone now, evaporated away. Maybe Sally would be covered with snow, a smooth white lump in a clean white drift at the edge of the porch. *God.* "Gran and Grandpa," she thought. "I could call them. But--"

"Ben," Artie said, "What about the cell phone GPS thing?"

"What do you mean?" Mose demanded.

Tim said, "Cell phones can be traced to the nearest tower, not a good idea if you don't want to be located."

"Well, we'll be quick," Ben said as if he had decided that it was a risk worth taking. "And I just remembered that Gramps checked on the towers. The nearest one is on top of—is at least 30 miles away, so that's a good bunch of square miles to look for us in. We can probably chance it, once or twice, for everybody who still has a phone."

"But hey," Mose went on, "what about this thing written on the blackboard? Talk about weird."

Everyone crowded close to see the pinched writing at the bottom of the board.

"Well, creep-ee," Lainey pronounced. "Who did that? Who wants to star in *Dismember 2, the Cabin?*"

The others looked from face to face. For a long moment, no one spoke, then everyone spoke--saying basically, *it wasn't me, it wasn't me.* Everyone except Paleface.

Andy suddenly raised his head and said, "Paleface. What about her? If it wasn't any of us, it was Paleface!"

In a blur of jeans and gray sweatshirt, Paleface ran from the kitchen into the larger bedroom and slammed the door. They all heard the immediate click of the lock.

"Paleface, you come on out here and answer our questions!" Carlos shouted, "Or we will break the door down!"

"Nobody's breaking down any doors," Ben said. "I can open that door quite easily if it's necessary. But let's let Paleface calm down for a while and then maybe Artie can get something out of her. Paleface kind of gravitates toward Artie."

"Yes, Ben, but we need to know," Kaylee commented. "A man followed us here? I don't like the sound of that. At all." Lainey and Shandy nodded.

"Nobody goes outside alone until we figure this out," came Mose's deep voice. "Ok?"

"Good," Andy said. "Good idea, Mose. Hear that, girls? Nobody goes out alone."

Tim muttered something to Ben, but Artie was too far away to hear.

"Hey, speak up, Mothy," Lainey said. "Do you know something about this? Maybe you wrote it."

"All right." Tim said, getting to his feet. "I was just saying that tomorrow in the daylight we should go around the backs of all the outbuildings, look at the sides of the buildings we can't see from the house, and see if we can find any tracks. See if anybody has been sneaking around."

"Brr, that gives me the snakes," Lainey said, though she looked perfectly composed. "A sneaker."

"Good idea, though," Ben said.

"Aaahhh, it's probably just Paleface being stupid, trying to get us stirred up," Carlos said, yawning.

"I'm going to heat up corned beef hash, and canned green beans, and make blueberry muffins tonight," Artie thought to herself suddenly. "Without eggs, the muffins will be crumbly, but I don't care. There are cans of beans and hash, and at least one big can of blueberries in the basement, so I won't have to go out to the old bunker or to the chicken house tonight in the dark, if there is something bad out there. And there are some jars of honey in the pantry, so we can have honey on our muffins." Artie thought of butter, real butter melting into steaming, tender muffins, tall muffins made with eggs, and sighed. Someday. She headed into the kitchen for the oil lamp.

"Hey, Artie." Carlos followed her. "Hey, get Paleface to come out here and tell us why she wrote that on the board."

Artie looked at Carlos for several seconds before turning away. She simply found that she had nothing to say to him. It was time to bring those cans up from the basement, anyway.

"I am talking to you, Ames," Carlos said, crossing the room and putting out an arm to stop her.

Ben was there in the kitchen, as suddenly as if he had materialized from the air. "No," he said. "Settle down, Aguirre. Or if you want to go out and check the outbuildings yourself, my headlamp is on the hook beside the back door."

"Well, *Scavenger,*" Carlos said, grinding out the word, "what I do want is to get Paleface out here and make her tell us what she knows and why she wrote that on the board."

"Nobody's going to make anyone do anything," Ben said.

Mose joined them. "Hey, relax, Carlos. Chill. Paleface has to come out sometime." He put a big hand on Carlos' shoulder.

Carlos shook off the hand angrily and stalked off into the living room, where he fell backward onto the couch, arms tightly folded around his ribcage as if he were trying to hold in his irritation.

Artie set the lamp on the kitchen table and lit it with a match from the wall holder. "I'm going to start cooking," she said to no one in particular. No one moved to help her. Paleface was still in the locked bedroom. "Figures," Artie said to herself, and scratched another match across the bottom of her shoe to light the kindling she had already stacked inside the stove.

"Better get the fire going," Artie heard Ben say to Mose as she started down the basement stairs with the lamp. "It's dark enough now. Since we all can't fit into the kitchen to eat, we might as well keep the living room warm."

When Artie began serving the corned beef hash, Ben saw Paleface venture out of the bedroom. Artie went to her at once and guided her to the table, running interference between the small girl and the others. Artie sat Paleface down at the kitchen table and gave her a notebook and pencil.

Then Artie sat herself down and said, "Did you write 'Man followed us here' on the blackboard?"

The others crowded around, picking up bowls and serving themselves, but standing close with their food, waiting to hear. Ben didn't like the avid look on some of the faces. "Vultures," he thought.

But Paleface nodded. She picked up the pencil and wrote, in the same cramped printing, "Man followed us here. Followed from my house. The first farmhouse."

The others all began to ask questions together, but Artie put a hand on Paleface's wrist and asked simply, "What's your name?"

Ben was floored. Of course the girl would have a name, a real name. He felt a familiar tightening of his gut. The Others had called the girl "Paleface" in the same casually cruel way they called him "Scavenger." And he had, for the duration, joined in.

Artie smiled encouragement, and after a moment Paleface took up the pencil and wrote, "My name is Sylvie Morgan."

"Sylvie," Artie said. "That is lovely."

"But what about the man that followed us?" Lainey demanded.

Sylvie dropped the pencil, and Artie turned to glare at Lainey. "Slowly," she said to Sylvie. "When you're ready."

Sylvie looked at Artie for a long moment and then moved the notebook closer to the edge of the table. "My house," Sylvie wrote, "when you all came there. I hid in the barn. When you left I was going to stay. Try to find Mom and Dad. But that man came. Stranger. I followed you. Didn't want to be left there with him. He followed you. Us. I was scared to stay anywhere. He kept following."

"But how did he find this Place?" Ben found himself wondering aloud. "It's not—" he caught himself. "—It's a long way from that shed to the Place. And it was a blizzard."

"Don't know," Sylvie wrote. But Ben had figured it out already. He wondered if Tim and Artie had, too. When Ben and Artie had driven to the shed in the storm, reversed and pretended to be coming from the south, the man could have been there in the night, somewhere not far from the shed, watching. He could have followed the truck tracks back to the Place during the time Ben was taking the others on their wild goose chase. Or he could have gotten to the Place even before that, if he had followed Ben and Artie back from their recon trip on foot, before they came back with the truck. Ben shook his head. "God," he thought. "The Place, found out. Now what?"

He looked around the room and met Tim's eyes. Yes, Mothy had figured it out. Artie glanced up, met his eyes, too. She had figured it as well. A long, cool shiver ran up Ben's spine. "Something bad is coming," Artie had said this morning. This morning, did she already know about this man? What did she know? Why didn't she come right out and say it this morning, then and there?

But Sylvie was still writing. "Coming back from the barn today. Saw a shadow around the corner by the barn rocks. Saw him. Saw his head around the corner. Same man. He went away quick." Ben saw her put the pencil on the table with care and fold her hands together.

"OK, good, Sylvie," Artie said. "Good to know. I am really sorry I didn't think to get you a pencil and paper before. But can't you speak at all?"

Sylvie hesitated for a long moment, then wrote, "Can't now. Don't know why."

"No big," Artie said. "Keep the notebook and you can talk to us that way. Now, let's eat, before the hash and beans get cold. And I had better get the muffins mixed and into the oven."

Ben looked down at the bowl he held: hot, slightly browned corned beef hash out of the can and fried, and a helping of steaming green beans. It was a simple enough dinner to make; except for the muffins, anybody could have done it, with the possible exception of Timothy. He watched Artie pouring water into the mound of Bisquick she had dumped into one of the large steel bowls. A big can of blueberries sat on the table as well, and a squatty can of Crisco. "It's time I did something about the cooking," Ben thought with a sigh. "I was hoping that the others would pitch in, but Artie is doing most of the cooking, and it isn't fair. I hate this leadership thing. Gramps said I would fall right into it naturally if I needed to, but . . ."

Ben heard his own voice, raised slightly, "OK, it's time for you guys to fit into the cooking schedule." He looked around at the faces: Artie furiously stirring batter with Paleface—no, Sylvie— watching; Shandy, Kaylee, Turk, and Lainey sitting side by side on the sofa, their bowls on their knees; Tim off by himself, sitting on the floor with his back to the bookcase; Carlos, Andy, and Mose on the floor near the fireplace. To a person, except for Turk, they paused and looked at him.

"Who wants to cook next time?" Ben said, had to say, hating it.

"Well, crap," Carlos said around a forkful of hash, "I can't cook." Andy and Mose nodded vigorously, agreeing.

Shandy looked thoughtful. "I can, a little," she offered, rubbing her arm through its pillowcase sleeve. "I can try. I don't know anything about wood stoves, though, Ben."

"Good, Shandy," Ben said. And she had called him "Ben," not "Scavenger." Ben made himself smile at her and took a deep breath. "And?" he said.

Lainey and Kaylee laughed at almost the same moment. "Not a chance," Lainey said, pulling a face. "I'm the queen of take-out. Anybody who ate my cooking would curl up and die. In agony."

"Yep, me, too," Kaylee said. "Even my mom can't cook unless it's all laid out for her. Dad grills sometimes. In the summer. We microwave. Or send for those Home Chef or Plated boxes. Or we go out."

Ben clenched his teeth on several smart remarks he would love to make. Were these people used to having everything done for them? Would they try? Then a thought came to him, a thought that Gramps might have had. "Well, we'll have to do teams, then," he said. "Artie has been cooking, so she can lead a team." His eyes sought out Artie's blue ones. "That OK?"

"OK," she said, straightening up after closing the oven door and going for the wind-up clock on the mantel. "Ten minutes."

"Ten minutes and you will lead a team?" Kaylee said, rolling her eyes.

"Ten minutes until I check the muffins," Artie replied shortly.

Ben said, "OK, Shandy, since you have some experience, you can have a team, so choose two people. And Artie can choose two, and I will have a team."

Shandy looked at Ben blankly for a moment. Carlos was tugging on her jeans. Shandy said, "Carlos. Carlos and, and—Lainey."

"I'll choose next," Ben said, "Mose and Tim."

"So that gives me Andy, Sylvie, and Kaylee," Artie said.

"Can't I be on Shandy's team?" Kaylee said, edging closer to Lainey, her voice suspiciously close to a whine.

"You bet," Artie said with a little too much haste.

Ben hid a smile. "OK," he said. "Artie's team is on for what's left of today. I'll do tomorrow, and then Shandy's, and then Artie's again. Finding stuff and bringing in the food and water, cooking, and cleanup. Should work."

Tim ventured, "We have a list of what food we have and where it is. I can make a copy to put up on the wall. We should have more than one copy of it anyway."

"Sweet." Ben let his shoulders sag a little. He found himself wondering where the idea of teams came from and if it would work. Then he saw Shandy watching him from across the room, a small smile lighting her thin face, and thought, "Well, could anything be worse than Tim's green beans?" He smiled back at her, holding his breath. He hadn't deliberately smiled at one of *these* girls since he was about ten years old. Nothing happened this time, no one called him *Scavenger*, no one laughed. Maybe he was just *Ben* now, possibly to everyone but Carlos Aguirre and Lainey. He let out his breath in a long sigh. He could get used to being just Ben. This was a start.

⚒ ⚒

Hands inside two bright red quilted oven mitts, Artie pulled out the two pans of blueberry muffins and set them on the stove's upper warming box. "Teams," she thought. "Not a bad idea. Guess I couldn't be on Ben's team because I have sort of learned how to cook on this big beast." She sighed. "Ughs. But at least Andy isn't

Carlos, and Sylvie has been helping me already." The muffins were lumpy, golden, and smelled delicious.

She shivered and looked around the bright, warm kitchen. She still felt uneasy. Bear sat staring at the back door once more, slowly sweeping his tail back and forth on the floor, ears canted forward, focus never faltering. For a few minutes, the bad thing coming had slipped her mind.

"Man followed us here," Artie thought. "Bear is focused on that. He knew before any of us, even me." She shivered again, made herself fill a bowl with the last of the hash and beans, sat at the table with Sylvie, and bent her head to the food.

When she had finished her bowl, Artie snagged a muffin each for herself and Sylvie.

Tim's voice came from the living room. "Looks like your phone is charged, Carlos," he said. "It says 33 percent, and the charging-battery image is up. That should be enough to do the job."

Carlos set down his fork and bowl so fast that they skidded a few inches on the planks of the floor. "Yeah!" He snatched the phone from Tim's hand. Artie saw the flat face of it blink in the firelight as Carlos lifted it to his ear.

Artie found herself holding her breath as Carlos' fingers scrolled and then tapped. She looked around at expectant faces and found that she wasn't the only one holding her breath.

"What the—" Carlos' shouted. He held the phone out for all to see. "No bars. There are no bars here, none!" He thrust his phone angrily toward Ben, who was sitting on the floor next to Tim. "You knew this, Scavenger! You knew all along we couldn't get cell reception here. I ought to—"

"Stop." It was Tim's voice, thin but loud enough to be heard over Carlos' accusation. Artie had never heard Tim use that tone of voice. "Stop that right now," Tim went on. "I've called here from Hailey on my cell. When I did, I got all the bars. I got

Ben. Do you understand that? I called here from Hailey and got through just fine two weeks ago." He looked at everyone, each in turn, as if to gather their attention. "That was then," he said simply. "Don't you get it? *Then,* there were bars, and I got through. *Then.* This is now."

"New times," Artie whispered to herself. "These are the new times."

"What's going on?" Shandy asked. She looked for a moment as if she were going to burst into tears. "I've got to talk to Mom and Dad. I've got to see if they're OK."

Andy slid closer to her. "We'll get back to Hailey, Sis," he said, looking up at her from the floor. "When the snow melts, we'll go back."

"When we can get the truck back on the road, I'll take you," Ben added.

"That could be spring," Shandy said. "What if the snow doesn't melt until April? What if it stays all winter? They've probably been out looking for us for two weeks. They'll think we're dead." She buried her face in the arm of the sofa. Mose reached up and put a hand on her back, but as he did so, he turned and met Carlos' eyes and dropped his hand.

"We can try your phone next, Shandy," Tim said. "Maybe it will be different. Do you have the same carrier as Carlos? We can try at different times of day, too." But Shandy didn't lift her head. Mose handed Shandy's phone to Tim, and he plugged it into the charger.

CHAPTER 6
BAD THING

The house still smelled of dinner, and Artie was enjoying the warmth of the fire burning in the stove as she sat at the kitchen table. The water for dishwashing was on the stovetop and wasn't even warm yet. And tonight it wasn't her turn to care.

Lainey, Carlos, Kaylee, and Andy were playing cards in the loft. Turk was there, too. They had taken the oil lamp from the kitchen table up so they would have two, and Artie imagined that they were sitting very close together so they could see the cards. She heard laughter and the occasional curse.

Shandy sat on the sofa with her legs curled under her, with Mose sitting on the floor nearby. She and Mose were talking in low tones. Tim and Ben were reading in front of the fireplace, and Sylvie, as usual, sat at the kitchen table with Artie, trying to read by the light of a candle Artie had brought from the basement. Artie made a mental note: tomorrow she would have to find at least one more oil lamp, or else one of the LED lamps. One of her lists said that more oil lamps were in the chicken house, white barrel, southwest corner, bottom layer, one back.

But tonight, notebook in hand, Artie was making another list. She had been thinking about *days*. She had lost herself in the days before the others arrived, even while writing in her journal, but now she was oriented once more. Ben's birthday, Halloween, was three days away.

It would be odd, but not that odd, to celebrate Halloween with snow on the ground. Artie remembered the last year she went out trick-or-treating, the year she was twelve. Hailey had had about a foot of snow on Halloween that year. Artie had been a gypsy, and had worn a parka over her peasant blouse, and boots under her long patchwork skirt, unzipping her parka on each front porch and flashing homeowners with her costume as they doled out the candy. Rosa had been a gypsy that year, too. Artie didn't mind snow on Halloween. Snow made it easier to imagine ghosts.

She had noticed the pumpkins on the floor in the old bunker, and hoped Ben would agree to letting her cut at least one or two for jack o' lanterns. The day after, she could make pumpkin soup, pumpkin muffins, even pumpkin pie, so the pumpkin flesh wouldn't be wasted. And to give the jack o' lanterns life, there were barrels of candles at the Place.

She had a birthday present for Ben, sort of. Artie rubbed her nose with an index finger. She wasn't sure she should give it to him, or what he would think if she did. But several days after she had given Ben Gary's dogtags and wallet, she had found Gary's little glass frog bead jammed into the bottom of one of her pockets. She had found a string for it so it could be worn as a necklace. Ben might like to have that. Or not. Or maybe she should save it for Christmas.

But in any case, Artie wanted to bake him a cake. She looked down at her list: cake pans, powdered sugar, granulated sugar, Crisco, vanilla, flour, baking powder, cocoa . . . The list ended there. Artie laid her pencil on the table. How could she make a cake without eggs? All the muffins and batches of cornbread she had made without eggs were very crumbly and fell apart even before the first bite. That wouldn't do for a cake. There must be some way to bake an actual cake without eggs.

"November 6 is Mom's birthday," Artie found herself thinking. "Was." Tears burned her eyes and she blinked them back. Her lips moved. "I'd have made you a great cake, Mom," she said to herself soundlessly. "And Dad would have taken us all out to dinner, and Gran and Grandpa would have come, too. We might have gone to a movie after dinner if anything good was playing. Maybe we would even have gone to Twin Falls for dinner." Artie's thoughts marched steadily ahead through a door she was trying to keep closed and locked. "L. L. Bean had the most beautiful rust-colored cashmere scarf, just perfect for Mom," she remembered. "One hundred percent fine cashmere, 60 inches long." She could picture the scarf now and imagined the rich, buttery softness and the feathery fringe. "I was going to order it. And I was going to make you a card using—" It was too much. Artie put her forehead down on her arm and pressed her cheek to the oilcloth on the table. The very day it happened, the morning she found her mother's body, had been the day she had planned to go up Quigley Gulch to collect bright leaves and the last of the year's wildflowers, so she could press them and make cards during the fall and winter.

Artie struggled to get her breathing under control. Crying wasn't good, wouldn't do any good—and above all, she didn't want the Others to hear her. She lifted her head and found herself looking into Sylvie's pale blue eyes. "Sorry, Sylvie," she said. "I just got to thinking about my mom." Laughter, Lainey's laughter, tinkled into the kitchen from above. Artie wiped her sleeve across her eyes.

Sylvie nodded and for a moment laid her hand on Artie's sleeve.

Artie stared at Sylvie across the table, then dropped her eyes back to the notebook. It had been a scratchy day. First, today was

Shandy's team's turn to cook, and for breakfast they had turned out burned oatmeal thicker than cement.

Then Ben and Mose had made yet another circuit of the buildings of the Place and had failed to find any new sign of the intruder. And there *was* an intruder.

The morning after Sylvie had written on the board, Tim and Ben had found that someone wearing man-sized shoes had been peeing and pooping in the snow in the upper meadow at some distance from the barn and had worn a path from that area to the back door of the barn. Inside the barn, they had found a little nest of food wrappers, empty food boxes, and towels in the hay near the back wall, a little cave inside and hidden by bales of hay. Whoever it was had eaten boxes of powdered pudding, sweet drink mix, and mashed potato flakes—plus several foil pouches of tuna, some boxes of crackers, and dozens of granola bars. Every day after that discovery, everyone had searched the entire Place, but found nothing more. Both bunkers, the wood-shed, and the house were now kept locked. They left the barn door unchained, hoping that the intruder would come back there for food and they could trap him inside.

Dinner tonight had been scorched chili from cans, nothing else. Artie thought that Shandy seemed ashamed of her team's minimal effort, but Carlos' smirk had erased all thoughts of sympathy. And then after dinner Carlos had confronted Ben.

The confrontation had quickly become nasty. Artie replayed it in her mind for the tenth time.

"Hey, we've been here more than a week, and it's time," Carlos had said, leaning back into the dark leather easy chair in the living room.

"Time for what?" Ben had asked, his eyes wary.

"Time to break out the supplies," Carlos said with a cocky grin. He spun one of the throw pillows on his index finger. "You know. The booze, the blow, the weed. All that stuff. Whatever pills you have stashed, too."

Ben had dismissed Carlos' question, saying, "There is no booze here. Gramps and I don't—I don't drink. And I wouldn't drink the first aid alcohol if I were you—it's poisonous."

"And?" Carlos was relentless.

"And, what?" Ben had put aside his book, his lips in a grim line.

"Cigarettes. Other smoke-able deliciousness. And pills," Carlos rapped out. "Any and all, legal, illegal, or paralegal." Kaylee and Lainey had laughed.

"Pills we have," Ben said. "But there isn't any oxycontin, oxycodone, vicodin, or anything like that. The pills are mostly antibiotics, aspirin and ibuprofen, immodium, calcium, and vitamins. The Place doesn't have any cigarettes, tranquilizers, or anything you can smoke or cook in a spoon, or shoot up. Gramps didn't stock any of that."

"Cra-zy Fra-ank Elli-ott," Carlos said, singsong. He pushed back a lock of black hair that had fallen over one eye. "Crazy Frank bought thousands of dollars worth of stuff. Crazy Frank Elliott got a truckload of diapers, but didn't get anything good, not even booze? Do you expect me to believe that?"

"I don't care what you believe," Ben said, turning back to his book. "What is, is."

"Come on, Carlos," Andy said nervously. "We won't be here much longer. The snow is bound to melt off at least once in the next couple of weeks, and then we can—"

"Aaaah—" Carlos had made an obscene gesture and climbed the ladder to the loft.

Artie was worried. Carlos, never very civil, seemed, literally, to be going stir crazy. "Cabin fever," Gran had called it. Carlos' version was taking a vicious turn. An image of her grandmother came to Artie without warning, and she had to smile, "No inner resources," Gran was saying, shaking a finger at some video of a criminal on a reality TV crime program. "This is the kind of thing that happens when someone has no inner resources." Gran had laughed then, as she always had when she was half serious. She faded, was gone.

Coming back to the moment, Artie looked down at her list and wrote, "Find cookbooks we brought in from the barn." Maybe one of the cookbooks would have a no-eggs recipe for cake. "Start small," she wrote, in sudden inspiration. "Find recipes for brownies and cookies." Artie smiled. Cookies and brownies would be good practice, and she knew there were cookie recipes without eggs. She wondered why she hadn't yet thought of making cookies. "Hey, Sylvie," she said, indicating the notebook Sylvie now carried everywhere. "What's your favorite kind of cookie?"

Sylvie didn't hesitate. "Peanut butter cookies," she wrote quickly.

Artie leaned forward to read the cramped letters and smiled. "We can do that," she said. "When it's our turn to cook, we'll make them for dessert." Memory flashed her an image of making peanut butter cookies with Gran last Christmas vacation, of Gran's long fingers holding the fork and pushing down on each cookie to press the pattern of crossed tines into the dough before they were baked, rows and rows, plates and plates of cookies made as gifts for friends. "Do you know about making the pattern on peanut butter cookies with a fork, Sylvie?" Artie asked.

Sylvie nodded, then ventured a small smile.

"Good," Artie said. "We'll do that. But I wonder about all these little traditions. I wonder if they are going to survive."

Sylvie wrote, "We will keep doing it."

"You're right," Artie said. "We will keep on doing things, just like generations of cookie-bakers before us."

Sylvie looked out the black window as if seeing something Artie couldn't see. "Maybe she is remembering baking cookies with her family, too," Artie thought.

"Sylvie," Artie said suddenly, "what do you think happened to your family?" She felt stupid and selfish that she hadn't thought to ask this before.

Sylvie wrote in the notebook for some time, then passed it over to Artie.

"Night before the Hailey guys came to our farm," Artie read. "Last Friday. Got home from school on the bus. Mom and Dad went to Twin. Took the pickup. Mom needed some groceries and some hen scratch. Dad needed some part for the lawnmower. Wanted to mow the grass one more time before it froze. Lawnmower was not working. They were going out to dinner in Twin. I didn't want to go. They said they would be back after dark." Artie looked at Sylvie, who pointed impatiently to the rest of her writing. "Mom and Dad never got home. Never answered their phones. Hailey kids came next morning. Scared of them and hid. Kids stayed three nights. Then the man came just before the kids left. I was scared of the man so I followed them. Mom and Dad never came back. Do not know what happened. Bad."

"Bad," Artie echoed. "Tell you what. When the snow goes away and after we get this following guy out of here somehow, we will go to your farm and see if your mom and dad came back." Sylvie nodded eagerly and reached for Artie's hand across the table, held it in her own small one for a moment. "And—" Artie could not help adding, "hen scratch? Did you have chickens?" Sylvie nodded, then held up her hands, flexed both hands twice, three times. "Thirty chickens!" Artie exclaimed. "Sure wish we had them right now!" Artie sighed and picked up her own notebook and sighed. *Eggs. Wouldn't that be lovely?*

Sylvie smiled and took up her book.

Artie reread her list and found nothing to add. Suddenly she felt very tired. It was pitch dark outside, but it was too early to crawl into bed. The faint crackles of wood burning inside the stove and its comforting heat lulled her.

She put her head down on the table, as she had done so often lately, and in the wavering shadows of the candle flame, stared at the uneven plank floor, the plain white walls, and the back door made of some dull gray metal. This kitchen was nothing like the bright kitchen at home, which was three times this size and sported stainless steel appliances and sinks, a black glass cooktop and up-to-the minute convection wall oven, a gray flagstone floor, an island and countertops of gray and black marble, and a back door of polished red oak with a large window. And in that kitchen there was no Bear.

As he had for a number of days, Bear sat facing the door, ears alert. "It's OK, Bear," Artie heard herself whisper. The dog flicked an ear but didn't change position or turn his head. "You watch, boy, and wake us up if you hear something." Artie felt herself sliding toward sleep and let herself go.

Barking. Ben woke up to the sound of frantic barking. He had fallen asleep on the floor by the fire. Again. He shook his head; how long had he been asleep? The fire had burned down to sleepy coals. It felt late. What was happening?

He scrambled to his feet and ran to the kitchen, where Molly and Moonie were hurling themselves against the door, barking hysterically. Artie stood there as if paralyzed, with her hand on the knob. "Bear!" Ben heard himself shouting. "Artie, where is Bear? You didn't let him out by himself in the dark." He felt his heart contract. "How could you?"

And then he heard it, barking from outside, and he knew it was Bear out there. He grabbed his headlamp from the hook and jammed it onto his head, then pushed Artie aside, shut the door tightly behind him to keep Moonie and Molly in, and ran out into the night. Without a coat, he felt the cold hit him like a wall, but it didn't matter. He switched on the headlamp. *Bear! Where was Bear?*

Ben could hear someone opening the door behind him, saw a slice of light spill onto the snow between his feet as he ran, a fan of light that gave him a shadow. "Don't let Molly and Moonie out!" he shouted over his shoulder. He heard the door slam, and the slice of light vanished.

His headlamp made a small, white tunnel in the blackness, moving back and forth over the crusted snow. *The barn.* Bear's barking was coming from the direction of the barn, and it wasn't happy barking. Something was wrong. "Oh, my God, if the coyotes have him cornered--" Ben thought. But he wasn't afraid of coyotes. He knew they would slink away from him. If he could just get there fast enough-- He ran down the path to the barn, moving his head from side to side, his light sweeping the snow, searching for Bear.

And there he was, Bear, a black mound of fur with teeth, crouched in the snow not far from the barn doors, barking and growling as he had never done before. Ben's headlamp swept from Bear to a dark, moving blotch against the side of the barn. The blotch was huge. It was no coyote. Bear moved toward it warily, growling deep in his throat.

"Help!" Ben's light hit her full in the face. Lainey. Lainey with her strawberry hair falling into her eyes, struggling. Lainey being held from behind by a tall man with a black beard. Ben saw a glint like ice at her throat. "Help!" she screamed again.

At their feet another figure struggled to stand, and a booted foot shot out with a kick to the side, and connected. The third figure was Turk. Another kick from the bearded man, and Turk sprawled face-down in the snow, unmoving.

"Let her go," Ben shouted over the barking, trying to stay calm. He had to do something, *something. Now.* Then the realization hit him like a raft of snow sliding off a roof. This was the intruder who had made that nest of food wrappers and towels in the barn. This was Sylvie's "man followed us here." And he had Lainey and a knife.

"Let her go?" the man echoed mockingly. "Do tell."

"Tim! Tim!" Ben shouted over his shoulder, with as much volume as he could muster. "Help! Top shelf of the safe, right!" He hoped that Tim could hear him and would know what to do. From the corner of his eye, Ben saw light fall onto the snow once more. Someone had opened the back door. "Tim! Artie! Safe! Top shelf, on the right!" Ben shouted again. Faintly, he could hear Molly and Moonie barking.

Ben focused on the man, on how he was moving. He had begun to drag Lainey toward the barn door. The long knife was very close to her throat; she wasn't fighting. Her hair swung away from her face. Ben could see tears running down her cheeks. "Let her go; I mean it," Ben said, taking a few steps closer.

The man stopped his progress and turned the blade so that it flickered in the beam of the headlamp. "Maybe Mose and Andy and Carlos will come out and we can all rush him," Ben thought. "Let her go and move away," he said.

"And you'll do what, kiddo?" came the man's voice, deep and harsh. "Throw a tantrum? I think you had better take off—all of you--and leave this place to me." The man lifted his head and Ben heard feet crunching in the snow behind him. The others had come out, at least some of them. "Leave this place to me, kiddos," the man continued, raising his voice. "Move somewhere else and I might even let this one go when I get tired of her."

"Not a chance," Ben said through clenched teeth. The man began dragging Lainey again. Ben heard someone come up behind him, close, and he froze, hoping. A small, warm hand felt for his own right hand, and then Ben felt a shape of metal that was not quite as warm, and very, very familiar. Tim had understood. From the weight of it, Ben knew the gun was loaded.

"Let her go, you bastard," Mose was yelling. "If you cut her, you won't get away!"

A row of yellow teeth appeared in the black beard. The man appeared to be enjoying this. "I don't have any problem cutting this one if I have to," he said slowly. "You have other girls here. I seen them."

Ben brought up the revolver and aimed it. He inclined his head slightly so that the backwash from his light would make the gun visible to the man. "Let. Her. Go. Drop the knife," he said, pulling back the hammer on the revolver.

The smile stayed. "Right, kid. You aren't going to use that toy."

Ben said, "This .38 look like a water pistol?"

The man laughed as he wrenched Lainey around between them, using her body as a shield, still with the knife at her throat. He started again for the barn door.

"Oh, God," Ben thought. "If he gets her inside the barn, how will I get Lainey away from him? How can I get him without shooting Lainey?'

But Bear had other ideas. Now the man's back was to him, and Bear sprang, teeth snapping in the air, paws on the man's shoulders. Overbalanced by Bear's weight while in the act of taking a step, the man fell on Lainey, driving them both into the snow. A bright yellow light showed him on hands and knees, scrabbling to rise. Lainey kicked and screamed. A flash of the knife and she stopped, motionless and silent.

Mose and Andy appeared at Ben's side. Mose had a flashlight, the source of the yellow light. "Keep the light on him," Ben said to Mose. The man was scrambling to his feet, pulling Lainey up with him.

Ben knew he had only seconds and ran forward. The man was in the act of straightening his back, one arm holding Lainey by the waist, the other with the knife at her throat.

Ben took two more steps and was there. He jammed the gun barrel behind the man's ear and felt him go still. Bear barked hysterically only a few inches away. "I'll shoot," Ben heard himself saying. "Let go of her, *now.*"

The rancid stench of the man was overpowering.

"You won't do that, kid. You can't shoot me in cold blood," came the deep voice in a cloud of foul breath, confident as if he were giving directions to the nearest gas station. "And I can kill her before you twitch a finger, so back off. Here, I'll cut her so you'll know." Lainey screamed.

Ben shone his headlamp at the angle of the gun barrel, located Bear by his barking, and thought, "If the bullet exits the skull, it should hit the barn." He pulled the trigger.

Ben fell backward into the snow as the man's arm backhanded him. His headlight pierced its beam of light into the blackness of the sky, clear to the stars. Then Bear's head was there, eyes squinted nearly shut against the light, pink tongue flapping wetly onto Ben's cheek.

Ben heard footsteps, and gathered himself. He almost fell over Turk, who was now sitting in the snow, his hands full of crystalline redness and gobbets of gray, the snow bright with blood and brains.

Ben saw Lainey pull away and run toward the house, falling into the arms of two people standing on the path.

He tried breathing, took a few shaky breaths. "Killed a man," his thoughts chanted. "Killed a man. You killed a man." He felt the weight of the gun in his hand and held it away from his body. His headlamp made a dazzle of the blued metal and wetly shining red glaze. "Gramps would have," he heard himself saying.

The same small hand reached for the gun and Ben relinquished it at once. Tim. Then an enormous, heavy hand came down on his shoulder.

"What did you just say?" Mose asked, but Ben shook his head. Mose stepped forward and shone his golden light on what was left of the bearded man. "Dead," he said after a moment. "Yep. Couldn't be deader. You nailed the sucker. It's cold out here. Let's go in," Mose said.

Mose went over to where Turk sat, wiped Turk's face with a handful of snow, dredged Turk's crimson hands back and forth through the snow until they looked clean, pulled him to his feet, and walked him up the path to the house. It seemed to Ben that Mose was moving slowly and with great precision. Everything seemed very, very slow, even the wagging of Bear's tail.

Ben watched Mose on the path ahead, and after a few moments he felt anchored in time once more and followed, Bear at his heels and Tim bringing up the rear. "Let's see if Lainey is all right," Mose said over his shoulder. "What a bastard. I'm glad he's dead."

CHAPTER 7

THE USEFULNESS OF BARRELS

Once back in the kitchen, Ben realized that he was cold—in fact, he was shivering—or perhaps shaking would be a better term for it. He made sure that Bear was in the kitchen and then locked the door. Artie stood just inside.

"Ben," she said. "Are you all right? Is Bear? I didn't let Bear out. I wouldn't. Please, I didn't let him out."

He rubbed his arms and said, "We're OK." Artie seemed to be shaking, too, and he was sorry he had shouted at her before. His brain had been on automatic for that last strange segment of time, and now it seemed to have thawed. A few things dropped into place. He felt heat stain his cheeks and was glad that the kitchen was lit tonight by only a candle.

"Of course you didn't let Bear out, Artie," he said, looking straight into her eyes; he wanted Artie to know he believed her. It had become obvious to him in the past few weeks that Artie had come to love the dogs, and next to himself, when it came to the dogs, she had been the most careful person at the Place. And it had become obvious to him on the way back to the house who *had* let Bear outside. "I'm sorry I shouted at you before," Ben said, had to say. "I know it wasn't you. I know who let Bear out."

367

He took a deep breath and looked at the Others, now gathered in the living room around Lainey, where Mose was kneeling on the hearth and building up the fire. "Of course you didn't do it, Artie," he said, his brain fully in gear now. "It was Lainey. Bear must have gone out with Lainey, when she went outside. Lainey and Turk."

Artie relaxed, leaning against the wall near the door. "Thanks," was all she said, but her eyes were bright.

Ben gathered Bear into his arms and felt him all over, making sure he hadn't been hurt by the intruder during the struggle. Bear *was* all right.

Tim appeared in the kitchen doorway. "Back in," he said briskly. "While they were all over Lainey, I put the gun back in the safe."

"You saved the bacon," Ben said to him, barely audible. "I didn't want that man—or the Others--to know that someone was going for a gun. I didn't want to say that, didn't want to say, 'Get a gun.' But I didn't want him to get her inside the barn."

"Yeah," Tim said, unconsciously wringing his hands together. Two spots of pink glowed on his cheeks.

Ben nodded. He felt himself collapse onto a kitchen chair, and held out his hands to warm them at the stove. Artie was bustling around in the pantry and came out with a box of cocoa mix.

"I'm making hot chocolate," she said. She looked at Ben and set the box of cocoa on the table. "Are there any empty barrels?"

Ben stared at her. Maybe his brain was still sludgy after all. "You're going to make hot chocolate in a barrel?"

"I'm going to make hot chocolate in the chili kettle as soon as I've washed it," Artie said. "But the dead guy." She stopped for a moment and then continued very softly, "We can't just leave him out there. If, *when* he goes all stiff, then—" she shut her eyes briefly. "Rigor mortis," she said finally. "And then he's going to freeze solid. I thought if there was an empty plastic barrel, I could put him inside and--and he would be hidden. And—contained. He wouldn't stink and he wouldn't—wouldn't *leak*. We could figure out what to do with him later on."

"Oh." Ben said, taken aback. He hadn't got that far in his own mind. Artie wasn't easily rattled, that was for sure.

"That's smart," Tim was saying. "Sure. Rigor mortis, like they talk about on TV. '*The First 48. CSI. New Blood.*" He looked at Ben.

Ben tried to jump-start his brain. "Barrels," he said. "New barrels. Empty barrels. Yes, there should be half a dozen in the barn. They're in the front east corner, I think. Good idea. Let me get warmed up and I'll do it. He is—was—a big guy, Artie. I don't want you to try stuffing him into a barrel by yourself. And really—you don't want to see him up close, what's left of him."

"I'll do it," came a voice from the doorway into the living room. It was Mose. "It *is* a good idea. Me and Andy will stuff him. You stay here, Ben. You've done your deal. We'll go out right now and do him, then roll him inside the barn and smooth out the snow. If another one of those white helicopters shows up in the morning, we don't want him lying out there for the world to see."

"Good, Mose, Andy. Thanks." Ben stripped off his headlamp and handed it to Andy.

"I'll come, too," Tim added. "I'll shovel snow over the blood."

"Or we can just shovel the bloody snow into the barrel on top of the dude, don't you think?" Mose said to Tim. "Yeah, come on. Know where a shovel is?"

Ben felt a wash of cold air as the three of them went out, but the slightly incredulous look on Tim's white face warmed him. He wondered if Tim had ever before been included, invited into an activity by anyone who wasn't an outcast. "More than one first today," he thought, shivering.

Artie was dipping hot water from the big dishpan into her kettle for the hot chocolate. She saw him watching and said, "I think we need cocoa more than wash water right now. Go sit by the fire if you want. I'll bring you some when it's ready."

Ben nodded and pushed himself out of the chair. He took three steps toward the living room and suddenly there was Lainey, hair swirling, arms wrapping around him, her body pressed close to his. He felt his own arms come up to hold her. "What—"

"Oh, Ben, Ben," Lainey was saying, a catch in her voice. "Thank you, thank you. You saved my life. You saved me."

His brain turned a notch and he thought, "Yet another first. Hugged by the popularity queen of Wood River High." He heard himself saying, "It's all right. It's all right. And if it hadn't been for Tim—"

"No," Lainey interrupted, "it was you, Ben. You saved me."

Ben felt his arms drop. "Lainey," he said after a long moment. He couldn't think of anything else to say. He walked past her to a warm space of floor in front of the fireplace and with care lowered himself into a sitting position. He felt strange, as if his balance were off, as if he were only a few degrees from falling. *Killed a man.* The phrase started ticking over behind his eyes. *Killed a man. Killed a man.*

Lainey followed. Near the fire Ben saw Shandy's lovely, narrow face, Kaylee's beautiful profile, and Carlos' dark frown as they crowded around.

"We didn't see everything, Ben. Tell us!" Kaylee demanded. Lainey sat on the floor between Ben and Turk, who had been lying full length in the shadows.

"Not much to tell," Ben said, staring into the fire. The flames caught the new pine wood that Mose had added, and crackled merrily. Gratefully he felt the heat beating against his knees, his hands, his face. "I think we were all asleep after dinner. Molly and Moonie started barking and jumping on the kitchen door. That's what woke me up. I went to see why, and heard Bear barking outside, so I went out to get Bear. And saw the guy in the snow with Lainey, headed to the barn with her. I saw him kick Turk away. And he wouldn't stop."

Ben took in a sharp breath, remembering the sinewy, powerful hands, the black strings of hair, the deep-set eyes, the high and narrow nose. The nauseating stench of him. "He wouldn't let go of Lainey. He had a knife. And he laughed." Ben took another breath and said, "Tim knew where the .38 was and brought it. But I couldn't get a clear shot; he put Lainey in the way. Then, when the guy turned to drag Lainey to the barn doors, Bear jumped on his back."

"Really?" said Lainey, wide-eyed. "Bear jumped him? I didn't see that. I just felt the guy falling on me."

"I don't think you could have seen Bear from your angle," Ben said. "And I knew that was the moment I needed." He stopped there, not wanting to say it. Bear heard his name, trotted into the living room, and curled up between Ben's knees. "Bear's a hero," Ben said, scratching behind the velvety ears.

"And you got him," Kaylee finished the thought. "You just stepped up there, and *snap*! He was toast. Well, not toast. More like jam. The back of his head, anyway. I went and had a look." Suddenly Kaylee swallowed, as if she'd had enough of blood and brains.

"Hero city," Lainey said. "Boy and his dog."

Ben didn't know how to feel about Lainey's remark. But there was something he had to ask. "Lainey," Ben said slowly, holding out his hands to the fire. "What were you doing out there? It's the middle of the night. Did you have to go to the outhouse, or what? Why did you let Bear out?" Lainey moved closer to Ben, very close, and Turk crawled on hands and knees to sit behind her. One of Turk's hands came up to splay across his ribcage on one side.

Ben felt strange, suffocated. He had killed a man; how *was* he supposed to feel about that? He'd killed a tall, strong man in

371

his prime—a guy with a long face, long hair and beard, long-fingered hands, big, booted feet-- "Hey," he asked suddenly. "Has anybody checked Turk? I think that guy kicked him pretty hard."

Carlos, Kaylee, Shandy, and Lainey exchanged looks. "No," Carlos said. "I wasn't out there. Did Turk get kicked?"

"Yeah, the guy kicked him pretty hard, all right," Lainey said quickly. Ben noticed that she hadn't answered his questions.

Shandy went to get a lamp from the front bedroom, lit it at the fireplace, and moved it close to Turk as Lainey lifted his t shirt. "Oh!" Lainey drew in a sharp breath. Two large, red swellings marked his taut skin.

Ben ran his fingers over Turk's ribs as Shandy held the lamp. Turk sat motionless, not even flinching as Ben probed his skin. "No broken ribs," Ben said at last, rocking back on his heels. "He could have a cracked rib or two, but everything is in place." Ben felt uneasy. He had checked dogs and cats, sheep and goats, cows and horses for broken ribs many times before, with Gramps, but had never run his hands over another person's ribs. And this was *Turk*, Turk, who had always baited Ben, had always laughed at him, taunted him for being different, for wearing old-fashioned clothes, for being non-athletic. Ben looked into Turk's eyes, but the eyes were flat, indifferent. *Nobody home,* least of all the old Turk Thomas. "This is creeping me out," Ben thought. "I've never been able to stand the guy, but he's not even in there any more. Not much is." Ben pulled down Turk's shirt and slid away from him, back toward the fire.

"He's going to have a monumental set of bruises tomorrow," Ben said, "but I don't think there's any serious damage."

"Good," Lainey said. "How did you learn how to tell broken ribs, Ben?"

Ben felt awkward with a beautiful girl so close. Especially Lainey. "You know that Gramps was a vet," he said, eyes on the fire. "It's just vet stuff. I used to go with him on calls after hours and on weekends. Even after he retired, Gramps still went out on calls when the other vets were tied up."

"Of course," Lainey said.

Ben took a breath. She was so close he could smell the fragrance of her hair, of her skin, some kind of fresh spice. What was she doing? Was she going to—no, Lainey belonged to Turk, had been welded to him since that night at the shed, and many months before, at school, in town, everywhere. Ben remembered his unanswered question. "What were you doing outside, Lainey?" he asked again. "Why did you let Bear out? It's not safe for him to be out alone, especially after dark. That's one of the Gramps Rules. It's really late. And you knew that there was someone sneaking around here because of what we found in the barn a few days ago. It wasn't safe for you, either."

She shook her head with irritation and moved a little closer to Turk. "Yes, but the sneak hadn't been in the barn for days, right? Because you guys were looking every day. And you hadn't seen anything else, any more tracks or any sign of him. I thought the sneak was gone. So I went out to look in the barn. I had my penlight and I went out to look in the barrels." She drew herself up defiantly but said no more.

"To look for what?" Ben persisted. "You could have gone through the lists of what is where," he went on. "They're on top of the bookcase right here."

"Yes, but the deal with the solar charger shows that not everything is on those lists," Lainey said, glancing at the others for support. Kaylee and Carlos nodded.

"And you wanted to find . . . ?" Ben said, unwilling to let it go.

Lainey threw up her hands and gave a short laugh. "All right, all right. I couldn't sleep. I'm not sleeping well here. You guys, all of you—you were asleep. I wanted some pills. There have to be some pills around here for that. You know. Ambien, Lunesta. I had some in my bag that night on the bus. I always carry them.

And last night I ran out. I mean, your gramps thought of everything, didn't he? So--"

"I don't know if there's anything like that here, Lainey. But you are welcome to look tomorrow. And Bear?" Ben didn't want to press it, but this was *Bear*, and he didn't want Bear let out in the night again, ever.

"The dog was sitting right at the door," Lainey said. "I mean, he wanted out. It was obvious that he wanted out, and as soon as I pulled the door open a few inches—bam! He was out like a shot. I figured he would come back in with me. So I took off— Turk and I took off—for the barn, and we were halfway there when this guy just jumped out of the dark and grabbed me."

"So scary," Kaylee murmured. "So awful for you. I would have screamed and screamed."

"I did scream once or twice." Lainey held aside her glossy curtain of hair and exposed one side of her neck. Ben could see a small cut there, and a trickle of drying blood. "He cut me. Do you think it will leave a scar?" she asked.

"Probably not." Ben couldn't keep himself from responding. "Little one, maybe."

Lainey let her hair fall and leaned back against the side of the couch. Carlos put out a long-fingered hand and stroked her hair. "Well, you can tell the story for years," he said, running a long strand through his fingers like a ribbon. "Escape from worse than death and all that."

"Yeah," Lainey agreed, but Ben thought her face had suddenly turned pale.

Artie came into the living room with two steaming mugs. "Ben and Lainey," she said, holding them out. "More's on the stove. Cups are on the table."

Everyone but Lainey, Turk, and Ben got up and made for the kitchen just in time to meet Andy, Mose, and Tim coming in from outside.

"Artie," Ben heard Mose saying. "Got to wash off. Can we get one of those steel bowls and take some water outside?" Ben watched as Artie gave Mose a steel bowl and the red quilted hot-pads. He held the bowl while she poured in a saucepan of hot water from the dishpan on the stove. Tim and Andy followed Mose back outside.

"Funny how everyone assumes Artie is in charge of the house," Ben thought, hands wrapped around the welcome warmth of the cocoa mug. "It's not even her team's turn to cook." But suddenly Carlos' face was thrust into his view.

"You've got guns here," Carlos said. It wasn't a question.

"Yes," Ben replied warily. He waited.

After a long moment, Carlos said, "Where are they, and what do you have?"

"Gun safe in the bedroom where I sleep, in the closet," Ben replied, trying to sound casual. "Just the family guns Gramps and I had, nothing fancy. Couple of rifles, couple of shotguns, couple of handguns. It's just a family gun safe, not an arsenal."

Carlos got up at once, strode to the bedroom door, and disappeared.

Ben sipped the hot cocoa, feeling it travel down to his stomach, warming him inside. He waited, knowing what would happen. "God," he thought. His arms felt so heavy. "Am I going to have to fight Carlos now?"

Carlos was back in the living room immediately. "Dark as a cave in there," he muttered, and grabbed the oil lamp from the side table where Shandy had deposited it minutes before. With a glare at Ben, he disappeared again, only to return shortly with his lips pulled back from his very white teeth.

"It's got a combination lock, a dial," Carlos said through his teeth, setting the lamp on the side table with exaggerated care.

"That's why it's called a safe," Ben said, realizing an instant too late that this was the wrong thing to say to Carlos.

"The combination," Carlos demanded, hands fisted on his hips.

"No," Ben replied as calmly as he could.

"No? You are telling me 'no,' Elliott? You?" Carlos' face darkened and he took a step forward. "You are giving me the combination."

"Are you good with guns, Carlos?" Ben went on, trying to think what he could say to get Carlos to back off. "Are you a good shot? I am." From the expression on Carlos' face, he knew he had hit a nerve. Carlos clenched and unclenched his fists, then looked away. "Bet he has never shot a gun," Ben thought. "And he knows the others will know that, because they spend so much time together. Small-town syndrome. We all know each other's lives too well. Now, time to shut this down."

"You don't need a gun tonight," Ben said mildly. He heard Mose, Andy, and Tim stomping back into the kitchen and the clink of metal against ceramic as Artie ladled cocoa into cups.

"You don't get it, *Scavenger,*" Carlos said, with cruel emphasis. "You are giving me that combination, or I'm going to—wait!" Carlos stood motionless. "Wait. Mothy Rich got the gun and brought it out there. He put it back in, too. He knows the combination. I can easily get it out of that little—"

Mose came into the living room with his cup. "Take it easy," he said, a hulking presence in the small room. "Fade, Carlos. We've had enough gun drama for tonight. Everything is handled." He sat on the floor near Ben and added pointedly to Carlos, "That was a fun task. I didn't see you out there helping us fold up that bloody SOB and stuff him, Aguirre." Mose's arms, sleeves rolled to the elbow, were dripping with water and pebbled with goose-bumps. He flung droplets from one hand and they sizzled in the fire. "Think I got all the blood off me, though. Brains, too."

Lainey patted the sofa behind her and said to Carlos, "Come and sit," and Carlos obeyed, still fuming. Lainey leaned back against his knees.

"I'm getting that combination, one way or another," he muttered under his breath.

"I'm going to ignore that," Ben told himself, very glad of Mose's presence. "I'm not even going to look at Carlos for a while." But he knew that Carlos was going to be a problem.

Tim flopped onto the floor next to Mose and Ben, set down his cup, dug in a pocket, and laid out a few things on the floor near the fire. "Wallet," he said producing a black leather wallet cupped and worn shiny from riding in a back pocket. "Knife, big. Knife, small. Box of matches. Hard candy." The clear candy wrappers sparkled in the firelight as Tim sprinkled the floor with a handful of peppermints and Jolly Ranchers. "Piece of newspaper," he continued, tossing a much-folded bit of paper down. "Let's see what's in the wallet."

Andy joined them, and Artie, with Sylvie, as usual, her shadow.

Tim opened the wallet and held it near the fire. "Three twenties and three fives," he said, laying out the bills. He smiled thinly. "A fortune. MasterCard, name of William P. Schuler. Debit card, Wells Fargo, William P. Schuler. Wells Fargo Platinum VISA, William P. Schuler. Little photo of two blond kids about four years old, twins. 'Marty and Matthew' written on the back. Idaho driver's license, William P. Schuler. Lives in Twin Falls."

"Well, the world is better off without William P. Schuler," Lainey remarked, drawing her feet under her.

"Too bad we can't take these cards and go spend his accounts down," Kaylee added. "He won't be needing them."

Tim held the driver's license close to the fire and suddenly said, "Wait! The dead guy is somebody else."

"What do you mean, Tim?" came from Andy.

"Look at the license." Tim held it out.

Ben had a look over Andy's shoulder. William P. Schuler was bald and had a round face with delicate features, height five feet six. The dead man had been at least six feet tall, with a strong nose and a full head of long black hair. Ben shuddered as he remembered that hair, clotted with bloody brains. He hadn't killed a short bald man. The dead man was not William Schuler.

"This wallet is stolen," Ben said. A finger of cold probed the back of his neck and he wondered if William P. Schuler was still alive, if the little twins Marty and Matthew still had a father.

Tim was busy opening the folded bit of newspaper. Ben could see that it was a large article, occupying almost half a newspaper page. The thing was mostly photograph, with a headline at the top that read, "Blue Lakes Murderer to be Sentenced."

Artie leaned forward and tilted the paper so she could see it. "Oh!" She exclaimed. "That's Mack Eldredge, Cormack Eldredge! You know. Murdered two teenage girls and their mom last year around Christmastime. In their house. They lived in Twin, somewhere close to Blue Lakes Mall. Remember? It was all over the news." Ben watched Artie tip the paper toward Mose. "Is that the guy you just put into the barrel?"

Mose nodded. Tim said, "Yep," and handed the paper to Lainey. "Congratulations. You escaped a triple murderer tonight."

Ben heard a sob in the dimness behind Artie's shoulder. Sylvie got up abruptly and ran for the large bedroom. Ben saw Artie gather herself to follow, but Tim was already on his feet, and she sank to the floor again. Tim and Sylvie disappeared through the dark doorway. "That's the first sound I've heard Sylvie make," Ben thought. "Maybe she will be able to speak someday."

Lainey held the newspaper article near the oil lamp. "Says here that on October 1 he was in the Twin Falls County jail awaiting sentencing, and his sentencing was supposed to take place on October 29."

Artie laughed, looking as if she had surprised herself. "That's today, or—it's very late now—that was yesterday."

"The county jail would be easier to escape from than the state pen," Shandy commented.

"Who knows what's going on in Twin now?" Andy put in. "Maybe everything is chaos, and he just walked away."

"God." Lainey shuddered. She looked at Ben and raised her mug to him. "Well, Eldredge totally got the death penalty, didn't he?" Ben felt profoundly uneasy and looked away from her lovely, flushed face. She held out her empty mug and Artie took it to the kitchen, refilled it, and brought it back.

"Anybody else?" Artie gathered several mugs, filled them, and returned to the fireside with her own mug as well. "I took the cocoa off the stove, so if anyone else wants some before it cools off, now's the time," she said. No one else got up.

Shandy said, "I can't get my head around this. There's no cops here, nothing, nobody to call. It's just us, and—and we had to take care of this. You did, Ben. And Mose, Tim, and Andy. As soon as we can get on the road, we have got to get back to Hailey." Heads nodded.

Ben and Artie looked at each other across a few feet of glossy floorboards painted with reflected light from the fire. Ben was the first to look away. "If there were cops here, would I be a criminal?" he thought. "It was self-defense, or *defense*, anyway. And Tim and Mose and Lainey were there, so I have witnesses." He felt as if his spine were melting, not entirely from the heat, and moved a little further from the fire.

Suddenly Ben remembered something from last week, and turned to look at Artie once more, but she had moved away and was reaching for her journal in the bookcase. "A bad thing is coming," he seemed to hear Artie saying again. "Something bad is coming."

"And that was before we found Sylvie's note on the blackboard," Ben thought. "Or could Sylvie have written that before we all went out to the barn to look for the solar charger, and could Artie have seen it just before she went out the door?" *Bad thing coming.* He looked at Artie, at her head bent over her journal, and wondered.

⊷╋ ╋⊶

CHAPTER 8

SMALL TREASURES

The day before Halloween dawned bright and clear, but with an edge. Outside, the wind was fierce, and drifting ice crystals formed a thin, twinkling mist an inch above the surface of the snow. Artie had looked at the outdoor thermometer an hour earlier: one above zero. Cold enough, but not winter-cold. No more snow had fallen and on the south-facing slopes, where they hadn't drifted deep, a few bare places showed sage and soil.

At ten in the morning, people were scattered around the Place. Carlos, Mose, and Andy were down at the woodshed chopping wood, a new task they had taken to as a competition. Ben had seemed glad to let them take over that particular chore. Artie was glad, too. It was a relief to get Carlos, in particular, out of the house in a way that let him blow off steam and wear himself out.

This morning at breakfast, the kitchen sink had refused to drain, and Tim was under it with a wrench, his legs sticking out into the kitchen. Sylvie was sitting on the floor near his knees, ready to hand him things. She had her notebook and pencil out so she could communicate. Artie had to smile at them together. "And no matter what, friendship is a good thing," Artie thought.

Lainey, Kaylee, and Shandy were in the front yard with three buckets of warm water and a bottle of shampoo, washing their hair. Turk was standing there with them, draped in towels, unmoving as a totem pole, the towels flapping around his arms in the strong wind. Through the windows, Artie could hear a faint but steady stream of shrieks and giggles; that was good, too.

Ben, taking the Shelties, had gone out to the barn—"To find something," he had said, but he hadn't told her what he was looking for, and Artie understood from his expression that he wanted to look for whatever it was, alone. She had watched Ben go out the kitchen door, looking almost jaunty for the first time since the Others had come. Artie pinched her arm; yes, this was real. That was really Ben going out the door. After the incident with Cormack Eldredge, nothing seemed certain.

Artie was enjoying the big leather chair and ottoman in the living room, cozied up under the red plaid throw and flanked by two pillows. Tucked at her sides were two cookbooks and her journal. Ben's birthday was tomorrow, Halloween, and she was finalizing her plans.

At dawn, Artie had brought up four pumpkins from the old bunker. The old bunker wasn't freezing inside, but it was cold enough, and Artie wanted to let the pumpkins warm to room temperature before she carved them. She had also brought in a jar of mayonnaise. In the darkness before dawn, going through cookbooks by oil lamp as she heated water for coffee, she had at last found a recipe for chocolate cake that used mayonnaise instead of eggs and cooking oil. The recipe had started with a boxed cake mix, however; Artie hoped that with just flour, sugar, cocoa powder, and baking powder, she could make it work.

Yesterday afternoon she had also found a dozen dusty old metal cake pans stacked in a dark corner of the basement, round pans with a strange, thin, and pivoting slider attached to the bottom of each. Ben said the pans had been his grandmother's and hadn't been used since he could remember. Artie had brought eight of the pans upstairs, and they had cleaned up just fine. She planned to make four cakes. Artie knew how boys devoured cake, and she was hungry for some, too. For frosting, she had powdered sugar, vanilla, food coloring, and Crisco. Gramps and Ben hadn't bought any prepared frosting.

"Now if this old stove will just be nice to me . . ." she thought. At least there would be plenty of split wood. She hoped that the boys' wood-splitting macho would extend to carrying the split wood from the woodshed to the back porch.

Ben and the Shelties burst in through the kitchen door with a blast of cold wind. Ben was wearing a huge necklace and a huge grin. Artie didn't think she had seen him smile like that since school let out for the Christmas holidays when they were in the seventh grade. He was carrying a large plastic shopping bag from Target and slid it onto the kitchen table. "Got some stuff, Artie," he said rather shyly, but still with the smile. "Want to have a look?"

Artie abandoned her comfortable chair at once. Ben proceeded to unwind his necklace.

"I picked up a few things in Twin just before everything came down," he said, stepping over Tim's legs and placing glittering loops and two strange flat panels on the table. "Look—these are strings of solar-powered lights, Halloween lights. I got them at Home Depot."

"Ohhhh," Artie said as she saw the little LED bulbs gleaming along the thin, dark wires as they lay on the table. "Fabulous, fabulous." Artie laughed out loud. She loved Halloween. And she was thrilled that Ben had waited until nearly everyone else was out of the house to bring in these treasures.

"Target was the last store I went to when I was in Twin getting the final supplies for the Place on that Last Friday. Target had their Halloween stuff out, and I grabbed a few things to use up the very last bit of Gramps's money," Ben went on. "Look in the bag."

Eagerly, Artie dived in. Her hand closed around something soft and rubbery, and she pulled out several handfuls of black plastic bats. "Wow, these are perfect!" she said. She had been wondering if bats cut out of white notebook paper would be acceptable, but now--

"I figure we can hang them with fishing monofilament," Ben said. "I bought lots of that. And I got a few bags of Halloween candy—candy corn and those little chocolate pumpkins, little Snickers bars, and some licorice bats."

Artie, intent on discovery, returned to the bag and found a small witch dressed in tattered gray fabric, just right to display on a table or bookcase—and here inside a plastic packet was an orange and black spiderweb tablecloth. She laid everything out on the table— spiderwebbing stuff and a bag of plastic spiders, the black and orange candles and the skull candelabrum, and the candy. Ben had brought Halloween to the Place.

Artie felt tears stinging her eyes when she looked up at Ben, who hadn't said another word as he watched her empty the Target bag. She could have hugged him, felt very tempted, and something of that must have shown in her eyes.

Ben backed away a little and said, "Glad you don't think it's stupid."

"No," Artie said. "Far from it. We are going to celebrate!"

Tim slid out from under the sink, and Sylvie stood up to have a look. Tim scrambled to his feet and dusted off the seat of his pants. "Hey," Tim said, surveying the tabletop. "Wow, Halloween. Look at this stuff! You and your Gramps thought of everything."

At Tim's shoulder, Sylvie smiled.

"Man," Tim continued, "you have solar Halloween lights! Serious, total finatory bits." He fingered the wires and the small flat solar panels with their black plastic stakes. "Hey, if we want to have these lit up tomorrow night, we had better figure out how to run these wires in through the windows or something, and we need to get these panels right out into the sun."

Ben nodded.

"I'll do it, OK?" Tim said, already gathering up the lights and panels. "It'll be fun. Come on, Sylvie, get your coat. Come on, Smoke. Don't worry about the sink. Almost done. I'll be back."

Artie watched them going out the kitchen door, and smiled. "It's going to be my team's turn to cook tomorrow," Artie said to Ben as the door closed behind Tim and Sylvie, "and I know it's your birthday. So what would you like for dinner?"

"Don't make much of my birthday," Ben began, but even as he spoke, Artie saw a change in his gray eyes. "Actually, why not at least do a Halloween special dinner?" he said thoughtfully. "After last night, I think we need something good to happen, don't you?"

Artie nodded. "Yes. A celebration would be really good. We don't want anybody else whining and issuing threats like jerkoid Carlos."

Ben began sorting the bats from the other Halloween things and making a pile of them on the table. "Yeah. And Artie," he said, looking up, "if he finds out that you know the combination to the gun safe, he'll be after you. Tell me if that happens and I'll deal."

"OK," she said. "Glad to. Carlos has always been fairly 'what I want, I get.'"

Ben smiled. "Got that right. Well, I guess ice cream is out, unless we have snow ice cream," he said, going back to dinner plans, "but snow ice cream has to be made with new snow, anyway, and we don't have any new snow. I'm not big with ice cream, though. What would be really nice, would be cake. Would that be possible? Gramps didn't buy any cake mixes, but I did. I got a bunch at Target the same day I got this Halloween stuff. Can you do cake, Artie?"

"I'm going to give it a try," she said, and thought, "Cake mix!" She said aloud, "I've got your grandma's cake pans now, and I found a recipe that doesn't use eggs. It uses a boxed cake mix, so it's great that you got some! The recipe uses mayo instead of eggs—who'd have thought? Glad you got some mayo."

"Busted," Ben said with a small grin. "I'm a mayo freak, so I got a bunch of jars of Best Foods that last week when I was buying, even though mayo wasn't on any of Gramps' lists. I don't know how long it will keep."

"Me either," Artie pronounced, "but it's certain to be good at this point. How does chocolate cake with frosting sound?"

"But—I didn't get any frosting!" Ben wailed. "Erg. I didn't think of frosting. How dumb is that? Can you do frosting?"

Artie laughed out loud, and it sounded good to her after last night's horror. "Sure! Powdered sugar and vanilla and Crisco—and I found some little bottles of food coloring in the pantry. Frosting is better when you make it with butter, but Crisco will do fine."

"Great. Awesomely great. Now I have to get the fishing monofilament so I can hang these bats. And I will get the cake mixes from the barn," Ben said. "Dinner-wise." He hesitated. "There's a bunch of canned hams and some great big cans of turkey. How about turkey?"

"OK," Artie said. "I haven't practiced the bread thing yet, so bread stuffing is out. Got any canned mushrooms? I thought I saw canned mushrooms on the list of things here in the house somewhere, but I haven't seen them."

"Yep," Ben said, laying the bats out in two neat rows. "I think that most of the cans of mushrooms are lined up on the floor in the loft."

"Good," Artie said, "Do you like mushrooms?" He nodded and she went on, "With mushrooms and an onion from the saw-dust barrels, I could make rice dressing to have with the turkey. There's lots of rice stored in the henhouse and some in the old bunker, too. There's sage and basil and thyme in the pantry, and pepper."

"Great," Ben said again. "That sounds perfect. And mashed potatoes with gravy?" he added hopefully.

Artie smiled. "Sure. And lots of gravy. Green beans, too. We have to have something green."

Tim and Sylvie, with Smoke, came back into the kitchen. "Green beans?" Tim echoed indignantly. "What about green beans?"

Artie and Ben dissolved in laughter. "Let's have canned peas instead," Ben said. He grew serious. "On Halloween night Gramps and I always told ghost stories after dinner. He had some stories he made up, and would tell a few of them. And every year he told this one he swore was true, a story that his grandfather told him when he was a kid. And I would make up a couple of stories, and so would Gary. Gramps would turn out all the lights. We'd sit there on the floor in front of the fireplace—not here, in Hailey—and have cake or pie with coffee or cocoa and tell them all. I'd like to tell ghost stories after dinner tomorrow night." He sighed. "Gary's stories always had him jumping out at you at the end—gotcha! Like that."

Artie was silent, thinking of Gary lying dead at her feet in the leaves.

Ben must have seen something in her face; she heard him saying, "Oh, God, sorry. I'll always miss Gary. And Gramps. Artie." He turned to her and he was so close that she caught her breath. "Artie, some of these Others might think that the ghost stories and the jack o' lanterns and things are stupid. But, you know—this is the Place, and I don't care. Gramps said he started the Halloween ghost stories when Dad and Uncle George were little, many years ago, way before I was born. And I want to keep on."

"Not at all stupid," she said. "I'll think up a story to tell, too."

"Going to get the turkey and rice and the cake mixes," Ben said, taking a step toward the back door. She saw him blinking; one hand came up to wipe at an eye. "The monofilament is in the barn," he said as he shrugged into his parka. "I've been meaning to move it to the fishing cabinet in the loft. I'll get you an onion from the bunker, too, when I get the turkey." He went out quickly, with the Shelties, and shut the door.

"Hey, where do you want the lights?" Tim was asking.

Artie turned to Tim just in time to see the hair-washing bunch come back into the house. "Lights?" Lainey said. "What lights? Let me see." She came stomping into the kitchen, shedding clumps of snow at every step.

"Oh my God, tomorrow is Halloween!" Kaylee chirped as Lainey lifted a string of lights from Sylvie's hands. "Look at all this stuff. It's Halloween stuff! And there's chocolate!"

"Oooh," Shandy added softly. "Look! Plastic bats. Is that sweet, or what?"

Artie whisked the candy back into the Target bag. "Yes," she said, "we're going to have a big dinner tomorrow night and then tell ghost stories."

"Good thing it's your turn to cook tomorrow, Artie," Lainey remarked.

"Good thing," Tim responded, nettled.

Artie wanted Ben to have a good birthday, or at least as good a birthday as she could manage. She took a deep breath. "You had better be decent to me," she said casually, turning to put the candy in the pantry. "I'm making chocolate cake."

"Cake!" That was Shandy. "But how can you make cake without eggs? I mean—"

"There's a way. You can help if you'd like," Artie said. "Any of you can help."

"It won't be my turn," Kaylee said. "Thankfully." Kaylee and Lainey removed themselves to the living room, where Lainey pushed Turk, damp towels and all, into the chair Artie had vacated. Sighing, Artie retrieved her cookbooks from the chair, as well as the towels, and brought them into the kitchen. She draped the towels over chair backs; they would be dry by dinnertime.

"Cake without eggs," Shandy persisted. "Do you have a recipe?"

"Look here," Artie said, opening one of the cookbooks. "Do you want to help, Shandy?"

Sylvie came to the table and sat, nodding and nodding. "Of course, I know you will help, Sylvie," Artie said. "And you are on my team, anyway."

"But this is special, a special night," Shandy said. "I would love to help. Have you figured out what else to make for dinner?"

Ben and the Shelties chose that moment to come back in, Ben laden with the things he had promised to bring from the old bunker. "Got 'em," he said, tumbling cans and a cloth bag onto the table. "Canned peas, an onion, rice, and a big canned turkey breast from the old bunker. Now I'm going out to the barn," he said. "Man, it's cold today. Come on, dogs."

"Thanks!" Artie said. "This is going to be great. Look, Shandy, we are going to have canned turkey breast with rice and mushroom dressing as a kind of casserole, mashed potatoes, peas, and turkey gravy. Ben said the cans of mushrooms are in the loft."

"I'll get Andy to bring some mushrooms down," Shandy said. "I'm not much for climbing ladders. And I can make frosting."

Artie found herself deep in plans for tomorrow's dinner with Sylvie and Shandy.

Presently Ben came back with a spool of fishing monofilament, and the three girls busied themselves tying varied lengths of line onto the floppy black bats. "I'm going to hunker down in my sleeping bag for a minute," Ben told them. "I'm freezing." He disappeared.

The woodchopping party arrived and attacked a box of crackers, several cans of sardines from the basement, and the peanut butter. Carlos and Andy took their lunch into the loft, but Mose hovered around Shandy, took the bats as they were strung, and found places to hang them—from rafters and beams, and from the loft railing.

Artie folded up the red-and-white checked oilcloth, tucked it into a corner of a pantry shelf, and spread the orange spiderweb tablecloth, then centered it with the skull candelabrum, complete with orange and black candles. The little witch she placed on the fireplace mantel.

Artie was surprised that the Others didn't sneer at her Halloween preparations. "Maybe if you're the only game in town, that makes you a good game," she thought.

Shandy and Sylvie were poring over a cookbook together and Tim was still working with the strings of lights. It was time to start thinking up a ghost story. Artie smiled. Since the threat of what turned out to be Cormack Eldredge had gone, the strange tension Artie had been feeling for days had evaporated, and she wanted to be alone to think and to sing. "I'm going for a walk up to the aspen grove," she told Shandy and Sylvie. "Thought I'd get some little branches to put around the witch on the mantel. Back before dark."

The cold wind met Artie's face as soon as she opened the kitchen door. She was glad she had put on Gran's gray hat and scarf. Jamming her hands into the pockets of the blue Gramps parka, she went out the door, skirted the barn, and set out toward the little aspen grove.

Ben had made a new rule that said, "Go where you need to go but don't make new paths," so she felt a little guilty striking out toward the pale trees, but she found that if she kept to the west side of the granite outcrops along the barn and then jumped from bare patch to bare patch, she left only an occasional impression in the snow.

Artie began to sing to herself as she left the barn behind. The harsh wind brought searing cold through her scarf and gloves—as well as her jeans--but her feet were warm in Gran's boots, and the windproof blue parka protected most of her body. She felt freed of a burden and tried not to think of Mack Eldredge and the creeping shadow he had somehow cast in her mind since the Others had come. Today's sky was wide and clear, today's wind was fresh and clean, and tomorrow would be good. She would *make* it good, she would see to it that it *was* good, end of story.

Artie reached the grove and, using one hand to steady herself, jumped across the sheet of rough ice that was now Spear Creek, caught like a shattered mirror among the rocks. Tiny beads of snow hissed as the wind drove them across the thick ice of the creek and onward through the aspen grove and over the narrow meadow into the sage beyond.

Near the stream, Artie found a fallen aspen with several small, clawlike branches poking up from the trunk through the snow. The tree had fallen recently, because some of the branches had brown leaves still attached, perfectly preserved on the black and white branches. "These will do nicely," she thought, breaking off several of the branches.

Something flickered at the edge of her vision and she looked up to see a glossy raven looking down at her from a high perch. The bird cocked its head, pushed with both feet, and launched itself into the air with a great croak, dodging among the trees and then flapping itself up into the sky and over the western ridge of the gulch.

Artie stood on the trunk of the fallen aspen and considered. "A ghost story," she thought. The ice on the creek sparkled in the afternoon sunshine, striped with the blue shadows of the naked trees. In one place, if she watched closely, she could see a trickle of water bubbling slowly under the ice, still moving, still alive. "I wonder how cold the water is," she asked herself, and with her heel, kicked at the ice until it gave. A cupful of water welled up from the hole and she removed a glove, then knelt and dipped in her hand.

"Oh!" Artie exclaimed aloud. She withdrew her hand at once and rubbed it along her jeans to dry it, then made a fist and jammed it into the pocket of her parka. Her hand felt not chilled, but *burned* with cold.

She gathered a few more branches and headed back. Tonight would be very cold, possibly the coldest night she had spent at the Place so far. "Good," she thought, "I'm going to have the stove heated up for a long time after dinner baking those cakes, so at least I won't be driving people crazy with too much heat."

In a cottonwood near the barn, both of the big owls sat hunched on a thick branch near the trunk, heads sunk into breast feathers and bodies lowered so that their belly feathers covered their feet. Artie looked up at the owls for a long moment, and the ghost story came to her just like that: complete and crystalline, just so, like a faceted gem set precisely into a ring. She smiled as she tramped back to the house.

CHAPTER 9
GHOST STORIES

Outside, the sky was already black, pricked with a few early stars; the east ridge, swallowed in darkness, couldn't be seen. Artie smiled and moved away from the window. It was Halloween, Halloween night, and she was ready for it.

Ben and Tim were taking the dogs out for a potty run, and the Others, all except Shandy and Sylvie, were asleep. A long afternoon nap seemed to be the order of things at the Place for most of the Others, even on a special day.

Both strings of solar lights, orange and purple, wove in a bright tangle through the aspen branches on the mantel, and the small witch's glass eyes glittered with points of reflection so that the wizened little face seemed alive with malice.

Sylvie had positioned a bowl of mixed candies on one of the end tables, convenient for anyone sitting on the sofa or the big leather chair. Bats hung from rafters and railings, swaying eerily in invisible air currents. Spiderwebbing veiled some of the windows and was punctuated here and there with inch-wide black spiders.

On the living-room bookcase, four newly carved jack o' lanterns stood unlit but complete with candles inside. Artie had gutted and carved them all, since no one else seemed to want to try. They looked good, good and scary, classic Halloweeny, if she did think so herself.

In the kitchen, the skull candelabrum on the orange table-cloth was ready to light. Artie had stacked plates and silverware there, too. The countertop sported four round two-layer cakes in a row, nicely frosted in orange by Shandy, who had also made the frosting. Each cake was topped with a licorice bat, Sylvie's idea. One cake sagged somewhat on one side, but Artie figured that she herself could take the saggiest piece of that one. She was proud of the cakes. The wood stove had, indeed, been kind to her late last night, and so had the chocolate cake recipe that substituted mayonnaise for eggs and oil.

The oven was beginning to send out delicious hot-turkey smells. Artie had found a deep rectangular steel pan, and in it, the turkey breasts were baking on a thick bed of seasoned mushroom-onion rice. The mountain of mashed potatoes was done and set aside; Artie had thought a dinner with two starch-es rather odd, but Ben had requested both rice and mashed potatoes.

Shandy was about to put a modest pot of peas on to boil, and, using the turkey-can liquid, Sylvie was making gravy in the cast-iron frying pan. Both coffee pots sat on the stove as well, for after-dinner coffee, and a gallon jug of apple cider, centered in a group of mugs, rested in a bed of granular snow in the sink. The afternoon's preparation had actually been fun, almost a thing of girlfriends working together, Artie thought. Except for Rosa, Artie hadn't really had girlfriends, not *girlfriends* girlfriends. "Interesting," she thought. "Maybe even promising. But at least we have made it happen."

Artie fingered the glass frog bead in her pocket, now strung on fishing monofilament. She had decided to keep it at least until Christmas.

She so hoped tonight would go well. For part of the afternoon, she had sat herself on a granite boulder on the uphill side of the barn and, in the cold, had refined and practiced telling her ghost story. Tomorrow she would write it down, she decided, so she could keep it, because by tomorrow the story would be part of the history of the Place. She hoped the Others wouldn't find her story stupid, but hope was as far as she would go with them; she would tell it anyway because of Ben and because it was Halloween. "Besides, I am a storyteller," came a thought from somewhere very deep inside. "That's what I am and that's what I do."

Artie closed her eyes and let her mind range down the creek, down to where Spear Creek's meadow narrowed, then up to the Hand and its sweeping view of hills and little gulches to the southeast. She thought herself into the aspen grove to the north, the sage flat nearby, and the west ridge on the Castle Hills side-- and finally, up into the black air toward the stars. The coyotes were silent so far tonight; she hadn't heard coyotes for two nights before, but that wasn't disturbing. Artie let out a long breath. Nothing bad was coming. Tonight the Place felt clean and bright and—and *safe*, that was it. And safe.

Ben, Tim, and the dogs pushed into the kitchen, laughing. Bear and Molly were jumping straight up, barking, having caught the flavor of excitement from the boys. "Hey," Ben said, hanging his parka and hat on the hooks beside the door, "it smells outrageous in here. When do we eat?"

Shandy looked up from the pot of simmering peas, pushed back a lock of hair, and smiled. "Any minute," she said. "You'd better be hungry!"

Having shed his coat, Tim sat at the kitchen table and took Smoke into his lap. "Ben said we can break out some treats for the dogs tonight," he said to Artie, looking around. "This place looks great. I've never been much for Halloween, but you three have outdone yourselves."

"Thanks," Artie said, taking a moment to sit down beside Tim. "You got the lights figured out, Tim. And they look perfect." She heard noises above and figured that the Others in the loft were now awake, thanks to the dogs. She saw that Tim heard them, too, and his expression changed; he looked wary. "Tonight has to be good," she told herself. "I'm not going to let Carlos or the girls take over or be nasty. This is going to be fun. We are going to have fun. We need some fun, all of us, especially after Cormack Eldredge."

Shandy stepped away from the stove and swiped a hand across her flushed face. "Peas are done," she said. "The coffee water is heating up, but slow. I have the pots pushed to the side here. I'm not going to dump the coffee into the pots until after dinner—that OK, Artie?" Artie nodded. Shandy was a very pretty girl, with her slender body, narrow face, delicate features, huge brown eyes, and long hair like a fall of melted chocolate—and unexpectedly, Artie was finding that Shandy was a thoroughly nice person as well. The cut on Shandy's arm was healing well, Artie noticed, but the scar likely would always be nearly an inch wide, the skin there stretched and shiny.

"Great," Artie told her. "I think we are ready. Tim, do you want to light the candles? Don't forget the jack o' lanterns, too."

"Sure." Tim set Smoke on the floor and went to the match holder for some wooden matches. "Be a lot easier if we had one of those long thingies."

Artie laughed. "Great vocabulary there," she said. "And you might light the fire in the fireplace as well. We're going to want it burned down to coals by the time we start on the ghost stories."

Shandy drained the water from the peas into the gravy skillet and poured the peas into a bowl, and Ben got four hard biscuit bones from the pantry and distributed them to the dogs.

The Others clumped down the ladder and crowded into the kitchen. "Oh, my god," Lainey said, tossing back her hair. "It smells freaking fabulous in here. I could eat a cow."

"Turkey," said Artie pleasantly.

"What?" Lainey froze in place. "What did you call me?"

"We're having turkey," Artie continued placidly. She had learned a lesson or two from Ben and how he handled things. Artie turned to Carlos and said, "No cake until after dinner."

Carlos stared at her for a moment and then took himself out the kitchen door, followed by Lainey, Turk, and Kaylee. "Outhouse run," Artie thought. "I wonder what they do up there in the loft, besides sleep." She decided that she didn't want to think about that and instead went into the living room to see the jack o' lanterns glowing for the first time. Tim had already lit them and was on his knees lighting the fire.

The scent of warm pumpkin filtered into the room, and Artie's breath caught in her throat as she stood in front of the four jack o' lanterns lined up on top of the bookcase. The candles inside flickered, and a bat turned on its invisible string above her head.

"Memories," she thought, feeling them suddenly swirling around her head. "Helping Mom get Turner ready to go trick or treating. He was a cowboy last year, of all things. A *cowboy*. Hanging paper bats in my window. Gran and I lighting our pumpkins and carrying some of them onto her front porch. Giving out candy to the trick-or-treaters. Reading ghost stories by flashlight under the covers at midnight in my room. And." She came to a full stop and swallowed. "And smelling that sweet, scorched jack o' lantern smell, just like this. Got to stop," she thought, "or I'm going to bawl. Not now, Artie, you idiot," she told herself sternly. "Tonight is Ben's night and it's going to be good," she told herself again. "It's going to be fun, and nothing will spoil it." She heard the Others coming back inside and decided that it was time to take the turkey and rice out of the oven.

Artie leaned back against the base of the leather chair in the living room and savored the last bite of chocolate cake, thick with frosting. She had positioned herself where she could see the fireplace, the tiny lights sparkling in the branches on the mantel, and the row of jack o' lanterns on the bookcase.

The turkey and mushroom rice had been savory and delicious, the peas just fine, the mashed potatoes and gravy very satisfying, but the cake—the chocolate cakes were perfect, the perfect finish to a great dinner.

Artie was tired from all the preparation, but it had been worth it to see Ben's face this morning when he had found the cakes all lined up on the kitchen counter waiting to be frosted. And worth it to see him eating this fabulous dinner. She reached high and put her plate on the end table so the dogs couldn't get at the smears of frosting. She slid back into a sitting position, gathering Moonie into her lap and holding her close. "Food coma approaching," Artie thought, feeling pleasantly sleepy in the warmth from the bright fire. "But I can't fall asleep. It's Halloween night."

Above her, Tim had claimed the big chair, with Smoke in his lap. Artie could feel one of his knees poking her shoulder, but that was all right. Lying half under the end table on the floor next to Artie was Sylvie, finishing up her piece of cake, her head propped on her elbows. Her pale hair fell loosely around her shoulders and shone with strawberry glints in the ruddy firelight.

Ben, Andy, and Mose lay on the floor near the fire. Bear had curled into Ben's side and rested his head on Ben's shoulder. Molly lay flat beside Bear.

Kaylee, on the sofa between Carlos and Lainey, also put her plate aside. "I know," she said. "Let's do charades!" She looked at Ben from under long lashes. "I know we're going to do ghost stories later, but how about charades now?" Kaylee tugged one foot out from under the prone body of Turk, who lay on the floor like a log rolled up against the base of the sofa. He began to snore softly.

"Yes, let's." Lainey added her voice to Kaylee's, but for the first time Artie noticed dark smudges under Lainey's eyes, and thought that Lainey's smile seemed a little forced.

"OK," Carlos added, "and let's do charades of horror movie titles, since it's Halloween. I'll be first."

"Typical," Artie thought, trying not to roll her eyes. "OK," she said. "Carlos, why don't you go first?"

He turned to look at her rather sharply, but soon was hunched over in a strange posture, lunging at Lainey and Kaylee, his hands curved into rigid claws. Kaylee shrieked happily, and Lainey edged away from him, leaning into Shandy at the end of the couch.

"Aaaah!" Kaylee squealed. "Stop, Carlos! I know, I know. You're that guy in *The Hills Have Eyes Four.*"

Carlos collapsed to the floor, narrowly missing Turk's feet. "How did you know I wasn't Freddie?"

"You had that walk," Shandy said, cradling her coffee mug in both hands. "You know, Carlos, that walk the guy had. You nailed it flat. Creepee." Carlos laughed and took a gulp of cider from his cup.

"You're next, Shandy," he said. "Think of a title."

Artie stole a glance at Shandy. Eyes alight, she was leaning forward, thoroughly enjoying herself. Artie had to smile. Tonight seemed enchanted. Even Carlos' off the wall suggestion of horror movie charades was working out well. Ben's face faded in and out of the light as the fire leaped and fell back. Artie couldn't help but think of the night she had held him, when he and Tim had cried in the dark. She remembered the scent of his hair, the fine sandpaper of his cheek, his quiet breathing, the warmth of his arm around her waist. Of all memories since that Last Friday, the memory of her first night at the Place was the best.

Ben slid his body a little back from the fire; his forearms were baking. He could smell the hot flannel of his shirt and hoped it wasn't scorched. He shook his head at his own carelessness. Gramps would have been irritated. Things, all things, were precious now, including flannel shirts. Bear grunted and moved as well.

Ben pulled himself into a sitting position, leaned back against the bookcase, and gathered both Bear and Molly into his lap. The charades were winding down now. Shandy had made the coffee, and everyone was holding a mug and sipping either hot coffee or the remnants of their cider.

Tim, the last holdout, had finally been prevailed upon to do a charade, and he was worming his way along the floorboards with both hands waving in the air above his head. "Antennae?" Ben thought idly. Kaylee and Lainey, heads together, were laughing so hard they were holding their sides, and even Carlos let out a snort or two. Tim's foot connected with the inert body of Turk, still lying against the couch, and for a moment Turk jerked as if startled, then turned his head slowly in Tim's direction. For just an instant, the firelight gleamed in Turk's eyes and he looked *aware.* Ben held his breath for a moment. By degrees, Turk's eyes closed once more, and the long, muscular body relaxed into sleep, or what looked and sounded like sleep. .

"I know!" Artie was saying to Tim. "It's a really old movie, right? It's Vincent Price, a Vincent Price movie?"

Still inchworming his way toward the fire, Tim nodded.

"It's 'The Tingler.'" Artie pronounced in triumph. "You are 'The Tingler!'"

"Yeah, you got it," Tim told her, brushing off his jeans and climbing past Artie into the big leather chair again. "I always liked that one. Did you know that back in the day, some theaters would rig a few seats to vibrate during every showing, and people would scream their heads off?"

"But ancient," Lainey said. "Way ancient."

"Mistress of the put-down," Ben thought, and wondered what to say.

"Good one," Mose commented unexpectedly. Ben had almost forgotten the big Shoshoni there in the shadows; he had been so quiet for so long.

Ben hoped that everyone was settled down, because the fire was low, the jack o' lanterns were flickering, and by the glowing numbers on the wind-up clock sitting at one end of the mantel, it was almost eleven o' clock. Time for ghost stories. Though in a way he hated bringing out Gramps' favorite story in front of the Others, Ben was determined to continue Gramps' tradition.

Ben looked at the firelit faces. Mose and Andy, near him, seemed calm and expectant; that was good. Turk, for all practical purposes a piece of wood, began snoring. The three girls on the sofa all held mugs of coffee and were leaning forward, their beautiful faces eager. Artie looked just like—just like Artie always looked, and he knew that she and Tim wouldn't make fun of a story he told. Nor would Sylvie. And then there was Carlos. Ben stared at Carlos, who was jammed onto the sofa next to Lainey, with his head lolled back onto the top of the sofa, his pale throat exposed. Carlos would be the problem, as usual. But—Ben leaned toward the sofa and looked more closely. Carlos had fallen asleep. Ben smiled. "That's pretty damned lucky," he thought. It was time.

Ben set his coffee mug on the floor. "Happy Halloween," he said softly. "It's time for ghost stories now. Gramps and I and Gary always told ghost stories as the last thing on Halloween, and

Gramps always started with the same story. Gramps said his own grandfather told him this story when he was ten years old, and swore that it was true. So I'll start."

He watched the girls on the sofa. Lainey smiled and draped her arm around Kaylee's shoulders. Shandy leaned still farther forward, staring into the fire.

"A few years after the Civil War," Ben began, "Gramps's family decided to move West. They sold their farm in Virginia and put all their possessions into two big trunks and a few suitcases. Carpetbags. They were actually two families, two brothers who had owned the farm together, and their wives and their children. Rob was older than Will, and his children were teenagers, two girls and two boys. Will had twin boys that were only two or three years old. The brothers determined that they were going to go to Oregon. They had heard that land was good out there, and they figured that if they were careful, they could buy their way to Salem and still have enough money to buy a farm big enough for both families. So they started out riding stagecoaches." Ben shifted his position and Bear moved and resettled himself, while Molly got up and padded into the kitchen. Ben could hear her lapping water from the bowl between the stove and the wall.

And then Ben could also hear Gramps' voice somewhere back in his head, a thin voice, but *Gramps'* voice, and he tried to let it flow through his own, to let Gramps tell this story once more.

Ben continued. "So they would take a stagecoach, and when it stopped at an inn they would eat there and stay the night, then take another stagecoach in the morning or whenever the next one took off that was going their way. They kept doing that for a about ten days, and pretty soon they were in Ohio." Ben ran his hand over Bear's soft head and felt the warmth of the fire on the black fur.

"One night it was raining hard and the stage was late getting to the inn because of the muddy roads, and it was dark when they stopped for the night. The two families ate dinner downstairs and got a room on the second floor. A porter brought up their suitcases and the trunks. They slept on straw-filled mattresses on the floor. They thought it was a lucky room, because the chimney of the big fireplace on the ground floor went through the room, so it was warm, just like the loft is here.

"The room was dark, though. The innkeeper had been a rude guy and hadn't given them a candle or a lamp, even when Rob told the man he could pay for one. There was a window, but it was late and still raining outside, so it didn't let in much light at all. They couldn't see anything. So they felt around in the dark and got settled on the floor. Pretty soon everybody fell asleep.

"And then—" Ben paused here for the effect, just like Gramps had always paused, "—and then, one of Rob's teenage girls, Violet her name was, woke up and whispered, 'I hear somebody crying.'

"Her mother said, 'Hush, Violet, you will wake the little ones.' But after a while, Violet said again, 'Mother, I hear somebody crying. Don't you hear it?'

"And her mother said, 'No, all I hear is the rain on the roof and on the windowpane.'

"Oh," Lainey interrupted, "it's just like a real ghost story. There's always three times."

Ben sighed. He felt like telling Lainey, "It *is* a real ghost story," but decided it would be better just to go on. "And after another bit of time, Violet said, 'Mother, there is someone moaning inside the chimney!'

"And this time her father answered.

"'Violet, no one can be inside the chimney,' Rob told her in a whisper. 'There's a fire in the fireplace down below, and the chimney is full of smoke and hot air. Roll over and put your hand on the bricks. Careful, though, or you could get burned. Just reach out for a touch. Then you'll know there can't be anyone inside the chimney.'

"So Violet rolled over in the dark and put her hand on the bricks of the chimney, and the chimney was stone cold, ice cold. And she said, 'Father, the chimney is cold as ice.'

"And her father took himself over the floor to the chimney and put out his own hand. 'You're right, my dear,' he said to her in surprise. 'The bricks *are* cold as ice.'

"And then a deep, moaning wail shrieked up the chimney!" Ben tried to make it sound sudden and frightening, the way Gramps always had, and was rewarded with gasps from some of the girls.

"And Rob said, 'Something strange is going on here.' And then the wail came again. And again and again. Everyone in the room was awake by this time, and they held onto each other in the darkness. The little ones started crying.

"Then a voice came out of the chimney, right through the bricks, a man's voice, and it said, 'Don't be afraid. I mean you no harm and no harm will come to you. But you are the first people who have heard my cries and I need your help.'

"And the one who spoke up first was Violet, and she said, 'What do you need us to do?' And the voice said in a raspy whisper, 'The innkeeper who took your money tonight doesn't own this inn. He worked for me and one day in the cellar, he took a brick and hit me on the head and murdered me. That was five years ago.'

"Violet and the others were shocked.

"The voice said, 'I cannot find peace until a man of God lays me to rest in consecrated ground. Tomorrow, find some excuse and go down into the cellar. Dig in the southwest corner there, and you will find me. Please, for the love of God, take my bones and bury me properly, so I can sleep. My name is Joshua Sandborn; I give you my name so the preacher can say my name over me when I am at last laid to rest.'" Gramps' words came to Ben effortlessly. He blinked, hard. It almost seemed that Gramps was in the room now, that he had made it to the Place after all. Ben took a deep breath.

"Then the voice said no more, and they never heard it speaking words again. The next morning, as soon as it began to be light, Will and Rob crept down the stairs and through the main room of the inn, where they took a candle off the bar. Will struck his flint and lit the wick, and they quickly found the dank stairs to the cellar and went down."

"Ooo," Kaylee put in. "I like it that there's a dank cellar. That's where you're never supposed to go."

"But always do," added Tim.

Ben smiled. They were into it. He'd hoped he was doing Gramps' story justice.

"And when they got down into the cellar, they saw a great many bottles and jars and boxes and barrels of supplies. But the cellar floor was dirt, and the southwestern corner was empty, except for a shovel leaning there against the wall. At once, Rob set down the candle and picked up the shovel.

"By the time they began to hear noises from the room above, Rob had dug a hole three feet deep in the floor of the cellar. Will took a turn next, and almost right away he struck something. Both brothers started using their hands and dug in the dirt like dogs. They felt cloth and then bone. Will reached for the candle and Rob smoothed the dirt away from the thing they had found.

"They saw a skeleton lying on its face. Its bones had on rotting pants and a brown linen shirt, and underneath its belly they saw that it wore a long leather apron, an apron like an innkeeper would wear, with straps that tied around the waist and the neck. Will touched the back of the head and the matted gray hair slipped off in his hand. There was the skull!"

"Ewww," Shandy contributed.

"They saw the skull," Ben went on. "And it was smashed in, in the back, a black crater. And then they heard someone coming down the stairs, fast, coming right down the stairs.

"It was the innkeeper. 'What the devil are you doing in my cellar?' he shouted at them, and Rob picked up the shovel to defend Will and himself. But—" Here Ben paused once more as Gramps had always done. "But Will said, 'This is Joshua Sandborn and you murdered him five years ago.'

"And a shriek like a spike rose straight up from the shallow grave. The innkeeper stood stock-still for a moment and then ran up the stairs. The brothers went after him and watched him run out the inn's front door and keep on running. The innkeeper never came back, and no one ever heard of him again."

Everyone was silent for a long moment. Ben looked at their faces and then into the fire, where the remnants of the flames were dying into coals. This was good. It had been good.

"But what happened to the inn?" Kaylee asked, swirling the coffee in her mug. "And what did the families do then?"

"What happened would never happen today," Ben said. "Rob and Will and their wives took over the inn, since it turned out that Joshua Sandborn had no family to inherit and the murdering innkeeper had no family to quarrel with them. They arranged for a Christian funeral for Joshua and had him buried in the local cemetery. They ran the inn for three or four years and made a pot of money. Then they sold the inn and started west again. And they never made it to Oregon." Ben drained the last of his coffee, which had gone cold in the mug. "They left the Oregon Trail east of Twin Falls and homesteaded a big acreage near Rupert. By then there was another set of twin boys for Will, and one of them, Aaron, was my Gramps' grandfather."

Lainey laughed. "And they lived happily ever after."

"Pretty much." Ben edged closer to the fire and put on another stick. He looked up at the lights on the mantel, and in the gloom near the ceiling, he could just make out a few bats turning slowly on the invisible monofilament. The jack o' lanterns' toothy grins glowed bright orange from the top of the bookcase.

He took a deep breath. With the fire and the pumpkins and the story, the night now felt like Halloween. The Place even *smelled* like Halloween. He smiled and found that Artie's eyes were focused on his face. "OK," he said, hoping, hoping so hard that he felt his hands clench into fists. "Who is next?"

No one spoke. Kaylee stirred her coffee with a finger. Carlos' dark head slid slowly down the back of the sofa until it rested on the arm near the end table. He gave a soft sigh and then began to snore. Lainey and Shandy stared into the fire, and finally Tim said, "I don't know any, Ben." Andy and Mose remained silent. Ben thought, "Well, at least they listened to the story I really care about, so tonight isn't a complete bust."

Then Artie lifted her chin and said, "I have one."

Ben thought, "Of course. Good old practical Artie always comes through. Give her an assignment, and she does it, every time. But at least she has a story." He moved from the wood floor onto the rag rug and said, "Go for it, Artie." He glanced at the glowing numbers on the wind-up clock and felt a little ripple run down his spine. "Look there at the clock. It's two minutes to midnight."

Artie hesitated for a moment, then drew up her knees and clasped them. The fire snapped twice, and Artie spoke into the silence that followed. "The Owls," she said. "That's the title."

She took a deep breath, and Ben closed his eyes and settled his head on his folded arms to listen. "This," he thought, "this is really Halloween. It's not Gramps telling me a story and it's not Gary, but it's a ghost story I haven't heard and it's happening now."

"On a Sunday afternoon in January, Patrick and Ramona were married in Sun Valley, at the Opera House, " Artie began. "They were childhood sweethearts. Patrick was tall and dark, with brown eyes and hair the color of ravens' wings. Ramona was tall, too, tall and graceful, with green eyes and long hair the color of frost, the color of the surface of the snow, the color of milk and foam and clouds."

Ben opened his eyes. *Patrick and Ramona?*

Artie gazed into the fire. "Patrick wore a white silk shirt and a black tuxedo, and Ramona was fair in her long white satin dress embroidered with crystal beads in curved patterns like frost on a windowpane in the morning. They danced and danced at the Opera House. Ramona felt weightless as she swayed under the starry canopy of lights in her new husband's arms, and Patrick felt strong, stronger than he ever had before. He felt like he could do anything, lift anything, move anything, regardless of its weight. For the first time in his life, he felt powerful.

"Then Ramona tossed her bouquet of white star jasmine and Patrick bundled her into his wedding present to her—a stunning long fur coat, a lynx fur coat—pale cream fur all dappled with tawny and brown and black and rust. They stepped out into the snowy night and the full moon shone on them and their happiness. They climbed into their little red Jeep and began the journey to their new home."

Artie stopped to take a few breaths, but no one moved and no one spoke.

"They had a long ride ahead to get to their home, a cabin up a gulch near Challis, surrounded by pines. They had spent all summer and fall finishing the place and furnishing it with their things. Patrick was a writer and Ramona was an artist, so they didn't need daily contact with the rest of the world, and looked forward to being alone in their home with just each other for company.

"Forty below zero it was, and the first full moon of the new year rose over the Boulder Mountains, so bright above the snow that the stars were dimmed.

"Up over Galena Summit they drove, and the winding road was as black as the tongue of a vulture. When they started down the other side, the moon showed them the Sawtooth Mountains, the White Cloud range, and the valley between, everything clean and white but the trees, which stood stiff and dark, each one with a sharply defined shadow.

"They passed through the town of Stanley without meeting a single car.

"Ramona hugged her beautiful lynx coat to her body and blew little trails in the soft fur. Patrick concentrated on the driving as their Jeep plunged into the deep canyon, and the narrow black road followed every bend and twist of the Salmon River.

"Above, the moon shone through the window and turned Ramona's pale hair into a fall of white taffeta. It cast barred shadows of pines across the road and Patrick stole a glance at his new wife's clear profile in the reflected glow of the headlights and the glancing light of the moon.

"The river was frozen in places, but where it narrowed and tumbled through rocks, the water was still alive, even in the cold. Above the water a thin mist curled and went slithering over the riverbanks until it touched the road and left an invisible glaze of ice. The road arrowed ahead like a crack in the world, black as the pit of hell.

"Patrick laughed as the Jeep swung around a curve above the river. He thought, 'Tonight the road is ours and the river is ours and the night is ours. No one but Patrick and Ramona ride the Salmon highway on this cold night.'

"But he was wrong. High above the river a great owl glided on frosty wings and looked down on Patrick's Jeep, its twin beams of light piercing the dark of the canyon and the noise of its hot engine shattering the silence. And the owl thought, 'This is my canyon and my moon and my night. How dare they intrude?'

"And without another thought, the owl hurled himself down and down and flashed across the highway in the glare of the Jeep's headlights.

"And Patrick saw the owl, so sudden, so close. And he swerved."

From the sofa, Ben heard someone gasp, but he couldn't tear his eyes from Artie's face.

"The jeep slid into space and, crashing through two inches of ice, dropped into the river.

"Patrick shoved open his door and came up at once, even as he felt his breath snatched and his limbs stiffening from the cold water.

"In the moonlight, he searched the broken-mirror surface of the river for Ramona but she was nowhere to be seen. The heavy fur coat dragged her down. Patrick flailed at the surface of the water to stay afloat, knowing that he had only moments before he would be overcome with the cold and would drown.

"But at last he saw one white hand break the surface near him. His own hands were slow and sluggish, but he got her arm, still enveloped in sodden fur, and he held to a boulder, then dragged her to the bank and over the rocks that were glazed and shining with ice, and laid her there on the pristine snow.

"Her face was colorless and lovely, already glistening with frost, and Patrick knew at once that it was too late. He did all the right things, but he knew that Ramona was dying in his arms though she held his hand in one of hers; it felt like a cold metal vice.

"He was so cold--so cold that he could feel his suit freezing to his body and the breath freezing in his lungs. But he gathered her into his arms and took a final breath, breathed into her face as if he could breathe for her, his last breath to tell her that he loved her.

"And the great owl, high above, saw them huddled together in the moonlight, dying from the cold, and for the first time in his long owl life, he felt remorse and was sorry for what he had done.

"And Patrick lifted Ramona's head one last time to look into her eyes and he lifted her and lifted her, and she lifted into the air.

"She kept his hand and he followed, borne, carried, *dragged* into the sky after her, straight toward the moon. Ramona took a breath and let go Patrick's hand. She was cold. Weightless; she felt weightless.

"And Patrick found that he had wings, soundless wings, great feathered wings, and he flew close after Ramona, and saw that she bore wings as well, great, soft wings of cream and dark brown and tawny and buff and rust.

"Ramona flew on. The moonlight sparkled on her claws, and the ice fell away from her wings and her hair and her feathers as she rose into the sky. She turned to look at Patrick and her eyes were wide and gold and reflected the moon, and she saw that his eyes had turned from brown to the amber of icy ale.

"They flew and flew, up toward the moon, out of the canyon, over the mountains and down and down, tiring after many hours, looking for a place to call their own." Artie paused here and smiled faintly at Ben, but Ben didn't see Artie. He saw stars in a black sky, and snow, and mountains blanketed with dark trees, and rivers like threads of silver far below.

"And as the moon went down in the pink glow of early dawn, Patrick and Ramona came at last here, to the cottonwoods of the Place, where they could live undisturbed, and here they live still," Artie continued. "They sleep the days away hidden in the branches of the cottonwoods beside the barn, and in the dark they hunt the narrow meadows.

"And in the summer they call softly to each other in the long, warm twilight as they hunt the rich, grassy meadows and the silvery sage of the hills.

"But in the winter--in the winter they remember the cold and the death and the frozen blackness of the river, and they *scream*."

A silence, long and warm, fell upon the room.

Then a voice came out of the shadows at Ben's elbow. "Bravo," Mose said. Ben could only nod.

Andy added, "Good one, Artie. Got me there at the end."

And Tim and Shandy added together, "Good one."

"Thanks," she said, and got up to stand at the north window in the living room, one that had very little cobwebbing around it. Ben saw the moonlight fall on her face, with a bar of shadow across her eyes cast by the strut of wood between the panes. He stared at Artie, barely noticing when the Others roused Turk and Carlos and trooped together up the ladder to the loft. Ben watched Artie standing at the window for some time looking out into the snowy landscape, one hand resting on the sill.

"She's just Artie," he thought, "just ordinary, practical Artie, who has been just Artie during all these years we've gone to school together." But somewhere on another level he thought, "I didn't know she had *that* inside her. Not something like *that*."

Bear suddenly sprang up, on high alert. And from the north, Ben heard a faint, long-drawn, keening howl. Bear growled. Ben scrambled to his feet to look out the window. "Not again," he thought, thinking of Cormack Eldredge, the dead man bent and frozen in a certain barrel in the barn. *Trash*, Mose had labeled it in black marker.

Ben came to stand just behind Artie at the north window, so close that he could hear her breathing. He wondered if he should just put a hand to her shoulder and pull her four inches back against his chest, but he had never done anything like that and he didn't know how, or what might happen after, or what *should* happen after.

Artie lifted her hand and pointed out the window. "Look, Ben," she whispered. "Look out in the meadow."

Ben looked past the barn, past the bare lilacs, out to the flat meadow where the moon made diamonds on the snow, and he saw them, four of them, running.

"Wolves," he breathed.

And Artie nodded. "Wolves." After a moment she added, "They're beautiful."

Then Ben's hands came up to her shoulders and gently drew her back; it was as if his hands had a life of their own; he didn't have to learn how. He held her shoulders close and felt Artie tense, then relax into him. An unfamiliar, electric warmth flooded his heart as Artie leaned back against his chest. "What am I feeling?" he thought. "What is this?"

He remembered the first night at the Place for Artie and Tim, when he had gone to her for comfort. He remembered his arm around her waist, and her soft hand on his cheek, in his hair. *Comfort.* Then, Gramps had just died. Then, he had just lost his best friend. Losing Gary right after Gramps had been hard, almost the last straw. Terrifying. But, *now.* What was happening now?

The wolves galloped south, straight down the meadow, down Spear Creek, and out of sight in the willows beyond the water-wheel. He thought of the deer that belonged to the Place, of the buck and of old Jane Doe, and hoped they were in a place safe from this pack tonight. "About the wolves," Artie was saying, whispering. "I don't want to tell the Others. Not yet."

"Our secret," Ben whispered into her hair. "Halloween story for another year." Artie's hair smelled faintly of the lemon shampoo that Gramps had bought in such quantities last spring. Ben tightened his hands on her shoulders and wondered if he should kiss her. That would be a first, and he felt paralyzed. That would be best when they were alone, and there were two other people still in the room.

Ben looked over Artie's shoulder into the starkly beautiful landscape of gray and white curves and planes and diamonds. "If I could just stay like this for hours," he thought. "For hours, while I figured out what I am feeling and what I should do."

Then Tim was there at the window standing beside Artie and the moment shattered.

"What?" Tim was saying. "What are you guys looking at?"

Ben released Artie and hoped Tim hadn't noticed. "Can't have this now," he thought. "Put it in a box. Box this feeling up. I can do that."

Artie was up to it. "The moonlight on the meadow and the hills," she said. "Isn't it lovely out there tonight?"

Tim peered through the window. "I suppose," he said. "Looks cold, though. Have you seen Patrick and Ramona?"

"No," Ben replied. "Not tonight."

"Awesome to put them into the story like that, Artie," Tim said, wagging his head from side to side. "Awesome."

"Thanks, Tim," Artie said, moving back from the window. "It's time to take the dogs out for a minute, isn't it?"

"Yep," Ben heard himself saying. "Just for a minute. Let's go." He watched Artie walk to the dim kitchen for her hat and parka, and wondered again what he was feeling.

"I will paint that story," Ben thought. "I will paint the road, the owls, and the river."

⟞⟞ ⟝⟝

CHAPTER 10

CARLOS

Artie zipped her sleeping bag all the way up and lay still in the warm darkness of Halloween. She had brought one of the jack o' lanterns into the larger bedroom; Shandy had been asleep by then, and Sylvie had no objection.

Artie propped her head on one hand and watched Jack's candle flickering, inhaled the warm scorched-pumpkin smell, and smiled to herself. "A good Halloween," she thought. "Ben . . ." She couldn't even put her thoughts into words. Ben had touched her, had held her—had held her, sort of—and had whispered that small secret into her hair. The jack o' lantern grew wavery and dim.

Artie felt moisture on her cheek and wiped the tear away with her fingers. She wondered what would have—what might have happened if Tim hadn't chosen just that moment to get up from the leather chair and wander over to the window. But that was what it was. She would take what she had been given and treasure it, a perfect small memory. And tomorrow? Tomorrow would have Ben in it, all day. Tonight, that was enough for Artie to dream on.

In the morning, Carlos was gone.

Sylvie shook Artie awake, and after Artie had pulled on her jeans and sweatshirt, Sylvie took her arm and dragged her into the kitchen, where everyone was gathered around the table.

"What?" Artie said, looking from face to face. Everyone was there—except Carlos.

"Carlos is gone," Tim said calmly. "He must have got up in the dark, while everybody was still asleep, and he took off. He took the parka you gave him, Ben, and the hat and gloves, and what was left of the Halloween candy from the candy bowl."

"But what are we doing to *do*?" Lainey was almost shouting, looking from Tim to Ben and back to Tim. "Why haven't you gone after him? It's really cold out there, and he doesn't know where he is going."

Artie looked around for the dogs, hoping that Carlos hadn't let any of them out. "Wolves," she thought. "My God, wolves." She grabbed at Moonie, who brushed her knee under the table. "The dogs," she said aloud.

"Oh, the precious dogs are all here," Lainey said. "No worries about the animals. But a person is out there alone. Lost."

Mose spoke up, laying a big hand flat on the table. "Carlos left tracks up to and over the east ridge," he said. "You can see his trail out the front window."

"But Carlos doesn't know how far to go or which way to go!" Lainey cried. "And he won't answer his cell. Something has happened to him!"

Artie clutched the fur on Moonie's back with both hands. She felt sick suddenly, cold and nauseated. As if from a distance, she heard Ben saying slowly, "Well, I guess we'll have to go after him. I hate leaving a trail in the snow that ends at the Place, but we don't have a choice, because Carlos is already doing that. Who's up for it?"

Artie was summoning up the courage to volunteer when Mose pushed his chair away from the table and said, "I am. Someone has to drag the poor bastard back here, and I can do that."

"Good," Ben said. "What do we have for breakfast today? Oatmeal and coffee? OK, let's eat, Mose, and get some of that coffee into a thermos."

Artie sprang up to get a thermos from the pantry and fill it from the coffee pot. She was thankful that today's team had at least done coffee and hot water for the oatmeal. She filled the thermos and scrabbled in the pantry for crackers, a bag of lemon drops, and the last of the granola bars that were in the house. Ben put his day pack on the table and Artie loaded it with the thermos and the food while he and Mose wolfed some oatmeal and sluiced it down with coffee laced liberally with canned milk. Lainey, Andy, Shandy, and Kaylee watched intently.

Artie shifted from foot to foot near the stove. The strange feeling at the pit of her stomach wouldn't go away. She wondered how long it would take Ben and Mose to catch up with Carlos. Carlos was athletic, in shape from football. What kind of head start did he have? "Got a light, Ben? A flashlight or your head-lamp?" She asked.

"I'll put my headlamp in," he said, " but I hope it won't take us that long to find Carlos and get him back here. Or," Ben lowered his voice, "or send him on down a road with some good directions to a--a town. I'm not going to drag him back here if he fights us."

"Oh, no, " Kaylee said. "It's too cold out there and we're too far away from any of the towns to let him go on, aren't we? You have to bring Carlos back. He's got his phone. Keep calling him. I've been calling him on mine but I'm not getting any answer."

"But if he gets to the highway, or to a town," Andy said, his hand on Kaylee's shoulder, "think. If he gets out, he could send someone here to get us."

"What I'm afraid of," Ben commented shortly. Kaylee and Lainey exchanged glances.

Mose knocked back the dregs of his coffee and grabbed his parka from the wall. "OK, Kaylee. You keep calling Carlos. We're out of here." His eyes found Shandy for a moment, and then he started toward the front door.

"Artie." Ben stood and he, too, lifted his parka from the wall hook. He zipped himself into it and jammed on his watch cap.

"Yes?" Artie shivered. Something, something was bearing down upon them like a—Artie couldn't put words to what she was feeling. Like a storm? A heavy weight? Or a snowplow? How could she let Ben just—just walk out the door?

"You and Tim take care of the dogs," Ben said. "Take extra care of them. You know why. And Bear will try to follow me, so you will have to take him out on leash or shovel out the dog run and stick him in there to go potty. The leashes are hanging in the pantry."

"I know," she said, then roused herself and smiled. "Of course. Don't worry about the dogs. Have you got a cell to take?"

Andy reached into the pocket of his jeans and pulled out his phone. "Here, take mine, Ben. It's charged. It was my turn yesterday for Tim to put it on the solar charger. Carlos's number is in there, and Lainey's and Kaylee's. You can call here by calling Kaylee or Lainey."

Ben took the phone. "Thanks, Andy."

Another wave of strangeness shook Artie and she knew she had to tell him. "Ben," she said, "you have to take a gun."

He turned abruptly and stared at her, as did the Others. "Because?" he said.

417

She told him the only thing she could say. "Something bad is coming," she said, almost a whisper, one hand on the kitchen wall to steady herself. She knew it would sound stupid, but she had to say it. "Be careful. Something bad. I can feel something bad. Be really careful."

Lainey's silvery laugh cascaded into the silence that followed.

Ben, however, smiled and said, "Gun's already in the front pocket of the pack, Artie. I took the .357 and left the .38 for you and Tim. You be careful, too. All of you," he added with a wave of one arm. And with a small, fading grin, he strode into the living room and followed Mose out the front door.

Artie had the presence of mind to grab Bear by the scruff of the neck as he shot past her on his way to Ben. "No, Bear," she said, pulling him toward her. "Not this time." Artie walked with Bear to the front window and watched as Ben and Mose, following Carlos' tracks in the snow, began to climb the east ridge. Slowly they made their way up the slope through the deep snow and the dense sage, walking in Carlos' tracks up toward the Hand.

Artie stood silent, Tim and Sylvie at her side, as she watched them gain the ridge. At the top, Mose turned and lifted a hand, but Ben didn't even pause to look back. The rising sun crested the ridge and turned Mose into a haloed saint, and Ben after him. Then the hill was empty, the sky was empty, and they were gone.

Artie felt as if her heart had been dragged up the ridge and thrown down the other side. The bad thing, the bad thing coming was a taste in her mouth, grit on her tongue, ashes and sandpaper and ice. "How can I just wait here?" She thought, staring at the trail trampled into the snow and at the place where it disappeared on the crest of the ridge near the Hand.

Tim's soft voice broke into her thoughts. "Artie, are you all right? You look funny."

"I'm all right, Tim," she said. "I just have a bad feeling about this."

"Nothing we can do about it," he said. "Come on, let's go back to the kitchen and have some oatmeal and coffee. I'm hungry."

"All right," she muttered, pulling Bear with her, "but if they don't come back by dark, I'm going to freak."

"If they're still gone, I'll freak with you," Tim said, just above a whisper. "But I'm glad Carlos won't be here while Ben and Mose are gone."

Ben started down the hill from the Hand, passing Mose, but after a few steps, stopped and surveyed what he could see.

Mose came up beside him. "I don't see him," Mose said, jamming his gloved hands into his pockets. "Why would Carlos climb up here instead of staying down on the road? I mean, the road is covered with snow, but it's so smooth that it shows up plain as plain. I don't get it."

"Vantage point, probably," Ben answered absently, shading his eyes and marking the spot on the next low ridge to the east where Carlos' tracks disappeared. "He doesn't know where he is, so maybe he'd get up high to see what he can see. Can't see that much from here, so there his tracks go to the next ridge over."

"Huh," Mose grunted. "Guess I'm not much of a Shoshoni," he said.

Ben turned to face him. "I didn't mean to imply anything, Mose."

"I know." Mose surveyed the snowy gulches, meadows, and ridges soberly. "I am a Shoshoni," he said after a few moments. "Full blood, both Mom and Dad. Got a share in the tribe and everything. But Dad left when I was two. Went to Montana and never looked back. I don't remember him at all. And Mom doesn't know squat about tribal-type stuff. You know, what plants you can eat and how to tell what animal made some tracks and whether or not it's going to snow. Like that."

Ben started downhill again and Mose followed. After a hundred yards, Ben said over his shoulder, "Artie knows things like that. She could teach you. And I know some things."

Mose barked a short laugh. "Artie?"

Ben said, "Yeah. Her mom is—was—a botanist, and Artie is interested in that kind of thing. When Artie and I and Tim were going through the books in the barrels before it snowed, we were picking out what books to bring into the house for the winter. Artie's pile had a whole bunch of plant and animal books. And anyway, you know her. She's always been into that stuff."

"Never paid much attention. Think she would teach me?" Mose said, as they had crunched their way halfway the hill.

"Sure," Ben said. "Don't see why not." Ben found that he felt comfortable with Mose at his back; that was a puzzle. The only other person Ben had ever felt that way about, besides Gramps, had been Gary. And now Tim; Tim was growing on him.

Mose had never been a friend. Starting in grade school, he had always been one of the jocks, a big, muscle-bound guy who hung with the bullies who had tormented Ben for years, though Mose himself had rarely taken an active part in the bullying. Ben spied a sparkle of plastic on the snow. "Carlos," he thought. He smiled, knowing Mose couldn't see the smile. "I'll let Mose find it," he thought.

"Look." Mose lifted the bright scrap from the surface of the snow. "Here's my first native tracking thing, *Kemo Sabe*. Candy wrapper." He held it out to Ben. "Carlos."

Ben took the wrapper and shoved it deep into a pocket. "Good spot," Ben said. "And Carlos is going to push himself as

420

hard as he can today. He'll want to be somewhere, somewhere indoors, by tonight."

"Yeah," Mose said. They continued downhill into the small draw. "And you know, I just thought. You and me, we have boots on. I have my boots because I had them on the Friday night when the bus crashed. And you have yours because of the Place. But all Carlos has on is his running shoes."

"Right," Ben said. "His feet will already be wet. Nasty in this cold."

"Sucky," Mose said. "But Carlos has been doing wind sprints for football every day since August. He's in shape."

Ben echoed, "Wind sprints?"

"Grief, man, you are truly out of the mainstream," Mose said as they began to walk again. "You know, wind sprints. You run fast, without pacing yourself, just as fast as you can run, until you can't breathe, and then you stop. And the distance you can do gets longer over time."

"OK," Ben replied. "I get it." Yes, he was out of the mainstream, all right; he'd always been out of the mainstream. *Wind sprints.* He was probably the only guy in high school across America who didn't know what that meant. He lifted his eyes to the south horizon and the gentle curves of the hills there, and after a few more steps, he nodded. "But I *do* know where I am," he thought. They trudged on in silence for half a mile in Carlos' tracks and began climbing the next ridge to the east.

"Carlos isn't too tired yet," Ben thought. "His tracks are just as far apart as they were when he started. He hasn't stopped to sit in the snow for a rest. He's going on fitness, adrenaline, and sugar." Ben sighed. He *so* hated leaving a trail in the snow that led back to the Place. He pushed himself to walk a little faster. "When I get tired, I'll ask Mose to lead for a while," he thought. "Hope we can catch Carlos before he gets down to the Fairfield highway. What an idiot."

Carlos—Carlos was a bully, had always been a bully. He was good looking, well-coordinated, and lively—all the things Ben was not. Carlos had always been quick with a deft put-down, a snide remark, some cutting phrase that really hurt—all things unpleasant. But, Ben had eventually come to realize, Carlos had a way with him. He was charming, and his charm and ready smile deflected the usual results of bullying, so he was very popular. His family doted on Carlos and spoiled him; their family car was years old, but Carlos drove a new SUV, a black Range Rover that often cruised around Hailey crammed with his friends.

Ben shivered inside his parka. If Carlos didn't want to come back, what would they do? Would Carlos run from them? Would he fight? How could they make him come with them if he refused to listen? "Not that I really want Carlos back at the Place, " Ben thought. "I'll leave the convincing-Carlos part to Mose. Maybe it won't matter, anyway. Carlos might be so cold and tired that he will be glad to come back." Ben used a thick bitterbrush branch to pull himself the last few feet up to the crest of the second ridge. He looked east and south over a newly revealed system of washes, gulches, and flats. No Carlos was to be seen, only two ravens flying east in the far distance, disappearing over the next ridge but one, which was higher.

Ben shaded his eyes with one hand. The glare from the sun on the snow was fierce. He wished he had thought to look for a pair of sunglasses or ski goggles. He knew there were a few stashed in the barrels somewhere in the chicken house.

Ben saw that Carlos' tracks dipped into the meadow below, then climbed the next ridge, his footprints pooled in blue shadow, as obvious as if they had been painted on the snow. "Another ridge? He's an idiot," Ben thought. "We'll catch him before dark. It's obvious that he doesn't know how to conserve energy and find his way in the back country."

"Huh," Mose grunted as he came up beside Ben on the crest of the ridge. "What the crap is the matter with that dude? Why does he keep climbing and then going down? It doesn't make sense." He shook his massive head. "When we get to the top of that next one, let's break out that thermos and stop for some coffee."

"Suits me," Ben said, and began plunging down the hillside, breaking through the crusted snow in some places, wallowing in Carlos' tracks in others.

⊨⊦ ⊧⊨

Artie, full of coffee and oatmeal, had just come in from taking the dogs for a run in the meadow. She had kept Bear on leash and was relieved when she found that he would potty on leash just fine. The dogs stopped still and bristled when they encountered the wolf tracks; Bear growled and left a yellow stain of urine to mark the spot.

Artie hung up her coat and hat and decided it was time to write in her journal. But before she got to the living-room bookcase, Andy intercepted her. "Hey," he said, holding up a hand. "Come on up to the loft. Lainey isn't doing too well."

"Lainey?" Artie echoed. Dutifully, she climbed the ladder to the loft, and found Turk sitting crosslegged in a corner staring at the wall, and Lainey, flanked by Kaylee, lying flushed and restless in her sleeping bag.

"She's really sick," Kaylee said when she saw Artie's head appear at the top of the ladder. "You've got to do something."

Lainey turned her head this way and that and unzipped her sleeping bag. "Too hot," she said moving a leg outside its folds. "Way too hot."

Artie crawled through two pairs of shoes and scattered cards and came up to the floor mattress. Lainey's complexion looked darker. Beads of sweat dotted her forehead and upper lip. The beautiful strawberry hair lay on her pillow in damp strings. Artie thought, "Oh, my god, what if she has something contagious? Or something dangerous? How can I figure this out?"

But then Kaylee supplied the answer. "I think it's withdrawal, Artie," she said.

Artie sat back on her heels, surprised. "What? Withdrawal from what?"

Kaylee sighed and pulled the sleeping bag up around Lainey's shoulders and stuffed the extended leg back inside. Lainey seemed to be shivering now. "Sleep stuff," Kaylee said. "You know, stuff like Ambien or Lunesta. Lainey takes a lot of them. Her mom has a prescription, but doesn't need them any more, but Lainey tells her mom that she can't sleep and has to have them. So her mom keeps getting it refilled. Lainey really does have to have them. She can't sleep without them."

Artie froze for a moment and suddenly a few things fell into place. "Of course," she thought. "Lainey was going to search the barn for that stuff when she went out and got grabbed by Eldredge."

Artie turned to Kaylee. "Why is Lainey going through withdrawal now? The night Eldredge was there, she had run out of pills and was going to look for some in the barn but didn't get that far. Why didn't she go through withdrawal then?"

Kaylee made a small intention movement as if she wanted to head for the ladder. "Well," she said, hesitating. "Well, I found that I had a bottle in my purse. Lainey and I were both wearing our bags the night the bus crashed. I had about half a bottle of Ambien that I got at my grandma's. I don't take it. Hardly ever, anyway," she amended. "I carry it in case we go somewhere and Lainey needs some. But I forgot I had it. And for a while here, she had hers, so I didn't think about it. But after, after that guy—" Kaylee swallowed. "After that night, when Lainey said what she was looking for, I remembered, and I gave her what I had left. And yesterday she ran out for real. What are we going to do, Artie?" Kaylee reached for Artie's arm. "What can we do?"

"I'm going to get the *Medical Advisor* and see what I can find out," Artie said, backing away. "You stay with Lainey and keep her covered up." Artie stood, took a few steps, and reached for the ladder, when she thought of something. "Kaylee, do you have the empty bottle? I need to know what's in the stuff, what chemicals. Maybe that will help me look it up."

"I'll look," Kaylee said. "I'll bet it's in Lainey's bag."

"OK." Artie slid down the ladder and found herself swearing under her breath. "Bad thing coming, all right," she thought. "Ben's out there away from the Place, we've got wolves, and now this."

She pulled the *Home Medical Advisor* from the bookcase and flipped it open to look for the publication date. "1996," she read. "Revised, 2010. Could be worse." She stretched out on the floor near the fading coals in the fireplace and began to search. Bear padded over to sit near her shoulder, but wouldn't lie down. Artie put one arm around him. "I know," she said to Bear. "I know, boy. I feel the same. It's not going to be right until Ben gets home."

The afternoon was growing old, and it was colder. Slanting yellow light fanned across the snow and made long shadows from those sagebrush and grasses tall enough to show above the crusted surface.

Ben lifted the binoculars to his eyes and scanned a hundred eighty degrees, all ways south. A sharp little wind hissed past his cheeks and stung them with ice crystals.

Ben and Mose were standing behind a blocky four-foot-high outcrop of black basalt just below the crest of a ridge and were peering over it. Mose said, "Well, if we turned around now, we wouldn't get back until after dark as it is. We're past the point."

Ben heard Mose rubbing his gloves together but didn't take the binoculars from his face. Below their vantage, he could see a dark figure moving at the end of the line of tracks they had been following all day. "I've got him!" he said. He handed the binoculars to Mose. "Look down there." He pointed, feeling his shoulders sag with relief. "Look. He's not even that far away. You don't even need the binocs; he's been in that draw. That's why I didn't see him at first after we got to the top here. He just popped up from that little draw. He's tired now. Look how slow he is."

Mose took the binoculars and scanned. "Yeah," he said after a long moment. Yeah, that's Carlos, all right. He's not the only one who's tired." He took the binoculars away from his eyes for a long look at the lumpy snow-covered slope below. "Hey, isn't that the Fairfield road down there? The state highway? Look at those green mile markers sticking up through the snow. Carlos is almost up to the highway. But it hasn't been plowed."

"Yes," Ben answered. "That's the state highway. So now what? He hasn't seen us. Do you think we should shout and wave our arms? Or should we just walk on down there? Or—should we just let him go? He'll know that's the state highway."

Mose pushed away from the chest-high outcrop, where they had been resting their elbows, and sat himself on a rock at its base. "God, I am freezing solid," he said. "Let's have some more coffee. It's not like he can get away from us now. And you said it--look how slow he is."

"OK." Ben slid down beside Mose, leaned against the basalt wall, and dug in his pack for the thermos. He poured the lid full for Mose and drank his from a plastic cup Artie had put into the pack for them. The steam warmed his hands and chin, and the coffee was still hot enough to burn his tongue. It was wonderful, coffee was. Two swallows and Ben felt his insides warming just a little. He took another mouthful and held it. The wind sent tiny ice beads against the basalt behind his head with a tiny zinging sound, and—

"Mose!" Ben held up a hand. "Listen. Do you hear a motor?"

Mose began to stand up so he could look over the basalt wall, but Ben shot out a hand and clamped it on the big forearm.

"No, Mose," he said, whispered. "Wait. Let's be cautious." Ben held his breath.

"It's a motor, all right," Mose said after a long moment. He tossed the last swallow of coffee into the snow and handed Ben the thermos lid. "Almost sounds like a truck. But there's something different about it."

"Let's take a peek over the rock," Ben said then, capping the thermos and shoving it back into his pack. He zipped the pack, shouldered it, and gradually lifted his head until he could just see over the outcrop. East. The sound was coming from the east.

Ben saw it first. "It's a snowcat," he said into Mose's ear. "It's one of the big ones, the kind they use to get around on the ski mountains. It's on the state highway, coming this way."

Mose nodded. "But this one's all white," he said. "The Sun Valley snowcats aren't white like that." Mose glanced at the hillside below them. "Look, Carlos has seen it. See? Look at him running. He's trying to get to the highway before it goes past him."

Ben watched Carlos running, almost floundering, toward the snowcat and waving his arms. He was shouting something, but Ben couldn't make out the words. "Oh, no," Ben thought, and his heart sank to his boots. "He will lead them straight to the Place. What can I do?" He felt paralyzed. The words "what can I do" seemed to ricochet around in his brain. *The Place, the Place, the Place*, he thought with each breath. What was more important than protecting the Place?

The snowcat accelerated as Carlos ran toward it. The cat's large windows made it easy to see inside the cab as the machine drew closer. Suddenly Ben realized that the snowcat had two occupants, and that they were both wearing white. "I don't like this, Mose," he said softly. "Are those the white soldiers we have heard about? I am not liking this at all." *Bad thing coming. Take a gun.* Artie's words dropped into his mind like cold stones, and Ben slung off his pack and scrabbled inside for his revolver. "Revolver?" he found himself thinking. "What I need is a rifle."

"What are you doing?" Mose said. "What are you going to do?"

"Chill, Mose," Ben said. "I won't do anything if I don't have to. You take the binocs and focus on those guys in the cab. Tell me what they're doing."

Mose grabbed the leather strap and slung the binoculars around his own neck. "OK," he said. He twirled the focus wheel. "OK, they are almost up to Carlos. They stopped the snowcat. One of them is climbing down. He's down. Now the other one is handing the first guy something, something, it's—it's a rifle! And Carlos has stopped now and that guy, he's pointing the rifle, and—"

Ben saw. He laid his left arm on the hard basalt rim and braced his right hand with it. He sighted down the barrel of the .357 and found the man with the rifle. A voice inside his head said, "You have a revolver and it's a hundred and fifty yards and that guy has a rifle and Carlos is only 25 yards from him, and—"

Crack! Ben saw the shooter stagger back a step with the recoil.

At first it seemed as if nothing had happened, as if the shot had gone wild. Then Carlos began to fall backward into the snow. The shooter lifted the rifle and leveled the weapon at Carlos once more. Ben could hear the man's loud laughter; he was glad the man was laughing; his own hands steadied.

Ben sighted down the barrel again, held half a breath, and pulled the trigger. *Crack crack!* There was a prolonged report; they had fired at almost the same moment. Carlos completed his fall into the snow and lay flat on his back. And slowly, very slowly, the man in white fell onto the near tread of the snowcat. Ben heard the clang of the rifle as it hit metal there, but his eye was on the second man, who jumped from the cat and grabbed for the rifle, swung the barrel uphill toward their position.

Snap! Ben fired again. The second man fell.

Mose sprang up, ready to charge downhill, and Ben said sharply, "No! Wait! Got to see if they're really down. Because if they aren't, they are going to be damned irritated. Keep the glasses on them and see if they move."

"God," he thought, "I sound just like Gramps."

Mose said simply, "Oh," and lifted the binoculars again.

They waited, shivering. Ben thought, "What if Carlos is bleeding out, what if he's not dead, what if he's dying, what if those men are just playing possum? Ohmygod, ohmygod." Mose's deep voice broke into his thoughts.

"Nobody's moving down there, " he said.

Ben zipped his pack closed and tossed it over the rim. He watched it roll twenty yards down the hill before it smacked into the top of a sagebrush and stopped. Still nobody moved at the snowcat.

"OK, *Kemo Sabe*," Mose said. "This is where we do the Lone Ranger and Tonto, and I'm not the Lone Ranger. I go down, you cover me."

Ben nodded. It was the only thing to do.

Mose crept over the rim and then launched himself downhill in great bounding strides, the crust on the snow crunching and shattering with the impact of his boots, powder underneath puffing out, little pieces of crust sliding downhill on the surface.

Ben kept the revolver sighted on the bodies at the snowcat. Still nothing moved.

Finally, the dark, upright figure that was Mose arrived at the cat. Ben watched him bend over the fallen men. "Dead-oh!" he shouted, holding out an arm and turning thumbs-down. Mose made for where Carlos lay in the snow. Ben kept the revolver in one hand and started down the hill, snagging up the strap of his pack on the way.

When he reached Carlos and Mose, Mose held up a bloody glove. Ben knelt in the snow beside Mose. Carlos was very pale, his face not much darker than the snow, and he was unconscious, completely out, but he was breathing.

"Not good, but could be worse," Mose was saying. "Look." His finger probed a bloody hole in Carlos' parka. "Got him right below the collarbone here. And I looked on the other side, on his back." Ben began to focus and tried to make sense of what Mose was saying. "The bullet went right through Carlos and came out on his back. He's got blood on the back of his head, too. He fell on this rock that was right under the snow here, see? And his head hit it dead center."

"Holy crap," Ben said. He turned Carlos' head to one side and felt in the straight black hair where the blood was seeping out. He probed with a finger all along the bloody patch of black hair. "His skull feels intact to me, Mose," Ben said. "I hope it's true." He looked at his own hand and suddenly realized that it didn't have a shadow. Nothing had a shadow. New clouds were eating the sky to the west; it felt warmer, and the wind was rising.

"Gonna get dark soon," Mose was saying. His voice broke. "What are we going to do, Ben?"

Ben felt a chuckle building in his throat that he hoped wasn't hysteria. "OK, Mose," he said. "We're going to unzip Carlos, rip off a couple of pieces of his shirt and jam them into his bullet holes, zip him up, and take him over to the snowcat. Those things have good heaters."

Mose whistled and said, "Oh, yeah. Yeah. You're the man. Sweet."

Ben looked east and west down the state highway and saw no other vehicles. "Let's get a move on," Ben continued with another glance at the sky. "I don't like the look of that sky. Or maybe I do."

CHAPTER 11

WHITE CAT

Two hours earlier, Artie had commandeered Andy and Kaylee to move Lainey downstairs. Lainey now lay on her sleeping bag near the fireplace with some clean rags and one of the stainless steel bowls near her on the floor; she had been throwing up all afternoon, as well as suffering cramps in her arms and legs. To keep it clean, Artie had pulled Lainey's hair into a ponytail.

During the last few hours, Lainey had finally stopped vomiting and had managed to keep down a half a mug of water.

Artie glanced at Lainey, could just make out her pale profile in the dim room. Lainey seemed to be sleeping peacefully. "She's still beautiful," Artie thought, with a touch of envious resentment. "If I had spent the afternoon heaving my guts out, I'd be all patchy and blotchy. I'd have eye bags. My nose would be red and running. But after all that, Lainey looks beautiful, as always." Artie shrugged away the ungenerous thoughts. "Looks like her addiction wasn't terribly serious," she thought. "That's good; I am already tired of taking care of her and it would be horrible to have to take care of Turk." She peered out the south window again.

Outside, twilight was deepening. Artie had been checking that window every ten minutes or so all afternoon. Ben and Mose were still out there somewhere.

About an hour earlier she had felt sick with dread. She had felt like screaming, like shaking everyone left at the Place and saying, "Something terrible is happening right now. *Now.* Do something!" She had been one step away from assaulting Kaylee and ripping away her cell phone to call Ben. But then, curiously and almost instantly, the feeling had passed as gently as a cloud lifts over a mountain, and was gone.

She felt relief, but couldn't have explained why if her life had depended upon it. And now, she just felt—empty. Where were Ben and Mose? "They have decided to hole up somewhere for the night," she told herself for the hundredth time. "Ben knows these hills. He would know a good place where they won't freeze. If anything awful happened, they would have called us. They'll start out again in the morning. They'll be back by noon tomorrow." Artie tried to make herself believe it. And Carlos. Artie tried to worry about Carlos, but found that a futile exercise and gave it up. Back in her mind somewhere, the thought kept beating, "But why don't they call? Why don't they call?"

Shandy appeared at her elbow. "Wish they'd get back before it's really dark," she said, voicing Artie's thought. "It's Ben and Mose and Tim's turn to cook tonight, " Shandy went on, "and it's going to be time to light the stove in just a few minutes. But Tim's the only one of that team who's here. There's leftover turkey and rice from last night, so we could have that. I can help Tim out."

"Good idea," Artie said. "We don't have any cake left, but we could make some cookies." Making cookies sounded good; she needed something to fill up her mind so she wouldn't go crazy and take off in the dark after Ben.

"Great." Shandy rubbed her thin arms. "We could make plain sugar cookies and frost them. I could make some more frosting. There's a lot of supplies for that."

"Sounds good." Artie said. "Let's get started." Artie added, "Let me take the dogs out on a potty run first, before it gets really dark. When I get back we can light the stove and get going."

"OK. How's Lainey doing?" Shandy asked. "I've been asleep for a while."

"She had a bunch of arm and leg cramps," Artie said, "and she's thrown up, or tried to, all afternoon, but she finally went to sleep. Maybe she'll be OK when she wakes up."

"Good enough," Shandy said. "My cousin Jenna got hooked on her mom's oxycodone and when Aunt Lil and Uncle Jason found out and took her off them, she was pretty sick for two weeks."

"Two weeks!" groaned Artie. "Did the doctor give your cousin anything to help her with the withdrawal?"

"I don't remember," Shandy said. "Maybe. I don't know."

"Well, we'll just have to do what we can do," Artie said. "The *Medical Advisor* told a couple of drugs to give somebody doing withdrawal from zolpidem, but we don't have those. At least that stuff isn't on the lists of things we have here. Water, and calcium pills." Artie sighed. "Those were the recommended things that we *do* have. When Lainey wakes up, we can try to get some calcium down her."

"Maybe." Shandy looked dubious. "At least Andy has taken over babysitting Turk for the time being. I sure don't want to be the one taking *him* on potty runs." Shandy wrinkled her nose in disgust.

Shandy peered out at the darkening landscape. "It's getting dark, Artie. You'd better take the dogs out. I'll get some kindling and get the stove ready to light."

"OK." Artie took Bear's leash from the nearby chair.

⇥ ⇤

Twilight thickened around the snowcat, and Ben looked down at Carlos, lying on the floor between the two seats. He still hadn't regained consciousness, but the rag-stuffed wounds had stopped bleeding almost at once. He now had some color in his face and had stopped shivering.

Ben put up the binoculars and did a scan, horizon to horizon. "Nothing," he said. "But somebody is going to miss these two soldiers and this cat and come after them."

Mose stretched his arms over his head. "Well, at least they left the motor running," he said. "Feels good to be warm. And being warm is a good thing for Carlos, too. What do you want to do, drive this thing back to your Place?"

"I've been trying to think," Ben said with a sigh. He took off his cap and ran a hand through his hair. "Huh," he thought. "My hair is getting long. Weird." He looked at Mose's big body overflowing the padded seat, a seat made for an average-sized man, and felt like bursting into laughter. That *was* weird. Ben slid his cap back on. He must be having some reaction from shooting those men. Hinch and Marshburn. Their strange whitish uniforms had the names embroidered on the chest. He had killed Hinch and Marshburn.

Ben shook his head. He had to stop dwelling on it, at least for the moment. Carlos was stable now, and warm. They couldn't just sit here. Ben needed a plan.

"Well," he said aloud. "We need to get Carlos back to the Place. They have helicopters. They'll have a helicopter out looking for these guys and this cat come morning, and this thing is going to leave a huge track. Maybe they even have something up there searching right now. They'll have a Blackhawk, maybe."

"Blackhawk? What do you mean?" Mose turned to face Ben.

"Blackhawk helicopter," Ben said. "You know, the National Guard out of Boise has them."

Mose winced. "Ow," he said; then added, "How do you know this stuff?"

"Gramps."

"Oh, sure. Well, we have to figure something out. Me, I like this machine. It's warm. And it can go anywhere. And how are we going to get Carlos to the Place if we don't use it? Also, what about these guys, these bodies? Dumb to leave them on the road, right?" Mose looked anxiously at Ben, and Ben suddenly realized that in all the years they had been in school together, he had very rarely heard Mose venture an idea of his own or be the first to make a suggestion. He glanced at Mose, who was leaning forward in his seat. "Waiting," Ben thought, "He's waiting for me to tell him what to do."

"Seventeen Oh Six, Seventeen hundred." A radio bolted to the dashboard barked out the words.

Ben and Mose both jerked as if they had been shot. "Jesus!" Mose hissed through his teeth.

"Seventeen Oh Six, Seventeen Hundred," the voice came again. And a pause. *"Seventeen Oh Six, Seventeen hundred."* And a pause. Then, "For Chrissake, Hinch, come in! Over."

"What is it?" Mose was saying. "What does it mean?"

Ben knew. Thanks to Gramps and his ex-military buddies, he knew exactly what it meant. "Hinch," the voice had said. *Hinch.* One of the dead men.

Ben turned to the dashboard, found a microphone, took it, punched in the button, and held it. "Seventeen Hundred, Seventeen Oh Six," Ben said, deepening his voice as much as he could manage. He released the button. Mose sat transfixed.

"Seventeen Oh Six, where the hell are you?" crackled through the radio. *"Shit, I hate operating when the whole GPS grid is down. Are you still in Carey? Over."*

"Roger, over." Ben replied, desperately hoping that was the right thing to say. His hand on the microphone was trembling; he tightened his grip. If only this Seventeen Hundred would think the snowcat was in Carey.

"Seventeen Oh Six, Seventeen Hundred. What's taking you so long? You guys haven't been joyriding around again, wasting gas, have you? Did you locate any food there? Over."

Ben took a deep breath and silently thanked Gramps for teaching him military radio protocol on ancient walkie-talkies when he was eight years old. "Seventeen Hundred, Seventeen Oh Six. Yeah, we found some food. Not a lot. Couple of hundred cans. Got—got stuck in a ditch," he improvised with the first excuse that popped into his head. He hoped it would fly. "Took us until just now to get out, over."

"You and Marshburn flag the locations of the cans? Over."

"Roger. Over."

"Well, get your asses back here asap, Hinch. Ditch? Got a cat stuck in a ditch and were too feeble to answer your radio for three hours? Beyond brilliant. You'd better not be drunk. And get a move on. Seventeen Hundred out."

"Roger. Seventeen Oh Six out," Ben said, and released the microphone button. He reached forward to hang the mic in its slot, but his hand was shaking, and Mose took it from him and fitted the mic into its clip.

"Holy shit, Ben," Mose said. He let out a long whistle. "I mean, holy *shit*. What the freak are those numbers? What just went down?"

"Those numbers are call signs assigned to people," Ben said. "Every soldier has one. Seventeen Hundred was the call sign of the guy who called and Seventeen Oh Six is—was--that guy Hinch. You say who you're calling, and then you say who you are.

Seventeen Hundred was calling Seventeen Oh Six, so he said, 'Seventeen Oh Six, Seventeen Hundred.' It's like saying, 'Calling Joe; Nick here.'"

"I'll be damned," Mose said, scratching one ear. "I wouldn't have had a clue. But now the guy thinks we're over in that little town on the way to Craters of the Moon--Carey, right? That can't be too bad."

"Right. So let's figure out what this all means," Ben said, thinking aloud. "These guys were a military patrol sent out to look for food—not to bring it back, just to find stuff and mark the locations of stuff they found. That means some truck or something will go to Carey to pick up the food that's supposed to be flagged by these two guys."

"Maybe they did go to Carey first and flagged where they found some food, and then decided to ride around and see what they could see," Mose offered tentatively.

"Good, Mose. Yeah, Seventeen Hundred said they had been out joyriding before. I hope that's what brought them out this way. And I hope they did flag some food in Carey. But even if they did do that first, sooner or later the cat tracks will lead the military straight to this spot. We don't know where their base is, so we can't be sure how much time I bought us. But—I would bet that Carey is a day trip for them, there and back. Just from what the guy said about expecting them back earlier, I bet it's a trip that can be done there and back in a day. Got to think." Ben dropped his head into both hands. He sat like that for some time, feeling the welcome heat from the cat's blower whisper past his ears.

Ben raised his head suddenly. "Time to get these bodies out of sight, don't you think?"

In the dim twilight of the cab, Mose nodded. "Hinch and Marshburn," he said.

"Yes, and--" Ben began but then said, "Wait. Wait. They have uniforms. They'll have ID. They have a rifle. Those uniforms

---

and ID may be useful to us sometime. The rifle, yeah. OK, Mose." Ben looked out at the expanse of snowy indigo hills. To the east, two stars pricked the darkening sky over the more distant mountains. To the west—to the west, there was nothing but a vague dimness. "What?" he thought. Ben sat up straight just in time to see the first wind-driven snowflakes splat onto the cat's windshield and slide down toward the wipers. He turned to Mose, smiling. "I've got an idea," he said with a tight grin.

Artie and Shandy, with some help from Tim and Sylvie, reheated the food and served dinner to themselves and to Kaylee and Andy. Andy fed Turk, who opened his mouth every time a fork touched his lips, and chewed with his mouth open. Occasionally, globs of rice fell from his mouth and were instantly licked up by Molly, who had stationed herself under Turk's chair.

On the floor in the living room, Lainey slept, still; Artie could see her shape in the flickering light from the low flames in the fireplace. Tim had kindled a small fire there as soon as it was dark.

They were so few that they could all sit around the kitchen table to eat, and they lingered there over coffee and pink-frosted sugar cookies.

"I'm going to call Carlos again," Kaylee announced, dusting cookie crumbs from her hands. "Then I'm going to call Ben. Nobody has called them for quite a while."

Artie sat silent while Kaylee's fingers moved over her phone. Kaylee pushed back her coffee cup and slumped forward with her elbow on the table and the phone to her ear. Artie tried not to hold her breath. "It's ringing," Kaylee said.

"Hello?" she said. "Carlos?"

Then Kaylee flinched so abruptly that she almost dropped the phone. Artie couldn't breathe.

"Mose?" Kaylee's voice sounded thin, sharp as a blade. "Why is this Mose? Where's Carlos?"

Artie gripped the sides of her wooden chair to keep her hands from snatching the phone away from Kaylee. "What about Ben?" she couldn't help saying.

"Mose, what is going on?" Kaylee asked, waving Artie away. Then she nodded. "What? What?" She was silent for a few moments, listening. "You OK?" Kaylee looked down at Artie's fingers suddenly clamped around her wrist. "Ben OK?" Kaylee nodded to Artie and Artie watched her own fingers release Kaylee's arm.

Another silence stretched out, and after what seemed an age Kaylee said, "OK. Yes, we're set for the night. Everything here is fine. OK. See you tomorrow."

See you tomorrow. Artie blew a long breath. "*See you tomorrow,*" she thought, "what a great expression." "Give," she said to Kaylee.

"Carlos ran into two soldiers, and they shot him," Kaylee said to her eager audience, giving it full dramatic flair. "But—Carlos is OK. Or semi OK. He was shot in the shoulder, high up, Mose said. But Ben and Mose have got Carlos. They got away from the soldiers. They are hiding for a while."

"What?" Andy said, coffee cup halfway to his lips.

"Yep. Carlos is shot in the shoulder, Mose says," Kaylee recited, smiling.

"God," Artie thought. "Kaylee would have a great career as a news anchor."

"So Ben and Mose are OK," Artie said aloud just so she could hear the words.

Kaylee nodded. " Yes, Mose says they are fine."

But they're out there in the dark," Artie couldn't help adding. "They'll freeze tonight."

"Mose said they are in a safe place, and they are hiding for a while. He said they found a snowcat. He said to expect them before it gets light in the morning, and not to panic when we see lights coming. Oh—almost forgot," Kaylee added, pushing her chair back from the table. "Mose told me to go outside for a minute and look. He said it's snowing."

⊷⊶

Ben tried not to think of the naked bodies of the two soldiers Mose had jammed into the back cargo box, but was very glad that Mose had the strength to lift them and stuff them inside.

It had taken them a while to strip the bodies and make a bundle of the uniforms and gear.

They had found some other things in the snowcat's cargo area before stuffing the bodies there—a shovel, two space blankets, a first-aid kit, a box of wire-stake flags, and a small roll-up tool kit.

Behind one of the seats in the cab, Mose found an olive-drab metal box that was obviously a lunchbox and contained two apples, four chocolate-chip cookies, four ham sandwiches in little baggies, a pile of orange peels, and a few crusts in wadded-up baggies, from sandwiches already eaten. "Their lunch and dinner," Mose said, grabbing the food out of the box. "Look, little mustard packs, even. I am star-*ving*." He had made short work of loading the bodies so he could get to the food.

The wind had risen and was howling around the dark cab as Ben and Mose ate their way through the lunches. Snowflakes tumbled down the windshield and made a smooth roll of white on top of the wipers. Carlos didn't stir. Ben found himself wondering just how hard Carlo's head had smacked onto that rock. "All we need is another zombie like Turk," he thought, "and if that isn't the insensitive thought of the year."

Ben hadn't realized it until the first bite of sandwich, but he had been starving, too. The food made him feel warmer and stronger. He polished off the last cookie and said to Mose, "Let's get rid of these bodies now. In this storm, they probably wouldn't send a Blackhawk to look, not in the dark. But we've got to get ourselves out of here."

After a few abortive lurches and stalls, Ben found that he could drive the snowcat. The cat negotiated the two feet of snow on the state highway without effort. Twin beams of light from headlamps, four feet above the level of the snow, penetrated only a few yards ahead into the manic whiteness.

Ben liked the feel of the wheel in his hands, but he noticed that Mose was leaning far forward, his whole silhouette tense. Ben said, "Don't look so worried, Mose. I know where I'm going, and this *is* a cat, you know, a *cat*--the classic tracked vehicle for getting around on snow. We'll be fine." He shot another glance at Mose, who was turned sideways and had a foot braced on either side of Carlos' lolling head to keep it from banging against the bases of the seats. "Remember that little road branching off from the highway, going south? You could see it when we were at the top of that last hill looking down on Carlos, from that outcrop."

"Nope," Mose said, with a kind of glum resignation. "I don't remember any side road."

"Well, it's there, and we're almost up to its turnoff, and I know where it goes, and I'm taking it," Ben said, thinking, "Mrs. Phillips would kill me for that sentence." He negotiated a dip in the highway and went on, "It goes down to a dirt parking lot at Magic Reservoir. And the reservoir will be the perfect place to get rid of these bodies."

"Hope it isn't frozen over," Mose remarked.

"Aren't you a ray of sunshine," Ben said with a grin. "Guess we'll find out. Look. Here's the road, see?--right between these two markers." He turned onto the smaller road, a narrow line of unblemished snow with no sage tops to break its smoothness. "Less than half a mile," he said. He could feel the ground descending as the cat tracked downhill.

Carlos' body began to buzz, and a raucous song blasted from his pocket. Ben flinched, but Mose patted Carlos' pockets and came up with his phone.

"Kaylee, it's Mose," Mose said, answering. "You guys OK?" There was a pause. "Yeah, we're OK. We got Carlos, but he's shot.'" Another pause. "Yeah, some white soldiers shot him through the shoulder, high up. Ben thinks he will be OK, though." Mose lifted his head and stared at Ben. His dark eyes looked glassy in the reflected light from the cat's instrument panel. Mose looked steadily at Ben. "Yeah, we got away from the soldiers and we're— hiding. We are hiding. Ben? Sure, he's OK." Mose smiled, his teeth a pale slash in the twilight of the cab. "Hey, we've got things to do, but we will be back before the sun comes up. We—we found a snowcat, so don't freak when you see its lights coming up the road. OK. And go have a look outside. It's snowing. Bye."

Mose ended the call and shoved Carlos' phone deep into one of his own pockets. "I thought that Carlos might not remember that you shot those soldiers," he said. "You know, he was already hit, already falling when you shot the first guy. So why give anybody any ammo against us? We don't know what's going to happen down the road."

Ben smiled; his face felt stretched tight. "Good job, Mose," he said, meaning it. "Good job."

He brought the cat to a stop when the headlights showed him nothing ahead but a swirling void. He changed gear and pulled on the emergency brake. "I'm going to leave it running," he said. Ben fished his headlamp from his pack and strapped it on.

Ben and Mose climbed down from the cab into the wind-whipped darkness, and Mose shoved open the lid of the cargo box. He tugged on a bare arm, then grabbed its companion and gave a mighty yank. A dark-haired body clad only in under-wear, fell to the snow. Mose returned to the box and pulled out the second body. Their limbs were floppy. "Glad we got these guys out of there," Mose said. "It would be awful if they went all rigor on us and we couldn't get them out without chopping them."

"Hold that thought," Ben said. "I'm going to walk down to the water and see what I can see." Even with the headlamp, he could barely make out more than his own feet in the blowing snow. The water was low, as he knew it would be, and he stum-bled down several step-terraces before he got to the flat, snow-covered sheet of ice stretching away south across the reservoir. Ben moved closer, onto the ice, which broke under his weight and let him down through a space of air onto more ice an inch or two below.

He leaned forward, squinting into the weak beam of light from the headlamp. Ten feet out from the edge, a blackness gaped: unfrozen water. He hurried back to Mose through the deepening snow.

"We can get them into the water, Mose," he said. "There's open water a few feet out. Come on."

Together they dragged first one body, then the other out onto the ice, and crunching through it with their boots into a few inches of freezing slush, pushed the corpses, one at a time, ahead on the ice until the white feet dangled into the water. Then Mose, hands on the bare shoulders, gave each a great heave, and with one splash after the other, sent them skidding across the ice into the black hole.

Ben and Mose made haste back to the snowcat, and Ben was very glad to climb into the warmth and shut out the storm.

"That second one," Mose was saying. "The one that was Hinch. He had a tat." Mose pointed to his left bicep. "Right here. '168th

Cav.,' it said. Blue and red one. And it had a flag, and some stars around it. And a tank underneath."

"Hmm," Ben said. "Never know when that info might come in handy."

Mose said, "Uh. Uh, won't they float? I don't know anything about dead bodies, but aren't they going to float?"

Ben said, "Well, if they're anything like deer or porcupines, yeah, they might float. For a little while, a few minutes, but not long. They'll sink. They'll float again after a couple of weeks. Might take a lot longer for them to come back up since the water is so cold now. They won't rot as fast now as they would in the summer. The rot is what brings them back up; it makes gas. And after they come back up for a while, they'll sink for good. With luck, they'll be sunk while the search is on. It's going to freeze and thaw a bunch of times before next summer, so I'm hoping that by the time anybody comes along here next spring, they'll be sunk for good."

"OK," Mose said agreeably. "Your Gramps teach you that stuff?"

"Yeah," Ben said. "And we saw things here and there." For a long moment Ben looked at Mose over the body of the unconscious Carlos, and he realized that he liked what he saw. "Mose," he said deciding something he had been thinking about while driving down to the reservoir, "I don't want to take these uniforms and this ID back to the Place."

"But—" Mose protested, incredulous, "—but it would be crazy to leave that stuff out here in the snow. Wouldn't it? We don't want anybody else finding the stuff, for sure. And you said yourself that the things could be useful. And there's the rifle. Are you talking about tossing the rifle into the reservoir?"

"Oh, let's take the rifle with us," Ben said. "And the knife that the one guy had on him. But there's a place close by where we can stash the uniforms and the ID and they will be safe."

Mose drew himself up in the seat and stared at the driving snow caught in the headlight beams. "Are you nuckin' futs?" he said. "What do you mean?"

Ben sighed and said, "I mean that Gramps and I made a cache here, a drop for a few supplies. And I'm going to show it to you. And you have to swear not to tell anyone else about it, ever."

Mose's eyes bulged and his eyebrows lifted. "You're the man," he said eventually. "And have I said 'holy shit' already? Sure. OK. I swear not to tell anybody else about this place, if it exists. That work for you?"

"Good." Ben took a close look at Carlos and pinched a fold of skin on his neck. He wouldn't put it past Carlos to wake up in the dark and take off with the cat. But Carlos didn't react at all. "He's still out for the count," Ben said. "Let's do it. It won't take long." Ben reached behind the seats and gathered the rolled bundle of clothing, boots, and ID they had taken from the soldiers. He jumped down from the cab, followed closely by Mose.

With his headlamp to guide him, Ben walked straight east and made his way cautiously up the slope of snowy, blocky lava talus to the currant bush, now just a fan of bare sticks, and to the narrow entrance of the cave just beyond.

He heard Mose whistle behind him as they entered the blackness. In the far recess, the two garbage cans gleamed, coldly silver.

Mose swore, then said, "Well, I'll be a black-assed bastard."

"We call this 'Magic Rim Cache,'" Ben told Mose. He lifted the lid of one of the cans and with some force, pushed the bundle inside. "There. Ready when needed."

"What else is in these cans?" Mose demanded, close.

"Two sleeping bags, matches, some food, coffee, a pot, things like that," Ben said. He saw no need to mention the hidden gun or the other caches. "This was in case Gramps and I needed a hideout when we were away from the Place. And now you have a hiding place, too."

Mose darted his flashlight around the little chamber. "It goes farther in," he said. "But I couldn't fit through; it's too narrow."

"I can't, either," Ben said. "I've tried to squeeze through. But I don't think it would be too hard to chisel off an edge of one of those rocks and widen that gap. I'd like to see how far back it goes sometime."

"Yeah. Come on; let's get back to the cat." Mose turned and started for the entrance. "It's freezing," he said over his shoulder.

When Ben stepped from the cave into the shrieking wind, his foot slipped on a bare rock and he nearly fell. "The wind is keeping some of these rocks clear of snow. It's drifting already," he shouted to Mose, and he grinned in the dark. "Let's go home. In this storm, the cat tracks will blow away behind us just like magic."

"Like magic," Mose said, and the wind blew his words back to Ben. "Like Magic Reservoir." Ben saw Mose turn his head toward the blackness that was the reservoir and heard him mutter, "Sink, baby, sink."

CHAPTER 12

BACK

Everyone else had gone to bed an hour before, but Artie knew she wouldn't be able to sleep.

Six feet away on the floor, Lainey was still fast asleep. Kaylee had folded the top layer of Lainey's sleeping bag over her before climbing the ladder to the loft with Turk and Andy. Tim and Smoke had taken themselves into the small bedroom, and Artie could hear the soft breathing of Sylvie and Shandy through the open door of the larger bedroom.

Artie had rolled herself up in the red plaid couch throw and was lying on the rag rug surrounded by close-pressed Shelties, trying to read by firelight. *The Vicomte de Bragelonne*--with its Musketeers and nobles, kings and dukes and queen, glittering jewels, and lavish parties--was a far cry from a ragtag bunch of teenagers and dogs crowded together in an isolated western cabin. Artie was glad she had pulled the Dumas trilogy from that barrel in the barn before the snow came. It was proving to be excellent escape material.

Outside, the wind screamed and howled, and Artie was reminded of the night she and Ben had brought back the Others in the same kind of snowstorm. She wondered if she could be hearing the howls of wolves through the shrieks of the storm, but, after thinking about it, decided that wolves with any brains would be curled up in a den tonight, sleeping with their tails over their faces and leaving the howling to the wind.

Every half hour or so, she had been getting up to stare out the south window in the living room, watching for the lights of the snowcat. "I'll never be able to hear its engine above the wind," she told herself.

Behind the events in the *Vicomte*, behind the piney scent and the crackling of the fire, even behind the sounds of the intermittent blasts of wind, Artie thought about what Kaylee had said. "Soldiers," she thought. "Shooting Carlos. Why would they shoot an unarmed boy? What were the circumstances? And—Ben and Mose are hiding from them now. I hope the soldiers are lost in this storm. Surely they can't find Ben. Surely they can't. But Ben has a gun." Her mind wouldn't let it go. *Ben has to be safe, he has to be safe.* "I'm the one who told Ben to take the gun, because I felt weird, like something would happen. But Ben already had it in his pack, Artie, you idiot," she reminded herself. "Something bad, something bad." Her mind tugged at the thought like a dog with a toy, and she felt strange. The *something bad* feeling had wisped into nothingness during the late afternoon, and despite her worry, what she felt now was--nothing.

Nearby, Lainey turned over in her sleep. "Don't know if I want to go," she muttered. Her lips parted and Artie heard the whisper of a long sigh. "Wear that one, Lenny. The green," Lainey said distinctly. "It will be brilliant." Lainey turned again, and all Artie could see was the curve of her hip under the sleeping bag, and a spill of firelit hair.

"That's what life has been for the Others," Artie thought. "Where to go. What to wear. How to triumph over lesser beings. I wonder what I might say in my sleep." She shook her head, thinking suddenly of Rosa. If she were still alive, where would Rosa be in this storm?

⊷⊷ ⊶⊶

Ben guided the snowcat uphill to the Fairfield highway and turned west, toward the Horner Ranch Road turnoff. Under the snow, the road was smooth.

Mose kept glancing at Ben and then looking away quickly, nervously. "It's fine, Mose. I'll get us there," Ben said. "Just keep on keeping Carlos from rolling around. I'm thinking that this cat is going to fit inside the new bunker. Gramps had us build it tall so it would take Dr. Lucy's tall fifth-wheel trailer. But if the cat doesn't fit, after we drop Carlos at the Place, we could drive it back down to that shed where we found you guys. It will fit in there."

"But that shed is miles from the Place," Mose protested. "If we leave it, we'll have to walk back. I don't want to walk miles and miles to the Place in a snowstorm, in the dark."

"It's not as far as you think, Mose," Ben said. He sighed. He might as well come clean; Mose would have it figured out by the time they got to the Place, anyway. "That night I got you all, I took a really long way home to make you guys think it was farther than it was."

Mose stared straight ahead into the snowflakes streaming through the twin beams from the headlamps. "Oh," he said. After a long silence, he added, "If we switched places, I'm not sure I would have taken you in. Us. All of us. You know."

Ben decided that he'd tell it exactly like it was. "If Turk had been his normal self, I don't know if I would have," he admitted. "But I could tell that he was really out of it. So—"

450

Mose interrupted. "How did you know Turk was out of it? You came driving up and got out and yelled. It was a night like this. Black as black and snowing just like this. You could hardly see a hand in front of your face. You didn't know who we were or how many of us were in that shed. You just saw the fire and stopped to check. Right?"

"Sort of," Ben said slowly. A snowshoe hare, cream-colored against the white of the new snow, shot across the road, and Ben slowed the snowcat just in time to miss the second rabbit. "There are almost always two," he could hear Gramps whispering in his mind. "Benny, if it's jackrabbits or snowshoes, there are almost always two of them, so slow down when you see one. And with the jacks, they'll double back across the road in a heartbeat and go right under your wheels, so don't speed up until you are well past them. But the snowshoes won't do that. Snowshoes won't double back like jacks. They'll just keep on going."

Ben said, "That *was* a night like this, Mose, just like this. Why would we be out driving around?"

"What are you saying?"

Ben replied steadily, "Just that I scouted you first. Artie was up on a hill above the Place when it was getting dark and saw a light down there. I scouted you. I came down to the shed in the dark, to the back, and sat in the storm, and watched through a crack in the boards. I saw who you were and after a while I figured that there was something majorly wrong with Turk. Then I went back and got the truck."

"But—"Mose sputtered. "But that means it couldn't have been all that far. You walked it? You walked it?"

"That shed is less than three miles from the Place," Ben said.

After an interval, Mose said, "If you hadn't showed up, we would have walked on by. We were going east toward Timmerman Hill, following the Fairfield highway, and we took a chance leaving the highway and going up one of the side roads because we were looking for a farmhouse, a good place to spend the night. But all we found was the shed, and it got dark on us. We would have gone back to the highway in the morning. If you hadn't come, we never would have seen the Place."

"Probably not," Ben agreed.

"But why did you take us in? I mean, why? None of us has ever been your friend."

Ben took one hand from the wheel and rubbed at the back of his neck. "Right thing," he said. "Gramps said to take people in if they weren't dangerous. And Shandy—I heard Andy saying that something was wrong with her."

"Huh." Mose sneezed into his hand. "I should have said this before, but I'm sorry about your Gramps, man."

"Thanks," was all Ben could manage. He kept his eyes on the road, glad that the sagebrush on both sides showed him where to aim the cat. The road shoulders were steep here, and the last thing he needed was to roll the cat.

"I mean, he wasn't Crazy Frank Elliott at all," Mose went on. "If anything, he was Genius Frank Elliott and we were all the crazy ones."

"You must be worried about your mom," Ben said, trying to turn the conversation away from Gramps; it was too painful out here in this wild, black, night, to think of Gramps, who of all people deserved the sanctuary of the Place, but who had been left behind in cold, burned-out Hailey.

Mose barked a short laugh. "My mom?" he exclaimed. "My mom doesn't give a rat's for me," he said. "Not a dirty rat's ass. She's gone."

"Gone?" Ben glanced at Mose. "What do you mean, 'gone'? Your mom is dead?"

"No. She took off," Mose said, eyes forward. "I'm on my own."

"Crap," Ben said, thinking, "The things you don't know about people." Aloud, he said, "Since when?"

"August," Mose replied promptly. "Some guy from Colorado showed up in a big, new Dodge Ram crew cab, bright red. Flashed some cash around. Bought her stuff. Took her to dinner, things like that. She cleans up really pretty, still. Steve Makes is his name, would you believe? The guy's whole name is 'Steve Makes-Dust.'" Mose grinned silently. "He's an Arapaho and filled Mom with a bunch of shit about how much cooler it would be for her at his place in Colorado. She did leave me a note. Wrote down his address so I could send along her monthly checks from the tribe. As if."

"I'm sorry," Ben said. "How have you been managing?" he asked, adding hastily, "not that it's any of my business, especially now, but with football you really didn't have time for a job."

"Oh, I've been cashing her checks from the tribe, and mine, too, that she's supposed to sign," Mose said. "The guys at the bank are used to me bringing in both checks and depositing them every month. I've been signing her name for so long they'd probably think Mom's real signature was a forgery. It hasn't been easy since she left, but I was making it. Barely. I've been working at the restaurant—you know, the Pine, where she was working before she left. At night I clean the kitchen, do the floors and other crap." Mose wagged his big head from side to side. "I didn't tell anybody she was gone," he said. "I'm the one who takes the rent check for our house to old man Lester every month, have been for years, and he thinks she's still around. I'm 17 and I've only got 9 months to go before I turn 18. The last thing I need is to have Child Services dragging me off somewhere."

"I hear you," Ben said. "Somebody sicced them on Gramps a few years ago because he was teaching me to shoot and that freaked them. But I was 12 and had my license. It was legal. They had to back off. But what a pain." Ben stared into the whirling whiteout and thought of Mose, so calm at school, so self-contained, and how it must have been for him to come home night after night, dog tired after work, to an empty house. "There's some strength in there," he thought, with another glance at Mose. All he could see was a dark silhouette hunched in the seat.

"Yeah." Mose paused for a moment and then added, "If your gramps hadn't taught you to shoot, Carlos would be dead, and probably Lainey, and you and me, too."

"Maybe," Ben conceded with a sigh. He slowed the big cat at the bottom of a long, swooping hill. Visibility was as bad as he had ever seen it. But the Place was his Place, and he *knew*. Like a compass needle, Ben felt pulled toward it in the darkness. He felt that he would be able find the Place blindfolded, or even with his eyes gouged from his skull. He smiled. There, just where he had expected to see it, was the bent sagebrush, and there were the three sheep-sized boulders together, humped under snow, only a few feet off the highway. And there, partly hidden by a small drift, was a green mile marker, the one that leaned a little past true. He couldn't read its number, but that was all right. Horner Ranch Road was close now. They were almost to the turnoff.

Ben squinted, his face close to the windshield glass. Yes! There it was. He turned north and began to whistle.

"Man, you are seriously—" Mose broke off.

"Crazy?" Ben said, feeling a little twist at his heart. "Like Gramps? Crazy *Ben* Elliott?"

"I'm sorry," Mose said. "I mean, I am, really, sorry. I haven't been a good friend to you," he went on slowly, as if the words pained him. "I haven't been a friend to you at all, and I should have been." From the corner of his eye, Ben saw Mose clasp his hands together between his knees. "This last year, I should have been. After what happened with Mom, what you did. And you never told."

"I told Gramps, is all. He saw the blood on me when I got home," Ben said, "but I asked him not to tell." He still felt unsettled about that strange episode, didn't want to think about it.

"The deal is, is that football is about all I've got," Mose said. "Sure, the popular kids let me hang with them. They joke around with me at school. I'm the big man when I fix it so one of those guys can score, and when we win. And it's fine for me to run around with them—get something to eat, go to the mall in Twin, ride around town: like that. But nobody comes home with me. I can go home with some of them, but that's it, the end. None of them would come to my house if their lives depended on it. Like to go there would give them the plague or something. And if I didn't have football, nobody would give me the time of day. Big dumb Indian here—oh, sorry—Native American. Good for blocks and tackles. Good for changing a tire on a Land Rover."

Ben glanced at Mose again, kept driving. He felt the ground rising under the tracks of the cat. They had almost reached Gray Creek Gulch. Soon after, they'd be on the downslope to the meadow. He wondered if the old shed would show in the headlight beams when they got to the far end of the long meadow, and if Mose would notice.

Mose said, very deliberately, "You would."

"I would what, Mose?" Ben asked, eyes on the road, searching for the turnoff in the drifting snow.

"You would give me the time of day if I didn't do football," Mose said. He said nothing more for some time.

Ben found the fork in the road and turned northwest onto Gray Creek Road. "Yes, I suppose," he said finally. "Some of the things those guys care about, I don't care about at all."

"My mom, you know what she is," Mose said then.

"Mose, you don't have to—"

Mose cut him off. "It's OK. These past three months, I've come to terms with it. When she said she might take off with this Steve Makes, I told her, 'Great. You're done with being a Shoshoni like me. Now you're an Arapa-ho.'" Mose laughed, and to Ben it sounded hollow and bitter. "She smacked me a good one for that."

Ben knew they were on the long meadow now. The cat's head-lamps showed the downed gate, with a few loops of snarled wire still visible above the moving surface of the snow, but in the near-whiteout, the shed was not to be seen. "Home stretch," he said to Mose.

"If this cat is too tall to fit inside the new bunker," Mose said, "are you really going to come back to that shed?"

"As a last resort," Ben said. "But I've been thinking that may-be we could take some of the boards off the west side of the barn and run the cat in there and then nail the boards back on," Ben told him. This solution had presented itself as he drove. "The cat is too tall to go in through the barn doors, but it's shorter than where the rafters start. We'd have to move a bunch of stuff, first. But I do think it will fit in the bunker."

"Huh," Mose grunted.

The cat lurched through a drift and began climbing. "Last hill," Ben thought with satisfaction. "Almost home, and we haven't heard a helicopter or seen any lights. But anybody would have to be crazier than the Elliotts to be out in a night like this." The thought of the Place's warm kitchen and Bear sleeping on the rug in front of the fireplace warmed him.

"Got to get Carlos in there," he thought without relish. "Hope he wakes up and we don't have another zombie like Turk on our hands." He thought of Artie bustling around the kitchen, and smiled. Tim, too, sitting cross-legged in the liv-ing room tinkering with the solar charger and the cell phones. And little Sylvie reading at the kitchen table. And the Others. "But I'm thinking wrong," he said to himself. "It's the middle of the night. Everybody will be asleep when we get there." He thought about how the Place was when it was just Artie, Tim, and himself, and what a kick it had been to paint Abbie on the roofs with Artie and Tim scurrying around like ground squirrels below. And the day of the helicopter, Abbie had worked, too.

Then there were the Others. "But they won't be there for much longer," he told himself. "Maybe. Hopefully. We have a snow cat now, and if we get another night like this, I can take them to Timmerman Hill and leave them." He had another thought, and spoke it aloud before he had time to change his mind. "Mose," he said, "after the Others go home, do you want to stay at the Place?"

"What?" Mose bent for a moment to steady Carlos' head. "Do you mean stay on, stay with you?"

"Yes. You. Not the rest of them."

"Wow," he said. "Thanks." Then after such a long time that Ben wondered if he was going to say anything more, Mose said, "That would be sweeter than sweet, especially if Hailey is all burnt out the way Artie said. And if more of those white soldiers are there. But." He came to a full stop and took a deep breath. "But, where Shandy goes, I'm going, and she says she has to go home and find her family."

"It's like that, is it?" Ben said.

"Yeah."

"Does Shandy feel that way about you?" Ben couldn't help but ask.

"Don't know," Mose said. "Doesn't matter, you know?"

"Yes," Ben said, with a new respect for Mose. "I get it." Then he added, "Shandy can stay, too, if it comes to that. Or—if you take care not to be followed, if Hailey is a ruin, you both can come back."

457

"Thanks, man," Mose said soberly. "Really, thanks. I can't imagine Hailey being much different, though. Guess I'll find out sometime." After a moment, he said, "Guess I need lessons in how to choose my friends. But Shandy? Shandy is for real."

CHAPTER 13
MIST

The Place was dark; Ben couldn't see even the smallest glow of light from the house through the storm as he drove up to the gate. Mose climbed down from the cat's high cab and pulled the gate open, dragging the wires through a drift, and then shut it behind after Ben drove through. With care and very slowly, Ben drove the cat downhill between the barn and the henhouse, and west to the double doors of the new bunker. He flicked on his headlamp and slid out into the storm.

Mose came right after him and made a little jump beside Ben in the snow. "Dude, you got it right," Mose said, and in his deep voice, Ben heard a note of glee. "Look! This sucker is going to fit right through those doors!" Ben felt a smack between his shoulder blades that nearly sent him face-first into one of those very doors as Mose clapped him on the back.

"Let's do it." Ben fumbled the key from his pocket, unlocked the padlock, and pulled out the chain.

They tugged the doors open, sweeping back ridges of snow, and holding his breath, Ben drove the cat into the dark bunker. Mose pulled one of the doors shut after, and climbed up into the cab again. "I've got Carlos," he said, sliding Carlos from the cab and slinging the limp body over one shoulder. "I can carry him."

"OK," Ben answered, shining his headlamp around the bunker. The cat had fit through the door by scant inches, but once inside, the cat's roof was at least twenty inches below the lowest cross-brace of the rafters. "God bless Dr. Lucy's tall trailer," he said to himself. "Who knew?" He lifted the lid of the cargo box and after a moment, shut it again. "Mose, I'm going to leave the rifle in the cat for now," he said. "Go on. I'll shut the door."

Mose staggered through a knee-high drift with Carlos draped over his shoulder like a rolled rug. Ben grabbed his pack, lugged the remaining bunker door shut, set the padlock and chain, and hurried to follow so he could light the way.

As Ben caught up with him in the dark and storm, Mose turned his head and said over his shoulder, "Holy shit, man. Holy-oly-ol-eee shee-it. It has been some day."

From the window, Artie saw the lights coming up the gulch at last, close, boring through the windblown snow, twin tunnels, dim at first but brightening. Artie hugged her own ribcage tight and thought, *"It's them it's them it's them,"* and spared a glance for the orderly assembly of things on the floor near the fireplace that she had prepared for Carlos—his sleeping bag and pillow brought down from the loft, a pile of hand towels, a few diapers, and the first aid kit from the basement. On the stove simmered a bucket of hot water beside a pot of coffee she had made only half an hour ago, hoping.

She saw the lights stop moving at the gate. Silhouetted by the headlamps, a black hulking figure crossed in front of the beams to open it, hunched against the blowing snow. "Mose," she thought, "that's Mose. So Ben must be driving."

Presently she lost sight of the lights as they disappeared behind the chicken house. By the time the lights reappeared, dimly, near the new bunker, she could feel the vibration of the engine in her bones, though she couldn't hear it over the howling of the wind. Bear felt it, too. He scrambled to his feet and took himself to the kitchen door, and Artie followed. The lights went out again.

Then, after a minute or two, she saw a faint glow coming closer and closer. "The headlamp," she thought. Artie pinched her wrist. She couldn't just throw herself at Ben when he came in. "Calm," she thought. "Be calm, Artie, just like you usually are. Now you *know* he's safe. Mose would have told Kaylee if anything had happened to Ben. Surely he would have."

In no time, Mose had flung open the kitchen door. "Carlos," he said, nodding at his burden.

"Living room," Artie responded, moving out of his path. "I brought his sleeping bag down. Just put him there next to Lainey. She's been sick and is sleeping it off."

"Good deal," Mose said as he brushed past her. He laid Carlos, limp as a rag, on the sleeping bag and stepped back. Lainey didn't even stir.

But Artie had eyes only for Ben. "You're all right?" she couldn't help saying as he came in, closing the door against the storm and shaking snow from his coat before hanging it on the hook. Bear jumped around him in sheer delight.

"Yeah," he said. He peeled off his cap and headlamp, and hung them up as well. Ben looked at the stove and took a lungful of air. "God, Artie, do I smell coffee? Did you make coffee?"

She flew to pour him a cup. "You bet," she said. Their fingers touched for a moment as she handed him the steaming mug.

Artie blinked. Even in the dimness of the kitchen, she saw Ben looking straight into her eyes. She held her breath.

"*Bad thing coming*," he said very softly, the last thing she expected to hear. "'*Take the gun,*' you said. Artie." His voice was a breath warm on her cheek. "You knew."

"Yes," she whispered. "Sometimes I know. I don't know how I know, but I know."

He held her eyes another moment. "I was going to take the gun anyway, but I almost didn't," he said. "Thanks."

Artie nodded. She couldn't speak.

Then Ben dropped his eyes and sipped from the mug.

Mose stomped into the kitchen, shedding clumps of snow with every step. With a sigh, he dropped into a chair and began to pull off his boots. Artie poured him some coffee and went to have a look at Carlos. She walked back into the kitchen and said, "Why is Carlos out of it? Is it a really bad wound? Has he lost a lot of blood?"

"His wound isn't too bad. It punched in and out, right under the collarbone—didn't even break a bone. He didn't bleed much. But the shot knocked him clean over and he hit the back of his head on a rock," Ben said. "I'm going to be freaked if he doesn't wake up pretty soon."

Mose grunted. "At least we got him back. Stupid SOB that he is. But," here Mose's teeth showed in a grin, "we got a snowcat out of the deal, too. A really nice one."

"That is a good thing. Wow, this whole day has been really weird," Artie said, unconsciously echoing Mose's thought of a few minutes before. And she told them about Lainey and her addiction withdrawal.

Ben took another swallow of coffee and then his lips thinned into a hard line. Artie wondered where his thoughts had taken him. "This coffee really helps, Artie," he said when he saw her expression. "As soon as I get this down, could you help me with

Carlos? We got him kind of plugged so he isn't bleeding, but I'm going to have to sew him up, and it would be better—so much better—if I could do that while he is still out of it."

"Sure," Artie said. "I'll get another lamp."

"That's OK," Ben said. "My headlamp will do fine." He looked over at the stove. Artie saw him register the bucket. "Ha," he said, almost a laugh. "And you have water ready." Ben smiled then, a real smile, and Artie felt her heart turn over. He drained the cup and she followed him into the living room, ready to help him do what had to be done.

⊨⊣ ⊢⊨

Ben washed his hands in the last of the hot water at the bottom of the bucket and dried them on a kitchen towel. Artie had just taken the dogs out to potty, wearing his headlamp and carrying another bucket to pack with snow to melt for breakfast coffee water. The sky outside was still black and starless, and it was still snowing.

Ben was heartily glad that he'd finished with Carlos, at least for the time being. "I am really clumsy, compared to Gramps," he thought. "Carlos's two holes may look funky with my stitches, but at least they are clean and closed up." And again, he wished for Gramps, Gramps' experience, expertise, and calm wisdom. Ben shook his head and hung the kitchen towel on the wall rack near the stove. Then he poured himself a cup of sludge from the bottom of the coffeepot, added a large portion of evaporated milk, and fell into a chair at the table across from Mose, who had also given himself more coffee from the dregs of Artie's midnight pot.

"I went and looked out about ten minutes ago, while you were finishing up," Mose said, stretching his legs and wiggling his toes in his stocking feet. "It's hard to tell because of the drifting, but

I think it's snowed about eight inches so far tonight, and it's still snowing and blowing pretty hard out there. Any tracks we made with the snowcat are long gone." He smiled, teeth white in his coppery face.

"Yeah," Ben said, downing a slug of gritty coffee. "Home free. Now if Carlos will just wake up . . ." Ben frowned. Carlos could be in a permanent coma from that impact to the back of his head, for all he knew. But the only thing to do about Carlos was to monitor his wounds, and wait. That's what Gramps would say.

"When he does wake up," Mose said, sounding unworried, "he'll have a hard time living that action down. Dumber than dumb, going off like that, without a clue, straight to the enemy, and getting himself shot."

Ben nodded. There was no arguing with that. *The enemy.* Ben stiffened in his chair. *The enemy had been too close to the Place for comfort.*

Mose went on. He rubbed one finger under his chin. "You know, we could have framed Carlos big-time," he said. "Could have stuck your gun in his hand and just left him there with the snowcat for that Seventeen Hundred and his guys to find. But," here Mose paused thoughtfully, "but it didn't occur to me at the time. What *did* occur to me then was getting ourselves warm, fast, and getting the crap out of there. And if we had left Carlos there, the next soldiers who came along the state highway would wonder where Carlos came from, and they would be out in these hills looking for the place where Carlos had been holing up. So . . ."

"Got that right," Ben said. That *had* occurred to Ben at the time, all of it, but he didn't want to tell that to Mose. It was good for Mose to let go of his long-standing role as grunt man of the jock pack and start thinking for himself. Ben felt a little chill slide down his spine. One thing he had to consider was what Carlos would remember, that he might remember Ben shooting that first soldier. Mose—Ben thought he could trust Mose. Carlos? Not a chance, and it was impossible to tell what the laws and courts might be like now, if there were any. But when Ben had fired, Carlos hadn't even been aware of Ben and Mose above him on the hill. "I don't think he'll remember, but there's nothing I can do about that," he thought, and lifted the now-tepid coffee to his lips. He gulped down the rest of it, grounds and all.

Even with caffeine from three and a half cups of coffee coursing through his veins, Ben felt exhausted, wrung out. The distance from the kitchen to the small bedroom seemed vast and foggy, darkening. He did feel warm now, however; Artie had obviously kept the stove stoked to keep the water and the coffee hot, and the heat felt as if it were melting his bones.

As his eyes closed, Ben heard the back door open and felt the cold draft, heard footsteps and paws dancing and the shutting of the door. Artie was coming in with the dogs. A dog pressed its head to his knee.

Ben was glad he had taken off his boots; that would be an effort beyond him right now. "Got to get to the bedroom," he thought, attempting to sit up straight. "Artie," he said. "Going to bed. Come get me if anything bad happens with Carlos."

"OK." Artie's voice sounded far away as Ben placed both hands flat on the tabletop and pushed himself to his feet. "Going to stay on the couch to watch him," she was saying. "I'll take the dogs out in the morning." That made some kind of sense, probably. Ben had to think about placing each foot as he made his way to the bedroom. He swung open the door and blackness greeted him. That was good. Tim was snoring. That was good, too.

Artie stamped the snow off her boots and stood the broom in a corner of the kitchen as she came inside with the dogs after their first potty run of the day. She hadn't really needed the broom to disguise their tracks. It was still dark and still snowing and blowing.

She rubbed her hands together and decided to build up what was left of the fire in the stove. She used a spoon to lift the latch on the firebox door and looked in. Yes, the box was half-full of cherry-red coals. She took some sticks from the wood box and shoved them in on top of the coals. "Not my team's turn to make breakfast this morning," she thought, "It's Shandy's team's turn. But we are kind of mixed up right now, and I need coffee." She heard little snapping crackles as the new wood caught and began to burn. The kitchen was still delightfully warm, and Artie felt almost sinfully comfortable as she eased herself into one of the kitchen chairs.

"Aaaaa." A low moan came from the living room. Artie hurried to Carlos, noticing that Lainey's sleeping bag, along with Lainey, was gone. While Artie was out with the dogs, Lainey must have moved herself back into the loft.

Artie got to Carlos just in time to see him open his eyes in the dim light of the fire dying in the fireplace. "Aaaah!" This time the moan was almost a scream. Artie bent over him.

"Carlos," Artie said. "It's all right. You're back at the Place."

"Jesus H. Christ," he hissed, one hand fumbling at the bandage she and Ben had tied around his shoulder. "Hurts. Hurts! This is batshit crazy. What is going on? My head, my head." His eyes widened. "My shoulder. It's on fire!"

Artie knelt on the floor and rocked back onto her heels. "Don't you remember?"

"What did you guys do to me? What did you do to me while I was asleep? Ahhhh, my head." Carlos made a quick movement as if to sit up, flinched, and lowered his head back onto the pillow.

Artie wondered what to tell Carlos as he demanded, "What did you do to me?"

Sylvie's small face appeared in the doorway of the large bedroom. She lifted an eyebrow at Carlos and made her way to the back door.

Artie bent over Carlos again. "What do you remember?"

"What do you mean, Artie?" He peered at her closely, squinting. "Artie, something is wrong with you. Really wrong. Your eyes. You have too many eyes."

Artie leaned away from Carlos. Had the bump on his head made him crazy? Then she realized what must be happening and held up a finger. "How many, Carlos? How many fingers?"

"I don't know," he said irritably. "Two? Two fingers. Who gives a—"

"Concussion," she told him. "You'd better lie still. Look, Carlos. You took off out of here yesterday morning. You ran into some soldiers and got shot, remember?"

Here he struggled to sit up, abandoned the effort, and turned to lie on his uninjured side. "Right," he said out of the corner of his mouth. His dark eyes narrowed again. "Sure I did."

"You got shot in the shoulder, high up, just under the collarbone. And you fell backwards and your head hit a rock, Ben says. Ben and Mose got you out of there and brought you back."

Carlos worked his mouth as if he were gathering spittle, and Artie drew away. "You ask Mose when he wakes up," she told him, getting to her feet. "I'm going to bring you some aspirin. Not that you deserve any."

"Holyshit," Artie thought, all one word, a word that rarely emerged inside her mind. She poured a cup of lukewarm water from the pot heating on the stove and shook three aspirin from the bottle in the pantry. "This is quite weird," she thought as she snapped the bottle lid shut. Then she realized that she was getting the giggles, and clapped a hand over her mouth, leaning her forehead for a moment against the cool edge of a pantry shelf. "Nobody has ever told me I had too many eyes before," she thought, squeezing her eyes shut. "That's the funniest thing I've heard for a long time. Or maybe I am just too tired."

She held the cup for Carlos as he downed the aspirin, and managed not to laugh in his face. "Not enough sleep, Artie," she told herself. "You are getting punchy."

At that moment Sylvie came back into the kitchen and hung her parka on the wall. She took her notebook and wrote in it, then brought it to Artie. "What is the deal with Carlos?" Artie read by holding the page close to the fire. She handed the notebook back to Sylvie.

"Carlos got sewed up by Ben last night," Artie replied. "He woke up just a few minutes ago. Carlos," she said, "when you have to go to the outhouse, yell for the guys and they can take you. And when Ben gets up, maybe he can find you a stronger painkiller. I'm going to do the coffee and breakfast, and then get some sleep."

Carlos grunted and turned away, pulling the edge of the sleeping bag over his face.

"You're welcome," Artie told him. She left him there and joined Sylvie in the kitchen. "Lainey and Carlos are out of commission, and everyone else is asleep, Sylvie," she said. "I think we've only got about half an hour of darkness left this morning, so if we're going to have breakfast today, we can either wake Shandy up now or make breakfast ourselves."

Sylvie pointed to herself and then to Artie, and nodded vigorously.

"OK," Artie said. She could feel herself smiling and thought, "I am so glad Sylvie found her way to us."

"Let's do it," she said to Sylvie. "What shall we make?"

Sylvie lifted her notebook from the kitchen table and scribbled into it. "Biscuits and Spam," Artie read.

Artie laughed softly. "Biscuits and Spam, and apricot jam," she said. "And after I have some, I am going straight into my sleeping bag."

Sylvie headed for the pantry.

——◁┼ ┼▷——

Ben and Mose sat on a big granite rock on the uphill side of the barn, sipping hot cocoa from plastic mugs. Overhead, a crystalline blue sky arched into deepest blue, and down the canyon, Ben could see a kestrel hunting, flying low over Spear Creek Road, which was drifted shoulder-deep in places, and swept almost bare in other stretches. Not a suggestion of snowcat tracks remained.

Mose was nodding to himself as he cupped the warm mug in both huge hands. "Well, I'm satisfied that Carlos doesn't remember anything about the soldiers or the shooting, or even the snowcat," he said. "Are you?"

"Yeah," Ben returned. "That doesn't mean he won't remember it in the future, though."

"Nope. But there are two of us and one of him when it comes to telling what happened." Mose smiled. The kestrel knifed out of sight down the meadow. "Ben, everyone is going stir crazy here," he said after taking a swallow of cocoa. "They know we have the snowcat. If we don't take them as soon as Carlos is healed up, everybody is going to start walking to Hailey."

Ben sighed. Midafternoon, and already the shadows were long and blue. "I know," he said. "Everybody but me, Artie, and Tim, you mean. And Sylvie."

"Right." Mose stood for a moment and then sat on the boulder again, in a different place.

"We can cram them all into the snowcat," Ben said, fully aware of the fact that he had said 'we,' not 'I.' "We'll go as soon

469

as we get another storm. I am not going to leave a snowcat track from the state highway to The Place." He looked hard at Mose's expression, which was bland and unreadable, and added, "The new bunker is locked with the chain. The key to that padlock and the keys to the snowcat are in the gun safe."

Mose nodded calmly. "I don't think Andy and Carlos have a clue how to hot wire something even if they could get in. But I hope we have another snowstorm before too long, or things might get ugly."

"You won't stay?" Ben knew the answer, but had to ask again. Somehow, Mose wasn't quite one of the Others any more. He was—was a friend, Ben thought suddenly, startling himself. Yes, Mose was now a friend. Scavenger hadn't had many of those.

Mose shook his head. A cold wind was rising and whipped strands of glossy black hair across his cheeks and forehead. Mose resettled his Gramps cap, tucking up his hair, and smiled. "Shandy's bent on going home, so I'm going. We talked about this before, Ben."

"Sorry." Ben resettled his own cap. He smiled as well. "I'm going to keep asking. But the very next storm that drifts, I'll fire up the snowcat and do it, so you can tell that to everyone. In the dark. I'm not going to go all the way to Hailey. I figured the drop-off point would be Timmerman Hill, the rest stop there at the bottom. That's a good-sized building. It's heated, has plumbing, and there's a cell tower on the hill right above it."

"Good. Hadn't thought about that building having heat, but it does. Did. Who knows now? And it's on the main road to Twin," Mose added. "Somebody will come by there."

"Yeah," Ben agreed. "I'll get together a box of food to go with."

"We're going to go back to civilization," Mose said after gulping the last of his cocoa. "Won't need it."

Ben stared downcanyon, then lifted an eyebrow. "You think?" he said.

Mose didn't answer.

$$\Longleftarrow\!\!+\,+\!\!\Longrightarrow$$

With her hands wrist-deep in dough, Artie blew a wisp of hair out of her eyes.

Lunch was done; Ben and most of the boys were out chopping wood. The Other girls were lying on the braided rug in the living room near the warm coals in the fireplace, coloring. Kaylee had discovered a stack of coloring books in the loft's tall dresser, and right after breakfast, Ben had gone out to the old bunker and brought back a fat 64 box of crayons for them. Turk sprawled on the floor near the bookcase, snoring. Carlos lay above them on the couch; Artie could hear his occasional remark and the resulting giggles. "I got coloring books for kids that might come here in the future," Ben had told Artie in a quiet aside when he passed through the kitchen earlier on his way to the living room with the crayons. "But I got some of those adult coloring books, too. Personally, I can't imagine coloring in someone else's artwork." Artie had smiled and whispered, "Whatever keeps them occupied. And adult coloring books seem to be a thing."

Ben had also brought four metal loaf pans for Artie, and in a large bowl, she had started the water-yeast-sugar-bit-of-flour mixture right after breakfast. Now she was kneading in heaps of flour, in hopes of making four loaves of bread as soon as the stove could be fired up when darkness came at the end of the day. Sylvie sat in her usual place at the table, watching. "Have you ever made bread, Sylvie?" Artie asked.

Sylvie shook her head, wrote something on her pad, and slid it across the table.

"Grandma did," Artie read.

"My grandma did, too," Artie said, "but not all that often. I've been kind of scared to try, but I guess the dogs can have it if it turns out to be a mess."

Sylvie nodded.

"But we need bread," Artie said rather grimly, pushing more flour into the sticky mix. "It will stretch the other supplies and make things seem more—more normal. And the cookbook said that if you're careful to keep it warm and fed, you can keep yeast going--for years, even--so you don't have to use up all your packets." She picked up the big spoon and added more flour to the dough, folding and folding it to incorporate the flour.

After a few minutes, Artie straightened to ease her back and said, "Look, Sylvie, it's turned elastic, just like the cookbook says!" Sylvie smiled. Artie said, "Now it has to rise. Then I punch it down again and make it into loaves in the pan. And when it rises enough to look nice, into the oven it will go. Sure hope I did the yeast right." She upended the big bowl and the mass of dough flopped out onto the table.

Sylvie gave her a thumbs-up, and Artie laughed. "Guess we'll see." She took a knob of Crisco from the tin on the table and rubbed the inside of the bowl with it, then folded the dough into a compact mass and dumped it in, turning it over so that the smooth top of the dough was filmed with the grease, as she had seen her grandmother do. Artie covered the bowl with a kitchen towel, grabbed the red wool throw from the back of a chair, and wrapped the bowl tightly, like a big plaid package. "Done, for now!"

Sylvie busied herself wiping flour off the table with the kitchen rag. The dogs had already taken care of the flour spilled on the floor.

Artie went to the large bedroom and retrieved her book, the middle one of the Dumas trilogy, *Louise de Valliere.* It would be good to escape for a little while and stop worrying about what the bread was going to do. Artie wanted to go outside for some alone time, but today's bitter wind made that seem like a poor idea. She opened the *Louise* to her bookmark and heard laughter from the next room.

"Yeah, we're gonna steal that pickup and get on out of here," Artie heard Carlos saying. "Better yet, the snowcat. Scavenger hasn't even let us see the snowcat," he went on. "If there is a snowcat at all. As soon as I'm back on my feet OK, I'm going to squeeze that little Mothy bastard and get the keys to that bunker. Got to get out of here," he repeated. "I wouldn't be surprised to find out that Scavenger is the one who shot me. He can get into the gun safe, after all."

Artie heard Shandy's soft voice. "Mose wouldn't lie about that, Carlos. Mose was there, and he says the white soldiers shot you. He says the snowcat is in the new bunker."

"Yeah, sure," Carlos returned.

Shandy raised her voice. "Mose wouldn't lie about that. He wouldn't!"

"Ice down, Shandy," came Lainey's voice. "Point is, we've got to get out of here."

"Don't I wish you would," thought Artie, trying and failing to concentrate on her book. She glanced into the living room, where a long rectangle of sunlight painted the floor. Suddenly she felt watched, and turned her head slightly to see Turk's blue gaze boring into her own. He looked aware, fiercely concentrating, angry, his head propped on both hands. Artie's harsh intake of breath startled Sylvie into looking up. "It's Turk, Sylvie," Artie whispered across the table. "He's watching me." Sylvie got up to look. But when Artie turned back to Turk, he lay immobile, his head resting on the wood planks of the living room floor, his eyes staring beyond her into nothing.

But even so, Artie felt a cold breath of dread as she studied Turk. He was snoring again, or appeared to be. She should be hoping that Turk would wake up and be fine. She should be hoping that he'd recover. However—she wasn't, and thought, "Might as well be honest with myself. It's not very kind, but truly--I don't want Turk back the way he was." Sylvie pushed her chair into the farthest corner of the kitchen, reminding Artie of the shy waif Sylvie had been those first days with the Others. Artie turned to Sylvie and was surprised by the fear in the pale blue eyes.

"Yes, he's creepy," Artie said, her voice just loud enough for Sylvie to hear. "And—so what if he looks harmless. He still creeps me out."

Sylvie hugged her own body with slender arms.

"Tell you what," Artie continued, with a sudden idea. "Wouldn't hurt if you had a knife, would it?" She waited.

After a long moment, Sylvie nodded.

"In the basement, to the left of the bottom of the stairs," Artie told her. "There's a coffee can full of silverware on a shelf, and I saw some knife handles sticking up. Like from steak knives, sharp ones."

Sylvie nodded again and padded quietly to the stairs, then turned and pointed at Artie.

"A knife for me?" Artie whispered. "I've already got one. I brought it from home." She promised herself that she would retrieve it from her pack at the next opportunity and stash it under her sleeping bag.

Ben and Timothy, laden with split pine and surrounded by frolicking dogs, made their way from the woodshed to the back door of the house. An inch of new snow had fallen in the early morning, and the dogs were jumping and rolling and barking.

"Cold," Tim said, trudging behind Ben in the path to the house. "I bet it's below zero right now."

Ben replied, "Bet it is. Bet it's about five below, but we can check when we get to the kitchen. I'm ready for some more coffee. Hope somebody filled the thermos this morning."

"I did that," Tim said, shifting his load a little. "Hope there's some left."

Ben squinted against the sun. The day was bright and brilliant, the clouds having vanished eastward in midmorning.

Clouds.

Ben stopped in his tracks. A column of pure white smoke rose, curling, from behind the barn. "Look, Tim," he said grimly. "Some idiot has built a fire in broad daylight. After I've told them and told them. Son of a bitch!" He dropped his armload of wood on the path and sprinted for the barn.

Tim set his wood down more carefully and followed.

The cold air knifed into Ben's lungs as he ran, his feet sliding in the new snow. He ran alongside the barn into the deeper snow, not caring that he was making a path, thinking, "God! Smoke in the middle of the day! On a clear day! I knew, I knew it was a mistake bringing the Others here. But Gramps said, Gramps said—" One foot slipped sideways on a root buried in the snow and Ben put a hand out to one of the cottonwood trees, steadied himself, and went on. The white smoke rose lazily in a puffy cloud just behind the barn.

"I bet it's Carlos," Ben told himself. "I can put the fire out with snow, and then--"

He came around the corner of the barn and saw it, the clean snowy meadow bisected by the faint linear depression in the snow that marked Spear Creek, the naked pale aspens beyond, the smooth shoulders of the hills bounding the gulch, the far shoulder of Cat Mountain, dark with pines. Ben stopped in his tracks. No one was in sight. No one.

Tim came around the corner of the barn and banged into Ben from behind. "What?" he was saying. "What?"

But Ben was trying to run through the deep snow in the meadow to the place where the white smoke was rising from the creek. He could hear Tim following.

Ben reached the sunken cleft in the snow that marked Spear Creek's path under its thick coating of ice and snow. Just on the far side was a willow, and just under the place where its shaving-brush branches met the snow, the white smoke rose and puffed into the icy air. Ben took a run at the creek and jumped it, sliding a little on ice at the far side.

"The little spring," he thought. "Under this willow is where the little spring comes out, the one where Gramps wanted to build the cooler out of screens." Ben tried to lift a foot and suddenly felt trapped. His boots were sinking into a slurry of mud, grass, and water. He jerked one leg. One foot popped from the mess with a sharp sucking sound.

Tim jumped the creek behind him, fell short, and crunched through the ice into an inch of water just behind Ben. He scrambled up the low bank.

Ben pulled off a glove and put a hand into the white smoke.

"What?" Tim was asking. "What is it?"

Ben jerked the other foot out of the morass, and stepped onto firm ground a few feet away. "Steam," he said to Tim as he moved to one side so Tim could see. "This isn't smoke—it's steam. We've got a hot spring!"

"What?" Tim repeated blankly.

Ben moved back to the source of the steam at the base of the little willow and dipped his hand into the little hollow there. "Ow!" he shouted. "It's hot, all right." Ben jammed his hand into the snow to cool it. On the stream side of the willow, snow was melting in a narrow path as the warm water made its way to the creek.

"I don't get it," Tim said. "How can there be a hot spring here today when there wasn't one yesterday? Doesn't make sense." Cautiously, he put his own hand into the steam just above the water-filled hollow. "It's plenty warm, all right." Steam curled on the surface of the water and parted around his arm.

Ben laughed out loud. "The interior of the earth," he said, as if to himself. "Cracks." He looked at Tim. "And *earthquakes*."

"Earthquakes," Tim mouthed silently. Then he said, "The earthquake! You mean it made this hot spring?"

"That's how the ones in Yellowstone were made," he said, "That's what Dr. Lucy told me once. The heat in the interior of the earth, earthquakes, cracks, and melting." Ben thought for a moment. "Don't know if this is a good thing or if we should be scared out of our minds. Hot water! But it also means the heat of lava close to the surface."

"Whoa." Tim tugged on his glove.

Ben laughed again. "I'll be damned. A hot spring."

Tim nodded.

Ben watched the steam glide over the surface of the little basin of hot water and skirl toward the east as a small gust of wind reached them from the meadow. "Tim," he said after a sudden thought. "When we get back to the house, I don't want to tell people about this until it gets dark. They'll come out here and trample this place like a herd of cattle when they hear about it. At least if they do it after dark, we can try to smooth the snow over before sunup."

Tim nodded. "Natural hot tub," he said. We should get one of those brown plastic tarps and some of those head-sized rocks from the other side of the barn to hold the tarp down, or they'll make the whole area into a mud bath."

"Good idea," Ben said, and meant it. He chuckled. "To think--I was all ready to read Carlos the riot act for building a fire in the middle of the day."

"He gets on my nerves," Ben heard Tim mutter. Tim raised his chin and looked Ben in the eye. "Always whining about something. I'll be glad when the Others are gone."

Ben stood up and brushed snow from the knees of his jeans; they were already soaked through. "Like I keep telling you," he said, with an effort to be patient, "the next snowstorm that drifts, I'm packing them into the snowcat as soon as it's dark, and they're out of here. They want to be out of here. They feel like I'm keeping them here. You know that."

"I know," said Tim. Ben jumped the creek again and Tim followed, this time more successfully. "But I've been meaning to mention something else," Tim said to Ben's back. "Or maybe you have noticed."

"What?" asked Ben over his shoulder as he trudged through the snow toward the barn, a little irritated. "Just spit it out, Tim."

"Well—it's Turk," Timothy said.

Ben stopped in his tracks. "What? Turk? Turk is out of it."

Timothy squared his shoulders and looked up at Ben, squinting in the bright sunlight. "Not any more. Not all the time. He's not out of it all the time."

Ben stared at Tim. Had he been missing something? A finger of cold tapped at the base of his spine. "What do you mean?" he heard himself asking.

"Turk is watching. Not all the time, but sometimes. More and more in the last few days. Yeah, most of the time he is dumb as a frozen turd, just stares off into space," Tim said, scratching nervously at the back of his neck. "But sometimes, he watches. I see him watching the girls; I see his eyes following when they move. Sometimes it's Artie, sometimes it's the Other girls. But most of the time—he watches Sylvie."

Ben saw Tim's black mittens curl into fists.

"And I don't like it," Tim said flatly. "Either does Sylvie. She hasn't told me, but I can tell. She is terrified of Turk, and I don't know why."

Ben turned toward the barn again, increasing his pace. "Hope for a storm," he said to Tim. "Hope for a big storm."

Artie dug in her pack and found the knife rolled in the dishtowel that she had brought from Hailey on the Last Saturday, and slid it from its loose wrapping. She sat on her bed and stared out the window. To the north, Cat Mountain loomed, dark with pines, remote and austere even on such a bluebird day. She felt a shiver of unease.

From the loft above came a faint, gutteral grunt.

Artie slid the knife under her pillow.

End of Scavenger Book 2

479

BOOKS 3 AND 4

Coming Soon!

A TASTE OF BOOK 3: WINTER

STIR CRAZY

The four loaves of bread came out of the old oven high and golden, fragrant and beautiful. Artie was proud of them. With Sylvie's help, she set the pans to cool on the pine countertop.

But no one noticed the bread. *Hot spring* was the topic of the evening. Shandy's team hadn't bothered to think about the evening meal. Andy had charged Shandy's phone and had found on it a directory of what he called, "Shandy's most marl playlist of the year." Lainey was busy gathering flashlights and towels. They were going to have a party, a hot tub party, in the dark meadow.

Mose and Andy had spent the early part of the evening scooping out a shallow pit in the newly thawed mud at the hot spring and lining it with a brown tarp held down by large rocks and metal fenceposts. "We'll all fit," Andy had said, coming into the house two hours earlier, his clothing splashed with freezing mud and water. "Our legs will mesh together, but we can fit in. It's going to be between two or three feet deep when it finishes filling, so we'll have to ooch down some."

Mose had gone out shortly after dark and had come back in triumph. "It's full," he said. "Let's do it."

483

Artie saw Lainey and Kaylee come down the ladder from the loft, wearing their shoes, but wrapped in towels. "Woo, woo," Carlos commented from the living room couch.

"Oh, stuff it, Carlos," Lainey said, laughing. "It's dark out there, totally black; who's going to see us in our underwear, anyway? Sure you don't want to come?"

"Arm," said Carlos, tight-lipped. "Shoulder. Next time."

Artie noticed that Turk was still in the loft. Lainey, leaning against the ladder, saw Artie's upward glance and said, "Yes, I've left Turk up there. He's asleep. I don't want to have to play nanny in the dark. Not fun. If he comes down, you can deal."

Artie shuddered. She'd be careful not to make much noise while the Others were gone. Taking care of Turk would be beyond horrible.

Mose, a big towel over one shoulder, handed Shandy a flashlight and headed for the kitchen door. "Come on," he said to everyone in general, and followed her out into the night, the Others, minus Carlos and Turk, trailing after. Artie heard a faint run of laughter as the door closed behind them.

Tim left the living room and sat himself at the kitchen table with Artie and Sylvie. "Guess we're not invited to the hot spring," he said. "Not that I care, but it's always like this, isn't it?" He spread his hands and looked at Artie. "It has always been like this, all through school. Them, and us. Or maybe we should be called 'not-them.'"

Artie looked from Tim to Sylvie and back to Tim, "Did you want to go with them, Tim? Did you, Sylvie?"

Sylvie shook her head with an emphatic *no.*

"No," said Tim, and his voice sounded both sad and tired. "No, but it wouldn't kill them to invite us."

Artie found herself smiling, and said, "You know, we don't need an invitation, Tim. I'll go out there with you if you really would like to go kick your legs around in the warm water with them. Still don't want to go?"

"Nope," Tim said. "Guess I am being stupid."

Sylvie shook her head again, but this time there was a grin.

"Tell you what," Artie said, getting up from the table and searching in a drawer for a serrated knife, "the bread is cool enough to cut now. Let's have some." She found a knife and got out a plate, a little apprehensive. But the loaf lifted cleanly from the pan and the first slices she cut looked perfect.

"At last," Artie thought, rummaging in the pantry for jam, "from now on, we are going to have bread and sandwiches and toast. Sure wish we had some butter, but at least now we can start using more of the flour. And," her thoughts slid deeper, "and I am not liking what is happening with Tim these days. He is trying to disappear so that the Others won't bully him." She shook her head. Her hand closed on a jar of cherry jam and she took it to the table. As she dropped into her usual chair, she heard a distinct *thump*.

"What?" came Tim's voice, almost in a whisper.

Thump. It came again. *Thump*. And again. *Thump*. Artie saw Sylvie look up at the ceiling and flinch when it came again, dull and measured. *Thump*.

Then it came to her. "Turk," she said. "Turk is up there. Turk is doing that." With each thump, Artie felt like she had been kicked in the stomach just a little. *Turk*. Turk the arrogant. Turk the bully. What could he be doing alone in the loft? Was his brain waking up?

"Well, I'm creeped out," Tim was saying. "Artie, do you want to run up the ladder and have a look?"

Sylvie's hands were clenched like white claws on the edge of the table; the oilcloth stretched taut under her nails. She looked frozen.

"Are you crazy, Tim?" Artie heard herself reply. "No, I don't." "But," she thought, "someone has to see what Turk is doing." She sighed and gathered herself to stand up.

At that moment, Ben came out of the small bedroom, a charcoal pencil in one hand. "What's going on up there?" he asked of the three of them in general.

"Everyone but Carlos and Turk is out at the hot spring," Artie said. She pointed to the ceiling. "Turk is up there."

Ben stuck the pencil over one ear and said, "I'll have a look." Grateful that she didn't have to do it, Artie watched him climb the ladder to the loft. She focused on what she could see of Ben, the cuffs of his jeans and his running shoes, as he stood on one of the high rungs for long moments. *Thump* came vibrating through the ceiling. *Thump. Thump. Thump.*

Ben slid down the ladder. "Weird," he said, pulling out a chair. "Hey, can I have some of that bread? Smells great." He flopped into a seat and reached for a slice. *Thump.* "Yes, it's Turk, all right" he said. *Thump.* "He's sitting on the floor right over our heads. Cross-legged. And he's hitting the floor with his fists." *Thump.* "He hits with one fist, waits a couple of beats, and hits with the other fist. He is staring at the wall. Just looks mindless." *Thump.*

Lightning Source UK Ltd.
Milton Keynes UK
UKOW01f1901230218
318415UK00001B/38/P